OIL IN THEIR

BLOOD:

The American Decades

Herman K. Trabish

First Editon, 2007
ISBN #978-0-6151-7750-2
WGA #1235495 (10-24-2007)

For Bebe, Abby & Lily.   To Teri.

…My head is full of pictures like a movie—different from movies I'd been sneaking into. The faked ones about outlaws, rich girls, playboys, cowboys and Indians, and shooting scrapes, killings, and a pretty man kissing a pretty girl on a pretty spot on a pretty day. It takes a lot more guts, I thought, to work and heave and cuss and sweat and laugh and talk like the oil field workers. Every man gritted every tooth in his head, and stretched every muscle in his whole body—not trying to get rich or rare back and loaf, because I'd hear one beller out, 'Okay, you dam guys, hit 'er up, or else git down out of a workin' man's way, and let me put in a G-ddam oil field!'
> …Woody Guthrie, *Bound for Glory*, 1943

Table of Contents

Illustrations

With a voice like a choir of angels and blue eyes that seemed to see you deep inside, the elegant elderly woman sang for her dinner party guests. After her performance, she called me over to the piano. I read your book about oil, she said.

It was 1973. American oil production would never again get bigger. The cost of gas had skyrocketed from 39 cents/gallon to $1.39/gallon. The Middle East was exploding. Again.

There is more to the story, she said. You don't understand.

Do you?

Delighted at my question, she smiled. Let me tell you a story, she said.

Part I: Wildcatting
February 1919

The crowd cheered. The burly old Frenchman with the big white walrus mustache walked from the apartment to the car waiting for him at the curb beside Number 8 Rue Franklin. A bodyguard followed. From beyond the gendarmerie barriers and lines of watchful officers, reporters shouted questions about the peace negotiations. The citizenry and rabble noisily yelled challenges and praise. The burly old man stopped beside the limousine and, while his bodyguard stepped graciously back and his driver held the door of the long elegant Pierce Arrow open for him and waited, he grinned and gleefully exchanged barbs with the reporters and citizens.

Fifty yards beyond them, behind a public urinal at the corner of Rue Franklin and Boulevard Delessert, a small, unshaven man in dirty overalls watched and nervously fidgeted with the revolver in his overalls pocket.

Nearby, a tall man in a French military uniform and worn, open army overcoat, with broad shoulders, thick black hair and intelligent, searching eyes, stood with his hands in his pockets and watched.

"Le Tigre," remarked the lean young man with shaggy blond hair and wide blue eyes beside him.

"He is a tiger, Charley," the tall man smiled, and added, his English heavy with a French accent, "but you told me if I brought you here you would speak English with me."

"Le Tigre," replied the blond man in a distinctly American accent. "Not just The Tiger. Le Tigre. I'm a reporter, LeFash. Got to get the words right. You know that."

LeFash, the tall, broad shouldered man in the worn army overcoat, did not answer. They watched the burly Frenchman. His small, narrow eyes sparkled. His heavy white walrus mustache fluttered with vigorous verbal bristles and rejoinders at questions from the crowd. He greeted some personally, continued to trade remarks and jests with others, and shook strangers' hands, the consummate veteran politician.

"Moves like a big cat, jovial like a schoolboy," the blond American reporter remarked. He took a pad and pencil from his overcoat pocket and jotted notes.

7

"They love him," LeFash smiled. "The Father of the Victory."

"On his way to join Wilson and Lloyd George," Charley scribbled. He looked at LeFash. "The most powerful men in the world."

"Except," LeFash interrupted, "when the heads of industry meet."

Charley glanced up. "Do you know something I don't know?" he asked LeFash.

LeFash just looked at him for a moment. "You know everything I do. Write your story."

Charley looked down at his notes.

Georges Clemenceau, Prime Minister of France, Le Tigre, stepped into the limousine. The bodyguard followed. The driver closed their door, got behind the wheel, started the vehicle forward toward the corner, and began the turn onto Boulevard Delessert.

The small unshaven man in the dirty overalls moved from behind the public urinals, catching the attention of LeFash as he withdrew the pistol from his overalls pocket and extended his arm, aiming. LeFash stared at him, rigid in uncomprehending terror.

BANG!

The crowd roiled. Heads pivoted, searching for the source of the shot. Charley ducked down, scanning. LeFash was motionless, looking at the shooter.

BANG!

Screams. People fell to the ground. Others ran.

"Get down!" Charley shouted at LeFash.

BANG-BANG-BANG!

The limousine's engine roared, its tires screeched and it accelerated up the boulevard. The small unshaven man in the dirty overalls moved into the street and aimed the pistol at the back of the car.

LeFash finally forced himself to act, charging the man with the pistol.

BANG-BANG!

Shots clanged against the car's rear panel.

LeFash tackled the man with the pistol.

The car disappeared around a corner in the distance.

LeFash and the gunman fell to the ground. Gendarmes' screaming whistles punctuated the on-lookers' shouts and curses as they all raced to the two men wrestling on the street near the urinals. Voices of rage rose in the crowd, calling for a hanging. An officer grabbed the pistol, bellowed to his men to take control of the mob and ordered others to protect the assassin. All the while, LeFash laid on the small, dirty, smelly man beneath him who wriggled viciously and grunted "Francais foutue! Le Tigre, le connard! Francais tringlee! Le Tigre, pute! Ninque Clemenceau!"

Finally, the gendarmes restored a semblance of order but could not quiet the mob's raging. They dragged the assassin to a waiting paddy wagon. Unsure of what LeFash's roll in the shooting was, they dragged him along and threw him in with the assassin.

Suddenly, Clemenceau's limousine came racing back down Rue Franklin. It stopped at the Prime Minister's residence just as the paddy wagon, its siren bleating, its engine roaring, its transmission grinding, raced off for the 16th arrondissement police station in the Avenue Henri Martin. The mob, LeFash's reporter friend Charley in it, followed the paddy wagon.

Behind them, Clemenceau's driver and bodyguard carried the Prime Minister into the Rue Franklin apartment.

*****

In a dingy, dank empty cell, in shadowy light, LeFash sat alone on a rickety stool. His face was a grim mask, revealing only that he had known worse places. Still in his uniform and shabby military overcoat, hands in the pockets, he stared at the ancient concrete rear wall of the cell. He took a deep breath and let it out, watching his breath appear in the chill air. Behind him, he heard distant noises echoing in the gray corridor outside his cell. He stood, pivoted and sprang to the black iron bars. Steps approached. In the dimness, he saw Charley. Behind Charley was a stout man in a gendarme's uniform carrying a key ring. Behind them were two men in very fine suits and overcoats.

Suddenly, behind the bars of a cell across and down from LeFash, the assassin's face appeared at the corner of his visibility and screamed, "Francias foutue! Le Tigre, le connard! Francais tringlee! Le Tigre, pute! Ninque Clemenceau!"

Charley, the gendarme and the men in fine suits halted, stared at the madman, realized he was behind bars and represented no threat, and turned to LeFash. Charley smiled. Relief passed over LeFash's face.

*****

Clemenceau's long, elegant Pierce Arrow rolled incongruously through an alley behind the 16th arrondissement jail. It came to a stop beside a heavy doorway in the wall, the door creaked open slowly and the stout gendarme with the key ring stuck his head out. He saw the car and disappeared within, though the door remained open.

The two men in elegant suits emerged, whispering between themselves. Clemenceau's driver jumped from behind the wheel and held the passenger compartment door open. The two men in suits, still whispering, got in. Behind them, Charley and LeFash emerged from the door in the wall and got into the limousine behind the men in suits. The driver closed the door firmly, jumped behind the wheel and drove quickly up the alley.

*****

As winter evening gray turned into dark nighttime with city lights twinkling on, the limousine drove slowly through a crowd, twice the size of the morning crowd, outside Number 8 Rue Franklin. The gendarmes cleared a path. LeFash, Charley and the men in fine suits moved quickly from the car to the apartment. Murmurs followed them. "The man who saved Clemenceau! The man who saved Clemenceau!" A few shouted hurrahs and, suddenly, there was cheering. LeFash glanced nervously at Charley, who grinned reassuringly.

Inside, the sitting room was quiet. A few men sat in chairs on one side of the room. A doctor stood beside the sofa where Clemenceau lay with closed eyes and an ashen grimace. The men in suits looked at the doctor.

"He is still in pain but he will live."

Clemenceau's eyes opened. "It is exhilarating," he smiled weakly. "I have never been assassinated before."

10

"And you have not now," admonished the doctor.

Clemenceau's eyes moved from the doctor, bypassed the men in suits and fell on LeFash. "So this is France's newest hero?"

*****

Following his brief interview with Clemenceau, the men in suits took LeFash out to the sidewalk in front of Clemenceau's apartment, introduced him to the grateful public and the voracious French press, praised his act of bravery and pointed out how this attempted assassination only underscored the importance of Le Tigre's agenda at the peace conference.

By morning, LeFash's fame was nationwide and all of France was talking about the importance of Le Tigre's agenda at the peace conference. President Poincare summoned LeFash to the Elysee Palace and, in a private ceremony attended only by LeFash, Charley, Poincare's men in suits and the voracious French press, praised the act of bravery, awarded him the Croix de Guerre and pointed out how the attempted assassination only underscored the flaws in Le Tigre's agenda at the peace conference.

LeFash next received an invitation to be an honored guest at the National Assembly. There, before the voracious French press, the morning session opened with all parties joining to recognize LeFash's bravery by a standing ovation. Speeches affirming, critiquing and denouncing Le Tigre's agenda at the peace conference followed. LeFash and Charley at first enjoyed their intimate look at the turning of the wheels of government. But after the speeches had gone on and on (and on and on), they were only too ready to excuse themselves for the next obligation on their schedule, a luncheon with Charley's colleagues in the voracious U.S. press.

They walked across the Seine toward the Place de la Concorde. It was a gray February day. Whitecaps kicked up on the greenish water. They laughed together about the politicians' speeches, trying not to be rude to the many, many women in black mourning who passed them by. On the Right Bank, the lawns of the Champs Elysee and Tuileries were green from the wet winter but the trees along the river and the boulevard and the garden walkways looked strange and surreal, with large random ugly gaps where trees were taken for firewood during the lean years of the war. They ambled past the obilisque and the fountain, where more widows in black lingered, to the Hotel de Crillon, the U.S. peace conference delegation's center of operations on the north side of the Place.

11

In one of the elegant hotel's private dining rooms, the reporters were already drinking. Hailing LeFash and Charley, a chubby man with a bright red face offered up glasses and a bottle of champagne.

Looking around the room at the laughing, drinking reporters, Charley grinned broadly. "Glad you people didn't feel obligated to wait for your guest of honor to get started."

"YOUR guesht of honor," corrected the chubby man slurringly while pouring them champagne.

"Colonel House's guest of honor is my guess," said a woman reporter, older and more dignified than most of the others, coming up behind them. Though the pourer, intent on filling glasses, did not read LeFash's quizzical expression, Charley saw his friend trying to figure out who the host of this party actually was. The woman looked at the silent faces around her and laughed. "Looks like I'm not the only one who needs more champagne!"

"Tarbell!" Charley blurted, diverting LeFash's attention. "This is Ida Tarbell, LeFash. The woman who personally brought down America's oil oligarchy."

Miss Tarbell shook LeFash's hand. "I have heard of your work," he told her.

"And I yours, Captain," she smiled. "I hope yours works out better than mine did."

"But Standard Oil is no more," LeFash smiled. "The world is better for that."

"So is John D. Rockefeller's fortune," Ida Tarbell replied. "Oil is a Hydra. It lost a head and grew nine more. The war left American oil richer than the Devil."

Other reporters in the room gathered quickly to them. Seeking to turn attention on LeFash and away from who the host of the party was, Charley's eyes flashed around the room for a distraction. The tipsy champagne pourer, still oblivious, saved him the trouble when, at Ida Tarbell's remark, he exploded. "Never mind the devil unless he's buying the booze—tell us your story, Frenchie!"

"Yeah!" another reporter chimed in. "What did it feel like to charge that man?"

"Feel?" LeFash pondered. "When I realized what I must do, I could only do it. Nothing else."

"What does it feel like to be a hero of France?" a reporter asked.

"All the people of France are heroes. None more than those who gave their lives for her."

Another reporter: "What do you think about the peace conference?"

LeFash turned toward the question and frowned.

"You don't like what they're doing?" asked the reporter.

"They are dividing up the world, taking what they want."

"Like Clemenceau giving Lloyd George Mesopotamia in exchange for Syria?"

LeFash gulped his champagne glass empty before he replied with a smile. "I like what Wilson says: The people there should decide."

"How can the peace conference leaders make that happen?"

LeFash frowned again and shrugged. "Like Wilson, I don't know."

"You're going to leave it to the peace conference?"

Protecting LeFash, Charley interrupted. "They're the most powerful men in the world, aren't they?" he asked.

"Except for the oil kings," LeFash added.

"Hey, Charley! This guy sounds a little red," a reporter called out. The room tensed.

"Not as red as the guy in prison who he saved Clemenceau from," Charley exploded. "Next question!"

From another part of the crowd around LeFash and Charley came a different line of questioning. "What are your plans?"

LeFash smiled again. "I need a job. Does anyone need a translator?"

"Hey!" Charley interjected. "You're MY translator! After all I did for you."

The crowd of reporters laughed, and then erupted into a jovial boisterous taunting of Charley, stopping only when a waiter entered to announce the meal.

*****

Under the firm leadership of John D. Rockefeller, the Standard Oil Company rose from a ragged alliance of oil refiners and shippers in western Pennsylvania and eastern Ohio in the post Civil war era to become an international force in the last decade of the nineteenth and the first decade of the twentieth century. In the process, the Standard Trust became the world's first completely integrated, full service oil entity, controlling crude supply, rail and pipeline transport, refining and end-product marketing and, thereby, controlling price.

As Rockefeller became the richest of the new American barons and typified the concentration of American wealth, populists and progressives protested, demanding considerations for the small businesses driving the process and the people who did the grunt work in the belly of the capital-producing machines. Among the most prominent of the populist, progressive publications was McClure's Magazine. In 1902/03, McClure's ran a series of articles over an eighteen-month period chronicling Rockefeller's cutthroat rise in and unsentimental monopoly of the American oil industry. Tarbell's condemnation of Standard Oil, subsequently published in book form, led a movement of what Theodore Roosevelt labeled "muckrakers" in a 1906 presidential speech: "...I hail as a benefactor every writer or speaker...who...with merciless severity makes such attack..." But, TR reminded the muckrakers, "...the attack is of use only if it is absolutely truthful."

Tarbell's journalism and Roosevelt's political leadership led to a long court struggle. In 1907, District Court Judge Kenesaw Mountain Landis famously ruled Rockefeller's Standard Oil to have engaged in monopolistic practices and leveled a $29 million fine. The Supreme Court made the conclusive decision in 1911, finding Standard Oil an unreasonable monopoly under the Sherman Antitrust Act of 1890 and ordering its dissolution.

The break-up allowed Rockefeller and his board of directors to reorganize into more competitive structures. The many "baby" Standards such as New York (Socony, Mobil), New Jersey (Esso, Exxon), Indiana (Stanolind, Amoco) and California (Chevron) stepped into mature, profitable independence, each a fully integrated, market-competitive entity. Rockefeller and his board, holding stock in them all, saw their wealth and power increase exponentially. With the rise of oil and gasoline-fueled technologies,

14

Anglo Persian, Royal Dutch Shell, Gulf and others formed integrated, oil-producing and marketing organizations to rival the Standards, providing service from the well to the pump across the U.S. and around the world. During the Great War of 1914-1918, an unprecedented hunger for oil by the warring nations brought these corporate entities unforeseen wealth and power, leaving them with a major stake in world politics and economics.

*****

Late that afternoon, the last reporters excused themselves to compose and file stories on France's new hero. Cheerfully, LeFash and Charley started to leave through the elegant Crillon lobby. A tall, pale, lean man in a dark, heavy, American diplomat's suit approached from the wide gleaming mahogany staircase and stepped in front of them. He nodded to Charley, looked at LeFash and asked in a heavy Texas drawl, "This our man, Clark?"

"Who is he, Charley?"

Without answering LeFash, Charley stared at the Texan, took a deep breath, let it out and nodded 'yes.' The man turned to LeFash and looked hard into his eyes. "The gent who bought you lunch wants to chat with you. How about it?"

LeFash looked at Charley, who again nodded 'yes.' LeFash looked back at the Texan. "It would only be polite to say thank you."

Up three flights of the wide, elegant staircase, on the top floor landing, two U.S. military guards stood at attention outside great, heavy mahogany double doors. The Texan made eye contact with one of the guards, who nodded them in. They passed through a reception area where two more U.S. Army guards stood at ease beside open French doors. Again a guard nodded them through, into an enormous, luxurious room with a high ceiling, white paneling and fine carpets. Reading a stack of papers beside a large gray stone fireplace with a blazing fire sat a small, pale, frail-looking man in a fine morning suit and shining black cowboy boots with a blanket over his knees.

He did not look up when they entered. The Texan led them over to the man beside the fireplace and they stood, waiting. Still not looking up, the man gestured toward a grouping of straight-back chairs across the room. The Texan nodded at Charley and LeFash and they brought the chairs nearer the old man at the fire. As they sat down, he finished his reading and looked up at them.

15

"Mighty kind of you to come up," he said to LeFash in a soft, gentle Texas drawl. "This old man is in awe of your bravery, Captain LeFash. I'm Edward House. Most folks call me Colonel." His hands danced as he talked. He reached one out to LeFash. It was almost delicate but it was calm. "Speaking for President Wilson and the United States government, it is an honor to meet you."

LeFash shook his hand gently but the man's grip was firm. House's eyes were friendly but LeFash saw himself being assessed in them. Suddenly, as House ended the handshake, a gleam came into the old man's eyes and his smile changed from one of greeting to one of decision. He glanced at the Texan and gave him a backhand wave. As House watched, the man nodded, got up and left the room. House looked at LeFash. "I hear you are looking for work, Captain."

"I was thinking of something in France, sir."

"Charley's editor wants you to write a column about the peace conference."

"He does?" blurted Charley.

"He does," smiled House, waving a cable. "I suggested it to him. Just got his cable back." He turned to LeFash. "You know, from a French soldier's point of view."

LeFash frowned. "But I can't write!"

"Charley will ghost write."

LeFash took a deep breath and looked straight at House. "What do you want?"

House's smile explained how much he liked straightforward people. "We want another set of eyes on the negotiations over the oil territories in Mesopotamia."

A fire rose in LeFash's eyes. "I want nothing to do with oil."

House lowered his head and turned it up at an angle, squinted at LeFash, said nothing for a moment and began working his small, pale hands as if he was holding something. "Well," House finally said, "I don't know that much about you but I know if I could get hold of the information I want, I surely could put a pain on Standard and Benchmark and that bunch."

16

"Benchmark?"

"They've got somebody passing information to President Wilson from inside Lloyd George's delegation."

"What is that to you?" LeFash asked.

"Men from Benchmark and Standard claim they have a memo from an American working in the Mosul region for Anglo-Persian, the oil developers. They convinced the President there's oil in Mesopotamia."

"An American working for Anglo-Persian? Do you know his name?"

"No. Why? Do you know somebody out there?" House's hands rested as he watched LeFash and listened.

LeFash held his face still. There was effort in his expression but Charley and House read it as decision roiling. They could not know he was thinking about Sam Wade, a young American who helped him win his first medal at the Battle of the Marne and who, he knew through a loose network of acquaintances in Paris, was now living in Persia with his wife and son and working for Anglo-Persian Oil Company. "Men I fought with went to the east to forget the war. But why do you worry about intelligence passed to your own side?"

As House began talking again, his hands began working again. "In the President's Fourteen Points he stood up for regional peoples to choose their own fate. Right now, Prince Faisal is talking to the Supreme Council, asking them to help his people create a great nation of their own in Arabia and Mesopotamia, just like it was agreed in Sykes-Picot and the deals with Lawrence. But now the American oil companies want Wilson to demand a place at the oil-deal table for them. They want to cut the desert up for the oil and let the peoples fall where they will."

"But you are a Texan. Why would you work against the big oil companies?"

"Son, I'm not in oil, I'm in politics. But in my heart, I'm a wildcatter. Nobody finds those big boys more disagreeable than me."

"So you want to find out what they know and how they know it?"

"And then maybe I can show the President they're working against his ideals for their own profits."

17

"And you think I can do that by pretending to be a reporter?"

"I'm working other sources." House looked hard at LeFash, his patience wearing thin. "I've got to be careful. If Faisal finds out Anglo-Persian is letting on what it knows about oil in Mosul, he will chop off that American boy's head. I don't want oil blood on my hands. Now do you want a shot at Benchmark or not?"

*****

In the Quai d'Orsay, the magnificent, neoclassical building overlooking the Seine that houses the administrative offices of the French Republic, Foreign Minister Stephen Pichon's great stateroom of an office was the meeting place of the Supreme Council. Abusson carpets covered parquet floors. Massive fireplaces, high windows, priceless paintings and seventeenth century tapestries lined elegant wood paneling up to decorative ceilings with elaborate crystal chandeliers. Heavy oak double doors across from the fireplace stood shut while French doors with glass panes looked out onto the gardens beside the river.

Beside the hearth in which a huge log burned, across from heavy tables with masses of documents, Clemenceau slouched in an armchair with thick carven legs and red and gold embroidery, staring upward, his white hair falling down over his high forehead, his white mustaches falling down over a mouth drooping with quiet. Facing him from the garden side, British Prime Minister David Lloyd George, a short, thickset man with a white face, high sagging cheeks, a high brush of white hair and a white Charley Chaplin mustache, sat in a straight armchair, twiddling his fingers and watching the oak doors with big anxious blue eyes. Beside him, in a slightly higher chair befitting his status as the only true head of state present, tall, angular, preacher-like President Woodrow Wilson, his jaw set with grit and determination, adjusted his pince-nez with long thin fingers to read a sheet of paper he held in his other long, lean hand. All three men had small tables beside them with stacks of their papers. Beside and behind each was a group of three secretaries, in small, straight, gilt chairs, taking notes and whispering.

Wilson turned, handed the sheet of paper to one of his secretaries and turned back to Clemenceau. "Where is this hero of yours, Mr. Prime Minister? We have delegates waiting."

Suddenly the oak double doors opened and LeFash walked through. Just inside the room, he stopped, came to attention and saluted while military guards took places beside each door. Clemenceau effortfully rose, went to LeFash, muttered "At ease," in French and turned to Wilson and Lloyd

George. "Gentlemen, this is the man who prevented me from experiencing assassination. Captain Leonid Chyrinski LeFash."

The British Prime Minister and the American President rose. But before they could step forward to shake LeFash's hand, two men came barreling in from the rotunda and burst past the military guards. The first was a lean swarthy man with passionate shining eyes, a broad nose, thick bottlebrush mustaches and beard and a warm smile, wearing long dark Arabian robes with golden trim and a matching kafiyya with a jeweled agal. The man following wore a British military uniform and a dark kafiyya with a simple golden agal. He was small, with deep blue eyes looking into an unknown distance, topping a long nose and a crooked smile.

The military guards at the door trained their rifles on the intruders. "Prince Faisal!" Clemenceau exclaimed, waving the guards off. "If you could wait just a few minutes more…"

When the guards stepped back, LeFash did the same.

"So you can find another way to avoid me?" Faisal barked at Clemenceau. "So you can make another deal behind my back?"

Lloyd George, his pale face suddenly bright red, stepped forward. "Prince Faisal, you know these things are complicated."

Faisal turned on Lloyd George. "And you make them more complicated when you promise my lands to others.

"We will work this out," Lloyd George said soothingly.

"You told my father we would govern ourselves from Mosul to Mecca!"

"And the Sharif promised military control!" Lloyd George snapped back.

"We fought like lions!"

Lloyd George turned to the man with Faisal in the British uniform and kafiyya. "Lawrence?" he asked dubiously. "Like lions?"

T. E. Lawrence remained calm. "The uprising was the response of desert lions," he said quietly. "Stealth, then sudden death."

"The Australians took Damascus," Lloyd George snapped at Lawrence, who grimaced.

19

"I rule it now," Faisal roared back. "Who will you give it to next? The Japanese? That crazy chef Ho from Indochina?"

"We are trying to work this out with the Zionists," Lloyd George answered.

"You are NOT!" raged Faisal. "I met with Weizmann. I can work it out with Weizmann. You stand in our way because you want us to fail! Then you will have your excuse to control our lands."

Wilson stepped forward. "Prince Faisal, I am Woodrow Wilson," he said calmingly. "I am…

"President Wilson!" Faisal exclaimed, stepping toward Wilson and bowing. "It is a great honor. Your Fourteen Points are the hope of the oppressed peoples of the world!"

Wilson smiled. "We," he began, sweeping his arm to include Clemenceau and Lloyd George, "wish only for you to live with the nations of the world in peace."

"As do we," nodded Faisal, studying Wilson.

"But there are resources…"

Faisal leaped back. "YOU, TOO! MY RESOUCES!" He pivoted and stomped for the door. "I am ruined! Come, Lawrence! My people are ruined!"

He disappeared into the outer rotunda. Lawrence stood a moment and looked from Lloyd George to Wilson. "This is not what I killed in cold blood and rode across deserts until I was blind with sun and crazed with heat for," he said quietly. "People are resources, too." He turned and followed Faisal out.

The room remained quiet as the three leaders looked at each other. Finally, Clemenceau's eyes fell on the U.S. President. "Resources, Wilson?" He turned to Lloyd George. "What does he know about resources? YOU GO BEHIND MY BACK? We have a deal over Syria and Mosul! Why do you have to bring this PREACHER in on it?"

"I did no such thing! OUR DEAL STANDS!"

"The hell!" answered Clemenceau.

Wilson's grim face turned grimmer. "Perhaps I should know about these deals?"

Clemenceau stepped forward unintimidated. "When you say 'resources' we all know you mean oil. So you know all you need to know."

Now LeFash stepped forward. "Monsieur Clemenceau, if my service to you allows me one liberty, may I speak now?" He did not pause. Clemenceau, Lloyd George and Wilson looked at him. "I was a boy in the Caspian region. I know how oil powers work. I see their hand here. They are dividing in order to conquer! Do not allow them to conquer your intentions!" He paused.

The three leaders studied one another, each reluctant to reply for fear of revealing secrets. Finally, Clemenceau turned to LeFash. "Do you have a proposal?"

"Surely you have other business," LeFash told Clemenceau. "Let me look into this and report back to you. Perhaps the dividers can be divided."

Again, the room quieted. Finally, Wilson spoke as he turned back to his seat. "Your hero is right, Clemenceau. Let him go to work. More information can only help us make our decisions." He sat down and faced Clemenceau and Lloyd George again, smiling. "We have other urgent matters. We have a world to remake."

The British and French Prime Ministers looked from Wilson to each other. Le Tigre shrugged and grinned at Lloyd George as he replied to the President. "It is an old world, Wilson. The simple plans of men are not necessarily enough to remake it."

"Still," Lloyd George smiled at Clemenceau. "We have an opportunity to assign your man to fact-finding and return to our work. How about it…" He turned back to his seat and, sitting, looked up at Clemenceau. "…once more unto the breach, dear friend?"

Clemenceau turned to LeFash. "Well, Captain," the old man said to LeFash. "It is agreed. You will look into the matter. Notify my staff when you are ready to report back. Your activities must remain confidential. Do you understand?"

LeFash nodded and saluted. The Prime Minister wearily returned the salute and dismissed him. Clemenceau slumped back into his chair by the hearth as the young soldier left the room with official permission to do what House had already set him to do.

21

*****

At the Closeries des Lilas in Montparnasse the next morning, LeFash vaulted the café patio railing and slipped in the rear door to join Charley in a booth by a window. "I filed your first column," Charley told LeFash as he sat down. "It praised the Big Three." Charley waved to his server, who came with brioche and coffee and took two orders for eggs and sausages.

"How is the old man?" Charley asked.

"Clemenceau? One tends to move slowly with a bullet in the back between the ribs."

A car rode past the café window with placards advocating the French Communist Party. Men on the sidewalk screamed in rage at it. It honked its horn and drove on.

"He was an Anarchist," said Charley.

"Who?"

"Cottin. The man who shot Le Tigre." Suddenly Charley smiled. "The patriots want to hang him but Clemenceau won't let them. He says because the man fired seven times and only hit him once he is too bad a shot to be a danger."

"Communists, Anarchists, patriots, capitalists. The city is on the edge of a volcano."

The waiter brought their food and, just as he left, two young attractive women walked through on their way to another table. One wore black. The other wore a black armband. LeFash and Charley looked down at their food and began eating in silence. Charley asked for an account of the meeting with the Big Three. LeFash gave it briefly, to Charley's astonishment.

"So now you have the assignment twice and both are secret."

"Yes."

"It is odd," said Charley after a moment of reflection.

"What?"

22

"None of them seemed to want to send a real spy."

"They are great politicians, masters of deception and denial."

"True. But it is curious."

"I'll tell you something even more curious," said LeFash, finishing his food. "I rang some oil company offices this morning to request interviews. When I said I was with an American newspaper, Anglo-Persian asked me to ring back. Same thing when I rang Standard and said I was with a French paper. But..." He finished his coffee. "...When I told Benchmark I was with a British paper, I was told I should ring the British delegation at the Hotel Majestic and ask for Mr. Tennet."

"Did you?"

"Not yet. I need more information. I need to get into the Majestic."

"That's easy."

*****

On the glistening hardwood of the Hotel Majestic Grand Ballroom dance floor, ladies in elegant free flowing gowns with scandalously rising hemlines and exciting décolletages danced with gentlemen in tailcoats and tuxedos. At one end of the floor, the orchestra played Charles Johnson's ragtime waltz *Cassandra.* The couples did hesitations to the raggy one-two-three. Europeans doing traditional closed figure rolls and whirls stared in awe and envy as American couples executed the syncopated side by side with spin and the open roll.

"Qu'est-ce que c'est!?!" LeFash, standing with Charley beside the dance floor, exclaimed.

"It's a girl!" laughed Charley, watching the dancers. "A pretty, young one. In all her paint and feathers. Not something we see much of."

The loud harmonious regularity of the waltz time and the sinuous elegance of the dancers galvanized their attention, satyrs and nymphettes gamboling like they never knew war. As the dance came to an end, they continued to admire the ladies as the couples paraded on and off the floor.

LeFash put his fingers between his collar and his neck and pulled to loosen it. "I would not want to see any of the politicians we meet with dressed like that," LeFash replied to Charley's appreciation of the girls' elegance.

"I'd like to see that secretary of Lloyd George's all gussied up."

"Unlikely," LeFash answered. "Maybe one of Clemenceau's mistresses. But they say Lloyd George is privately just as religiously prudish as your Wilson."

"Still," Charley laughed, not taking his eyes off the dancers. "He has an eye for the ladies."

LeFash pulled again at his collar. Charley looked at him. "Are you ready?"

LeFash laughed. "I always expect only something other than what I am ready for." He glanced around the ballroom. "Yes."

They circled the dance floor, moving between tables of partiers and diplomats and peace conference camp followers. "This is the place to be on Saturday night," Charley muttered while nodding and waving to journalists and other acquaintances.

"You seem to know everyone."

"How do you think I found out where they keep those oil documents?" Charley asked LeFash. They walked on. "Smile big," he suddenly said out of the side of his mouth. "That's my source."

"She's a girl!" LeFash whispered.

"A very nosey London girl who desperately wants an American newspaperman to rescue her from the drudgery of retyping Foreign Office business. Thank goodness she's got an escort tonight. Smile and wave and pretend I've just told you she's the prettiest girl in the room."

After a full tour around the ballroom in a widening circle, they wound up near double doors into the kitchen where there was a steady stream of waiters and bus boys.

"How do you know her information is reliable?" LeFash asked.

"I don't. Let's get on with it."

LeFash looked at Charley dubiously, breathed slow and deep, and took a cigarette case from his inner pocket. He held it up to Charley, who nodded and pointed through the kitchen doors. With the nonchalance of a pair of Lotharios headed out for a smoke, they went into and through the hot steamy noisy kitchen, and then out the rear kitchen door into a hotel freight delivery hallway. LeFash put the cigarette case away. "This way," he told Charley.

"At least the information you got about the hotel is good," Charley whispered as they walked the long hall.

"Because I got it myself. Not from some silly girl." He spotted the freight elevator at the end of the hall and pointed. "There. Now."

Charley suddenly acted stumblingly drunk. Just as they came in sight of two British soldiers guarding the freight elevator entrance, he seemed to lose his balance and leaned into LeFash. LeFash half dragged Charley to the elevator. He spoke rapid-fire French to the guards and gestured that he wanted to take Charley up the freight elevator. Charley babbled drunkenly about wanting to go to the dance and "…get at those slutty British nurses and typists…"

Neither stopped talking. It was a hilarious cacophony of rapid-fire French and American vulgarity though it exasperated rather than amused the British soldiers, as was their intent.

"Just put them on the elevator and get them out of our faces!" One soldier finally told the other.

Moments later, LeFash and Charley were riding the elevator toward the top floor of the Majestic. When it opened, they stepped out into a silent, shadowy hallway. Charley pointed to a pair of elegant carved wood double doors at the end of the hall and they moved stealthily toward them. "Saturday night," Charley whispered. "Nobody at the office."

At the doors, LeFash whispered back "I hope you are right" and tried the handle. It gave. "Just like the British," LeFash whispered, smiling. "Military guards and Scotland Yard emptying the waste, but they don't lock the doors."

They slipped into the room. It was dark until Charley found a switch and turned on the overhead electric light fixture. Dim bulbs cast a yellow glow. A long oval conference table and chairs occupied most of the room. On the wall by the chair at the head of the table was a large map. While Charley went to it, LeFash walked around the table, studying the nameplates at each chair and the papers on the table by the nameplates.

25

The map was of Europe and Asia, with England on its western side and China on its eastern side. It went as far north as the Arctic Circle and south to the Horn of Africa and the Indian Ocean.

"Look at this," Charley said quietly. LeFash looked up. A section of the map at the center had a bold red line around it. "Somebody explaining why Europe's shorthand for the Levant is the 'middle' East?" Charley speculated.

They continued to study the map. The red line encircled the former Ottoman Empire: Turkey, Syria, Mesopotamia and the Arabian Peninsula. "It is the territory to be divided," LeFash said.

"Odd that it does not include Persia," Charley commented. "You'd think they'd want to protect Anglo Persian."

"Maybe Anglo Persian took it off the table," LeFash said.

Charley looked down at the nameplates and files at each seat and walked slowly around to the side opposite LeFash, reading as he went. "Sykes at the head of the table. Nicholson at his left."

The Frenchman also circled and read. "Bell. McMahon. Here are the French. Domergue."

"Oil companies," Charley interrupted.

LeFash looked up instantly and strode to the reporter. "Where?"

Charley pointed. "Standard. Royal Dutch. FINA. Benchmark."

At the Benchmark place card there was, like at all the other places, a stack of papers and folders. On the top folder was a business card. LeFash picked it up and studied it. Charley looked over his shoulder. "Johnson. I know that guy," Charley suddenly said. "I tried to interview him. Little prissy guy, perfect dresser, wouldn't say a word about why Benchmark is here. Just said to ask his boss."

"Did he say who that is?"

"Guy named Bennett. Couldn't get to him. Separate offices and accommodations from the peace conference bunch."

LeFash handed Charley the business card and picked up the file under it. He turned over a few pages until he came to something he read intently.

"What?" Charley demanded.

Suddenly, from the hall, there was the sound of a door opening and closing. Then there was the rumble of male voices. Charley and LeFash moved quickly to the door and listened. LeFash held up two fingers, indicating he heard two men.

"Who could it be?" Charley whispered.

LeFash started to shrug that he didn't know, then caught sight of a full wastebasket in the corner of his vision and pointed to it. "Scotland Yard."

"On Saturday night?"

LeFash shrugged. "Their way of getting into the party?"

The voices came nearer. Charley moved to flick off the lights. LeFash grabbed his hand, shook his head 'no' and pointed at the bottom of the door, where the light fell into the hall. They could hear the men talking on the other side of the door. The handle began to turn. LeFash stuffed the file into his coat pocket and muttered to Charley. "Get ready."

Two Scotland Yard detectives, oblivious to any danger, came through the door thinking only of emptying the wastebaskets and getting to the party downstairs. Suddenly, LeFash charged them, hit one in the chest with his right shoulder and the other with his left, and sprinted down the hall. Charley bolted by them at LeFash's heels. As they passed the elevator, LeFash saw by the arrow above the door that the car was downstairs. He kept running. Behind them, the Scotland Yard men gathered themselves and began pursuing.

When he reached the far end of the hall, LeFash lead through the door to the stairwell. Breathing hard, Charley started downstairs. LeFash grabbed his shoulder. "No!" he whispered. "Up!" Taking the stairs two at a time, he lead Charley to the hotel roof. They slammed the door behind them and LeFash jammed the opening mechanism. Out on the shingles, they caught their breath and looked around.

"Now what?" Charley demanded anxiously. "They'll break it open soon."

"The fire escape!" LeFash exclaimed, looking around desperately. But he saw no fire escape. They heard the Scotland Yard men slamming themselves against the door.

Charley looked at him in terror. "What do we do!?!"

LeFash looked across to the building nearest the hotel. "We jump." He pointed. "There."

Charley looked to the rooftop across the alley. "Are you crazy?"

"We are spying, Charley. It is treason. They will shoot us."

"But…"

LeFash hesitated no longer. He ran to the edge of the roof and leapt across to the next building. It was not as difficult as it seemed. Catching his balance, he turned and looked at Charley.

The Scotland Yard men broke through the jammed door. Charley looked back at them, then across to LeFash, took a deep breath and ran. At the edge, he leapt desperately but slipped. He flew, flailing, across the alleyway, fell short of the roof on the other side where LeFash stood waiting and helplessly watching, slammed against the wall of the building with too much force to hold on and fell, screaming, until he landed with a dull thud in the alley below. LeFash dropped flat on the roof where he was and peered over the edge, down at Charley's body. His searching eyes clouded with grief and his face frozen in a complex expression of terror and regret and the pain of loss he knew from experience would only grow worse.

Suddenly he heard the wild blaring of whistles from the hotel rooftop. He looked up. It was the Scotland Yard men. In the dark, they did not see him. They would not try the jump but they were signaling for help. He looked down. The whistles brought British military guards swarming into the streets below. The Scotland Yard men and the military guards began yelling at one another.

LeFash took the file from his pocket, removed the memo that was of such interest to him in the conference room and scanned it's conclusions one more time:

In summary:

1. Gas vents and geologics strongly suggest presence of oil, as in Caspian

2. Recommend secure control of Mosul with the object to exclude all other would-be exploiters and thus curtail competition with Persian development
3. Curtailing competition will prevent forced merger with other oil producers

for Anglo Persian Oil Company

Sam Wade

LeFash stared a long last moment at the signature, tore the page into bits and carefully chewed and swallowed some of it while scattering the rest in the breeze. He put Johnson's business card into his pocket and then dropped the file over the edge, into the alley, where the authorities would find it near Charley's body. "Thank you, my friend," he whispered. Finally, he raised himself into a crouch, glanced around the nearby rooftops and, before the Scotland Yard men could react, bolted across the rooftop he was on and leapt to another, nearby.

Seeing movement and noises in the darkness, the Scotland Yard men began blaring their whistles again. The British soldiers and the Scotland Yard men again began screaming at one another. Shots rang out on the street below. Meanwhile, in a time honored tradition, LeFash escaped over the Paris rooftops. Two blocks away, near the Arc de Triomphe, he came down to the streets. He caught a taxi on the Champs Elysee and took it to Monmartre, where he disappeared for the night into the keeping of old friends, dance hall entertainers.

In the chill gray of the next morning, while only Paris newsboys, milk men and kitchen maids stirred, LeFash made his way by back streets toward the Hotel Crillon. In the sidewalk litter from the previous night he found newspapers, extra editions, bannering headlines about him. "HERO TURNS SPY" and "AMERICAN NEWSMAN DEAD."

Using the Crillon's service entry for deliveries and hotel staff, he slipped in among morning freight handlers. Finding his way to the rear stairwell, he climbed to the third floor and confronted two sleepy marine guards awaiting dayshift relief. They had yet to see the papers. He spoke to them in rapid-fire French, frequently repeating House's name.

"Whoa, whoa, whoa!" exclaimed one. "English, pal."

LeFash replied with more rapid-fire French, again repeating House's name.

"He wants to see the Colonel," said the other marine.

"Yeah, and I'd like to see Queen Marie of Romania," said the first.

"No! No! No!" LeFash exclaimed. "House. HOUSE!"

The first marine started shaking his head 'no' but LeFash continued being insistent in French. Finally the marines decided they'd better find somebody who spoke French. One turned and opened the rear door to Colonel House's suite. The instant the door was open and the marines' attention divided, LeFash burst through.

Wending desperately through the hotel suite's hallways, LeFash finally found his way into House's small bedroom. The marines and house staff were at his heels, the soldiers ready to shoot him. Sitting by the fireplace with a lap blanket over him, House looked up from reports he was reading.

"I must talk with you!" LeFash exclaimed as the marines grabbed him.

"Let him go," House told them, wearily flicking them away with one of his small hands.

*****

With respect to the Levant, the political goal of the Paris conference was to bring order and peace to the remnants of the Ottoman Empire. To the governments of the conquering nations (Britain, France and the United States), this was not the same as reaching a mutual understanding with the governments and leaders of the local populations. Wilson's idealistic pronouncements about self-determination did not erode the clarity Lloyd George and Clemenceau drew from European history: Might makes maps. Self-determination was fine where it was possible; economics were more important.

Before Wilson arrived at the Peace Conference, Lloyd George — knowing there was oil in the Mosul region of northern Mesopotamia — had seduced Clemenceau — who was less concerned with oil — into a private deal. France would give up claims to northern Mesopotamia (subsequently the Kurdish region of Iraq) and Jerusalem in exchange for uncontested control of greater Syria and including the Mediterranean coast (subsequently Lebanon). At the time, Wilson did not care to have the U.S. "entangled" in the region at all. Later, confronted with competing claims by Arabs, Turks, Zionists, the European powers and the oil interests they represented, the U.S. president agreed with his British and French counterparts to "submit the matter to further evaluation" or, in other words, to put off the tough decisions. Eventually, Arab leaders got a degree of self-determination,

Zionists got a gesture toward a homeland, the Turks got a protective mandate and the oil interests divided the entire region between themselves.

Before the war, Armenian Turkish millionaire Calouste Gulbenkian had masterminded the formation of the Turkish Petroleum Company, a joint venture in Mesopotamia between Anglo-Persian, Royal Dutch/Shell and German and Turkish banks. After the war, division of the victors' spoils required a satisfactory compromise with these interests. The compromise was the Red Line Agreement. It was a division of territory officially signed in 1928 but outlined some time before that by French and British diplomats in consultation with legendary oil company executives Walter Teagle (Standard Oil of New Jersey), Henri Deterding (Royal Dutch/Shell), Charles Greenway (Anglo Persian), Ernest Mercier (CFP) and Calouste Gulbenkian.

The Red Line Agreement created the Iraq Petroleum Company, in which all the competing oil companies would share. First, it included Turkish Petroleum Company claimants Anglo Persian, Royal Dutch/Shell and Gulbenkian. Second, it rectified Clemenceau's sacrifice of the French claim to Mosul oil by giving the CFP an equal share. And, finally, it made U.S. oil companies an equal partner through the formation of the Near East Petroleum Company, which was a conglomerate of the Standard companies of New York, New Jersey and Indiana, as well as the Gulf and the Atlantic companies. The primary restriction of the Red Line Agreement was that none of the participants could explore and take oil independently.

During the 1930s, the enormity of Persian Gulf region resources began luring these companies into finely crafted evasions of the Red Line's spirit, if not its letter. Anglo Persian used pre-war associations with local Sheikhs as an excuse to accept Gulf Oil Company funds for exploration in Kuwait. Gulf also set up a Canadian front with Standard Oil of California (SOCAL was not a member of Near East Petroleum) for a joint venture in Bahrain. Eventually, SOCAL obtained the first drilling rights from Ibn Saud in Saudi Arabia and all the major players began angling for a better position to exploit those fields. World War II obviated further aggressive maneuvering but, after the war, Jersey and Socony forced the formation of the Saudi Arabian and American Oil Company (Saudi Aramco) to replace the Red Line Agreement.

*****

The next day, by House's contrivance, LeFash boarded the departing transatlantic liner S.S. France II at the Le Havre docks. According to his passport, he was now Henry Livingstone, an American expatriate without resources to sustain himself in France. He was to work his passage as a

31

stoker in the ship's boiler room and, in New York, be sent ashore without pay or comfort.

He worked twelve-hour shifts as a quasi-slave under a big, hard, muscular crew chief with a coal dust blackened baldhead, a saggy face and sallow skin. The crew he worked with were men as desperate as himself and as brutal and coal dust blackened as their crew chief. The crew took its meals in rotations, two eating while the others kept shoveling coal. Despite their desperation and brutal natures, they had no strength to spare on each other during the working day and all they wanted to do during their bunk time was drink the day's allotment of brandy and sleep.

The work was mind numbing. The heat was sweat-exhausting. The smoky air was choking. But hard work drove strong men into a half conscious, pain numbing rhythm that left their minds, if they still had them, free to remember.

Shoveling, Henry Livingstone remembered being LeFash. He remembered a face associated with the name at the bottom of the APOC memo from Mosul in the Benchmark file. It was an axe-blade profile with a shock of brown hair and almost innocent deep brown eyes that could burn into you or light you up. Sam Wade. At the First Battle of the Marne, untested Lieutenant LeFash won a medal and became a hero because of an idea Wade shared with Paris Governor General Joseph Gallieni: They would use fleets of Paris taxis to get desperately necessary soldiers to the battlefield. Despite Lieutenant LeFash's obstructive bureaucratic protocols, young Wade made the idea work.

But unlike Lieutenant LeFash, Sam Wade was not present when their medals were awarded. There was an explosion, a terrible accident, and Wade was rushed back to Paris with a broken body. LeFash was awarded his medal and promoted and ordered to the front. He saw Wade only once more. War-hardened, retrained and ready to use the impatient American ways Wade had taught him, LeFash took a leave in Paris before returning to the front. After a visit to his mother and his stepfather, he looked Wade up. Wade's body was healing. They had a brief but fine reunion and parted as friends. After the war, he heard that Sam Wade was living happily in Persia with his wife and son and working for Anglo Persian Oil Company.

Still shoveling, Henry Livingstone remembered being LeFash and watching Colonel Edward House, President Wilson's top adviser, work his frail hands over each other and thoughtfully assess the significance of LeFash's report about the Mosul memo. "This memo is why Lloyd George gave Clemenceau Syria for Mosul. This memo is why President Wilson gave up on Arab self-determination. Faisal will kill the man that wrote this memo. And this memo

32

explains this." He waved the report he was reading when the marines chased LeFash into his bedroom at the Hotel Crillon.

Henry Livingstone shoveled coal more forcefully as he remembered House reading out parts of the report to LeFash. "...Johnson...British delegation oil committee representative...found dead in his hotel room early this morning...authorities calling it suicide but circumstances are suspicious."

And Livingstone shoveled harder when he remembered what Charley Clark, dead American newspaperman, told LeFash about Johnson. "Johnson...Little prissy guy, perfect dresser...Wouldn't say a word about why Benchmark is here. Just said to ask his boss...Guy named Bennett. Couldn't get to him. Separate offices and accommodations from the peace conference bunch."

And then Livingstone shoveled furiously when he remembered what House next said to LeFash. "If this was Texas, I'd say whoever killed Johnson is going to want to kill you, too. Reckon we better get you on a boat."

And, finally, Livingstone shoveled like a madman as he remembered what LeFash did not tell House: He must do whatever was necessary to make sure this "guy named Bennett" did not reveal Sam as the author of the Mosul memo so, even as he fueled the fires driving his steamship west, he expected his transatlantic passage to be roundtrip. He had to go back and deal with Bennett.

When the S.S. France II docked at the South Street port, Livingstone was sent from the ship under the stern, watchful eye of the saggy-faced stoker crew chief. With his House-provided false U.S. identity and passport, he easily cleared customs, slung his few belongings over his shoulder and headed out onto the streets of lower Manhattan. Immediately Livingstone, with all LeFash's war-weary instincts, noticed a swarthy man with a young face and dark alert eyes in a fine suit following him. Calmly, he led the man into a blind alley off Front Street, hid behind ash cans, doubled back behind the watcher, dashed onto Water Street at Fulton, lost himself into the fish market crowd and, with some of House's U.S. money, bought a ride uptown in the first passing taxi.

Stepping out of the taxi into the bustle of pedestrians between Broadway and Sixth Avenue on 42nd Street, he immediately went into 130 West, located Wade Auto Works on the listing board in the lobby and took the elevator to the twenty-nine story building's penthouse level. At the reception desk outside the elevator, amid Oak paneling, oriental carpets, antique furniture and vistas to the rivers and the sea on all sides, he demanded to see Harry Wade. Though the receptionist and her support staff eyed him austerely and explained that Mr. Wade was in a meeting, he demanded they give Wade the name Henry Livingstone and told them they would be sorry if they didn't. Dubiously, the receptionist scribbled a note and sent a runner.

Moments later, the previously austere staff was deferential. One led him to an inner sanctum, an executive den. He declined smoke and drink and asked to wait alone. He sank into a soft chair, threw back his head, closed his eyes and began to think. He did not think long before he slept the sleep of an exhausted man at a destination he did not think he would ever reach.

The noise of a door opening abruptly startled him awake. A tall slender man with a receding hairline and shining brown eyes in an impeccable suit, his colorful tie askew, stood in the doorway. Behind him was a conference room. Men sat around a conference table arguing vehemently. The man closed the door on the conference room. Quiet returned.

"Mr. Livingstone," the man said, reaching out his hand, "I'm Harry Wade. I've been looking forward to meeting you since I got Colonel House's wire."

"He said you would help me," Livingstone said as he stood, shook Wade's hand and began to explain his needs. But a door on the other side of the room burst open and the swarthy watcher Livingstone had left on South Street burst in, exclaiming, "He slipped me, boss!"

Harry Wade introduced Livingstone to the swarthy watcher, Isaac Mawcasharrow, a younger, more innocent looking man than he had appeared to be on the streets of lower Manhattan. They shook hands and eyed each other.

"Mr. Livingstone," Wade said. "I'm in the middle of a meeting so I will be brief. We worked closely with the Wilson administration during the war. We believe in the president's just and lasting peace. We know there are forces working against him. According to Colonel House, you are a good man who served the president in Paris. That is enough for me. You remain in danger. Large business interests…"

"The oil companies at the peace conference," Livingstone interrupted him.

"Yes," Harry Wade nodded. "They fear you." Wade stopped and looked at Livingstone. "Because of something you know?"

Livingstone studied Wade and wondered how much he could reveal. Finally, he decided to say nothing of Wade's son, Sam. "I must return to Paris. There is a plot to influence the leaders at the conference. The Benchmark man behind it must be stopped."

"He is no longer in France."

"How do you know?"

"Wilson was furious about the whole plot. He told Benchmark that U.S. oil interests must be considered but they had to get that man – Wilson called him a "murdering spying slime" if I recall rightly – out of Europe if they wanted the president's cooperation. We haven't been informed of his identity but we heard a rumor the spy is on his way to Oklahoma to run an oil company's security operations."

"I must pursue him."

"Why?"

Once again, Livingstone hesitated. How much should he tell Wade? He glanced at the swarthy watcher and wondered if he should speak in front of this man. It was not his habit to say a lot. He thought of Charley's death. Once again, he decided to keep Sam's potential jeopardy to himself. "It is personal. I would appreciate your help."

"Go with Mr. Mawcasharrow," Wade told him, indicating the swarthy watcher. "He has my orders to see to your needs." He shook Livingstone's hand again. "The resources of Wade Auto Works are at your disposal." He turned and opened the door behind him. The din in the conference room went on. He started through the door, thought of something, stopped and turned back. "Mr. Livingstone."

Livingstone, starting out the other door with Mawcasharrow, turned back. "Yes?"

"Thank you for your service to my country."

*****

Exiting the room, Livingstone and his new companion walked down a quiet hallway. Doors opened into empty offices on both sides.

"The men from these offices are at the meeting, Mr. Mawca…Mawcasharr?"

"Mawcasharrow. Call me Gatch."

"Is that not an odd name?"

"Long story. You have a trunk or anything?"

"Just this." Livingstone indicated the duffle bag on his shoulder with a slight lift.

"We'll get you an apartment and some clothes and then start thinking about what you can do."

"I will not be staying in New York."

Gatch looked at Livingstone in astonishment. "You won't?"

"Too many very bad memories."

"You've been here before?"

"Where, exactly, is Oklahoma?"

Gatch stopped walking and looked at Livingstone. "You're going after that spy?"

"It is a long story."

In the quiet, they studied each other until they came to an unspoken understanding. "Let's check you into a hotel, get you cleaned up and fed and find you a new suit. Then we'll talk about Oklahoma."

*****

"If you do not get me out of this city soon," Livingstone said to Gatch a few weeks later, "I will go on my own."

Around them the biggest crowd ever to see a Yankee game in the Polo Grounds, a sea of dark suits, shirtsleeves, vests, bowlers, derbies and straw hats speckled with thousands of army and navy uniforms, cheery spring bonnets and bright outdoor fashions, roared as Alderman Robert I. Moran delivered a perfect ceremonial first pitch into the hands of umpire Tom Connolly.

*****

36

The Boston Red Sox were baseball's 1918 American League and World Series Champions, as they had been in 1912, 1915 and 1916. They were the sport's classiest act. The New York Yankees, the Red Sox opponent on Opening Day, 1919, had never won a pennant and only three times in their history finished as high as second place. But a new and controversial experiment involving one of the Red Sox pitchers, as well as a beautiful Spring afternoon, brought out a record capacity crowd of 30,000 fans. The game was played at the Polo Grounds, where the n'er-do-well Yankees were tenants of the baseball- and city-dominating New York Giants, perennial contenders in the opposing National League. Though none could know it on that gorgeous, warm afternoon, the experiment involving George Herman "Babe" Ruth would very soon turn everything in baseball upside down.

*****

"Why are you in such a hurry?" Gatch replied, reaching into a bag of peanuts.

Managers Ed Barrow and Miller Huggins walked to home plate to exchange batting orders and go over ground rules with Connolly and the other umpire while the alderman scurried back to a nearby box behind the Yankee dugout where Yankee owners Colonel Ruppert and Colonel Huston gave him a hail-fellow greeting. The boisterous fans gibbered and shouted, many still settling, as the bright red hands on the right field clock over the freshly green outfield fences newly devoid of hard liquor billboards clicked to two p.m.

Livingstone snapped a peanut free of its shell and watched Gatch, waiting to think of a better answer to Gatch's question than the truth he did not want to reveal.

"Most folks think the Great White Way is the place to be," Gatch told him between munches.

"They have not been to Paris."

They watched the managers return to their dugouts and the Yankees charge onto the field. The crowd roared.

"True enough," Gatch admitted.

"So?"

George Mogridge, the tall lean Yankee lefthander, started throwing his final warm-up pitches as Harry Hooper, the Boston leadoff hitter, watched.

37

Gatch leaned in close to Livingstone and whispered. "Too many questions."

Livingstone looked at Gatch with surprise and whispered back. "I ask too many questions?"

Gatch leaned back and laughed. "Naaahhh." He leaned in again. "The trucking companies I'm trying to put you with. They want to know too much about you. Look. Here we go."

Hooper stepped into the left hand batter's box. Mogridge wound and delivered. Umpire Connolly's hand exploded upward. "STRIKE!" The crowd roared.

Gatch leaned in again. "I can still get you that job driving for Benchmark," he said quietly.

Livingstone looked at Gatch with a complicated expression, half fury and half futility. "Stay in a city I hate or work for a company I detest?"

Hooper lined Mogridge's next pitch into right center field, rounded first and held. Yankee right fielder Sammy Vick returned the ball to shortstop Roger Peckinpaugh at the keystone, who walked it over to Mogridge.

Gatch and Livingstone watched quietly and munched their peanuts without pursuing the question of Livingstone's future. Jack Barry, the next Boston hitter, grounded to the infield, forcing Hooper, but beat the throw to first. Mogridge wild-pitched Barry to second before he got Red Sox centerfielder Amos Strunk on a pop-up to shortstop Peckinpaugh.

As Strunk trotted to the dugout and the next Red Sox hitter strode to the plate, three men in fine pin-striped banker's suits came down the aisle in the box seat area.

"Look," Gatch nudged Livingstone. "It's Mr. Wade."

Livingstone studied the men as they moved into front row seats behind the dugout. "Do you know who he is with?"

"That's some of the big oil men who keep offices here in town," Gatch told him. "That might be Mr. Teagal of the Standard. I think the other man is from Benchmark."

As the men took their seats, a tall batter with broad shoulders, a barrel chest and a big round face stepped into the left hand batter's box.

"This is that pitcher Barrow is playing in the outfield," somebody behind Livingstone remarked.

"Crazy bastard," said the man behind's companion. "Risk a great pitcher like that."

"The kid can really hit, though," the first man said. "Hell, he hit eleven home runs last year and was mostly a pitcher."

"WALK HIM!" a voice in the crowd yelled.

"You think Huggins ought to have Mogridge pitch around him?" asked the companion behind.

"Too early in the game."

Just as Mogridge went into his stretch and wind up, a muscular man in a worn ill-fitting suit came down the same aisle as Wade and his companions. The man behind Livingstone screamed "DOWN IN FRONT!" as Mogridge delivered. The man walking down the aisle pivoted quickly and scowled a blood-freezing violent scowl. The batter swung hard and hit a vicious low line drive to centerfield. The crowd came to its feet and the face in the aisle disappeared into a sea of screaming fans.

Duffy Lewis, the Yankee centerfielder, charged but the line drive sank sharply to the hard outfield turf and then suddenly bounced up over Lewis's shoulder. The outfielder whirled and chased it but the ball kept bounding along the slightly sloping outfield and finally rolled all the way to the centerfield wall. Before Lewis retrieved it, Barry trotted home with the first Red Sox run and Babe Ruth wheeled around third and scored run number two standing up, his first home run of the 1919 season.

The fans settled back into their seats. Voices in the upper decks screamed "LUCKY BASTARD!" and "SOMEBODY GET US A LUCKY BUM LIKE HIM!" Livingstone and Gatch watched as the muscular scowling man walked the rest of the way down the aisle to Wade and the oil men. As Stuffy McInnis batted against Mogridge, the muscular man leaned across the oil men and said something to Wade. Wade nodded, got up, squeezed by his companions and followed the muscular man back up the aisle.

As Mogridge disposed of McInnis for the third out of the inning, Livingstone leaned to Gatch without taking his eyes off Wade and the muscular man as they walked up the aisle. "You know who that is?"

Gatch glanced up. "Name's Bennett," Gatch said. "Works for Benchmark. Arranged the tickets, I think. Takes Mr. Wade out to Belmont to play the horses."

"I'm going to the men's room," Livingstone instantly replied, jumping up.

Thinking nothing of this, Gatch continued watching the players move on and off the field until, after an instant of flashing, connecting thoughts, he looked again at Livingstone, who was quickly moving toward the aisle. "That's the spy!?!" Gatch exclaimed, jumping to his feet and falling in behind Livingstone. Striding purposefully, the Frenchman did not answer.

In the wide passageways at the rear of the seating area, Livingstone just caught a glance of Wade and Bennett as they moved deep into the shadows of the inner recesses of the stadium far behind home plate. They stepped behind a girder. Bennett glanced around, spotted a heavyset man with narrow eyes nearby and nodded. The man and two other thuggish looking characters of similar build moved out of the shadows and gathered around Bennett and Wade. Livingstone and Gatch slipped behind another girder where they could watch.

With cold dead eyes Bennett stared at Wade and held out his hand. Wade took an envelope from his inside suit-jacket pocket and handed it over with an equally cold if not so dead stare. As Bennett put the envelope into his own pocket, one of his men spotted Livingstone and Gatch watching. "Boss!" he exclaimed, pointing. Livingstone ran. Gatch did not. While one of the thugs grabbed Gatch and dragged him to Wade, Bennett's two other men chased Livingstone.

Livingstone raced through the wide walkway between the third base box seats and the restrooms and snack stands at the rear of the stadium. He dodged around and between oblivious fans. Behind him, Bennett's thugs barreled through the crowd. Running hard and holding his lead on them, he rounded the curve in the left field grandstand corner and raced up the ramp leading to the Polo Grounds shuttle station. Coming out onto the plank platform, now almost empty, he looked around frantically. To his left was the immense train line storage and repair yard. Instantly, he knew he could lead them an endless chase there. But would that only give them time to get reinforcements? Who knew what kind of gang Bennett could call on? To his right, at the far end of the platform, Livingstone saw the shuttle leaving the station. Maybe he could make it. He dashed for it and breathlessly caught the last door as it closed on him.

He sat, breathing had, looked back and saw them watching the two-car train leave them behind, saw them suddenly decide to dash out of the shuttle station onto 8th Avenue. As he lost sight of them, he looked around with a sequence of desperate, flashing realizations. This shuttle only went a block, to the 9th Avenue El station at 8th and 155th Street. They would run, beat the train there and be waiting for him. There was no way out of these cars until the doors opened at the station. A plan formed in his mind.

As his shuttle came into the station, he saw them waiting on the concrete platform. They could only cover two of the four doors. He slumped inconspicuously down below the level of the window and watched for the doors where they would not be. The train stopped. The thugs stood away from the cars and waited for Livingstone to commit himself to an exit. He peeked over the edge of the window, watched and waited for them. They looked at each other impatiently. Finally, like a fool with too much rope, one moved for the rear door of the car Livingstone was in. Angrily, the other stood his ground between the doors of the next car.

Livingstone rose into a crouch and dashed for the open door. Without hesitation, he burst out and sprinted for the station stairs. The thugs, cursing one another, again gave chase.

He dashed onto 8th Avenue, turned the corner onto 155th Street and desperately looked for someplace to hide: Clothing shop and drug store, lunch counter and pawn broker, shoe shop, beer parlor, tobacconist and a service station. A 77 service station! Wide open, people and automobiles coming and going, stacks and lines of things waiting. Maybe a way to disappear.

He moved quickly into the front room of the tiny house beside the service station pumps, stepped behind the doorpost and glanced back to the street. He saw the thugs come around the corner onto 155th Street and look around in desperation, which meant they had not seen him come into the service station. While they walked the streets, looking into shop windows trying to spot him, he turned to the service station counter.

The attendant's back was to him, much smaller than he would expect a grease monkey to be. The attendant turned to face him. It was a girl in overalls with grease smudges.

41

She smiled. It was a brilliant, refreshing, happy smile. He stared and could not speak immediately. She was vibrant, healthy and lovely, with soft white freckled skin, fearless, inquisitive blue eyes and wisps of cornflower blond hair hanging loose from under a New York Giants ball cap. "What are you looking at?" she demanded.

"You are very lovely for a service station attendant."

"I'm only doing this to make my way until I get a part on Broadway. I'm an actress. What can I do for you?"

He looked around quickly but saw no place to hide except behind the counter at her feet. "Well, I am going to have to offer you the opportunity to demonstrate your acting talent and your sense of character." He glanced over his shoulder through the station's front window and saw the thugs coming up the street. "I want to hide behind this counter at your feet because," he began moving around the counter to conceal himself, "in just a moment some men are going to come in here looking for me. I think you will be able to decide in the moment whether to reveal me."

He slipped under the counter. Before she could ask anything, Bennett's thugs burst through the door. With a glance, she was instantly afraid of them.

"Some guy come in here?" One demanded. Both eyed her suspiciously.

"With or without an automobile?" she asked.

"Without, sister. Give!"

"Why would a guy without an automobile come in here?" She asked. "This is an auto service station, not a lunch counter."

"You lookin' for a swat, sister?"

She reached under the counter, picked up a crowbar and brandished it. "Come and get me."

He stepped forward but the second thug grabbed his shoulder. "C'mon, Sherman. We gotta grab this guy before Bennett gets pissed off."

The first man stepped back and both retreated to the street. "Consider yourself lucky, sister!" The first thug called over his shoulder as they moved off, looking for Livingstone.

"I ain't your sister!" She yelled, watching them disappear up 155th Street. "OK," she announced when they were out of sight.

He got up, uncurled, shook himself and smiled. "You know character."

"They were easy to read," she said, taking a stern, hard look at him. "I handled bums like that up and down Roosevelt and Kedsey." She tapped the crowbar she was still holding against her palm. "You I'm not so sure about."

"Believe me when I tell you I would like nothing more than to offer you the opportunity to make up your mind. But this is neither the time nor the place."

She smiled. "You got a better time and place?"

He studied her with an aching sense of opportunities lost. "Not right now," he finally said.

She shrugged and turned away, replaced the crowbar under the counter and walked off toward the service station garage. "Fair enough. You can't blame a girl for asking. Catch me in the footlights."

He watched her walk away and then, finally, he turned, looked at the street and walked out into the bright light of the afternoon. He waved down a taxi and took it straight back to the Algonquin Hotel, on West 44th Street between 5th and 6th Avenues, where Wade Auto Works kept him.

In front of the hotel, he did not get out of the taxi but waited. The hotel doorman came to the curb and opened the door. Livingstone slid farther into the car and whispered out the open door brusquely. "Did Mr. Mawcasharrow come in, Frank?"

"Mr. Livingstone!" the doorman exclaimed.

"SHSH!!!" Livingstone interrupted him from the shadows of the taxi. "Answer me!"

"Not since the two o'youse left this morning."

"Good. He's on his way. Tell him to meet me at the Public Library. And don't let anybody—ANYBODY—else know I was here. You understand?"

"Yessir."

"Good. Step away." As the doorman retreated, Livingstone looked at the taxi driver. "Drop me behind the Public Library at 41st Street."

A little later, lurking behind one of the Public Library's lions, Livingstone watched Gatch arrive alone and go up the wide marble steps. He followed. Soon they were huddling in an empty corner of the ground floor reading room.

"You're none the worse for facing off with those thugs," Livingstone observed snidely, then became direct. "Why was Wade paying off Bennett?"

"He wouldn't tell me," Gatch snapped back. "But he's not working with him, if that's what you're thinking. Probably lost at the track. I told you, they play the horses."

"Why should I believe you? Why shouldn't I think he was paying off Bennett to come after me?"

"And he arranged the payoff to be where you could catch him making it?"

"Then what's the payoff about?"

"I don't know." Gatch looked hard at Livingstone. "I don't like this thug, Bennett, any more than you do."

"Why did he let you go so quickly?"

"He don't want me, he wants you."

"Is he intimidating?"

"I've faced worse."

"You were in the war?"

"I was too busy trying to stay alive." Gatch took a deep breath and blurted out his story. "I went on an exploration expedition to Venezuela in 1915 for Mr. Lithachik, Mr. Wade's father-in-law. He was looking to put in a pipeline for the Gomez government." He shook his head. "Outlaws, hostiles, crazies, wild animals, you name it. I got sick in 1916. Malaria, dysentery. Lost forty pounds. When they got me back here in '17, I was skin and bone. Started getting better about the same time Europe did. Mr. Wade was old friends with my daddy so he gave me a job." He looked at Livingstone and saw he

44

was no longer listening but staring at a row of books and thinking. "What's your next move?"

Livingstone suddenly looked at him. "Get me out of New York."

"I've still only got the one job for you."

*****

Once again on the run from Bennett, heading west and believing once again he must eventually go back east and face the man he was running from, he drove a Benchmark Oil tank truck toward Chicago. While driving he finally had time to think. All his life he had been going back and forth between the east and the west. Before he was Livingstone, before he was Captain Leonid Chyrinski LeFash, he was Jacques Chyrinski Stonagall.

His mother was Marya Chyrinski, a former courtesan in the Czar of Russia's retinue, a product of the finest education, courtly world and elegant lifestyle the Czar's European pretensions could provide its brightest and most beautiful. Then she incurred the jealousy of the Czar's daughter and was put with the maids. Seizing an opportunity to escape this servitude, she made her way south to Baku, the Russian industrial port city on the western coast of the Caspian Sea. There, she survived by her wiles and charms. Under the Czars, Baku was one of the first places in the world to turn huge oil and gas deposits into immense wealth. Men soaking in oil money sought entertainment. Marya found rich investors and opened a house in which they entertained and were entertained.

Near the time she became pregnant with Jacques, one of her most active (and brutal) investors was murdered in the house. A crazy man who lived there as a janitor fled the same day and was never found. Nine months later, Marya delivered Jacques and never identified the father. Many whispered that the brutal investor had raped her, she had murdered him and sent the janitor away to bear the blame. For many years, she told Jacques only that his father was a good man and she had loved him.

Baku in the 1890s was an exciting place for an innocent youth. Jacques played and explored on wide muddy streets and in narrow alleys, at the crossroads of the world, full of exotics, Cossacks and Orientals, Europeans and Arabians, men of all races and kinds coming and going by ship and rail and horse and camel busily buying and selling and getting and spending. Then came the Communist uprising in 1905. It escalated from marching and chants and rock throwing to fires and guns and bombings.

Fearful for the safety and future of her son, Marya left her house to Arsineh, her beloved Armenian assistant, who would be protected by the Armenian oil field workers. She and Jacques went to Paris, a trip she had long dreamed of and promised him. They stayed in a fine house near the top of the hill in Monmartre, with LeFash, a Parisian man who had visited Jacques' mother in Baku. LeFash owned a nightclub down below in Pigalle.

At thirteen, Jacques found Paris exciting and frightening. His mother had taught him the language but the children of the streets were meaner than those he knew in Baku. They didn't want to know him and called him "Arab." LeFash, the nightclub owner, told Jacques he would win their respect by acting tough and daring the meanest one to fight him. LeFash seemed to know these streets and seemed certain of his advice.

The next day, when the group on the street again began teasing him, Jacques challenged the meanest boy among them to a fight. Unfortunately, the meanest boy seemed unafraid and, in fact, smiled when Jacques blurted out the challenge. The boy was a much better fighter. He punched and kicked until Jacques could not fight anymore and went home crying. He told Marya he had done what LeFash had advised. She screamed at LeFash and only calmed down when she cleaned and nursed Jacques' bruises, cuts and scrapes.

For the next few days, Jacques did not go outside but stayed in and studied the books in the house. He found exciting stories about French schoolgirls and their lovers. Then Marya announced he must pack because they were leaving for America the next day. The sea crossing was rough and he was sick much of the time. When he was not throwing up, he thought about how much he had liked his life in Baku and wondered if he would ever go there again.

When they got to New York, they took a room at the Fifth Avenue Hotel. After sleeping, he felt much better and was hungry. Marya took him to the hotel tearoom for breakfast. After eating, he began wondering what they would do now, in America. Once again, the language was not a problem because she had taught him to speak it. He looked at her. She had only nibbled at her porridge and was studying the contents of her handbag. She seemed worried. Then she came to a decision. Abruptly, she led him back to their room.

She dressed in a fine black gown with white lace trim and made him get into his best suit and boots. When they were both groomed to her satisfaction, they took a streetcar far downtown, to where streets called Wall and Broadway crossed. Near there, they went into a tall, anonymous-looking

46

brick building and up to the top floor. Marya whispered something to the lean man at the desk. He told her to wait. They sat a long time on a wood bench. A tall man in a dark, heavy suit came out of a door behind the desk, walked to Marya and said, brusquely, "Mr. Prophetta will not be able to see you."

His mother seemed to expect this. She smiled, thanked the man, shook his hand, leaned close to him and whispered something in his ear, nodding toward Jacques. The man looked very surprised and asked them to wait again. A few moments later he returned, shook his head grimly and firmly said, "Mr. Prophetta will not see you."

Rage rose into Marya's eyes, more furious than anything Jacques had ever seen. She protested, she screamed, she wept and she demanded to be seen. In response, the tall man in the dark suit summoned more men in dark suits who forced Marya and Jacques into the elevator. Raging in defense of his mother, Jacques was helpless in the crushing grip of a husky man, even more helpless than he had been in the fight against the French boy. The last thing he saw as he was dragged into the elevator was the Benchmark Oil insignia on the front desk. The men in dark suits rode with them in the elevator to the ground floor, forced them out onto the street and summoned a policeman to make sure they moved away and stayed away from the building. So vividly intertwined were his rage and the Benchmark insignia that even now, thirteen years later, his hands gripped the steering wheel in a knuckle-whitening death grip as he drove west, staring at the Benchmark insignia on the truck's dash, remembering.

Jacques and Marya walked all the way up Broadway to their hotel. That night he listened to his mother cry herself to sleep in the hotel bed across from him. The next morning, in the hotel tearoom, his mother again neglected her porridge and studied the contents of her handbag. Afterward, they dressed and groomed and went out again. Again, she led him onto a bus down Broadway, but this time not quite so far downtown. They got off the bus near a big park with a grand, stately building, walked back uptown a block and crossed a street called Chambers to a tall, elegant brick building on the corner away from the park. Again they went to the top floor.

After his mother passed a note via a secretary, a tall, handsome, fair-haired man with sparkling blue eyes and a sharply tipped handlebar mustache came out. He greeted Marya enthusiastically and introduced himself as John Montgomery Ward. Mr. Ward shook Jacques' hand vigorously, too, and then led them into his private office. The desk was covered with law books and the shelves were filled with mementos, trophies and pictures of the strange American sport of baseball.

Mr. Ward and Jacques' mother talked quietly of Baku and someone named Jack who they also call their "mutual friend," with mysterious sidewise glances at Jacques. Soon Mr. Ward explained he had pending appointments but promised he would handle the matter personally and would send her word at the hotel. On the way out, Mr. Ward asked Jacques if he knew how to play baseball. Jacques replied that he did not.

"We'll have to do something about that, won't we?" Ward smiled.

"That would be fine," Jacques smiled grimly. "But the sport I would really like to learn is boxing!"

Ward leaned back a bit and studied Jacques carefully while Marya apologized and assured him Jacques would love to learn baseball.

"No, no, no," Ward interrupted her. "If you're going to know baseball, its just as well to know a little about fighting, too," he smiled. "We'll take care of both," he promised Jacques as he walked them back to the elevator. "You'll hear from me soon," he told Marya and then, looking directly at Jacques, he added, "and so will you!"

Weeks of visits with the wonderful Mr. Ward followed. During this time, his mother was cheerful and hopeful as she led him on trips exploring the city and renewed regular schooling for the first time since they left Baku. Ward took a part in Jacques' education, too. They went to baseball games together and Ward taught him how to play the game. But on some Saturday mornings when Marya was told they were going out to Ward's country club on Long Island for a round of golf, Ward actually left Jacques at a gymnasium in the Bowery section of lower Manhattan, in the care of a smelly, mean old man named Marty.

Boxers sparred in the several rings around the big noisy room while others went at heavy bags and speed bags. Marty took one look at Jacques from tiny, deep-set, bleary eyes, sniffed and snorted a bulbous, pock-marked nose full of mucus, spit on the gymnasium's concrete floor, and shrugged. "Only one way to learn how to box, kid." And with that, he stripped Jacques to the waist, got him into a pair of gloves and put him in a vacant ring with another boy about the same size and age. When they were ready, Marty nodded and said, "Clang, that's the bell."

The boy moved toward Jacques, bobbing and weaving like a knowledgeable boxer. Jacques held up the big heavy gloves and hesitantly backed away. Then, much sooner than he expected, he felt the ropes at his back. The other

48

boy came at him with left jabs. Jacques managed to deflect the first two with the gloves but their force knocked his hands aside. Faster than Jacques could react, the boy delivered a swift right to his chin. Jacques' head jerked back, hit the top rope and bounced forward. The boy hit him with a roundhouse left, knocking Jacques to the canvas.

Marty spit. "Boxing lesson number one: How to get knocked down."

Laying on the floor of the ring, Jacques looked up. "I already knew that one."

Marty looked at Jacques in surprise and laughed. "Hey—you're ok kid. Maybe its time to
start on lesson number two – how to get up."

Livingstone smiled and his hands relaxed on the tank truck steering wheel as he remembered Marty and the boxing lessons. He did not take much interest in golf and baseball with Mr. Ward but he took to boxing with a passion. Whenever he could not find energy for practicing at the heavy bag or the speed bag, he pictured the Benchmark Oil insignia in his mind. Suddenly the fury welled up in him and he roared at the bags. If he was sparring with another boy and felt afraid, he pictured the Benchmark logo and rage replaced the fear. Eventually, Marty taught him the boxing lesson he called "How to be a winner without being a loser."

One morning Jacques' mother gave him an envelope to take to Mr. Ward's offices. Wearing his fine, law office suit and shirt, he walked down from the hotel, past the elegantly green Madison Square, to the IRT Twenty-third Street station and caught a downtown train for the ride to City Hall. At Canal Street, he noticed three roughly dressed rambunctious boys his age distract the men in the ticket booth, slip the turnstiles and jump aboard the rider-sparse train. They quickly noticed him in his law office finery and made jokes at his expense. When he ignored them, they laughed loudly among themselves and moved closer. Fortunately, the train reached the City Hall station before they got to him. Anxious to elude them, he immediately left the train but, perhaps sensing his desire to avoid them, they jumped up and followed him out of the station, past the grand City Hall building and up toward Chambers Street along the Green.

Sweating in the muggy late summer heat, he walked rapidly, hoping not to betray his fear by running. It looked like he could stay ahead of them the short distance to the law building a block up Broadway. But these boys were not going to be put off. Two of them dashed across Broadway and ran up the street, then crossed again and walked down his side of the street, coming at him. He glanced back. The third boy was still behind. In the middle of the block, the two in front stopped and stared at him. He stopped walking. He thought about racing into the park but he was a distance runner, not a sprinter. They would catch him.

"Hey, Carl," he suddenly heard the one behind him say from very near, too near. "Is that lace on his cuffs?"

"I b'lieve it is, Buff."

"I b'lieve we might have ourselves a Lord or somethin', Wayne."

He looked back at the one called Wayne behind him. Wayne smiled an intimidating, threatening smile. He instinctively backed up. Suddenly, he felt a hand against his back. He turned and heard Carl's voice. "Where you goin', my Lord?"

Jacques' head turned to look at Carl but the feel of the hand on his back suddenly took him out of himself. Maybe it was also a glimpse of something in a shop across the street or maybe not, maybe he remembered it or maybe he only imagined that he remembered it. A kerosene can, maybe with a Benchmark Oil label. What he remembered for certain was that a rage welled up in him, a rage that made him do and say things he did not know he would do or say.

"YOU'RE REAL BRAVE, THE GANG OF YOU!" he suddenly screamed. His eyes blazed in fury. He whirled around and stepped back onto the grass of the green. "FINE! COME AND GET ME!" His head whipped back and forth. "COME AND GET ME!" he raised his fists and without thinking lowered his voice, a fury coming into his eyes as he curled his body into a fighting crouch. "And come and get your beating."

For a moment, nothing happened. Wayne and Carl and Buff looked at each other, one train of thought between them: "This isn't fun, this isn't easy, I don't want anything to do with this." Without a word, each began backing away. Jacques remained in his fighting crouch. He did not yet see the shift in the situation. He remained ready to act on the lessons Marty had taught him. Not until the three ruffians had backed off, drifted away and disappeared beyond City Hall on their way to make mischief elsewhere did Jacques realize he had learned a new lesson, one Marty had not taught him but only prepared him for.

Remembering, his hands relaxed on the truck's steering wheel until a pit in the rough two-lane highway jolted him into a firmer alertness.

Despite John Montgomery Ward's best legal tactics, he could not prove Marya's claim that Jacques was the son of Jack Stonagall and therefore the grandson and legal heir of Benchmark Oil Corporation founder Johannes Stonagall. Because Ward and Jack had been Colombia College chums and close companions in the failed Players League venture, the lawyer worked every angle he could. But the Benchmark Oil corporate lawyers easily made Marya's claims on Jacques' behalf look in court like the schemes of a nefarious foreign courtesan.

It had taken all Marya's hope to get herself and her son to New York and put Jacques' claim in Ward's hands. But just as corporate might ruined Jack Stonagall's ambitions in the 1890 Players League debacle, it also ruined the promises he made to Marya in 1892. After he stabbed her tormentor Robert Cortezar dead and impregnated her, Jack promised Marya his legacy would provide for her if he could not and left in search of oil in the South Pacific. It was a quest from which he did not return and a promise which would not be kept. When her only remaining hope for her son was proved ruined by a passionless letter from a Benchmark legal clerk, it broke Marya's heart.

After the final judgment, she moved herself and Jacques to a cheap apartment in the lower East Side tenements, proudly concealing from Ward how low she had fallen. Nearly out of money, Marya was futilely looking for work when she got sick. Though weakening, she determinedly went on looking for work, coughing and feverish, until her strength failed completely. Jacques nursed her and managed for them with dwindling finances. When he became desperate, he went to Ward.

Ward was furious that Jacques had not come to him sooner. He had Marya put in a nursing home on Long Island and took Jacques to live with him and his vivacious young wife in their big, luxurious apartment on Livingston Street in Brooklyn. But it was too late. Marya died of pneumonia. After Marya was buried, Jacques stayed with the Wards until, after accompanying them as far as Paris on their golfing tour of Europe, they left him in the keeping of Marya's friend LeFash.

His adolescence in France made him French. Enrollment at Ecole Superieure de la Guerre, the elite French military academy, freed him from LeFash. He would only find out much later it was LeFash's money (and knowledge of a certain General's predilection for women with male genitals) that got him into the exclusive school. Matriculation in the summer of 1914 gave him the opportunity to prove his commitment to France. The Great War was upon them all. By 1918, he could have been proud that he had proved his patriotism if he had still cared.

It was night on the two lane concrete Lincoln Highway. He was driving past the sand dunes on the south shore of Lake Michigan between Chicago and South Bend, Indiana. The only sound was the engine rumble of the Benchmark Oil three-tanker-truck convoy rolling west.

"Why Benchmark?" Jacques remembered asking Gatch as he opened the truck's door in the Wade Automotive garage in lower Manhattan at the beginning of this journey.

"For the ten thousandth time," he remembered Gatch answering impatiently as Jacques climbed up into the cab. "Wade Automotive and Benchmark Oil have done business since we started making tankers." Gatch, standing on the garage's oil-stained concrete floor, banged twice on the truck's big tank, looked up at Jacques and smiled at the hollow sound. "We deliver the trucks to their regional offices ready to fill and send out. They stopped asking questions a long time ago."

"Still," Jacques smiled, pumping the starter and turning the key. "You'd think they'd want to know something about me," he yelled over the rumble and roar of the truck engine.

"They know you're our guy," Gatch yelled, waving as the two trucks ahead started rolling forward.

Livingstone leaned into the clutch, eased his vehicle into gear and rolled after them, nodding over his shoulder at Gatch. "Come see me in Chicago!" he yelled back.

Journeying six days, he had wondered why that touring car carrying four men in suits had trailed the three-truck convoy. He glanced in his side mirror: Still there.

*****

Coming east from Chicago on the same stretch of highway was another touring car with four men in suits.

"You shouldn't oughtta be doin' this," the small toad-like man with the bulging eyes riding in the front passenger seat said as he fidgeted with the peeling leather on the dashboard and watched out the front window, studying the dunes across the road beside the lake.

"So you say," replied John Torrio without looking up from an account book he was studying in the light of the flashlight the husky man sitting next to him held over his shoulder. "Little City, Little City—the finger!" he grunted out of the side of his mouth quietly at the husky man. "Follow the finger!"

"Sorry, John," the big man apologized through heavy lips, snapping his thick neck around to bring his gaze from the window beside him to the account book, where he lowered the glare of the light to the line John Torrio's finger was on. "I was watchin' the dunes."

"Listen: If we haven't seen the trucks, we won't see the thugs goin' after 'em," Torrio told him. "You see anything up ahead, Sylvester?" he asked the driver.

"No, Mr. Torrio," the lean elderly man at the steering wheel replied. "But my eyes ain't what they used to be. Not at night, anyway."

"I told you to let me drive, boss!" exploded the toad-like man in the passenger seat. "This old fart can't see a dog squattin' to shit on his foot!"

"Nice talk, Toad," replied the driver. "For a guy who doesn't know a clutch from a gat."

"Shut up!" Torrio hissed from the back seat, violence in the hiss. For an instant, the small, swarthy man's nondescript flabby, clean-shaven features and balding head transformed into the terrifying presence of a venomous snake. The car fell silent. The snake became again a meek accountant and returned to his account books. "Sylvester drove me in Brooklyn, he drives me in Chicago, and he'll keep drivin' me 'til I say otherwise. Keep your eyes on the highway, Sylvester."

"Yes, Mr. Torrio."

*****

The headlights were far behind his truck but Livingstone recognized the identifying flaw in the driver's side globe. It was a patch of tar. He had seen it close up when, ready to hit the road later than the other drivers in Washington, Pennsylvania, he was just climbing into his truck when the touring car pulled into the roadside café. They probably won't clean it until they get where they're going, he had thought to himself, wondering where that might be. He watched the four men get out of the car. Young, heavy set, mean eyes, well-dressed but not like they knew how to wear such suits; tired-looking. He got in his truck and headed west. After supper that night, after dark, he saw in his side view mirror the headlights and the identifying tar smear. Still there.

Suddenly a something, a shadow, came out of the sand dunes between him and the headlights and obscured them. Moving away from the scene behind his lead trucks, he could barely make anything of the diffused lights, the fire-like flashes and sparks, the strange shadowy sense of movements. And then it all disappeared into the darkness behind him.

He looked ahead. The lead trucks were leaving him behind. His thoughts flashed faster than lights in the night. He hit the accelerator, veered left into the lane for oncoming traffic, caught up with the second truck, and waved and yelled at its dull, weary-eyed driver. The man looked over at him like he had gone insane but slowed, took a hand from the wheel and held it forward in an "after you" gesture. Livingstone nodded maniacally and sped into the gap opening between the first and second trucks. A moment later, he accelerated again, again veered into the left lane, caught up to the leading truck and again waved and shouted like a maniac. The lead driver, just as weary-eyed but not quite so dull, realized something needed his attention and steered toward the highway's shoulder while waving his left hand out the window in a "come on, follow me' gesture. As the two other trucks braked and pulled off the road, Livingstone was just beginning to slow when he saw a big car emerge from a gap between the dunes ahead and block the highway. It was exactly like the shadow that had come out of the dunes and cut off the car behind them. Jacques' headlights illuminated shotgun barrels in the rear window of the car from the dunes now blocking their way.

Suddenly it all made sense to him: A hijacking! The following car was their escort. Now they had no protection and somebody wanted to steal these trucks! In sheer self-defense, he ducked low behind the truck's dash and accelerated directly at the side of the car. The weight and speed of the truck was enough to crumple its side and drive it across the pavement, across the shoulder and into a ditch between the highway and a farm field.

Assuming the gunmen in the car were neutralized, he put his truck into reverse, intending to back toward his fellow drivers. Then he heard gunshots. He checked his mirrors. Another car, probably the one that eliminated their follow car, was behind them in the middle of the highway, its doors open. Men with shotguns stood behind the doors, shooting at the truck drivers. The drivers grabbed their pistols from their trucks' glove boxes and returned fire from the cover of the trucks' empty tanks.

He now had to decide whether to speed up the road to the next town for help or keep backing and stand with the other drivers. They were dullards, he knew, but decent enough to him. Help them. Suddenly an idea popped into his head.

Leaving the gearshift in reverse, he pushed in the clutch and revved his engine. When the engine was roaring, he let out the clutch and accelerated backward, hard, at the gunmen's car. The gunmen had no time to react. Livingstone's truck smashed into the car, driving it into the dunes and knocking the gunmen all across the roadway. Braking and skidding to a halt, he threw the gearshift into first and rolled to his fellow truck drivers.

"Holy Hell!" screamed the dull second driver.

"Yes," agreed Livingstone and looked at the convoy's lead truck driver.

The man surveyed the bodies of the men in the road, some making agonized helpless attempts to get up. "Let's get out of here," the lead driver finally said. 'I got a lotta questions but I'd just as soon ask 'em in a garage in Chi."

"Yes," agreed Livingstone.

The drivers turned and started for their trucks while Livingstone sat and waited to assume his position behind them in the convoy. But the drivers did not walk away and when Livingstone looked up he understood why. He had not seen the headlights of the touring car coming east from Chicago. They had been on the horizon when he had accelerated forward into the first carload of gunmen in front of the convoy. And, while Livingstone was destroying the second carload of gunmen behind the convoy, he had not seen the touring car coming east roll to a stop up ahead. He had not seen or heard as Toad and Little City got out and shot dead the gunmen still breathing in the first car.

Now he saw them in the road ahead, the three of them: Toad, Little City and the car. Little City went to the car and opened the door. John Torrio got out and walked alone toward the trucks and drivers. He held his hands up above his shoulders, palms out. "The shooting is over, boys. I'm John Torrio and these are my trucks. I'm sorry this had to happen to you."

An arm came out of the driver's window of Torrio's touring car. It held a big handgun. Before anybody could react, a shot sounded. Livingstone and the two truck drivers looked at each other in terror. Then they heard a thud, and a clink behind them. A body lay on the highway. Its outstretched arm had dropped the gun pointed at the truck drivers when its head had exploded blood.

Sylvester's head popped out of Torrio's car's driver-side window. "Sorry, Mr. Torrio. I don't know what's wrong with my eyes. I was aimin' for the shoulder."

Torrio looked back at his driver. "Forget it, Sylvester." He turned to Toad and Little City and gave them an angry look and made a quick nod toward the bodies on the highway. His gunmen immediately walked down the road and put gunshots into the heads of the men from the second car.

Torrio stepped nearer the three truck drivers. "You boys climb back into them trucks and follow us into town. We'll take good care of you from here."

*****

As everybody in Chicago knew, John Torrio was as good as his word. There was no more trouble that night. He put the three drivers up at the Sherman House, right across the street from a police station in the heart of Chicago's Loop. He took care of the room bills and saw they were fed well and got all the girls and gambling they wanted. After a week of relaxation and recovery, Sylvester stopped by while they were eating breakfast in the Sherman House café, dropped his hat onto the table, folded his lanky body into the fourth chair at their table, grinned and offered them jobs driving Benchmark Oil tanker trucks on the Chicago-Milwaukee run. The other two drivers were quick to agree, especially when they heard what their salaries would be and that they could keep their Sherman House rooms.

Livingstone hesitated. If it was not obvious from the beginning, it was now clear that John Torrio had many business interests. "Does Mr. Torrio have any other jobs available?"

"What're you talkin' about?" The duller driver blurted out.

Sylvester glanced hard at the dull driver. The lead driver gritted his teeth. "Ea'cher breakfast!" he grunted and they both turned their attention to their eggs and ham.

Sylvester sat back in his chair and looked long and hard at Livingstone. Except for the sounds of the other two drivers eating and the muted breakfast noise around the cafe, it was quiet. Livingstone watched Sylvester study him. "Anything in particular you had in mind?" Sylvester finally asked.

"I'm as good with people as I am with a truck," Livingstone offered. "I was an officer in the war."

56

"You like shooting?"

"No," Livingstone snapped back. "No."

Sylvester continued studying him. "Un huh," he muttered, and then looked at his hat. He picked it up and adjusted its crown, as if he was waiting.

Livingstone watched, then quietly added, "When I was a boy, I lived in a house full of women. There was a bar and entertainment in the house. Later, before I joined the military, my stepfather ran a nightclub."

"Maybe you didn't hear about the Volstead Act?" Sylvester replied. "We go dry in January."

Livingstone glanced at the other drivers, who were finishing their breakfasts. He answered quietly. "There will still be a demand for wine, women and song, no?"

The convoy leader, who was taking a gulp of coffee, spewed it. Some splashed on the other, dull driver. "Hey!" he exclaimed, standing and slapping at the coffee on his shirt. "What the hell!?!"

Caught between the taboo talk and the dullard's ire, the convoy leader stood and shshsh'ed the dullard.

"Boys!" Sylvester interrupted, suddenly reaching threateningly into his inside coat pocket only to smilingly withdraw a pair of cigars and toss them onto the table toward the two drivers. "Go out into the lobby and have a smoke. Give me and your partner a moment."

*****

Prostitution has almost always been the unglamorous profit center of any organized gangster's criminal business structure. Though mobsters prefer to be known as nightclub impresarios, gamblers, drug dealers or bootleggers, they make their money managing the sale of female labor. The business had thrived in the "Levee" district of Chicago, from Clark Street to Wabash Avenue between 18th and 22nd Streets, since the birth of the city. William T. Stead's 1894 "If Christ Came to Chicago" provided maps to the district's many houses even as it railed the Levee's evils.

The Prohibition Era produced a dramatic expansion of the prostitution business. Glorious tales of gangland "action" belie the dirty truth that the

57

Mafiosi made their big money selling sex. Case in point: Alphonse "Scarface" Capone.

The difference between the thug criminal and the successful racketeer is the ability to organize. Johnny Torrio brought Capone, a hometown Brooklyn acquaintance, to Chicago to manage a brothel. When Capone showed he could run it successfully, he was promoted. Eventually, Alphonse and his brother, Albert, ran several mid-sized houses in the Chicago suburbs for Torrio. For a two-dollar session, each working girl earned one dollar, minus ten cents for "protection." The Capones were successful because they kept their girls busy.

For their success, they were promoted to the management of The Four Deuces, at 2222 Wabash Avenue. It sold booze on the first two floors, had gambling and offices on the third floor and a busy sex mill on the top floor. (The basement was used to brutally win over uncooperative citizens.) This promotion set Capone on his way to racketeering prosperity. He expanded his business, opening ever-larger brothels in the Chicago suburbs. Booze and gambling were always available but the biggest money came from the flesh trade.

Like most racketeers, Capone detested having to acknowledge the keystone of his success. Cicero investigative journalist Robert St. John made an undercover study of a Capone business establishment. He called the place a factory of sin, "...the carnal equivalent of the Western Electric plant..." and referred to Capone as a pimp. Not surprisingly, St. John soon was made to understand that his health would be better sustained by conducting his investigative journalism elsewhere.

Nevertheless, numbers don't lie. Ledgers obtained in a 1926 Chicago police raid on a Capone business called The Barracks in Forest View showed income and expenses for the week of September 6, 1926:

Category	Income
slot machines	$ 906.00
piano player tips	55.25
bar	2677.10
gambling	1800.00
prostitution	5891.00
Total Gross Income	$ 11,329.35
Pay-offs	(10%)
Expenses	$ 8540.00

*****

It was a simple clapboard house in the undistinguished suburb of Chicago Heights. The siding was cracking, the paint was chipping and the plumbing was noisy and leaky. The door to the enclosed porch was solid and locked. If the customers said "swordfish" they were allowed into the living room where there was a bar on the kitchen side, tables across the back for high stakes poker, and sofas everywhere else. On the sofas, girls in lingerie lounged, waiting for those who knew the password and could pay.

A door off the living room led to Livingstone's office. Another led into the hall where there were small rooms on each side all the way back to the rear of the house where there was a staircase and the first floor bathroom. At the top of the back stairs there was another bathroom and a hallway leading to the front of the house with more small rooms on each side. At the front of the house, the second floor hallway came to a locked door. None of the girls or the customers had ever been through it. It led into Livingstone's private bedroom and bath and the front stairs that went to down to his office.

There was a guard on the porch door and another on the front door. There was a bartender. There were girls for all the rooms and more girls for the poker tables. There was a cook in the kitchen and a full time cleaning lady and neither of them had any questions and both of them earned good money and were happy. Just like the bartender and the guards. Just like the girls who kept the customers happy. The poker players who won were happy. And if the poker players who lost were unhappy, they often got a few minutes to relax in a cubicle with a girl, on the house, and they seemed to like coming back.

Whenever Sylvester stopped by to pick up Torrio's cut, he found everything in order. If he ever had kids, he always told himself, this was how he wanted their school run. Sometimes the Chicago Heights cops and local pols protecting the territory waved off the payola Sylvester delivered, telling him Livingstone had already taken care of them. And then the Sox won the pennant and the World Series came to Chicago.

"John wants the whole house tomorrow night," Sylvester told Livingstone late on the morning of September 28, 1919, as he stepped into the house's office and tossed his hat on the chair by the desk. "Toad and Little City'll be by in the afternoon to help your boys throw everybody but the staff out."

"Everybody?" Livingstone asked without looking up from the account book he was studying. "I usually get the local police captains and their alderman tomorrow night."

"They won't want to be anywhere near here tomorrow night." When he saw this news presented no problem to Livingstone, Sylvester turned to watch the scantily clad girls in the living room chatting and giggling with each other as they whiled away the slow late morning hours. "The word is out to stay away."

"What's going on?" Livingstone asked, looking up, suddenly interested.

Sylvester looked away from the girls and back at him. "Plenty."

Suddenly, the telephone rang. Livingstone picked it up. "Hello?" He listened. "GATCH! How great to...WHAT?" He listened. "TOMORROW NIGHT? MR. WADE!?!" He looked up at Sylvester, who nodded. Livingstone suddenly understood. He turned his attention back to Gatch, on the phone. "Of course, Gatch. It's all taken care of. All you and Mr. Wade have to do is show up. That's right. See you tomorrow night." He cradled the phone and looked up.

"Guy named Bennett with Benchmark Oil has a party comin' to town to ride the train down to Cincinnati with the Sox," Sylvester told him. "Car company boys from Detroit, oil execs from New York and down south."

Suddenly, Livingstone was staring at him. "Did you say Bennett?"

"Yeah. From Oklahoma. You know him?"

Livingstone looked down at his desk. "I've heard of him."

"You look worried," Sylvester picked up his hat and smiled at Livingstone's stony expression. "Don't. Mr. Torrio has a special crew for VIP events. Classy types. Give your people the night off."

Livingstone did not look up. "Right."

"I can see you're gonna think this through, like you do everything," Sylvester said, putting on his hat. "I'm gonna hit the road."

"Right."

After Sylvester left, Livingstone went on staring at his desk, thinking.

The next night, Livingstone again sat at his desk in his office, waiting, thinking between the loud beats of his heart, watching the door, listening to the clock tick, occasionally wiping at dust on a chair arm or window sill, perking at the sound of guests arriving and Torrio's VIP staff greeting them, fingering the knife strapped to his ankle, slumping back as names were exchanged between the host and his guests and the name was not Bennett.

In a corner of the front room near the bar, a black man from New Orleans quietly sang jazz tunes to his own soulful accompaniment on a piano brought in from one of Torrio's Loop nightclubs for the occasion. John greeted his special guests at the front door as they arrived. Among the earliest were four men Torrio greeted with special enthusiasm. He even called Livingstone out to meet them. Torrio introduced "Sport Sullivan," a pudgy man with a pencil thin mustache. Silently, Livingstone shook the offered hand. Sport genially ignored Livingstone and spoke directly to Torrio, reporting in answer to Torrio that things in Boston were "...about to get juicy." They all laughed and Sport introduced Torrio to Mr. Brown, a tall man with dark, laughing eyes and dark skin.

Torrio told Sport he knew Mr. Brown from Saratoga. "How is A.R.?" Torrio asked Mr. Brown.

"Just superb," replied Brown. "He sends his respects and wants me to make sure you know he knows nothing happens in Chicago without that you know about it."

"I appreciate that," smiled Torrio.

"You know the boys, John?" Sport asked, indicating the other two men.

"Only from the ballpark," answered Torrio.

"Well, then," beamed Sport. "Shake hands with Chick Gandil, Mr. First Base of the American League Champion Chicago White Sox. And the best left-hander in the league, Eddie Cicotte."

Following hardy handshakes and jovial good-to-know-yous, Torrio interrupted the niceties. "I'm gonna leave you boys in the care of Mr. Livingstone. Help yourself to anything and everything, wine women and song, its all on my tab. We've got some fat cat car and oil company boys coming in later to play some poker, if you're interested." He looked across to the bar and nodded. A woman with a gleaming artificial smile and a stunning

61

figure in an elegant cocktail dress showing lots of skin walked toward them. "Have fun boys."

As the four men smoldered in the woman's heat, Livingstone muttered for them to come see him if Gladys couldn't get them what they wanted and retreated into his office. He resumed his post at his desk, waiting, thinking between the loud beats of his heart, watching the door, listening to the clock tick between the muffled piano tunes in the next room, occasionally wiping at dust on a chair arm or window sill, perking at the sound of guests arriving and the VIP staff greeting them, fingering the knife strapped to his ankle, slumping back as names were exchanged between the staff and the guests and the name was not Bennett.

Late in the evening a party of Detroit men arrived. Cautiously checking, Livingstone saw Bennett was not among them. Boisterous, they enlivened the house. Some immediately went into the rear rooms with girls and, returning refreshed, called together a poker game. Sport from Boston and Mr. Brown from Saratoga agreed to join in. Seeing the stakes would be high, the baseball players excused themselves with a bevy of the happiest girls to the rear upstairs, proclaiming a different game of "poke-her." As the ballplayers and the girls disappeared into the depths of the house, Livingstone was about to close his office door and return to waiting when there was another commotion at the front door and another boisterous bunch of men arrived, the oil company men. Amid the jocularity, he saw Harry Wade. He was just about to fade watchfully back into his office when Gatch appeared at the rear of the group.

"Jacques!" Gatch exclaimed, spying him across the room.

"Gatch!" Livingstone murmured, edging out of the office doorway nervously. Reading Livingstone's caution, Gatch immediately came across the room, clasped Livingstone's hand and arm in both of his and leaned in. "No Bennett. Didn't show. Relax."

A wave of relief swept across Livingstone's face and he smiled. Gatch turned toward the group of oil men. "Boss!" he called to Wade. "Look who's here!"

Wade looked up from the glad-handing going on between the oilmen and the Detroit men. "Jacques!" he exclaimed, immediately coming over. "How good to see you!" he added, as if he hadn't a worry in the world. On Livingstone's face was the obvious question: Would Wade acknowledge that the last time they crossed paths Livingstone ended up running for his life? Wade simply ignored that matter. "You look good!" He exclaimed cheerfully.

"So do you, Sir."

"I am! You know, son, before the war, the world belonged to the old Barons. But it's our world now! Ha! Ha!"

Gatch and Livingstone smiled at Wade's exuberance. They chatted.

"Well," Wade finally concluded through a genial smile. "You take Gatch over to the bar and catch up while I go lose a little money to the Detroit boys."

He jovially sat in at one of the poker tables where the rich oil and car company executives were cheerfully losing big to Sport Sullivan and Mr. Brown. Torrio's friends played with professional grimness. The execs joked and drank and did not let intoxication keep them from agreeing boisterously that Prohibition's imminence required immediate and severe indulgence.

Livingstone and Gatch retreated to the far end of the bar. Livingstone ordered a bubbly water imported from France and offered to mix in alcohol for his guest.

"No, no," Gatch laughed. "That's how the white man got my people."

"What do you mean?"

Gatch studied the Frenchman. "You wouldn't know anything about that, would you? Never mind, it's a long story. Look at you: Running a business. You like this?"

"I know what you are thinking," Livingstone smiled, reading the doubt in Gatch's face. "In your country, it is a dirty business, like slavery. But in the old world it is a way for a poor young woman to survive. No young girl grows up dreaming of this. I did not, either. But there IS something called circumstance. The important thing is how it is done. I do it well. My people survive. My young girls find their way."

Gatch looked around the room. "Yes."

"Tell me about Bennett."

"All I know is that he runs security for 77 Oil in Tulsa."

"Oklahoma?"

"Is there a Tulsa, France?"

Livingstone ignored him. "And he organized this party?"

"Yes. But not because of you."

"Then, why?"

"Bennett's the link between the big company men and guys like your boss."

"You're saying Mr. Torrio picked this house?"

"Far as I know," Gatch shrugged. "Prob'bly his best. How did you end up with Torrio?"

Livingstone thought for a moment. "My other choice was Benchmark."

"This IS against the law."

"Bennett is lawful?"

"Bennett is not exactly Benchmark."

"This is not exactly wrong."

"Well," smiled Gatch. "At least we can talk about baseball. Who do you think is going to win the World Series?"

"I know who is going to win."

"C'mon—the Sox aren't that good."

"I would not bet on the Chicago team if I were you."

Suddenly Gatch sat up straight and stared at Livingstone. "Are you saying what I think you're saying?"

"Two of Chicago's best players are upstairs right now with girls they cannot possibly afford. Torrio is paying."

Gatch grinned. "Aw, he's just showin' his home team a good time."

Livingstone nodded toward Sport Sullivan and Mr. Brown. "They are not here for poker. That is just to pass the time."

"They came to see Torrio?"

"They represent a man in New York named Arnold Rothstein. Do you know him?"

"The Big Bankroll. Makes his living fixing horse races and cheating at poker." Gatch stopped talking and thought for a moment. "Christ!" he suddenly exclaimed. "The odds against Cincinnati are huge. These guys will clean up!"

"But Gatch," Livingstone concluded, "You can't bet with this information. They will trace it back here and kill me."

"Christ! How do you know all this?"

"I don't, Gatch. I'm a Frenchie. I don't know anything about baseball."

And that is exactly what Livingstone told the Grand Jurors when his name came up in the 1920 investigations, which is why his standing in the Torrio organization became stronger and his wealth and independence grew.

*****

Rumors of the 1919 World Series "fix," popularly known as "the Black Sox Scandal," tarnished baseball's image throughout the 1920 season. It left fans dubious of the sport. The eight White Sox players were eventually cleared by a Cook County Grand Jury investigation tainted by the disappearance of confessions and evidence. The players were nevertheless banished from the game for life by newly appointed Commissioner of Baseball Kenesaw Mountain Landis, who was seeking to protect baseball's reputation. Landis, curiously, was the Federal Judge who in 1907 had ruled against the Standard Oil Trust.

Lured by the home run heroics of a young Yankee phenom named Babe Ruth, fans could not turn away from the game. The 1919 Red Sox experiment of using Ruth as pitcher and outfielder had been so successful (he hit 29 home runs with 114 runs batted in while pitching nine wins with an earned run average of 2.97) that Boston owner Harry Frazee could no longer afford Ruth's salary and sold him to the Yankees. In 1920, Ruth gave up pitching but hit 54 home runs (more than any other TEAM in the league that season) with 137 runs batted in and a .376 batting average. Although baseball fans

Babe Ruth's Home Run Hitting Changed Baseball Forevermore In The Early 1920s:

There was the Babe and then there was everybody else...

1919 AL

New York Yankees: 45
Philadelphia Athletics: 35
Boston Red Sox: 33
St. Louis Browns: 31
✳ **BABE RUTH: 29**
Chicago White Sox: 25
Washington Senators: 24
Cleveland Indians: 24
Detroit Tigers: 23

1920 AL

New York Yankees (minus Ruth): 61
✳ **BABE RUTH: 54**
St. Louis Browns: 50
Philadelphia Athletics: 44
Chicago White Sox: 37
Washington Senators: 36
Cleveland Indians: 35
Detroit Tigers: 30
Boston Red Sox: 22

1921 AL

Philadelphia Athletics: 82
New York Yankees (minus Ruth): 75
St. Louis Browns: 67
✳ **BABE RUTH: 59**
Detroit Tigers: 58
Washington Senators: 42
Cleveland Indians: 42
Chicago White Sox: 35
Boston Red Sox: 17

2001 NL

FOR COMPARISON, When Barry Bonds had the highest single-season home-run total of all time:

Colorado 213	Atlanta 174
Milwaukee 209	Florida 166
Houston 208	Philadelphia 164
Arizona 208	San Francisco (minus Bonds) 162
Los Angeles 206	San Diego 161
St. Louis 199	Pittsburgh 161
Chicago 194	New York 147
Cincinnati 176	Montreal 131

BARRY BONDS 73

were dismayed by the Black Sox betrayal, as well as the 1920 death of Cleveland shortstop Ray Chapman from a bean ball by Yankee pitcher Carl Mays, their attention in 1921 focused on the charismatic Ruth. The Babe affirmed their faith with 59 home runs, 178 runs batted in and a .379 batting average, leading the sport into a Golden Age and selling so many tickets the New York owners could pay for Yankee Stadium, "the House that Ruth built."

Though the eight players involved in or touched by the 1919 World Series fix were ruined for life, none of the gamblers who profited from it were ever brought to justice. Many, however, met gangland fates. On November 4, 1928, Arnold Rothstein was found shot in the service elevator of Manhattan's Park Central Hotel at 56th Street and 7th Avenue. He died in the hospital the next morning.

*****

In January 1920 Prohibition became the law of the land. People who went on selling alcohol illegally were arrested and ruined – or their business boomed. Livingstone, under the protection of Torrio's citywide arrangement with the Chicago authorities, quickly became popular and rich. By the summer of the year, Livingstone was enjoying more wealth and comfort than he had ever known before in his life.

In July 1920 the Republican National Convention opened in Chicago. Besides the usual customers, Torrio's organization now had a huge influx of conventioneers to provide with gambling, women and booze.

During the convention, Livingstone was leaving the Blackstone Hotel when he decided to step into the men's room. As he came out into the lobby, he saw a house detective he knew grab a disheveled young woman in a cheap evening dress by the arm. "Get the hell out of here until you're done bleedin', dammit!" The detective ordered her in a loud, angry whisper.

"Let go of me, you bastard!" she blurted.

"You filthy bleedin' bitch!" answered the detective, whipping the girl by the arm. "What did you think you was doin'?"

Because Livingstone knew the brutal Irish detective, he started to steer away from the trouble until something rang familiar when the woman snarled back. "The Roosevelt and Kedsey boys don't go down there with their tongue before they stick their damn thing in!"

Roosevelt and Kedsey, thought Livingstone. Where had he heard that before? He looked harder at her. The soft white freckled skin was now a little ruddier with make-up. The fearless, inquisitive blue eyes were now fiercer with fear and rage. And the wisps of cornflower blond hair now straggled from a fancy formal hairstyle atop her head. But it was the grease monkey who saved him at the service station in the Bronx.

The detective laughed. "Well, these ain't the boys at Roosevelt and Kedsey, they're Republicans—they're GENTLEMEN!"

"Yeah, and I'm the Duchess of Devonshire. Gimme my money."

"Like hell."

"You're not gonna pay me?"

"You didn't do the job, did you?" He put a heavy hand on her shoulder and pushed her. "Get out of my hotel."

"Huh!" She grunted, letting his push turn her away while she surreptitiously reached into her handbag. "Imagine—a house dick who's a pimp AND a welcher." She spun back to him and stuck a .22 pistol into his midsection. "Gimme my money you bastard."

Suddenly four men in suits started moving toward her from opposite parts of the lobby.

"Listen, you hag," said the detective. "There's a money belt two inches thick with Republican hundred dollar bills between that little pop gun and my gut. And no matter what happens, you don't get your money. Take a look around." Her eyes darted right and left and she saw the men approaching. "Take this any farther and you'll be bleedin' everywhere."

She gritted her teeth and quickly moved the gun to his chin. "Maybe I'll show you what it feels like to bleed first."

Livingstone decided to risk intervening. Hands behind his back, he moved in, smiling. The detective and the girl glanced at him. "Good evening, Albert. Is there a disagreement with the lady?"

"Back off, Jacques. This ain't no lady."

Livingstone held his smile. "It appears she becomes rather grouchy at certain phases of the moon. But she's done me a courtesy in the past and I'd like to repay it."

The girl glanced at him a second time and recognized him. "You sure know how to pick your times and places, buddy."

"Yes. But you helped me out of my difficulty and I'd like to reciprocate.' He looked at the detective, still grimacing from the gun barrel at his chin. "How much, Albert?"

"Just take the bitch off my hands. You can settle with her."

Livingstone turned back to the girl. "I'll pay you what he owes you and put you up for the night. How is that?"

She glanced from Albert to Jacques and, finally, lowered the pistol, released the hammer and slipped it back into her handbag, but kept her hand in the bag, on the gun. "Deal."

Albert let out a breath. "You bought yourself a real prize, Jacques. Good fuckin' luck."

"Thank you, Albert." Livingstone looked at her. "Follow me."

"Fine," she said, staring at him. "But remember I've got a gun."

"Yes," he said turning away toward the front door of the hotel. She followed him into the sweltering heat and heavy humid air of late night, midsummer Michigan Avenue. The hotel doorman handed him a key. "Thank you, Craig," he muttered.

"No problem, Mr. Livingstone," the young doorman answered with a smile. "I'll be by later to see Kimmie."

"I'm sure she's looking forward to seeing you." He walked to a big motorcycle parked at the curb, inserted the key, turned it, kick-started the engine and looked up at the girl.

"Jacques Livingstone?" She shouted over the roar of the engine.

He smiled. "That's right." He shouted back, reaching to shake her hand. "And you?"

"Katie Marie," she shouted. "Katie Marie Stannish from Chicago, Illinois, by way of Hell's Kitchen."

He looked down at the motorcycle, revved the engine, looked up, smiled and shouted over the roaring din. "Well, Katie Marie, how about some supper?"

She grinned back at him. "How about a fast ride along the lakefront first?"

Later, back at his house, they sat on a sofa beside his desk. The night was still hot and sticky and heavy. Empty plates of cold cuts from his kitchen sat on the coffee table before them. Outside the office door, they heard the muffled sound of the jazz piano in the house's front room.

"The music is good," she said.

"My partner sent him and the piano down to entertain at a private party and the girls liked him and he liked the girls and now he and his piano are regulars," Livingstone smiled.

Suddenly, she groaned and held her abdomen.

"The cramps?"

"Yeah."

"Why would you go to work at this time in your cycle?"

The cramping passed. "Most of them don't notice," She said, looking up. "It just makes it easier for me." She laughed. "Lubrication. And when I moan from the cramping, they think they're really hot stuff. If they see the blood, I turn on the water works and tell 'em it's my first time and they give me a bigger tip."

"So you are still performing."

"Yeah, I guess. How do you know so much about women?"

"I grew up in a house like this, full of women. My mother ran it. It is common in the old world."

"More common here than the goodie-goodies want to know," she replied.

"Why did you give up performing?" he asked.

She looked down. "The people who owned the 77 station where I worked invited me to a company picnic. Some company big shot heard me sing with the kids and offered me a singing job, a private party for 77 execs. It was fun. I had a few drinks and they kept tipping me, encouraging me to do "special performances." Nothing over the line, but I guess the guy who hired me got the wrong impression. He offered me a contract, said he would get me jobs singing at all the private parties. I couldn't have been happier."

"You signed a contract?"

She looked up. "Yeah."

"But you didn't read the fine print."

She hung her head. "I sang all through the holiday season. I was so happy. I thought I was on my way. He showed up one morning in January, said I owed him money. 'Transportation, representation and incidentals,' he said. I had no money. I was just living week to week. He said he would just have to collect from my family in Chicago." Still looking down, she stopped talking.

"You went to work for him?"

"Yeah. Until he sent me out here."

"You came home to your family?"

She looked up at him with pale terror in her face. "No! Never!"

"You are free of all of them now. You can start over."

Her face hardened. "Everything is changed now. But I made this life and I will live it." She stared at him defiantly.

"It is wearying to live with it," he replied. "Is there something else for you?"

"I still have music," she said.

"Good," he smiled. "Music."

"And I will kill him if I ever get the chance." She groaned again and held her abdomen.

"The cramps."

She nods 'yes.'

He put his hands over hers, on her abdomen, and rubbed in gentle clockwise circles. "Have you ever thought about the way sexual feelings make you feel good?"

71

"For the men," she laughed harshly, then added, "It only feels good to get them off me."

"For anyone," he said quietly. He moved around behind her and put his hands on her shoulders. "Just relax."

"Do your worst," she shrugged.

As they sat together on the sofa in the quiet, with muted jazz playing in the next room, he lightly massaged her shoulders, then her mid and low back.

"Mmmm," she moaned. "That feels good." Her eyelids drooped as her warm, sweaty body relaxed.

He moved his hands lower to her hips and buttocks and thighs, gently prodding away tightness. She momentarily tensed and then continued to relax. Her eyes closed. He moved his hands to her abdomen. "Now. Think about someone. A lover. Or someone you could love."

She opened her eyes and glanced sidewise at him over her shoulder skeptically. "Someone like you?"

He smiled and continued to massage soft circles into her abdominal muscles. "Is that so impossible to imagine?"

She closed her eyes and relaxed back against him. "No."

The room was still. His massage grew warmer, more intimate. "This is for you," he told her. He moved his hands to her small breasts. The nipples hardened under her thin evening dress. He tweaked them gently. "Let yourself have it."

She moaned and turned her head. They kissed. It was a slow, tentative kiss that slowly grew deep, probing and passionate. She began to turn toward him but he gently and firmly put a hand against her back, stopping her. "This is for you, to ease you." One hand continued its gentle caressing at her breasts while the other slid to her thigh and then beneath her gown. He gently massaged the swelling in her low abdomen and then the heal of his hand gently caressed downward, over the mound where her legs met. Finally, his fingers elegantly probed her moist center. Her body suffused with pinkness and the chemistry of delight and excitation was now all she felt. His knowing fingers entered her and spread her moisture over the tip of her inner self, from where electric sensations of pleasure emanated and played across her body into her consciousness. Slowly, they fell into a rhythm, her rocking up

72

with her pelvis, him massaging in with his fingers and around against her pleasure center with his thumb. She moaned and groaned and moaned and groaned and, finally, she grunted a deep, low growling release of her pain and pleasure and relaxed into him. She breathed deeply and for a moment the room quieted and all they heard was the distant jazz piano. She turned to him and kissed hungrily and, before his hand moved away, she began rocking against it again and he understood she wanted more. He began again, massaging rhythmically, and she began rocking again and their kisses grew hungrier and her moans and groans grew deeper because now she knew what was coming and come it did, greater heights of pleasure and a deeper growling, grunting, gasping finish.

For a moment, the room was again still. But it seemed to vibrate. The vibrations throbbed in him so intensely he could not move. They excited her. Giggling, she spun out of his grasp. "I must have you," she exclaimed, moving quickly to raise her tight skirt above her hips and straddle him. Before he could react, she popped open his trouser buttons, pulled his hard excitement out and took it into herself.

"You do not have to do this," he moaned, laying his head back in pleasure.

"I must!" she exclaimed delightedly. "For myself!" She began rocking on him.

"I cannot…" he began to moan.

"Don't!" she interrupted him, rocking more aggressively. "Give it to me! Give it to me!"

And with groans and grunts, they joined together in a moment of waves of pleasure, not sure whose were whose, until she came to rest and laid her head on his shoulder. Once again, there was stillness and deep breathing and the distant sound of the jazz and the hot, sweaty night.

"I didn't think you would want me," she whispered to him.

"I didn't think you would want me," he whispered back.

The next morning they were asleep in his bed when Sylvester pounded on the door of the second floor bedroom. Livingstone raised his head and looked at the door. He turned and smiled at Katie Marie, at his side and also coming awake.

She smiled back through sleepy blue eyes and a haze of blond hanging hair, pointed to a door in the corner and whispered, "Toilet." He nodded 'yes.' She slipped naked from the sheets and disappeared into the bathroom dragging her gown behind her.

Livingstone rolled up, pulled on his undershirt, shorts and trousers and talked to the door while he pulled his suspenders into place. "What?"

"Mr. Torrio wants all his best people at the Blackstone tonight," Sylvester, in the hall, said to the door. "Tonight's the big floor fight at the Coliseum and…"

Livingstone opened the door and finished the sentence. "…And the big poker game at the hotel. Good morning to you, too." He turned, walked across the bedroom toward the stairwell at the other side of the room, and added, "Let's go downstairs."

Sylvester followed, talking. "Mr. Torrio wants your best bartenders, dealers, girls…"

"Girls?" Katie Marie interjected, appearing at the bathroom doorway clutching her gown against her nudity.

Startled, Sylvester turned, saw her, stopped and took in her beauty.

"You'll definitely do," he smiled.

Coming back from the stairwell, Livingstone interrupted. "You stay away from the Blackstone," he snapped at her. "I mean…" he glanced at Sylvester, then back at her. "…Take it easy around here until you feel better."

Sylvester turned to Livingstone. "Mr. Torrio says he's gonna need all your best girls. I could…"

"She's sick," Livingstone snapped. He looked at Sylvester challengingly. "Is that a problem?"

Sylvester smiled in surprise at Livingstone's adamant attitude. "Nah. There's plenty of girls." He glanced back at Katie Marie. "Looks like she's at death's door."

"Come downstairs," Livingstone said sharply, turning back to the stairwell, then glanced over his shoulder at Katie Marie. "Go ahead and take a bath. Use my bathrobe. I'll have somebody bring you up a day dress."

By Friday, July 11, 1920, the seventeenth national convention of the Republican Party had failed through eight rounds of balloting at the Chicago Coliseum to select a nominee for President of the United States. The two frontrunners were Illinois Governor and former Congressman Frank O. Lowden and General Leonard Wood, winner of the Medal of Honor for heroism against Geronimo, former White House physician, commander of Rough Riders and former U.S. Army Chief of Staff. Late on that steamy Chicago Friday night, partying and caucusing Republicans all over the city debated the deadlock. In an elegant modern French Beaux Arts lake-view suite high up in the Blackstone Hotel, Chicago's finest, Benchmark Oil held a soiree for the most elegant and famous Republicans. The host was the company's Chairman of the Board. The bill of fare was a simple buffet and, in deference to the "dry vote," there was no bar. The topic of the night was "Lowden or Wood?"

In an identical suite one floor up with a better lake view, also on the Benchmark account, a smaller group gathered. The host there was John Torrio and nothing was too good for his guests. Some were special Chicago people and some, those in the "know," had wandered up from the party below. Mayors and Congressmen, Governors and Senators, businessmen and powerbrokers came here, without their wives, to smoke the best tobacco, drink the best booze, play the fastest, highest stakes games of chance and fondle the most compliant, responsive, beautiful women money could buy while they forgot the political bickering.

At a poker table in a quiet, cigar smoke- and aroma-permeated inner bedroom of the suite, over stakes far higher than the stacks of poker chips, four men studied the cards showing and those in their hands. Despite his protests to Torrio, Jacques Livingstone was this table's private host. Three burly men in expensive suits watched a short, pudgy, bald man in a cheap suit, his cards pressed between the fingers and thumb of his left hand. He flicked the cards with the first two fingers of his right hand and studied them.

One of the three burly men, California oilman Edward L. Doheny, was old. His shaggy hair and thick, bottlebrush mustache were white. But behind rimless spectacles his blue eyes shone more vividly than any of the others. "Not Lowden OR the General."

"Exactly," said the youngest of the three, Oklahoma oilman Jake Hamon, a lean man with shaggy hair, a pale sagging face and hard, knowing but weary eyes, like he had been too long at the party.

"Come on, Ohio—bet or fold!" exhorted the biggest of the three, Harry Sinclair, his broad pale face, high forehead and thinning black hair framing his famously small laser-beady black eyes and wide scowling mouth.

He was exhorting the small pudgy man in the shabby suit, Harry Daugherty, back-room power broker from Ohio by way of Republican Party power centers in Washington, D.C. Daugherty threw his cards on the table. "I can't play with you boys. You've got all the chips."

Sinclair's scowl suddenly turned to a big, broad grin and it became clear why he was one of the best deal-makers in the oil business when he picked up the cards from the table and shuffled the deck. "Daugherty, Daugherty, Daugherty." He started dealing and dealt Harry Daugherty in. "There's plenty of chips. We're putting together a company in Canada. It's going to buy oil just before the price goes up and sell it at the new, higher price. The profits are going to disappear into Liberty Bonds and the bonds are going to be donated to the party for the presidential campaign."

Daugherty looked at Sinclair, then picked up his cards. "That buys chips."

Doheny picked up his cards and smiled, almost grandfatherly. "Buys chips. But not for Lowden."

Hamon picked up his cards and set his jaw. "And not for the General."

Finished dealing, Sinclair set down the deck and picked up his cards. "So who?"

They studied their cards.

Jacques Livingstone, who first heard of the American democratic process as a little boy in faraway Baku and then heard it extolled as an adolescent in France, smiled inwardly at the irony. He had begged Torrio to put him in charge of the girls but Torrio said he needed his best man at his most important poker table. Perhaps, smiled Jacques to himself, democracy had its own inevitability. Perhaps things were the same in the new world as in the old. Despite Jacques' best efforts to avoid it, he was once again seeing big oil doing what it did best to democracy.

Daugherty glanced through the card room's open double doors, to the picture window across the front room overlooking the lake. A tall, expensively dressed clean-shaven stately man with a thick shock of black hair and smiling eyes had each arm around a buxom, giggling young girl. The girls held bottles of champagne and glasses and took turns dribbling gulps into the man's mouth. The man was telling the girls a story. "So this lady says to my friend, 'Sir, where I come from we stress breeding!' and my friend says, 'Lady, I stress it every chance I get but I don't usually talk about it in polite company. Wha'd'ya have in mind?'" The man and the girls burst into uproarious laughter. Others around the room, similarly debauching, took no notice.

Daugherty studied his cards and threw some down. "Two. Harding looks like a president. Handsome. The big smile and the "I'm gonna make you rich" look in his eyes. Got the sweet pipes, a real speechifier. Comes from Ohio, mother of presidents. Another McKinley."

Doheny threw in cards, wiggled two fingers at Sinclair, picked them up, glanced at the man with the two girls by the window. "Another McKinley. I like that."

Hamon passed a palm down over the table, signaling to Sinclair he would stand pat, then studied Harding. "He does. He looks it."

Sinclair checked his own cards, tossed some in, then picked up the deck. "Dealer takes three. Andrew Mellon is the man I'd like to see at Treasury."

Daugherty bet chips. "Sounds right."

Doheny dropped chips to stay in. "I do my business with Interior. What do you think about Senator Fall?"

Daugherty watched Doheny's chips drop and then looked at him. "Yes."

Hamon dropped chips to stay in. "What about Attorney General?"

Daugherty turned to him. "What about me?"

Hamon smiled broadly and threw in his hand. "Yeah."

Doheny hesitated, glanced at Sinclair and Hamon, then back at Daugherty. "Harding will go along?"

Daugherty's pudgy face suddenly became rigidly serious. "Harding will go along."

Doheny smiled and threw in his hand. "Yes."

Sinclair smiled, threw in his hand and pushed the pile of chips to Daugherty. "Like I said, there's plenty of chips."

*****

Later that night, John Torrio's big touring car pulled up by the curb in front of Livingstone's Chicago Heights house. In the back seat, Torrio turned to Jacques. "I don't hafta explain it, do I, kid?"

"No, Mr. Torrio."

"This ain't some local micks or wops I can deal with. You unnerstand? If any of what you heard at that poker table got out, it wouldn't be healthy for any of us."

"Hey, Mr. Torrio!" Sylvester grinningly exclaimed from behind the steering wheel. "He showed them guys pokin' into the World Serious fix, didn't he?"

"Showed 'em nothin'," Big City, grinning in the front passenger seat, grunted. "I'm a Frenchie," he said in a terrible mockery of a high-pitched voice. "No speaka da basabol!" Sylvester and Big City laughed.

"That's gonna come out," Torrio said grimly. "Those ballplayers are gonna go down. But they'll never get to the guys who made the real money."

"Thanks to stand-up guys like Jacques," Sylvester added.

"True enough," Torrio agreed, reaching past Jacques to throw open the sidewalk side back door. "Now get outta here. I gotta get home, my wife's gonna throw a fit."

"Hey, Mr. Torrio," Sylvester interrupted, winking at Jacques who, stepping out, stopped in the open door. "Is it OK to put a little something down on Harding? You know, a Christmas bonus."

Torrio glanced from Sylvester to Jacques, thinking. In the silence of the deep night, there was, from the house, an elegant, seductive female voice singing with the house piano.

*"I'm always chasing rainbows / Watching clouds drifting by
My dreams are just like all my schemes / Ending in the sky
Some girls search and find the sunshine / I always look and find the rain
Some girls make a winning sometime / I never even make a gain..."*

Torrio decided. "Yeah, bet on Harding. Just don't skunk the odds…" Suddenly, he added, "Where the hell is that beautiful music coming from?"

"Believe me / I'm always chasing rainbows / Waiting to find a little bluebird in vain"

"The house," said Big City, as the piano accompaniment cuts the night.

When the woman's voice took up the song again, Torrio said, "I gotta see who's singing." He pushed Jacques aside and started for the house, the others following.

"I'm always chasing rainbows / Watching clouds drifting by
My dreams are just like all my schemes / Ending in the sky
Some girls search and find the sunshine / I always look and find the rain…"

Seeing Torrio coming, the man at the front door opened it and stepped aside. As they entered, Katie Marie, beautifully made up and once again in her alluring evening dress, was standing by the piano player finishing another verse.

"…Some girls make a winning sometime / I never even make a gain…"

As if to confirm Torrio's impression of just how haunting and compelling the singer was, the girls, house staff and customers sat enraptured by her performance. When she saw Jacques, her face lit up and she sang directly to him.

"Believe me / I'm always chasing rainbows / Waiting to find a little bluebird in vain"
Believe me / I'm always chasing rainbows / Waiting to find a little bluebird in vain"

As she finished, the listeners applauded enthusiastically. She gleefully, if quickly, acknowledged them, whispered to the piano player to take over and rushed to Jacques.

Torrio grinned. "You didn't tell me you found a new girl singer!" he said. "She's something!"

Glancing nervously around the room, Jacques saw all eyes on him and no business being transacted. "Hey!" he exclaimed. "Let's get back to work!"

The girls, the bartenders, the dealers and their customers scurried.

Torrio beamed at Katie Marie. "Sing another one for us, girlie!"

"Don't mind if I do," she smiled, then stopped and looked askance at Jacques.

Hoping to keep her presence and his relationship with her quiet, he was not at all happy about this turn of events but, looking from her to Torrio, he saw he was the only one who did not want her to sing more. He shrugged. "Sing."

Still gleeful, she hurried back to the piano, whispered in the player's ear, then turned to her small audience with a sincere expression and eased into her song.

"Reuben, Reuben, I've been thinking / Said his wifey dear
Now that all is peaceful and calm / The boys will soon be back on the farm
Mister Reuben started winking and slowly rubbed his chin
He pulled his chair up close to mother / And he asked her with a grin..."

There was a bouncing bridge by the piano player and suddenly Katie Marie's face lit up and she launched her performance.

"How ya gonna keep 'em down on the farm / After they've seen Paree'
How ya gonna keep 'em away from Broadway / Jazzin around and paintin' the town
How ya gonna keep 'em away from harm, that's a mys-sterr-yy
They'll never want to see a rake or plow / And who the deuce can parleyvous a cow?
How ya gonna keep 'em down on the farm / After they've seen Paree'..."

Keeping with the song, she quieted and sang to the men like they were babies she was trying to lull. Attractive enough when she was merely standing near him, when she performed Jacques found he could not take his eyes off her. Neither could Torrio or any of the others in the room.

"Rueben, Rueben, you're mistaken / Said his wifey dear
Once a farmer, always a jay / And farmers always stick to the hay
Mother Reuben, I'm not fakin / Though you may think it strange
But wine and women play the mischief / With a boy who's loose with change..."

Suddenly, the piano player banged out a bridge and the room exploded with life and joy as she launched again into the chorus.

"How ya gonna keep 'em down on the farm / After they've seen Paree'
How ya gonna keep 'em away from Broadway / Jazzin around and paintin'
the town
How ya gonna keep 'em away from harm, that's a mys-sterr-yy
Imagine Reuben when he meets his Pa / He'll kiss his cheek and holler "OO-
LA-LA!"
How ya gonna keep 'em down on the farm / After they've seen Paree'?"

Like everybody else in the room, Jacques, Torrio and the other men burst into applause. "Encore!" Torrio yelled.

She grinned, curtsied graciously, whispered again to the piano player, rose from the curtsy and sang again, this time in ballad style, melodious yet melancholy.

"Private Perks is a funny little codger / With a smile a funny smile.
Five feet none, he's an artful little dodger / With a smile a funny smile.
Flush or broke he'll have his little joke, / He can't be suppress'd.
All the other fellows have to grin / When he gets this off his chest, Hi!"

She burst into the chorus.

"Pack up your troubles in your old kit-bag, / And smile, smile, smile,
While you've a lucifer to light your fag, / Smile, boys, that's the style.
What's the use of worrying? / It never was worth while, so
Pack up your troubles in your old kit-bag, / And smile, smile, smile..."

As she went, softly again, into the second verse, Torrio suddenly turned to Livingstone. "I can get this girl big time nightclub work."

Jacques thought a moment, then shook his head 'no.'

Torrio looked at him with surprise, then studied him. "Oh. It's like that, is it?"

"Yeah," Jacques said. "I guess so."

"That's no good, kid. Family is one thing. This life is another. Like oil and water, they don't mix. Oil floats, catches fire. Things blow up."

"She can sing here," Jacques said. "I'll make it work."

Torrio hung his head and shook it dubiously. "Good luck, kid." He looked up. "C'mon, Sylvester. It's late. My wife is gonna kill me."

Katie Marie smiled brightly as Torrio, Sylvester and Big City stood and left, waving as she sang. *"...What's the use of worrying? / It never was worth while, so / Pack up your troubles in your old kit-bag, / And smile, smile, smile."*

*****

A year later, in July 1921, on a hot summer night, John Torrio stopped by the Chicago Heights house to introduce a new lieutenant. When Torrio entered, the stranger, Sylvester and Big City trailing, Katie Marie, heavy with child and waddling, stood by the piano player delighting the house crowd of stockyard meat packers, Midwestern railroad men, Great Lakes seamen, Indiana oilfield roughnecks and Chicago clerks with her gay performance of "Hot Time In The Old Town Tonight":

"TWO nights ago, when we were all in bed
Old Mrs. Leary left the lantern in the shed
and when the cow kicked it over, she winked her eye and said
it'll be a hot time, in the old town, tonight!
FIRE FIRE FIRE..."

Around the room, the girls and their customers joined in. *"...it'll be a hot time, in the old town, tonight!"*

And then Katie Marie launched another verse. *"ONE night ago, when we were all in bed..."*

Waving to her and grinning, Torrio led the men with him across the room to the open door of Jacques' office. "Hey, kid."

Seeing Torrio, Jacques came grinning from behind his desk to the doorway and shook hands warmly with his boss.

Happily, Torrio waved his arm toward the room. "Everybody's havin' a good time!"

"Buying your booze, losing at poker and spending money on the girls to console themselves," Jacques grinningly told him.

Torrio stepped closer. "She looks good." He nodded toward Katie Marie.

"Thanks," said Jacques. "I told you."

"Yeah." He stepped aside. "I want you to meet Al Brown."

The stranger with Torrio stuck out a thick hand and arm to shake. Jacques studied him. Big enough, thick-chested. Scar on his cheek. Intense and intelligent Italian eyes. Genial smile – a façade. He had heard rumors that Torrio was bringing out a thug named Capone from Brooklyn to strong-arm his Chicago opposition. The rumors said this Capone was a mean character with a bad scar on his cheek from a knife fight.

"Brown is gonna be my under boss."

Realizing this introduction was important, Jacques decided not to question the name, stepped forward and grasped Brown's hand firmly. "Nice to meet you, Mr. Brown."

Behind them, Katie Marie launched a final chorus. *"Old Mrs. Leary left the lantern in the shed..."*

"Yeah." Brown shook Jacques' hand. turned sideways and swept his free hand over the front room. "You sure do take it easy with the help," he observed.

"The help?" Jacques asked.

Brown waved his arm again. "The girls. The product."

"...it'll be a hot time, in the old town, tonight! FIRE FIRE FIRE..."

Jacques looked at Torrio, who smiled at him and turned to Brown. "Jacques runs the most profitable house in Chicago, Al."

"Still," grunted the scornful Italian, turning and looking around the room. "It ain't the way to do business."

Behind them, the piano played the song's final bridge out, Katie Marie's little audience applauded, she awkwardly bowed and curtsied over her big belly and then came across the room to see Torrio.

Jacques laughed tactfully. "It works, Mr. Brown."

"Til' they turn tail on you," Brown answered without looking away from the activities around the room.

Jacques smiled. "If a girl is not happy here, why would I want her?"

83

"You gotta run 'em," Brown grunted, still not looking at Jacques. "Or they run you."

Jacques did not reply. He watched Brown watch the room.

Katie Marie interrupted, greeting Torrio with a warm hug. After a few quick comments about her belly, Torrio asked her to sing *"Mary."* Grinning, she said she could never say 'no' to him. She returned to the piano player, whispered to him, turned to the room and announced the next one was for Mr. Torrio.

As she started singing, Sylvester leaned over to Jacques and whispered, "Brown's looking for trouble."

Katie Marie sang softly.

"My mother's name was Mary, / She was so good and true;
Because her name was Mary, / She called me Mary too..."

"He won't get it here," Jacques whispered back.

"She wasn't gay or airy, / But plain as she could be;
I'd hate to meet a fairy / Who calls herself Marie..."

"Still," said Sylvester. "In this city he's not gonna hafta look too hard."

"...For it is Mary, Mary, / Plain as any name can be.
But with propriety, society / Will say Marie.
But it was Mary, Mary, / Long before the fashions came..."

Suddenly, she grunted, grabbed her belly, bent, there was a "splat!" and a puddle of water was at her feet. She looked up in terror, every eye in the room on her.

"Get her upstairs!" Jacques suddenly exclaimed. "Sylvester! Can you go for the doctor?"

The room scrambled and the chorus gave way to the next act.

*****

In November 1920, Senator Warren G. Harding of Ohio was elected
President of the United States, thanks in part to a richly funded Republican

Party machine. Harding's campaign manager, Harry Daugherty, was appointed Attorney General. Harding's old senatorial poker pal, Albert Fall of New Mexico, was appointed Secretary of the Interior, with the enthusiastic approval of oil magnates like Harry Sinclair, Edward L. Doheny and Jake Hamon.

Though Hamon's wife soon shot him (when she found out he was also married to somebody else) and the Chicago White Sox players involved in the World Series fix were banished from baseball, no big money gamblers or big oil Republicans faced serious consequences for their activities. The Harding administration is described by most commentators as one of the most identifiably corrupt in U.S. history. Harding was accused of sexual licentiousness and probably fathered at least one illegitimate child. Daugherty partied hardy and profited handsomely, despite the suicides of two men close to him in lucrative illegalities. Albert Fall grandly expanded and improved his New Mexico ranch with under-the-table money he earned for allowing Sinclair and Doheny to drill for oil on government lands at Teapot Dome in Wyoming and the Elk Hills in California.

Harding's unexpected death in August 1923 heralded a souring of fortunes. Calvin Coolidge, Harding's Vice-President and successor, was very Republican and pro-business but would tolerate no impropriety. Democratic investigations into Fall's activities turned into the Teapot Dome scandal. The quasi-surreptitious partying over which Prohibition violators giggled turned into a blood bath in the streets when rival bootleg gangs began struggling for power. Even the Bunyonesque Babe Ruth began to show a little humanity. He slowed a bit in 1922 (.315 BA, 35 homers, 99 RBIs), though the Yankees still won the pennant. He returned to form in 1923, though the rest of the league was catching up. In 1924, Ruth's team fell to second place. And in 1925, Babe got "the Bellyache Heard 'Round the World" (variously reported as appendicitis or indulgence in too many hot dogs and beer), had only 25 homers, 66 RBIs and a .290 batting average, and the Yankees finished seventh in an eight team league. 1925 also saw the first death of an active major leaguer in an airplane crash, when Cincinnati pitcher and Air Force Reserve pilot Marv Goodwin's plane went down on a training mission, heralding other coming changes.

*****

On a clear, warm spring evening in April 1924, Jacques (Stonagall LeFash) Livingstone folded back the top on his new, black, three-door Model T Sedan Touring Car and drove his wife Katie Marie Stannish Livingstone and their nearly three-year-old son Montgomery (Monty) Chingatchgook Livingstone from the suburb of Chicago Heights into The Loop. They drove up Michigan

Avenue, past sprawling Soldier Field. As they approached the green expanses of Grant Park, the suburban rows of short squat two- and three-story brick and frame houses and apartment buildings gave way to the grand procession of masterly renaissance and gothic architectural structures facing the formidable east across the park and the lake, structures built to endure weather and time and fire, announcing that come-what-may, Chicago was here to stay.

The sun set in the west, sending shafts of late afternoon white light between the looming buildings and casting long shadows from tree-lined Michigan Avenue across the park's fields and fountains. The deep blue lake beyond flashed back beams of glimmering golden tribute.

Jacques drove north, through the evening parade of taxis and cars and well-dressed, urban, ambitious and window-shopping society just beginning to become tuxedoed, gowned and bejeweled evening socialites and socializers. At Congress Parkway, he turned left in front of the Congress Hotel and drove between the big buildings to Wabash, where he turned left again. They moved slowly in the busier, less orderly back street through new and old cars, horse-drawn wagons and trucks, people in evening dress and business suits and working clothes, the freshly clean and the day weary. He came back south a short block and a half, turned left across the streetcar tracks into an alley between a speakeasy and a residential hotel and drove to the end, where he parked behind the Blackstone Theater. They used the theater's access walkway to emerge onto Balbo, and then walked past the theater and around the corner onto Michigan Avenue, where Isaac "Gatch" Mawcasharrow, Jr., Monty's godfather, stood waiting at the front door of the Blackstone Hotel.

When Katie Marie pointed out Uncle Gatch to little Monty, the boy ran to him. "We're goin' to the moving pichures Uncle Gatch!" he exclaimed as Gatch swept him lovingly up and whirled him around.

"I KNOW!" Gatch answered. "Sword fighting!"

"Yeah! But Daddy says I gotta be quiet for the kissin'!"

Laughingly agreeing, Gatch set Monty down and, after equally warm greetings with Monty's parents, the four walked north up Michigan Avenue, enjoying the reunion, Monty's antics, the warm evening and the bright lights of the street-level storefronts and theater marquees. As they passed the Hotel Sherman, two men in natty suits came out.

"Merde!" Jacques muttered.

"What?" Gatch asked.

Before Jacques answered, one of the men, the stocky, swarthy man with the scar on his cheek, exclaimed. "Livingstone!"

"Mr. Brown," Jacques answered unenthusiastically, mustering a smile and continuing to use Capone's nom de guerre. As the group stopped in the hotel entryway, Jacques went on. "You know my wife and Monty. This is Monty's godfather, Isaac Mawcasharrow, from New York. He turned toward Gatch as he shook Brown's hand. "Mr. Brown is Mr. Torrio's partner."

"Nice to meet you," smiled Gatch nervously, immediately alert at the mention of Torrio.

"Yeah," said Brown. "Nice-ta-meetcha-too." He did not bother introducing his companion. His gaze pivoted instantly to Jacques. "Gotta talk, Livingstone."

"We're on our way…"

"Now, Livingstone." He looked at Katie Marie. "You and the kid and the guest go on up the street. This'll only take a minute."

Pained expressions and shrugs went around until Jacques decided and looked at Gatch. "I will be quick. Take Monty and go on. I will catch up."

"That's right," grinned Brown mockingly. "He'll catch up."

As Gatch, Katie Marie and Monty turned up Michigan Avenue, Brown grabbed Jacques' arm and pulled him into an alcove of the hotel lobby. "Them broads o'yours are hittin' the streets and runnin' and I warned you about that."

"I don't want them if they don't want to stay. They are free to go."

"That ain't how you run a business," Capone told him angrily. "If a girl wants out…" He held up his fist. "…you talk her into going back to work."

"No, I let her go. She is advertising."

"You can't trust 'em. The cops grab 'em. They spill. You gotta send a message. Nobody quits on us."

"Wrong message. Let her go and new girls come. Everybody wins."

"In this town," said Capone. "I win. ME. I won't have runaway broads." He held up the fist again. "Deal with that cooze or I'll send somebody down there who will." Capone pivoted abruptly and walked away, out of the hotel and south on Michigan Avenue. His companion followed. Jacques watched for a moment, shaking his head sadly, remembered his plans, dashed out of the hotel and turned uptown.

He caught up to his family and friend at Adams and they walked together over to State Street, crossed, walked up to the Orpheum Theatre and bought tickets for "A Sainted Devil" starring Rudolph Valentino, Nita Naldi, Helena D'Algy and Dagmar. There was not enough sword fighting and way too much dancing and kissing for Monty. By the time Don Alonzo erupted in fury at the film's climax, the little boy was fast asleep in his mother's arms. When the movie ended, Jacques left Katie Marie and Gatch at the theater exchanging critiques of the film while he went for the car. On his way out, he heard her assure Gatch she could have played the female lead far better and then launch into a thorough disparagement of Nita Naldi's lovemaking. He smiled.

As he pulled the car up in front of the theater, he saw Katie Marie come out carrying Monty and still excitedly telling Gatch how Valentino's lover should be played, Monty still sleeping the imperturbable sleep of a three-year-old in her arms. She laid the boy in the front seat, gave Gatch a sisterly peck on the cheek, walked around to the driver's side of the auto, gave Jacques a more passionate, wifely kiss, took his place behind the wheel, and drove off to put Monty to bed, leaving the two friends on State Street, walking back toward the Blackstone.

They passed a little Italian restaurant on Wabash between Van Buren and Congress. "Man, that smells good," Gatch said, inhaling.

"You are hungry?"

"In the rush to meet you, I missed supper."

"Let's go in here. I know the owner."

A little later, following a warm greeting from the portly, bright-eyed, gray-haired Italian immigrant owner, they were sitting at a corner table with a red-checked table cloth ("Mr. Brown's table," the owner assured Jacques), sipping Italian Chianti and nibbling at antipasti while awaiting a hot dish.

Gatch looked at Livingstone. "You look tired, Jacques. And worried."

"I am fine."

"Is it Bennett?"

"I have heard nothing of him since before Monty was born."

"Is it Capone?"

"You knew?"

"Mr. Brown?" Gatch asked sarcastically. "Come on. With that scar, who does he think he's kidding?"

"It has all changed since he took over. His thugs are getting ridiculously rich selling rot gut. They beat or kill anybody in their way." He shook his head. "Thanks for asking," he concluded sarcastically, hanging his head.

"I'm leaving Wade."

Jacques looked up quickly. Studying Gatch, he saw there was more and waited.

"I'm a little worried."

"About what?"

"Well, for one thing, about the wire transfers between New York and Tulsa."

"Wire transfers?"

"To the GlennOil 77 Company."

"Is it not normal for an automotive giant to do business with an oil company?"

"To a guy named Bennett."

Jacques said nothing, just watched Gatch and waited.

"Thought I might go down there and ask some questions."

Jacques still watched and waited.

"You know they're finishing up the investigations into that Teapot Dome business?"

"I heard," Jacques smiled. "Just in time for the next election."

"Coolidge is kicking it to a couple of lawyers, Roberts and Pomerene."

"I hear they are aggressive."

"You know something about it, don't you?"

"I know where the money came from," shrugged Jacques.

"They know where the money went," said Gatch. "They're going to get Secretary Fall. If they knew where it came from..."

"They could get the oil guys, Sinclair and Doheny and the rest," concluded Jacques.

"You ever think about telling what you know?"

"They would kill me."

"Go to Roberts and Pomerene. They'll protect you. You could break the back of corruption."

"I would not do anything but leave my son fatherless."

Suddenly, Al Capone (nee Brown) stormed into restaurant, dragging a screaming girl by her hair, two thugs following.

"You see what I mean?" Capone bellowed. Then he leaned down, got his face right beside Jacques and, through clinched teeth, whispered viciously into Jacques' ear. "This bitch went to a copper with a story." He whipped her away to one of the thugs and flicked his hand toward her, implying that the thug get rid of the girl. He stood back. "She's one of YOURS! Dammit, Livingstone. You gotta put the product in its place!"

Jacques stood up, his face stern. "She is a human being. Not product."

Capone eyed Jacques and laughed. "People who talk to me like that sometimes have accidents, Livingstone. They happen to cross the street just when bullets come by."

Jacques leaned on the table. "That is it. I am closing the house. And leaving town."

Capone stepped back, put his hands on his hips and stared at Jacques. "One—you don't close MY house."

"YOUR house?"

"Yeah. Torrio's gone. This city is mine now. Two—girls don't run away on ME. What makes YOU think YOU can? This ain't Paris, Frenchy, this is Slaughtertown."

Jacques' face remained stern but implacable. Gatch, Capone and Capone's thug watched, waiting for Jacques to respond, none sure what he would say or do. Around them the restaurant was silent.

Finally, Jacques lifted his weight up off his arms and stood quietly, arms at his sides. "I understand. I will take care of the problem."

Capone grinned and laughed again. "Perfect."

*****

Early the next day, Jacques woke all the girls in the house and sent them away, telling them the house would likely be open again in a few days under a new manager and warning them about Capone's new policies, should they choose to come back. In answer to their pleas, he told them he was not yet sure where he was going.

After packing all night, Katie Marie slept in until Monty was up and about and then dressed and breakfasted him. She taught him the lyrics to *California Here I Come* while readying him for the road. As Jacques pulled the Model T into the driveway and was preparing to load it, Gatch arrived in a taxi. Quickly, they packed the car with all the luggage it could carry and piled in, Katie Marie and Monty in the back seat singing, Gatch behind the wheel and Jacques in the passenger seat, almost literally "riding shotgun" as he fingered a .38 revolver in his inside jacket pocket.

As Gatch started the engine, a seven-seat touring car came up the street. "Wait until that car stops," Jacques ordered. It stopped in front of the house and shut off its engine. "Capone's men," Jacques whispered to Gatch.

"Which way?"

"Drive!" Katie Marie demanded from the back seat.

Jacques pointed. Adrenalin and lust for the engine's roar fueled Gatch's reaction. He threw the gearshift to reverse and floored the accelerator. As soon as he was clear of the driveway, he whipped the car into a full turn, reversed the gearshift and accelerated. In the touring car, the Capone thugs yelled at one another until the driver restarted the engine and pursued.

"Step on it," Jacques shouted at Gatch. He pointed around a corner. "That way." He glanced back and fingered the pistol.

Gatch turned the car right. They flew over railroad tracks, roaring north.

Monty started crying. "I'm scared, mommie. Make him slow down."

Unperturbed, Katie Marie smiled at Monty. "Sing with me! *California here I come, / Right back where I started from, / Where bowers of flowers bloom in the sun...*"

"Mommie!"

"North? What the hell?" shouted Gatch. "You goin' back to Chicago?"

"Here! Left!"

Now they were headed west on the fine new concrete of the Lincoln Highway.

"Mommie, make him slow down."

"Sing, baby! *Each morning at dawning...*"

Jacques twisted toward the rear compartment and boosted himself over the seatback so as to see better out the back window but acted like he only wanted to join in the singing. "*Birdies sing an' ev'rything...*" he boomed to Monty.

Katie Marie grinned at him. "*A sun-kissed miss said, 'don't be late,' / That's why I can hardly wait...*" She led, both Jacques and Monty grinning and joining in. "*Open up that Golden Gate, / California here I come!!*"

Finally, Monty relaxed a bit, though he still clutched tightly to his mother as the car roared up the highway. She looked from her son to her husband and smiled.

"Where we goin'?" Gatch asked in the moment of silence.

"Joliet."

"What's there?"

"The road to Oklahoma."

"What the hell?" Gatch asked, befuddled.

Jacques looked back uneasily. "Is this as fast as it will go?"

"Yep. I guess it's just a question of who runs out of gasoline first now."

Jacques fingered the gun and looked from his son up to the rear window, studied the car trailing in the distance, fingered the gun again. "Maybe."

They outran the Capone gang to Joliet, driving west on Mississippi Road. At Douglas Street, near the junction of the Lincoln Highway and what would become known as Route 66, Jacques spotted a shed in a field a hundred yards off Mississippi and directed Gatch to steer into it.

"Now what, mommie?" Monty asked when the car stopped and Gatch shut the engine down to cool.

Gatch laughed. "Good question."

"Don't ask me, Monty," Katie Marie told her son. "Ask daddy."

Jacques looked from the boy to the adults. "Well, for one thing, we're all gonna go around behind this shed and make wee-wee."

"Good idea, daddy!"

While they stretched their legs, Jacques suggested that Katie Marie pull out the cold chicken she had in a picnic basket and fill their water bottles at the nearby spigot while he and Gatch refilled the radiator. After they nibbled on the chicken, he and Gatch walked up to a stand of trees and shrubs near the road.

"What the hell you plannin'?" Gatch asked. "Shootin' 'em as they drive by."

Jacques laughed. "It is good you weren't with the American Expeditionary Force. The war might not be over yet."

Gatch laughed. "Then what?"

"We watch," Jacques shrugged. "If they go south, we go Lincoln Highway."

"And vice versa?"

"And vice versa."

Sometime later, the Capone car drove past, the thugs inside yelling at each other so loud Gatch and Jacques heard them as they went by. At the junction of the highways, the car slowed and arms pointed out all the windows, in both directions. The yelling got louder. Finally, the car turned left and headed south on Douglas Street. Jacques and Gatch returned to the Model T and headed northwest. In Aurora, they gassed up. Late in the afternoon, they spotted roadside cabins outside DeKalb and stopped for the night.

They ended the next day by crossing the Mississippi River and spent the night in Clinton, Iowa. The next five days were long and hot and dry. The first ended in Cedar Rapids, the second in Dennison, the third across the Missouri River in Omaha, Nebraska, the fourth in Grand Rapids and the fifth in the middle of the endless prairies near Kearney.

After Katie Marie got Monty to bed the fifth night, the adults settled down in rockers on the porch of their roadside motor hotel cabin and listened to the crickets chirp, watched the fireflies dart and swatted mosquitoes. Gatch noticed Jacques looking worried as he studied their maps in lantern light.

"What is it?"

"By now those boneheads are back in Chicago and Capone has figured out that we are heading west on this route."

"So?"

"He's got telephones and he can hire killers all across the country."

"What do we do?"

"We need to conceal ourselves. Travel with somebody else or something like that."

Katie Marie laughed. "I always wanted to run away and join the circus."

They heard the sound of a night train nearby, then its whistle. They sat quietly and listened. Gatch was about to say something about the lonely sound of the train whistle when there was a louder, nearer sound of another train and another whistle, this one higher pitched and screeching. And then there was the frantic blowing of train whistles and horns and then enormous deafening crashing sounds, and then explosions and agonizing, terrifying distant screams and the night sky to the south towards Kearney was suddenly full of fire and smoke.

Jacques, Katie Marie and Gatch looked at each other in astonishment. Jacques spoke first as both he and Gatch came out of their chairs. "Get the car started." He turned to Katie Marie, who was already nodding her understanding as he spoke. "You will have to stay here with Monty."

"Go!" she replied.

By the time they reached the crash scene, locals were fighting fires in the nearby fields. Wreckage of two trains was up and down the tracks for nearly a half-mile. The air was thick with smoke, puddles of oil and piles of debris lay along the tracks and moans and screams and the murmur of voices came from everywhere in the eerie, flame-lit darkness. As Gatch and Jacques stood by the car, outsiders wondering what to do, a tall man in a worn suit with a broad face and a high forehead walked by. His tie and collar were undone, his shirt was wet with sweat, his eyes were deep and dark and purposeful, and he chomped on an unlit cigar.

"Can you carry a stretcher?" he demanded.

"Yeah!" Gatch snapped back.

"Go down there by those Red Cross trucks."

Soon they were carrying bodies from around the wreckage to Red Cross ambulances where the intense, tired man in the worn suit, Doc Baxter, decided which ones went into Kearney to the clinic and which ones went to the morgue room at his farm.

Gatch and Jacques worked together quietly. The work was wearying but neither complained, nor did the crews of locals working through the night around them. No one stopped for introductions but faces became familiar as they repetitively performed the grim tasks at hand. After an hour or two, as Doc Baxter was telling Jacques and Gatch to set a dead body on their

95

stretcher off to the side for later transport to the morgue, a pair of young boys came down from the highway effortfully carrying a heavy barrel. The short, shabby man walking beside them tapped the barrel with the two-foot dowel rod he carried.

"Right here, boys." The short stubby man turned to the group. "Barrel o'water, Doc. Why'nt you and the fellas splash your selves?"

"Good idea, Ben."

"We're runnin' outta floor space at the clinic, Doc."

"Floor space! These people need bed care!"

"Easy, Doc, easy. We ran out of beds hours ago. Then we ran out of cots. Now the floors are full with palettes."

" 'Scuse me," Gatch suddenly intruded. "We're stayin' at a roadhouse hotel up on the Lincoln Highway and most of its empty."

"Yeah," nodded Ben. "The old Honeymoon Hotel."

"Might be easier to get medical supplies there than to get all these folks into Kearney," observed Doc Baxter.

Ben pivoted his chubby body. "I'll get it done." He walked off.

The men doing the heavy lifting gathered around the water barrel, drank and splashed themselves, and quickly returned to their grim work. When the men went back to work, the women doing the nursing began dispensing water from the barrel to the wounded.

"Thanks," Doc Baxter said to Gatch as he and Jacques were about to return for another body. "Where you boys from?"

Gatch and Jacques glanced at each other, wondering what and how to explain. Doc Baxter stuck his cigar in his mouth, chewed at it, eyed them and waited for an answer.

"We left Chicago last week," Gatch finally said.

"How did this happen?" Jacques interrupted, changing the subject to the train wreck.

96

"Like this," a voice boomed from the darkness behind them.

They turned toward the voice. Two young men in scruffy pants and undershirts, pushed hard, came stumbling forward clumsily, banged into one another and sprawled on the bloody dirt and grass. Then a man walked into the light. "The tracks weren't switched," he reported. "So I checked the switching shack. Found a still and these two passed out. They claim it was the alkie fumes."

"You know this man?" Gatch asked Doc Baxter incredulously.

"Never met him," Doc Baxter replied, now studying the big stranger in the white Stetson with the broad chest, swarthy round face and small, dark, intense, intelligent eyes. When he took in the pair of pearl-handled pistols in the quick draw holsters at the man's waist, he took his cigar from his mouth and added, "But I'm guessing he's Two-Gun Hart."

"Agent Richard Hart, Prohibition Service," the man quickly corrected him, tipping his Stetson. "I'm tracking a St. Louis bootlegger and his toughs. I picked up their trail in my home territory, up near the Dakota border." Jacques and Gatch offered hands to shake but Hart was already stepping toward the two men on the ground. He grabbed strips of bandages and began binding their hands behind them. "These boys were working for the bootlegger. I promised them they wouldn't hang if they spilled."

"They've got a lot of blood to pay for," Doc Baxter interrupted. "But I've known them their whole lives and they're way too stupid to be evil."

"That's how I had it figured," agreed Hart.

"That fella from St. Looey's gonna kill us if you don't hang us," one of the boys blurted out.

Hart looked down at the boy. "He's not going to kill anybody son." Hart looked back at Doc Baxter. "For promising not to hang 'em, these boys told me where my man is." He finished tying them and stood up. "I'm going after him and his gang. Think I could get some help from your local sheriff?"

"Ben?" Doc Baxter laughed. "Not likely to be helpful."

"Anybody around here know how to handle themselves?"

"Well, me," shrugged Doc Baxter. "But I've got my hands full at the moment."

"Still," said Hart, fixing his expression, setting his gun belt at his hips and turning away. "It won't wait."

Gatch and Jacques glanced at each other. Jacques nodded 'yes.' "Hold on, Agent Hart!" Gatch called.

Soon they were following Hart's flivver into the Nebraska night in their own Model T.

"Did you notice how much Hart looks like Capone?" Gatch asked.

Driving, Jacques simply nodded 'yes.'

They could be brothers," Gatch muttered.

"Unlikely," Jacques replied.

"Maybe this is the guy we should be traveling with," Gatch thought aloud.

"Maybe."

Near the edge of Kearney, the flivver turned off the highway. A couple of miles up the side road, near a farmhouse surrounded by oaks and hackberry trees and chokecherry and sumac shrubs on a flat piece of farmland, the flivver pulled over and stopped. Jacques parked behind it. The farmhouse was a quarter mile on, on the far side of the tree and shrub windbreak. Stealthily, Hart led them on foot to the rear of the house, its windows bright with electric light. Inside, the radio played dance music and chatter and laughter carried across the prairie.

Fifty yards from the back door, Hart whispered to Gatch and Jacques that he would circle around to the front, where the automobiles were parked, light a match and wave it. When they saw the match flicker out, they were to lay down a barrage of gunfire against the back of the house. When the outlaws ran for their vehicles, Hart would round them up.

"You make it sound so damn easy," Gatch whispered.

"I've tracked plenty of these cowards," smiled Hart grimly. "Trust me: They ALWAYS run."

A few minutes later, Jacques and Gatch saw the match flicker and flicker out. They looked at each other, Jacques raised his eyebrows quizzically and

98

Gatch answered with a shrug. They turned toward the house and began shooting, Jacques with Hart's Thompson submachine gun and Gatch with Doc Baxter's shotgun. At their barrage, which tore into the house's rear wood slat wall and shattered its back windows, the lights went out inside and the voices and laughter stopped. Eerily, the radio went on playing in the moment of silence that followed the first barrage. After another exchange of answerless glances, Jacques and Gatch began shooting again. Gunfire was returned from the house randomly. Jacques and Gatch kept low and kept firing, stopping only to reload.

They heard shouts from inside the house but could not make them out over the noise of the guns. The music from the radio disappeared from among the noises of the night but return gunfire blared out intermittently. Then, though Jacques and Gatch kept shooting, the return fire from the house ceased and a heavy voice called out.

"I don't know what branch of the law you are, but if you'll take this roll of cash and be on your way, you'll save me the trouble of having to kill you."

Gatch and Jacques smiled grimly at one another, remembering Hart's words to the young alky cookers. "He's not going to kill anybody son." They raised their weapons and answered with a new volley. There was return fire for a few more minutes while inaudible shouting continued in the house. Then the return fire slowed and finally stopped, though Gatch and Jacques continued firing, according to Hart's plan.

During a pause to reload, something came flying from the house into the backyard. It hit the ground and exploded into flames.

"Molotov cocktail!" shouted Jacques.

Another flew from the house and exploded in the yard.

"Whatta we do!?!" Gatch yelled in panic.

"Shoot!" Jacques told him.

A third bomb flew toward them and exploded. They fired frantically.

After shooting non-stop in terror a few minutes longer, they realized no more bombs or gunshots were coming at them. They stopped shooting. The night became deeply quiet. Moments passed as heartbeats. Then they heard the clear crack-crack-crack of pistol shots, one after another, coming from the far side of the house. There was an instant of pause and then crack-crack-crack and crack-crack-crack again and then another silence. And they heard a voice, pleading.

"No, mister, I'm just a car driver, I..."

Crack.

"That's my WIFE, sheriff!"

A woman screamed. Crack.

"She didn't..."

Crack.

Silence.

In the darkness and quiet, they waited and watched the house. Soon they heard someone moving around inside the house, a light went on and they prepared to open fire again. Then the silhouette of Hart's big presence filled the back door, his white Stetson back on his head, a pistol high in each hand. "Come on out, men, its over."

They walked into the back door of the empty farmhouse as Hart exited at the front. They followed him. In the front yard lay seven bodies, five men and two women, each with a bullet hole between the eyes.

"That's some shooting!" exclaimed Gatch.

"And in the dark," Jacques muttered.

"How could you do it?" Gatch asked incredulously.

"I'm a sharpshooter."

Jacques turned to Hart. "Are they all killers?" he asked quietly.

"I don't know."

"But that's murder," Gatch blurted out.

Hart turned to him and stared. "I don't care."

They loaded some of the bodies into Hart's flivver and others into the back of the Model T and drove them to Doc Baxter's farm, the local morgue. Once again following Hart, Jacques and Gatch rode in silence until Gatch sighed and looked over at Jacques, who was again driving. "I guess Hart's not the one to travel with."

Jacques glanced back. "We still need cover to travel."

"But not Hart."

"Not Hart."

When they arrived at his farm with the bodies, they found Doc Baxter back from the wreck on the tracks. He was processing the dead so as to notify the next of kin. Wearily, he pointed at his icehouse and told them to lay the shooting victims out inside until he could get to them. Glancing as the dead were unloaded, he took his cigar out of his mouth and identified the locals as a childless farming couple but could not explain the presence of the St. Louis bootleggers in their house.

"No more wounded to tend?" Gatch asked Doc Baxter.

"Lots," Baxter replied.

"Why aren't you tending them?"

"Not my job."

"Not your job?" Gatch asked in confusion.

"I'm a vet. Specialize in pigs."

"And coroner?"

"You'd be surprised how much people are like pigs," Doc Baxter smiled, sticking his cigar back in his mouth and returning to the train wreck dead.

After they got all the bodies into the icehouse, Gatch went out of the cold room into the dark night. Jacques stood in the room's dim light and idly watched Hart go through the bootlegger's pockets for information about his operations.

"Hold this," Hart instructed, handing Jacques a flashlight.

Jacques took the light, watched Hart pull a telegram from the man's pocket and held the light so Hart could read the telegram.

"Who the fuck is Al Brown?" Hart wondered aloud.

Jacques quickly moved near Hart.

"Hold the damned light still!" Hart commanded.

Reacting defensively, Jacques lowered the light and eyed Hart challengingly in the dark cold room. For a moment, neither flinched.

"I need the light to read," Hart growled quietly through gritted teeth. Still, Jacques did not flinch. Unexpectedly, he raised the flashlight and shone it directly into Hart's brown eyes, where Jacques saw red raging.

"Fine," Jacques said quietly. He shined the light on the telegram. "Read."

Hart did not read aloud but Jacques now could read over his shoulder. The telegram was to a bootlegger Hart knew in Rapid City, South Dakota.

"Sam Palizzolla, may he never rest in peace," muttered Hart.

From Al Brown, Chicago, it read: IMPORTANT RELATIVES NEED HELP IN YOUR REGION STOP TELEPHONE BENNETT EARLIEST FOR ORDERS STOP

"Bennett?" Hart wondered aloud again. "Brown? Bennett? I thought I knew all the bootleggers in this neck of the woods." Quizzically, Hart looked again at the telegram, turned the page and then the envelope over. On the back of the envelope, he found pencil writing: Man woman little boy.

"Must've called in and got this information." Hart looked up at Jacques. "Mean anything to you?"

Jacques studied Hart momentarily. "Its obvious, isn't it? This man Brown has some relatives around here who want to buy booze and your bootlegger got the information on them from somebody named Bennett."

"Yeah," nodded Hart, "but this says there's a little boy and Doc Baxter said those farmers didn't have one."

"So now you know there are others involved."

"Yeah," grunted Hart. "But who?"

Jacques shrugged.

"Hell," Hart muttered, stuffing the telegram into his pocket. "Gimme my flashlight and get out of here."

*****

Vicenzo Capone was the older brother of the Alphonse "Scarface" Capone. Vicenzo left their Brooklyn family home at the age of 16 and rambled across America, winding up with the American Expeditionary Force in Europe in 1917-18 where he earned distinction as a marksman. After the war, while Alphonse was moving to Chicago, Vicenzo wandered to Nebraska and, seeking to conceal his Italian ethnicity because it met with discrimination, he took the name of Richard Hart in imitation of his movie hero, William S. Hart.

Just as Prohibition made the career of Alphonse, it also made the career of Vicenzo. He became a Prohibition Enforcement Agent and won fame for his skill at bringing down bootleggers and still-runners throughout the upper Midwest. He was promoted to the U.S. Indian Service and vigorously enforced Prohibition laws on South Dakota and Nebraska reservations, chasing "renegades" like his cowboy hero and earning the nickname "Two-Gun Hart." During a presidential vacation in the region, Hart served as a bodyguard for President Calvin Coolidge. Eventually, in the course of his efforts to run down a bootlegger, he was involved in a wrongful shooting death that brought him notoriety and controversy. Defended vigorously by the temperance movement behind Prohibition, he was eventually found innocent.

Eventually, Vincenzo became Marshal of Homer, Nebraska, where he married and settled down and raised four sons. Occasionally, he performed sharp shooting exhibitions, sometimes shooting cigarettes out of the mouths of his sons. Late in their lives, the Capone brothers briefly reunited. It is not certain they exchanged yarns about the "good old days" of Prohibition, but they certainly could have.

*****

Jacques walked out into the cool blue of the pre-dawn and found Gatch sleepily studying the stars on the horizon. They returned to the Model T. "Now what?" Gatch asked.

103

"Tulsa."

"But we need some kind of cover."

"Not Hart," Jacques repeated grimly.

"Then who?"

"I don't know."

"Let's go back to the roadhouse and get some rest," Gatch suggested.

"Right," concluded Jacques. "Maybe something will turn up."

At the roadhouse, they found activity everywhere. There were lights on in most of the cabins, vehicles all over the grounds and people were scurrying between arriving and departing vehicles and the cabins.

"Guess Sheriff Ben got the wounded out here," Gatch observed tiredly.

Jacques was too weary to do anything but nod. He turned and walked through their cabin's screen door. Katie Marie was asleep on the bed, her arms around Monty. He stopped and stood between the door and the bed, enjoying the peaceful beauty of his sleeping wife and child. Gatch followed him in but stopped in the doorway, holding the screen door open and staring out.

Jacques glanced and saw him. "What?" he whispered.

"What do you think the Ethiopian House of David is?"

"What?" Jacques asked again, this time irritably, as he stepped back to the doorway.

Gatch pointed. Next to the roadhouse office was a big bus with ETHIOPIAN HOUSE OF DAVID across its side. Inside it, men appeared to sleep, heads against the windows, eyes flickering in dreams. Around it were tents and smoldering campfires.

"Barnstorming darkies," Katie Marie whispered from behind them. "The roadhouse usually lets them rent cabins so they drove late into the night to get here."

"But the train wreck wounded got here first," said Gatch.

104

"Thanks to you, the way I heard it," she said, rising in her nightgown and moving across the cabin, pushing her sleep mussed hair from her face and kissing Jacques. "They were real heroes, especially the women, the way they helped us with those poor train passengers."

For the next two days, everyone at the roadhouse rested and recovered from the trauma, work and sleeplessness of the long train wreck night. Amid the hubbub of Red Cross caregivers, recovering train travelers and baseball barnstormers, Jacques kept his own pensive counsel, thinking about Capone's agents of vengeance and how to elude them, thinking about Bennett and how to get at him.

The barnstormers pitched tents around their bus and settled, continuing to help with the wounded while awaiting a weekend event in Kearney. Among them were two women, singers who played shortstop and second base and handled domestic duties for the team's ten men. Katie Marie quickly befriended them. By their second afternoon of friendship, the three were doing harmonies as well as laundry.

Gatch fell in among the fascinating, mostly outgoing and often outrageous entertainers who toured as a baseball team, taking on local semipro teams for sport, fee and wager. Their manager and catcher was Squeaky Dixon, a short, stocky, baldish power hitter with a firm eye and an odd, high-pitch to his voice. Seeing marketing possibilities in Gatch's "red Indian" Native American skin tone, Dixon got Gatch to admit he was once a pretty good third baseman and invited him to join the team's upcoming workout. Gatch gleefully reported the invitation to Jacques.

"They're headed south to a tournament in Tulsa," Gatch smiled. "Perfect cover."

Jacques smiled back. "Perfect. IF you can play with them."

In an empty field across the highway from the roadhouse, in hot Nebraska spring sunshine, the barnstormers laid out a rough diamond and, swatting away flies, mosquitoes, chiggers and gnats, began loosening up. Four took to the outfield to shag flies and jog. Two stood to the leftfield side of second base, chatting while fetching grounders slapped by batters hitting against Dixon, who sweated and grunted while throwing batting practice fastballs. Nothing else cut the quiet of the hot afternoon except the chink of bad pitches against their portable chain link backstop and the smack of wood bat on good pitches. Occasionally, Dixon shouted from the mound and the players rotated, from outfield to infield to batting. Along the third base line, Jacques waited with Gatch while Monty delightedly fetched bats and balls.

"These guys make it look easier than those guys at the Polo Grounds," Gatch observed of the players' simple grace and elegance.

"Can you play with them?" Jacques asked.

Just then, Dixon, satisfied with the batting practice, yelled "Spooney!" and walked toward first base. He waved a short, wiry man with thick black hair near second base toward home plate, then yelled at Gatch. "Get out on the infield and let me see if you can pick up grounders without getting your balls bruised."

"Now we find out," Gatch grinned at Jacques, and trotted out to third base. He pointed at one of the player's gloves and got the use of it.

Dixon nodded to Spooney, who slapped a hard grounder. Reflexively, smoothly, Gatch fielded it and threw hard across the diamond. Dixon took the throw, tossed the ball on one bounce to Spooney and said, "Hit it harder. Make him move." He also turned to the outfield and waved his right arm over his head. A tall lanky man with small piercing eyes nodded and started loosening up his right arm.

While Gatch chased grounders, Jacques noticed a fine new Packard drive up and park across the highway at the roadhouse. Expecting trouble, he watched the Packard and smiled when he saw Doc Baxter climb out, chomping on his ever present unlit cigar. Scanning the scene, Baxter spotted Jacques and strode purposefully to him. After an exchange of pleasantries, Jacques explained to Doc about Gatch's tryout as they watched him prove he could field the position and throw.

"Smart," Baxter agreed. "Folks in this part of the world'd never sit for a white boy, even a Frenchie, playin' with these niggers, but a INDIAN! Now that's a hoot!"

Dixon caught a bullet from Gatch, stopped, again turned toward the outfield and waved his right arm over his head. As the tall, lanky man trotted in, Dixon turned back to Spooney. "Climb into my catcher's gear, will you, Spooney? I wanna see if this guy can hit and Suitcase needs some work."

As Gatch trotted in to hit, the tall, lanky man walked slowly to the pitcher's mound. As Gatch selected a bat and Suitcase started throwing warm-ups to

Spooney, Doc Baxter spoke again. "Wanted to talk to you about those folks Hart shot."

Suddenly, Jacques felt uneasy. "What about them?"

"They didn't put up much of a fight, did they?"

Jacques hesitated. 'I didn't see," he finally admitted.

"You look ready, Suitcase," Dixon squeaked at the pitcher from his first base position as Spooney threw a warm-up toss back to Suitcase, on the pitcher's mound.

"Two more," the tall lanky pitcher with the high kick and the easy motion grunted, sweating and winding. His pitch slammed into Spooney's mitt, a burning fastball.

Beside the batter's box, Gatch swallowed hard and looked across the diamond at Jacques, both wondering how well this tryout would go.

"Those people were all shot right between the eyes," Doc Baxter said to Jacques. "As Coroner, I'd be required to report executions, even by a peace officer."

Suitcase threw another smoking fastball and Gatch gulped nervously again as the pitch slammed loudly into the catcher's mitt. Dixon waved at him and, uneasily, he stepped in to hit.

Equally uneasily, Jacques considered his answer to Doc's remark. "Hart's a sharpshooter," Jacques said. "He doesn't miss."

"He missed a telegram," Doc Baxter said.

Suitcase wound and pitched. Gamely, Gatch swung hard but the pitch slammed into Spooney's mitt before his bat got across home plate.

Suitcase remained all business on the mound but Dixon and Spooney laughed. "In'ian warrior a might slow for our league!" Spooney yelled.

"Hang on, hang on!" Gatch yelled, stepping back, shortening up on the bat and taking a few more practice swings. "I just gotta get my timing!"

"A telegram?" Jacques asked, not wanting to let on he knew of the telegram.

Suitcase wound and threw again. Again Gatch swung behind the pitch and missed completely. Hoots and jibes came from around the field. "Send him back to the reservation!" "Heap big squaw!"

"Yeah, a telegram," said Baxter. "Not the first one. I know there had to be a first one because this one just says PREVIOUS INFORMATION WRONG STOP LOOK FOR MAN WOMAN LITTLE BOY AND INDIAN."

Jacques looked at Doc Baxter. "What are you going to do with that telegram?"

"That's a tough one."

"Yeah," Jacques said nervously.

Gatch stepped back, put the bat between his legs, rubbed his hands together nervously, took the bat and determinedly stepped in again. Suitcase pitched again. This time Gatch let it go by.

"Well," squeaked Dixon. "I guess it was outside."

"You know it was," piped up Spooney. "In'ian maybe got an eye," he added as he threw the ball back.

"Ain't no good if he can't use the lumber," Dixon squeaked. "Let's go, Suitcase."

Suitcase wound and threw again. This time Gatch timed it perfectly, stepping forward and smacking it hard on a line into right field. He grinned at a different kind of hoots coming now from the barnstormers watching.

Jacques looked at Doc Baxter and smiled. "But what does it all mean?"

"See if you can do that again!" Dixon yelled at Gatch.

Still grinning, Gatch set himself to hit again. Dixon flicked his right hand at Suitcase, indicating a real fastball. Suitcase nodded and wound.

"You boys were somethin' else the night of the train wreck," Doc Baxter said.

"Just trying to do the right thing at a bad time," Jacques replied, maintaining his tight, nervous smile.

Gatch timed the next pitch right and again met it squarely, smacking it on a line into centerfield. Hoots and cheers came from all around. "Woo Woo Woo!" "He's on the warpath!"

Dixon walked onto the infield and intercepted the return throw to the mound. "Good enough for today, boys. Come on in. We got us a new infielder!"

Jacques turned to Doc Baxter. "We'll be leaving after tomorrow's baseball game."

"Yeah, well," Baxter replied. "You knew Hart better than I did and he's gone and not likely coming back this way anytime soon, so here." He handed Jacques the telegram. "If you see him, give him this. Me, I'm just a pig doctor and not likely to ever figure out what it all means." He stuck his cigar in his mouth and ambled off across the highway toward his shiny Packard. "I'll see you at the ballgame," he called back.

Still smiling, Jacques watched Doc Baxter off, then took Monty by the hand and joined Gatch among the barnstormers gathering their equipment.

"Well, I guess we goin' t'go on an' let you play with us tomorrow," Dixon said to Gatch as Jacques approached.

"Damn!" exploded Gatch. "Isn't that the most generous thing I ever heard."

"You complainin' already, In'ian?" Dixon grinned.

"You make it sound like you're doin' me a favor."

"Ain't we?"

"Look, Dixon, don't take this the wrong way 'cause I like you just fine and…" He gestured toward Jacques. "…so do my friends but this IS Nebraska where there're still lynchings and you ARE niggers."

"And what are you?"

"I'm not a nigger."

"No, you ain't," Dixon grinned. "an' don't take this the wrong way 'cuz I like you just fine and…" He gestured toward the other players. "…so do my friends but this IS Nebraska and it warn't all that long ago that these peoples' folks was gettin' arrows through they hearts an' hatchets in they heads an' you IS a In'ian. Chief PotCallsKettle is what I'm gonna name you." Still

109

grinning, Dixon turned to his teammates. "C'mon. Let's go get some meat and taters…" He looked back at Gatch. "…an' firewater."

Left alone with Monty, Jacques and Gatch walked back toward their cabin, silent and grim.

"The art of diplomacy," Jacques said.

"What about it?" Gatch asked.

"You lack it."

"Yeah."

"But you are a good baseball player." He smiled at Gatch and Gatch smiled back. "Go clean up and help Katie Marie with the dinner. I want to go into town and do a little research."

Gatch let out a deep breath, nodded his assent and they parted ways.

Late that night, after cooking, cleaning up and putting Monty to bed, Jacques, Katie Marie and Gatch settled down on their cabin's front porch. Even with all the roadhouse cabins and its grounds full, evening brought quiet and the undaunted mosquitoes and fireflies. As they enjoyed the peacefulness, a train whistle blew in the distance. All three turned toward the sound expectantly. There was only quiet.

"I love the quiet," said Katie Marie. "They say it's peaceful and quiet at night in the hills up over Hollywood."

Gatch and Jacques exchanged uneasy conspiratorial glances.

"What?" demanded Katie Marie observantly.

Jacques shrugged at Gatch. "About California," he began.

"What now?"

"We have to go to Tulsa first."

"Tulsa? Why?"

"It all goes back to Paris," Jacques said.

"The peace talks," she nodded. "Saving Clemenceau's life."

"What happened after."

"The oil companies. The murders," she nodded.

"Yes."

"I don't know if you've been reading the papers," she said sarcastically. "They've got a little oil business in Tulsa."

"And Mr. Wade," Gatch interrupted. "My boss. Ex-boss. Has been sending payments down there."

"So?" she asked.

"To the man who was responsible for the murders in Paris," explained Jacques. "I did some research at the public library this afternoon. The oil companies and the governments have completed their negotiations. Information about Mesopotamian oil…"

"It is now the Kingdom of Iraq," Katie Marie corrected him. "I read the papers, too."

Jacques gritted his teeth at the interruption and at the reminder of the way the Great Powers and the oil companies negotiated over the lands and peoples in the Levant the same way they slaughtered the people of Europe in the war. "I think the man in Tulsa," he went on, "is blackmailing Wade to hide the identity of Wade's son, who was important to me, important to France, at the beginning of the war."

"So you think you've got to stop this blackmail. And get the man responsible for the murders."

Jacques nodded 'yes.'

"And how the hell are we going to do this—with our CHILD—while Capone's monsters are out to get us?"

"That's why we're staying for the baseball game," Gatch interrupted.

"What the hell has that got to do with the price of beans?"

"We want to connect with the barnstormers," Jacques told her.

111

"Well, if we're staying for the game," she snapped back, "I'm singing with Cookie and Candy in the parade tomorrow."

"We want to travel south with them for cover."

"Whites traveling with darkies?" she asked.

"Gatch will be traveling with them. We will be with him."

"They're letting me play with them tomorrow. It gives me a chance to make myself valuable."

"How?"

Gatch looked from Katie Marie to Jacques and back to her. "Good question."

The parade through Kearney's Main Street to the ball field at the edge of town the next morning was a joyful entertainment. The barnstormers called it "strut and razzle dazzle." Candy, Cookie and Katie Marie, the three girl singers, led. Musicians among the ballplayers followed, accompanying the singers with snare drum, trombone, cornet and banjo. Next came the other players, dancing and pantomiming, making the crowds along the street laugh. One barked for the game while juggling Coca Cola bottles and baseballs while two more played a crazy kind of "pepper" with a giant inflated ball, glove and bat. The colorful Ethiopian Clown bus brought up the rear, Dixon driving slowly and the remainder of the team on top, playing what they call "shadow ball," an imaginary, slow motion game with an invisible ball. Folks all over town came out to Main Street to see and then followed along, rounding up friends and neighbors as they went, everybody gathering for the big game.

Arriving at Kearney's ballpark, Dixon pulled the bus up on the sprawling grounds outside the right field chicken wire fence. Jacques, following in the Model T, parked adjacent and at an angle, creating a private space in between where the team could relax in and around the bus and await the start of festivities. As the crowd in the bleachers around the infield grew, cars and trucks arrived and parked beyond left and centerfields amid wagons and grazing draft horses and mules. By mid afternoon, the small ballpark's grandstands were brimming and the townsfolk had spread out along each foul line. A family picnic area developed on a slope in foul territory down the left field line. Down the first base line and underneath the grandstand, not far from the Clowns' bus, there were portable chain link fences. On the fence gates were large "ADULTS" signs. Inside the gates, bartenders were mixing drinks from whiskey bottles and drawing tap beer from kegs over roughly devised barrel and plank wood bars. Nearby, money was changing hands at tables where hastily grease-penciled charts showed odds, records were scribbled into notebooks and scrawled receipts were handed out when bets were placed.

While Katie Marie conferred with Candy and Cookie about their next performance, Jacques set Monty chasing loose balls among the players and helped Gatch get ready for the game. Dixon walked over to them. "Gonna need your help, Frenchie."

"What?"

"Look." He pointed out the makeshift bar and betting parlor. They scanned nonchalantly until they noticed someone familiar talking to the man supervising the bookmakers.

"Is that Sheriff Ben?" Gatch asked.

"It is," said Jacques.

"Is he gonna break up their fun?" Gatch grinned.

Dixon looked scornfully at Gatch. "He their boss, boy."

"Is gambling legal in Nebraska?" Jacques asked in surprise.

Dixon turned to Jacques and gave him an equally scornful expression. "He comin' down here to talk with us. Stay with me."

Jacques looked at the barnstormers manager and shrugged. "Fine."

"Fine," concluded Dixon and pivoted toward Suitcase while Jacques and Gatch exchanged quizzical expressions. "'Bout time," Dixon said quietly to Suitcase.

Suitcase nodded, picked up his glove and waved to Spooney that he wanted to warm up. Just at that moment, the Kearney players started gathering on the field for their warm-ups. All the barnstormers looked, curious to see what they were up against. "Well, lookee here," said Suitcase loudly, grabbing Dixon's attention.

Dixon looked, saw what Suitcase saw, stopped, took a chaw from a bar of tobacco in his pocket, chewed while studying the lanky, gangling light-skinned black man warming up to pitch for Kearney, and spit. "Westin Smith."

"Done conned a pitcher's pay out of another bunch of hungry hillbillies wit' dat damned story about a Eye-talyan mama an' a Somethin-stannie papa," Dixon mutters.

Suitcase tucked his glove under his arm, took out a tobacco pouch and papers and began rolling a cigarette. "B'lieve I'll go down and talk with ol' Westy."

"Wait 'til I get done with the Sheriff!" Dixon told him. "Smith knows how to get under your skin."

"B'lieve I'll go," Suitcase repeated, starting toward the Kearney players.

"Shit. I've got to go see this Sheriff," Dixon muttered. He looked around at his people. "Go with him, Chief," he barked at Gatch. "Keep him out of trouble!"

While Jacques and Dixon awaited Sheriff Ben, Gatch followed Suitcase to where Weston Smith was warming up. Seeing one another, the tall, lanky, exact duplicate right-handers in lighter and darker tones nodded wordlessly in greeting.

"We gots to worry 'bout you, Westy?"

"Not me," grunted Smith, delivering a pitch and taking the return throw from his catcher. He paused to wipe a narrow brow with deep creases. "An' you needn't worry 'bout my heater and my hook neither 'cause ain't none of you gonna hit 'em," he grinned. He wound and pitched again, took the return throw and turned to Suitcase. "What you need to worry 'bout is Whitey Dark."

"Who?"

Smith gestured toward a Kearney player, then made another warm-up pitch while they looked. What they saw was a big strapping man with a boyish face and a full head of silky white hair, huge shoulders, chest and arms, a narrow waist and thick legs.

"He a boy or a old man?" Suitcase asked.

"He a id'yat," Smith reported, taking his catcher's return toss. "But he hits like a lumberjack and throws like a thunderstorm."

"Gotta kinda dull look," Suitcase observed.

"He a id'yat," Smith repeated, still throwing warm-ups. "But y'all better worry 'bout him."

"Where he playin'?"

"He don't start," grunted Smith.

Suddenly, Suitcase's temper flared. "You tellin' me I got to worry 'bout a man-boy-id'yat that ain't in the starting line-up!?! You son-of-a-bitch, you messin' with me!" Suitcase started at Smith and Gatch realized why Dixon sent him along. He pulled Suitcase away as Smith took the return throw and turned to them, grinning. "I'm tellin' you ain't nobody gonna hit me so you need somethin' ELSE to worry 'bout."

"Yeah?" Suitcase flailed against Gatch's hold and screamed at the top of his lungs. "Well, you and them farmers kin worry 'bout ever SEEIN' my fastball, let alone hittin' it, so WORRY "BOUT THAT!"

Smith stood with his hands on his hips while Gatch pulled Suitcase away. Fans in the immediate vicinity saw and heard the confrontation. As Gatch pulled the still flailing Suitcase across the outfield they rained down verbal abuse in defense of their own. By the time Gatch dragged Suitcase to the Clown warm-up area, the stands were hailing boos. Once out of sight of the fans, Suitcase relaxed and grinned. "Turn me loose, Chief." As Gatch let him go, he looked over at Dixon, Jacques and the Sheriff, who were concluding their meeting with a handshake. "That oughtta sweet up the bettin'," Suitcase proclaimed with a grin. Without another word, Suitcase turned and walked back toward Spooney, gesturing he was ready to warm up while Gatch watched in amazement.

Returning from the meeting with the Sheriff, Jacques walked over to Gatch. "Quite a show."

"You think any of it was real?" Gatch asked.

"All of it," Jacques shrugged. "A real show."

Gatch watched Suitcase warm up while Jacques confirmed Monty was still having a good time with the barnstormers. Then Gatch remembered to ask about the meeting with the Sheriff.

"Just like Chicago. Gambling and boozing are banned and booming. There is big money on this game. And Dixon has a side bet, covering all takers."

"The Sheriff's holding those stakes?" Gatch asked.

Jacques nodded 'yes.'

"What about umpires?" Gatch suddenly asked. "It could get ugly."

"Doc Baxter is the Kearney man."

"We have an umpire?"

"Me."

"You?"

Jacques shrugged, raised his shoulders quizzically and grinned sheepishly. "Dixon told them I was a French war hero."

"You told him?"

"No," smiled Jacques. "Another of his fabrications that only happens to be true."

A Kearney man in a white suit and straw hat with a deep voice consulted with Dixon and the Kearney manager and then walked to home plate and used a megaphone to welcome the fans. Having their attention, he asked them all to stand. "And now the Ethiopian Clowns girl trio, Candy, Cookie and Katie Marie, will lead us in the traditional singing of the National Anthem while we raise the flag in centerfield!" The three women stepped forward, the snare drum rapped a rumtumtum, they began singing and the crowd joined in.

My country, 'tis of Thee,
Sweet Land of Liberty
Of thee I sing;
Land where my fathers died,
Land of the pilgrims' pride,
From every mountain side
Let Freedom ring.

When the song ended and the flag was flying, the crowd let loose a vibrant cheer and the announcer in the white suit again stepped forward with his megaphone. "Ladies and Gentlemen, your Kearney Wildcats!" The Kearney team trotted onto the field. Jacques followed, and took his umpiring position behind second base. Doc Baxter walked out from under the grandstand, chomping away at his unlit cigar, took his place behind the catcher, growled "Play Ball!" and pulled a protective mask over his face without removing the cigar.

The Clowns' leadoff hitter stepped in. The Kearney announcer, calling through the megaphone, described her as "…one half of the prettiest double play combo in the history of baseball, partner of harmonizing shortstop and number two hitter Cookie Marion, the singing second basewoman Candy Cassidy!"

While Candy got ready to hit, the announcer added, "Ladies and Gentlemen, the Ethiopian Clowns benchwarmers are passing among you. Your contributions toward the entertainment would be gratefully received."

"Come back with yore hat after the game and I'll let you know what you're worth!" a leathery-faced local lady yelled. Those around approved of her humorous challenge. Nevertheless, a pair of Clowns players smiled broadly in Stepin Fetchit style and moved through the grandstand and standing crowd areas with upside down caps, gratefully nodding at the donation of pennies and nickels.

In the opening innings both pitchers made good on their bold bragging, staying nearly unhittable. The game was a scoreless deadlock. At the end of the Kearney third, after striking out the side to finish off the first nine hitters in order, Suitcase left the mound grinning and boldly proclaiming that Kearney was "…a bunch of farmers swingin' like ol' barn doors in a heavy wind." But he momentarily lost concentration at the start of the fourth inning and walked the Wildcat lead-off hitter. He sprinted to first base and immediately began jumping up and down on the bag, yelling at Candy and Cookie. "Here I come, spikes high, nigger girls. Get outta my way or I'm gonna stick you like a cheap whore."

Unperturbed, Suitcase pitched from an elongated stretch. The runner went for the steal on the second pitch. He slid into second base spikes high. Cookie took Dixon's perfect throw, agilely dodged the runner's spikes and tagged the man with a vicious gloved-hand thrust into his lowest gut. After Jacques called him out, the man rolled over, struggled to his feet and stumbled, bent at the waist, back toward the Wildcat bench.

"Hey!" Suitcase yelled at his back. "You still want to stick a cheap whore? 'Cause I knows where yore mama works." When the hunched over player did not respond, Suitcase looked at the other Wildcat players.

They glared meanly but said nothing until Westin Smith yelled for Suitcase to get back up on the mound "....and do yer pitchin' with yer arm insteada yer mouth!"

Smith pitched effortfully, sweating and grunting as he did during his warming up. But the Clowns could not, or did not, hit him. Gatch was unable to make any contribution aside from the laughter that came when the announcer introduced him as "...the third baseman and the best hitting member of the ten lost tribes, Chief PotCallsKettle!" Most of his teammates, it seemed to Gatch, were making little effort to hit or score, preferring to keep the game close but entertaining with a range of stock antics like running the bases backwards, sliding under pop ups, climbing on each others' backs to make throws and diving through each others' legs to make catches. When Gatch asked Dixon why they were clowning instead of playing to win, the team leader grinned. "I'm coverin' all the action that Bookie can get against us, fool. Why do I want to discourage the Rubes?"

Through seven innings, the game remained scoreless. In the bottom of the eighth, with one out, Suitcase decided it was time to use his old gag of loading the bases and calling in his outfielders. Dominating the Kearney team the way the pitcher was, Dixon saw little harm in the act and figured it would give one more boost to the betting against his team. So the catcher patiently went along while Suitcase intentionally walked the bases full and then went through the elaborate pantomime of signaling his outfielders in to sit on the grass around the pitcher's mound. "Don't need no outfielding!" Suitcase loudly proclaimed to the delight and agitation of the fans. At this moment, the Kearney manager surprised them by sending Whitey Dark up to pinch hit.

Gatch hurried to the mound and waved for Dixon to come out. But before Dixon got up out of his crouch, Suitcase put up a hand, stopping him, and then turned to Gatch and broadly waved for him to sit down with the outfielders. The pitcher made a comical show of cooling Gatch off. "Don't woooorrry, Chief! This boy a id'yat. Ol' Suitcase don't need no fielders!"

He again took the mound. The right-hand batting Whitey Dark, with an innocent grin on his boyish face under a floppy mop of silky white hair, swung with all the might of his huge shoulders, chest and arms and thickly muscled legs, driving Suitcase's first pitch so high and far beyond the centerfield fence that the team literally paused to watch the ball in flight

118

while the baserunners scored and the Whitey Dark happily galloped around the bases. "See," muttered Suitcase, looking away from the flight of the enormous drive and down at Gatch while the Kearney fans in the grandstand roared in delight. "Didn't need no fielders." Undaunted, he waved the fielders back to their positions and got the next two Kearney hitters, mere mortals of normal skill and mentality, on strikeouts.

The Clowns went to work with concentration in the top of the ninth and scored five quick runs on the tiring Westin Smith. Then, with the bases loaded and two out, the Kearney manager brought Whitey Dark in from left field to pitch to Squeaky Dixon. To the astonishment of Dixon and all the other Clowns, the strange, mountain-of-muscles man-boy threw three perfect pitches at such a terrific speed that the big power-hitting catcher could do nothing with them except strike out flailing.

"Why don't they use him in the starting line-up?" Dixon asked Doc Baxter when he resumed his catching position for the bottom of the ninth, holding a one run lead.

"Poor boy wanders away," Doc Baxter shrugged.

Confident he could hold their 5 to 4 lead, Suitcase quickly got the first two Kearney batters. As he returned to the mound after the second out, he noticed Westin Smith conferring with Kearney's manager. Suitcase and Dixon exchanged glances, wondering if Westin was disclosing Suitcase's one weakness. Sure enough, the next Kearney batter bunted. Before the lanky pitcher could untangle himself from his elaborate motion to field it, the runner was on. Suitcase was more cautious with the next batter, keeping his pitches high to prevent a bunt, but walked him.

Now the Wildcats sent a huge flabby hulk of a farm boy to bat. Dixon complained that the boy's enormous stomach protruded into the strike zone. Doc Baxter shrugged, pulled his cigar out from between the bars of his mask, yelled "Play ball!" and then stuck the cigar back in his mouth. Attempting to avoiding putting the hulky boy on base by hitting him, Suitcase's first two pitches were outside. Now behind in the count and irritated, Suitcase brought a belt high fastball right over the plate. Baxter called it a strike but, at the same instant, Fat Boy leaned in, twisted away and screamed.

"What?" Baxter asked.

"It hit me!" Fat Boy whined.

"It was perfect strike!" Dixon said.

119

"But it hit me!" said Fat Boy. "Look!" He pulled up his shirt, exposing enormous rolls of human blubber. Across one of the layers of flabby flesh was a red streak where the pitch grazed him.

"He's gotta try to get outta the way!" Dixon protested.

"I did!" the boy whined. "I don't move too good."

Doc Baxter pushed back his mask, took out his cigar and sighed. "No," he finally agreed. "You don't. First base," he proclaimed, gesturing down the baseline. "Next hitter."

Now the bases were loaded. And Whitey Dark once again came to the plate. This time Suitcase was more cautious with the baseball savant. Suitcase worked the count to three balls and two strikes before laying a daring and inhumanly perfect fast curve across the outside corner of the plate to the right-handed batting strong man.

Getting around late on the pitch, Whitey Dark hit a vicious line drive up the first base line straight at Fat Boy. Fat Boy ingloriously fell to the dirt, the quickest movement of his life, in sheer self-protection.

On his belly, Fat Boy watched the ball hit the outfield grass and bounce hard twice as the runners at second and third, running with the pitch, scored. He saw the Clowns' right fielder race over, glove the drive, look up and break into a walk, with the game lost and nowhere to throw. He also saw Whitey Dark run to first base and then get swooped up by his joyous teammates. Elated to be on the winning team, Fat Boy climbed effortfully to his feet, dusted himself off and trotted over to join in his team's celebration.

From across the diamond, Gatch noticed Fat Boy do all this while the Wildcats celebrated their victory. The celebration spread from the players to the fans, who streamed out of the grandstands and onto the field. Quickly, the scene was chaos. The ballplayers and the citizens of Kearney screamed joyously and danced jubilantly. Youths rode in on horses and mules from beyond the outfield, circling the celebration. Little boys in centerfield set off fireworks. The infield filled with celebrants as Gatch desperately began moving against the mad throng to get to Doc Baxter, at the same time struggling to keep track of where the ball was as the Clowns' right fielder walked toward their bench to get his gear.

Remaining aloof from the madness of the celebration, Westin Smith sat on the Kearney bench and watched. He saw what Gatch saw, and then he saw

Gatch get to Doc Baxter, yell at him, point at Fat Boy and point at the right fielder. Realizing what was going on, Smith quickly began fighting his way through the wild celebration toward Fat Boy. Quickly, amid the chaotic melee, it became a desperate race for second base. Gatch led Doc Baxter, the Clowns right fielder and, eventually, Jacques. Westin Smith dragged a very reluctant and whiney Fat Boy, who did not really understand the situation. Obliviously joyous Kearney fans and players and despondent, precariously outnumbered Ethiopian Clowns blocked all progress.

Suddenly, as the competitors neared second base, a siren was heard and a fire truck appeared from the outfield. Sheriff Ben, determined to stem the brewing riot, rode atop the truck. The white suited announcer was at his side screaming through his megaphone for calm. Men on either side of the truck held fire hoses. At first, the fire truck divided the crowd and it seemed to break apart and settle down. But as the truck moved through the outfield and neared second base, the crowd closed around it, swallowing it. "Victory! Victory! Victory!" the huge throng chanted. Sheriff Ben waved his arms madly and the man with the megaphone pleaded for calm. In defiant response, the chants grew more enthusiastic. Sheriff Ben pointed at the truck driver, who blasted the siren. The crowd found this fun and screamed in approval. The driver set the siren off in bursts. The horses at the periphery spooked and began bucking and twisting into the crowd, setting off more screaming and panic.

A wave of the mob pulled the Clowns right fielder away but Gatch grabbed the game ball from the man and fought on toward second base, Jacques and Doc Baxter struggling to stay at his shoulder. Across the infield, Smith came on, now behind Fat Boy and pushing him like a bulwark against the onslaught, Fat Boy screaming in fear.

In short centerfield, Sheriff Ben was desperate to get control of the crowd. He had only one option left. He waved his arms, signaling men at the rear of the truck. They opened up the truck's tank valves. The men on the hoses began blasting a jet spray of tank water into the middle infield. In moments, the soaked crowd parted and second base became a muddy morass.

At just this moment, both Gatch and the Fat Boy/Westin Smith entry broke through the mob. Gatch sloshed three strides forward in the muck and dove, his right fist holding the ball, his right arm aiming at the bag. With a deep grunt and mighty shove, Smith pushed Fat Boy, who slid through the sludge toward the base. Gatch's hand hit the bag an instant before Fat Boy came crashing down onto him with a groan and a thud, muddy water splashing up, both players sinking in. A moment later, Jacques, Doc Baxter and Westin Smith were standing around second base, peering into the muck.

121

"Was he safe or out?" Smith demanded of Doc. Doc looked at Jacques.

"Don't look at me," Jacques said. "I don't know what this is about." He looked around at the gathering crowd of suddenly quieting and suspicious Kearnians. "And I don't think I want to."

"Well," said Doc, taking his cigar out of his mouth, putting a foot on Fat Boy's bulk and using it to roll the huge man off Gatch, "if the Chief held onto the ball, Fat Boy is out, the runs don't count and Kearney lost."

As he said this, Fat Boy rolled away and a soggy muddy Gatch appeared in the muck, still clutching the baseball. He grinned at Doc Baxter, who stuck his unlit cigar between his teeth and threw his thumb up in the 'out' gesture.

*****

Gatch, Jacques, Katie Marie and Monty followed the barnstormers east on the back roads of southern Nebraska, playing small town teams in Minden, Red Cloud, Hebron and Belleville. The caravan turned due south through Kansas, with stops for games in Concordia, Salina, Newton and Wichita. For saving their money in Kearney, Gatch kept his spot in the starting lineup despite the fact that he turned out to be the team's weakest hitter and only an adequate third baseman. The barnstormers jokingly called him "the brains" of the line-up and it continued to delight the fans when the local announcers introduced him as "...the best hitting member of the ten lost tribes!" The games were nonstop fun, though nothing like the one in Kearney.

The caravan continued south, across the Oklahoma border and then east, toward Tulsa. One late afternoon, having agreed with the ball team on the small town of Bartle City as the day's destination, they let the bus get ahead of them as they took a slower, closer look at Oklahoma. It was flat country, farm fields and weedy plains cut intermittently by small up-thrusts of scrub-covered hills, an occasional east-west railroad line running through. Where the hills fell away into creek or river valleys, there were hardscrabble family farms. Where they fell away into dry canyons, there was desert.

Indiscriminately, there were oil derricks. Some were lone decaying dusters, a wildcatter's dream gone dry, and some were solitary green explorers, a dreamer's wildest hope. A highway sign announced that Bartle City was just ahead as they saw, on the horizon, a cluster of derricks, a wildcatter's dream come true. Driving nearer, they saw at the foot of the derricks, an oil-boom town. Even from the distance, they could see the town was frenetic with commerce and growing. At its outskirts, as they slowed to accommodate traffic, Gatch suddenly did a comical double take.

"What the???"

"Horsey!" Monty exclaimed, pointing.

"Yeah," Gatch answered, staring. "Four horsies. Pulling a brand new Cadillac full of Indians, like they're riding a wagon."

"In case they run out of gas?" Katie Marie asked in wonder.

"There's an oil boom," Jacques replied. "They're not going to run out of gas."

While his passengers gawked at the horse-drawn Cadillac, Jacques drove on. "Look at that," he uttered a moment later.

The other three looked across the road to the foot of a hilly up-thrust, where a mansion sat on a wide expanse of field-like lawn. Near a great old oak tree, away from the mansion, was a small Indian encampment. They saw teepees, campfires, drying hides and airing blankets, and a refuse area away from the camp.

"Who do you suppose lives there?" Katie Marie wondered aloud.

"Just who you see," Gatch answered after a moment of silence. "Look." He pointed to where the front door hung off its hinges. On closer inspection, they also noticed the glass windows broken in their frames.

"Buy a house and live on the grass?" Jacques muttered. Suddenly, he slammed on the brakes and the Model T skidded to a halt inches from the upturned hand of a huge man with sun-reddened brown skin, red bleary eyes and long straight greasy black hair hanging to his shoulders and falling in strands across his face.

"Drunk Indian," Gatch announced. "If he raises a tomahawk, I'll say something."

"He probably wouldn't understand your New England accent," Katie Marie said.

The big man peered at them through the highway detritus on the windshield and then, satisfied they were halted, turned to his left and waved for a group of children with reddish brown skin and straight black hair carrying worn baseball mitts and bats to cross. After the kids gleefully raced across the road and down the highway toward the lawn encampment, the big man wobbled back toward his curbside position, wind-milling his arm to send the car on.

"O.K.," grinned Katie Marie. "Go."

"Some traffic cop," Gatch muttered, as Jacques put the Model T back into gear. Just as he accelerated, there was a tremendous explosion in the distance, the car rocked with the concussion and Jacques slammed on the brakes again. A series of explosions followed, rocking the car in sequence. Monty began crying and Katie Marie scooped him into her arms, exchanging worried glances with the two men.

They all craned their necks, looking for disaster. The traffic-directing drunk did not react to the explosions. Neither did the children moving along the highway behind them, tossing a ball, laughing and shouting. Neither did the people at the encampment on the mansion lawn. Behind them, the horse-drawn Cadillac continued on its plodding, clopping way. Three brown skinned women in colorful homespun came along. The big inebriated man raised his hand to halt them. They laughed at him and, without stopping, crossed the empty thoroughfare and continued walking. Turning to watch the women, the big drunk saw the Model T in the middle of the highway. Glaring, he walked to it, slapped the fender with his big hand and adamantly waved them on.

"Drive!" Katie Marie ordered Jacques. "Whatever exploded doesn't matter to me as much as a meal and a hot bath!"

A few minutes later, as lights in windows along Bartle City's dirt and gravel Main Street twinkled on, Jacques steered through heavy traffic and mud puddles. They rolled slowly amid rough men walking worn plank sidewalks in heavy, worn, dirty boots, hard looking drivers in battered, rusty flatbed trucks hauling pipe and oil field steel, and weary, red-eyed teamsters cursing and driving neighing, sweating horses pulling wagon loads of derrick lumber, drill tools and pipeline parts. Splintery-planked buildings, tents and roofless frames lined the way, all busy with business, the hasty roiling tenements of Boomtown. Jacques pulled up beside the Ethiopian Clown's bus outside a three-story whitewashed plank building.

"The Broadway Hotel," Gatch read from the sign on the balcony spelling out the name in letter formations of little electric light bulbs. Then he looked around. "But definitely not Times Square."

"Who cares?' answered Katie Marie, climbing out and pulling Monty after her. "They've got bath tubs and they'll take the darkies."

Weaving through the early evening foot traffic crowding the wooden walkway in front of the hotel, they made their way inside, checked in and were given adjoining rooms on the third floor at the front of the hotel overlooking the street. While Katie Marie toileted Monty and got him ready to go to the dining room for supper, Jacques stood by a half-open window and looked down on the town.

Gatch approached from his room, drying his face after shaving. "You find the team?" he asked.

Jacques nodded 'yes.'

"Down the hall?" Gatch asked.

"Downstairs. In back."

"Nigger cabins?"

Jacques nodded 'yes.'

"They gonna meet us in the dining room?"

Jacques turned his head and looked at Gatch. His expression said the answer was a question too obvious to ask: If the hotel wouldn't have them in the main building, why would they be welcome in the public dining room?

At Jacques' non-reply, Gatch read the expression. "Just don't let anybody know I'm not Italian." Following Jacques' gaze, he looked to the street below.

Amid stacks of pipe, lumber, tools and supplies, a marketplace was changing from the dayshift to the nightshift. Lines of men looking for work became lines of men looking for women. Hand scribbled placards advertising oil field tools and jobs disappeared into the dark. Electric signs reading CAFÉ and POOL HALL, code names for cathouse, speakeasy and casino, lit up the street.

"Not exactly Montmartre," Jacques muttered.

"Honky-tonks," Gatch replied. "Same idea."

125

"Entertainment."

"And booze," agreed Gatch. "Prohibition or not." They watched men in working clothes mingle with ladies in heavy make-up and light, filmy dresses. Slick-looking gambler types rubbed shoulders with shabby drunks, newspaper boys sold four-sheeters to flabby working women. A hustler grabbed a pair of young boys in overalls by their arms and led them down an alley out of which an old bent man came coughing and spitting. "The Second Coming is at Hand!" a man in black preached. The stooped old man looked up at preacher, coughed harder, spit and walked by. "The day of judgment COMETH!" bellowed the man in black.

Katie Marie walked into the room with Monty. "Let's go eat," she barked. "I've got a date with that bathtub and all the hot water it can muster."

"Look at that!" Gatch suddenly exclaimed. Jacques, stepping away from the window, pivoted back and Katie Marie joined them. An Indian youth in a fine suit was walking slowly through the crowd on the street. From his pockets and buttonholes, paper money protruded. As he walked along, smiling, greeting the motley crowd, people helped themselves to the bills. As each bill was drawn away, the boy replaced it with another. The boy drew quite a retinue as he disappeared into the doorway of "Bill Bailey's Pool Hall."

"You think there's oil money in this town?" Gatch sarcastically asked.

"You think they know what to do with it?" Katie Marie answered in the same tone.

At that instant, gunshots sounded inside "Bill Bailey's." A bunch of men scrambled out and spread along the street. Right behind them came a lean, dirty man holding a revolver, his arms clamped to his sides by a hefty man at his back pushing him. The crowd opened up and scattered but, like the audience at a melodrama, could not turn away. When the big man, his face unshaven and without thoughtfulness, had pushed the lean man, eyes bleary, beard scraggily, clothes filthy, to the middle of the street, he stopped.

"Put that gun back in its holster, Morris!"

The lean man turned back and stepped forward. "Get out of my way, Bert!"

"I'd love to, Morris," answered the big man, blanching at the heavy, foul breath of the little man with the gun in his face, "but it's my job to be in your way. You know that."

126

"She'sh my wife, Bert!"

"I know that, Morris. But if you'll go home and sleep this off, you'll wake up and realize she ain't worth it."

Morris raised the gun. "Don't make me shoot you, Bert."

"You ain't gonna shoot me, Morris."

Morris suddenly swung the gun up, slamming the barrel against big Bert's chin, knocking him back. At the same instant, a barrel-chested Latin man in a clean black suit with a blood stain on his right thigh came limping through the door of "Bill Bailey's" with a gun in his right hand. With his left, he dragged a slender brunette in bright make-up and a scandalously diaphanous white and green gown, who pulled back desperately. Morris looked at them.

"No, No!" The woman screamed in agony, the only one of them who seemed aware this could not end well.

The crowd on the street retreated further but swelled in size. "Somebody get your sheriff!" A voice called.

"That Mexican IS our sheriff," was the reply.

Suddenly, Morris fired his pistol into the air and the crowd went silent. He lowered his pistol. "She'sh my wife, Jose."

"Widow or Divorcee, Morris. You pick."

"It ain't true!"

"Ask her."

The lean dirty man looked from the stocky Latin man to the woman. Her head hung down. She was weeping silently. Feeling their eyes on her, she looked up, terror in her eyes. "Don't make me choose! Don't make me choose!" she wailed. Then weeping overcame her and her voice fell off. "Don't make me…"

Suddenly, Morris raised his gun and started shooting. Reflexively, Jose shot back.

At the window upstairs in the hotel, Katie Marie suddenly stepped back. "We've seen enough of this," she announced, turning away from the window and pulling Monty with her. Gatch and Jacques hesitantly turned to her.

"I wanna watch!" Monty protested, pulling away and running back to the window.

She glared 'You see?' angrily at Jacques and Gatch. Immediately, Jacques grabbed Monty. He and Gatch distracted the boy, leading him out of the room, toward the stairs to the hotel lobby and dining room. Katie Marie followed, but only after a quick glance back through the window told her that Morris and his wife had several bullet wounds and were being carried to the town doctor while Jose still stood in the street, bleeding at the thigh and shoulder, tiredly waving his pistol and demanding that the crowd disperse.

She joined the two men and the boy in the hallway and led them downstairs. Between the second and third floors, they passed a big blond woman coming up carrying bedding. She smiled at Katie-Marie as they passed and spoke quietly with a Scandinavian accent, "You folks like mebbe t'buy some oil leases, yah?"

"I beg your pardon?" Katie Marie asked her.

"Leases," she repeated. "Best prices, I'm sure as shootin'."

Intrigued by the maid's lacey bodice and buxom blondeness, Gatch stopped, grinned and raised his hat. "I'm sure."

"Not interested," Jacques interrupted, pushing Gatch on and pulling Katie Marie behind.

"Leases?" Katie Marie asked Jacques.

"I'll explain while we eat," he told her, forcing their march downstairs.

As they took seats at a table in the middle of the bustling, noisy dining room, Gatch announced he had to "...see a man about a dog" and strode off toward the rear of the hotel.

"Why does Gatch like dogs so much, daddy?"

"Dogs?" Jacques asked.

"Everywhere we go, he always goes to see a man about one."

128

Before Jacques replied, Gatch suddenly came hurrying back into the dining room. "You gotta SEE this!" He grabbed Jacques by the arm and pulled him from the table. Exchanging a 'what can I do?' expression with Katie Marie's expression of irritation, Jacques impatiently allowed himself to be dragged to a back window looking out on the far side of town. Expecting little, he looked out. His eyes suddenly opened wide.

"I thought it was in Tulsa!"

"Probably corporate offices," Gatch answered. "That's a refinery. Bennett prob'ly runs security there, too."

Jacques stared at the sprawling plant behind the "77 Oil Corporation" sign across from the hotel. He remained silent for a few moments. "Let's go eat," he finally said. "And then get some sleep. Tomorrow morning we will ask around."

As they returned to the dining room, a waiter stopped them. "Hey!" he whispered, pulling them aside. "You fellows're new in town."

Jacques nodded. "What about it?" Gatch challengingly asked.

The waiter glanced left and right. "I've got some leases. Osage land. Don't ask me how I got hold of 'em. But I can let 'em go cheaper than anything you can get at the tree."

"The tree?" Gatch asked.

"No," said Jacques curtly, pushing Gatch off toward the outhouses in back of the hotel. "We are not in the oil business," Jacques told the man firmly as he pivoted away toward the dining room.

The waiter watched him go, shook off the rejection and turned toward the kitchen.

Jacques returned to the table and a few minutes later Gatch joined them. The dining room was crowded and busy. Monty hungrily munched at bread with butter while the adults looked at the menus that had come in Jacques' absence. Suddenly, the room rocked with a distant explosion and, while the four newcomers looked at one another in fright, more distant explosions followed, keeping the dining room shaking. Jacques, Gatch and Katie Marie froze and looked around in panic. The other diners nonchalantly went on eating and chatting. Monty dropped his bread and butter and threw his arms around Katie Marie. "Mommie!"

A man at the next table eating alone while carefully studying a large, thick, handwritten logbook looked up at Monty and laughed. "Don't worry, young fella. It's just my crew working late looking for oil."

"Looking for oil?" Monty asked. The adults with him were immediately attentive.

"You're blowing up instead of drilling down?" Gatch asked.

"You with 77?" Jacques interrupted.

"Yes," the man laughed, looking at Monty. "And no," he added to Gatch. "And most definitely no," he concluded, looking at Jacques. "I'm more or less on my own."

"A wildcatter," interrupted Gatch.

The waiter came to their table. "What'll it be?"

"More like a research scientist," the man replied to Gatch, a twinkle in his blue bespectacled eyes, a sprightly grin playing at the corners of the small mouth in his round, sturdy face. "I recommend the stew. Whatever you order is going to taste like the stew anyway."

"Fine," Katie Marie decided, handing her menu back to the waiter. "Stew all around."

The waiter took the other menus and departed.

The man next to them shifted his barrel-chested weight and continued. "I'm a geologist. DeGolyer. Everette DeGolyer. I was lucky enough to find a big field for Lord Cowdry down in Mexico before the war so he's financing this research in geophysics."

"Sounds more like war than research," Jacques observed.

"It came out of the war."

"Geo what?" Gatch asked.

"Geophysics," DeGolyer repeated. "Geo, like geography, mapping. And physics, the study of forces, like explosions. During the war the Germans developed a way to listen to the sound of the French big guns reverberating in the earth. They could pinpoint the gun by the exploding sound of the shot and then take it out."

"We learned to do the same," said Jacques.

"Not many people know that," said DeGolyer, taking a more careful look at Jacques.

"I wound up with the artillery. I learned the method. But how brilliant to apply it to oil exploration!"

"Yes," smiled DeGolyer, gesturing toward the logbook with an expression of frustration. "If my German professors could make it work."

The waiter returned with big bowls of chunky stew and served them.

"Smells good," Katie Marie said. She turned to Monty and got him started before taking up her own fork. Meanwhile Jacques and Gatch dug in.

The waiter took away DeGolyer's empty bowl as he left. "It is good," grinned DeGolyer. "They make it every night, so they have the experience."

While eating, Jacques went on talking with DeGolyer about the geophysical research. "Surely you simply map the variations in the expected sound wave reverberations," he thought aloud, showing a kind of excitement Gatch, Katie Marie and Monty had never seen in him.

"That's the idea. But it's hard to isolate a specific oil deposit. And you can't just stick a well in wherever you guess oil might be. Drilling is expensive. And before you do that, you've got to get your leases in order."

Quickly finishing his stew, Jacques set his bowl aside. "Let me look," he said, gesturing toward the logbook.

"Sure," DeGolyer smiled, handing it over. "Say, are you looking for work?"

In his interest to see the logbook, Jacques ignored the question and began thumbing through pages of topographic maps and profiles of the region's mountains and valleys. Angles were drawn between the sites of the explosions and the sites of the listening and recording devices. Then came pages of calculations, descriptions of the angles, the ellipses they defined and the irregularities in the ellipses that suggested irregularities in the layers underground.

Gatch lit up at the job offer and started to say something but held back as Katie Marie interrupted. "What's that about leases?"

"Leases?"

"Yeah. The hotel maid offered us leases."

"Yeah," added Gatch. "So did one of the waiters."

DeGolyer laughed. "I've had offers from barbers and car dealers and newspaper boys and madams."

"What's a madam?" Monty piped up.

A woman passed by with a water pitcher. Gatch grabbed his water glass. "Madam!" he called, waving his glass until she filled it. "Thank you, Madam," Gatch said, sipping and grinning.

"Oh," said Monty. "It's a lady." He looked at the woman with the water pitcher. "You got any leases?"

DeGolyer and Katie Marie laughed as Gatch spewed his water and the woman, understanding none of it, left their table quickly without answering Monty.

As Gatch cleaned up, Katie Marie pressed DeGolyer on the subject of leases.

"Indians and farmers and the government own all this land," he told her. "Oil people don't want to buy it if there's no oil and they can't afford it if there is and the sellers and buyers don't know which is which until the oil people drill. So they lease the mineral rights."

"In other words," she said, "they go partners."

"Exactly. Usually the deal is cash down plus an eighth of the returns. More or less cash and as much as a quarter or a half or as little as a sixteenth or a thirty-second, depending on how tough the drilling will be and how promising the geology is."

"So what's with every Tom, Dick and Harriet selling leases?"

"Well, when there's oil in the region, a market develops."

"So," Gatch interrupted, "a drunk farmer or Indian loses a bet in a poker game and the gambler sells to the guy who runs the local political machine and the town council finances drilling and the power broker gets rich and the town builds a monument to the mayor."

"Sometimes," smiled DeGolyer. "And sometimes the oil company gets involved."

"Here," Jacques interrupted, pointing at a place in the logbook.

"Just that value?"

Jacques shrugged.

DeGolyer looked at Gatch. "Not chatty, is he?"

"You lookin' for conversation or oil?" Gatch asked.

DeGolyer looked back at Jacques. "Right or wrong, you've got to come to work for me." He glanced at Gatch. "Both of you."

"Do you know anything about a man named Bennett with 77?" Jacques asked him.

"Sure," DeGolyer answered, suddenly eyeing Jacques suspiciously. "You know him?"

"No," said Jacques. "What can you tell us about him?"

"Not much. He runs security for 77. They're the big boys around here. He's their big boy."

"He is at the plant across the way?"

"He's in California. Spends most of his time there since they hit those fields in L.A."

"You know him?"

"Not really. The big shots back east like him. He does favors for them, I hear."

"What kind of favors?"

"Don't know."

"Hey!" Gatch interrupted Jacques' interrogation with a smile when he saw DeGolyer's sudden discomfort. "Jacques's only looking out for his wife and son, Mr. DeGolyer. Some big shot in Chicago told us to watch out for Bennett and we were just trying to keep out of his way."

"Good advice," DeGolyer said, looking straight at Jacques. Jacques looked down at his plate. "Well, folks," DeGolyer suddenly said, standing up. "I'm done and I want to get to my room and go over these numbers. So I'll try one more time. Come to work for me. Smart men are scarcer than poor Indians around here."

Jacques looked up and smiled a small smile. "We're not interested in the oil business."

"Wait a minute," Gatch interrupted again. He looked at Jacques. "Our friend in Chicago is bound to have lost interest in our deal by now. And he doesn't really know where to find us..." He put a hand inside his jacket to suggest a hidden pistol. "...if he wants to work things out, right?"

Jacques studied Gatch, then DeGolyer.

"Gatch is right," Katie Marie chimed in.

"So?"

"We stay here," Gatch told him.

"And work in the oil business?"

"Think about what we're after, Jacques. Is there a better business for us?"

Jacques shrugged. "Fine."

Gatch grinned. DeGolyer was delighted. "Go see my top driller, tomorrow," He told them, standing up. "Name is Gable. Clark Gable. Young kid, but cocky. Big fella, with a mustache and ears that stick out. He's easy to spot. He'll be the one bossing everybody else around. Tell him I sent you and to put you to work, teach you the ropes."

134

The next morning, beside the Ethiopian clowns' bus, Gatch, Jacques, Katie Marie and Monty shared a warm parting with the baseballers. After inadequate words, sentimental tears and, inevitably, laughter, the barnstormers boarded the bus and drove east. Katie Marie returned with Monty to the hotel. Jacques and Gatch turned and walked toward the sound of distant explosions.

At the fields north of Bartle City, a man supervising the field research directed them to DeGolyer's exploration well. At the well, they immediately spotted Gable or, rather, Gable spotted them. "Hey! You two! Look out!" he yelled, as they stepped up onto the muddy, greasy drilling platform to speak with him. Three men worked around the drill hole, using huge tongs to unscrew the drilling tool from the uppermost length of pipe, while three more were using a rope pulley system around a wheel at the top of the derrick to lift a huge length of pipe from a nearby stack and lower it to the hole.

As Jacques and Gatch stepped out of the way, Gable supervised the men in control of the pipe as they lowered it to the men at the hole. "Down, down, down—there—hold!"

The men at the hole slipped the tip of the new pipe into the tip of the pipe in the hole, brought the tongs back to the joint and tightened it. Next, the man at the top of the derrick used a second pulley system to raise the drill tool to the top of the new pipe. The roughneck crew on the platform fixed that end with the tongs. Men on the platform and the derrick waved 'OK' to Gable. He turned and nodded to a man by an engine. The engine was attached to a huge flywheel. The flywheel was attached to the drill string at the well by a huge belt. The man eased the throttle arm forward and the engine grunted into action. The wheel turned, setting the belt in motion. The hole started spitting mud as the drill string started rotating. A deep, distant grinding came up from inside the hole.

The job complete for the moment, Gable looked around at his men. Satisfied they were preparing for their next tasks, he jumped from the platform and strode to the visitors.

"DeGolyer sent us," Jacques reported, yelling over the sounds at the well.

"Yeah, I know," Gable answered, revealing a letter in the pocket of the shirt. At a grinding noise from the engine, he grimaced. "Either of you know anything about engines?"

"I can make that one sound better," Gatch told him.

Gable pushed his Stetson back on his head and eyed Gatch.

"I'll make it hum like a happy baby."

" A Dago good with tools? This I've got to see." He turned to Jacques. "What about you?"

"I do not know. DeGolyer hired me because I understood his geophysical research."

"That's right," Gable grinned, putting his hands on his hips. "But he wants me to show you a thing or two about the oil 'bidness' first. And the first thing I'm gonna show you is what a bunch of hooey this geophysics is."

"Hooey?"

"Yeah. You want me to tell you how to find oil? Creekology. First, you find a salt dome or some such right structure, see? Then you pick the anticline and you walk it."

"With the drilling equipment and crew?"

"What? No. That comes later. You walk the anticline with an Indian and a dog and a tin can and a silver dollar and a steak bone and a hammer and a wooden stake."

"Oh, science."

"Listen, buddy, this works. I learned it in Ohio and Kansas. Men got rich using this method."

"Go on."

"Now you blindfold the Indian and give him the silver dollar and turn him in circles three times and he throws the silver dollar as hard as he can. Then you tie the tin can to the dogs tail."

"Can you take the blindfold off the Indian?"

"What? I don't care."

"But the Indian would."

136

"Fine." Gable suddenly stopped and eyed Jacques suspiciously, an expression that asked, "Do you want trouble?"

Jacques smiled. "You tie the tin can to the dog's tail?"

Gable smiled, feeling he again had the upper hand. "That's right. And you throw the steak bone in the same direction as the Indian threw the silver dollar. The dog chases the steak bone. Wherever the tin can comes loose from its tail, you hammer in the wooden stake and send the drill crew out to spud in."

"And you find oil like that?"

"You find just as much oil that way as you do blowing everything up. You find salt water the same way. And dust."

"Hey, boss!" One roughneck yelled.

"Yeah, yeah," Gable answered, then turned back to Jacques. "Come on. Time to put another pipe length on the string. He proceeded to supervise the crew through the same series of maneuvers as before. When they finished, Gable again jumped down from the platform and started over toward the engine where Gatch was working.

"You do this over and over, all day long?" Jacques asked.

Gable stopped and looked at Jacques hard. "Listen, brother. That's what you do all day long on a GOOD day. When you don't spend your day fishing in the hole for broken pipe or a dropped tool or have your sands cave in and spend your day pouring concrete casing. There are so many things that can go wrong when you're drilling that I'm always glad to spend the whole day just doing that! Hey! Listen!"

"What?"

"Listen."

"What?" Jacques heard nothing but the boiler and pump engine and the drilling. "What?"

"That wop pal of yours has got my pump engine PURRING!" He pivoted and rushed over to where Gatch was working.

137

"It really is a fine piece of machinery," Gatch, greasy, on his knees and going at the engine with a wrench, grinned up at them.

"In the hands of the right mechanic," Gable declared. He stuck out his hand to Gatch. "You're hired."

"What about me?" Jacques asked.

Gable scowled. "When I say you're a roughneck, you join the 'perfessers' out in the field. Until then, you're just a roustabout and you do what I say."

"You will take me on?"

Gable glared at Jacques. "Say, listen, pal. When this well comes in, I'm on my way to Hollywood for wine, women and stardom. Until then, I take on whatever DeGolyer tells me to."

"Hey boss!" The roughneck yelled again.

"Alright, boys. Let's get to work!"

At the end of the long day, the second tour came on duty at the well. Gable invited Jacques and Gatch to join him for a drink. They cleaned up and walked to a rough looking place at the opposite end of Main Street from The Broadway Hotel. While they walked, Gatch asked Jacques about Katie Marie.

"I told her not to wait for us tonight," Jacques said.

"Good for you!" Gable interrupted. "No dames in your way. Love 'em and leave 'em."

"That's not quite what I am saying."

"Its what I'M saying. Now, listen—nobody likes the pretty little ladies more than this guy." Hand gestures and pelvic thrusts left little doubt about what he liked about them.
"But none of 'em are any good. Half of 'em are too clingy and the other half are loose."

"You have done the survey?" Jacques asked.

Gable grinned. "You bet I have, pal. More field work than all the perfessers in Germany. Housewives, debutantes and working girls. None worth the trouble they make."

At the edge of Bartle City, not far from where the east-west railroad line crossed the wrong end of Main Street, Gable led them into a rough plank building. As he threw back the door, he smiled. "Welcome to The Crystal Palace, where Mr. DeGolyer sends his crews for recreation." He pointed across the room, behind the bar, to a brassy blond woman in heavy make-up and crushed velvet. "The madam sold him his first lease."

Glancing over the plank structure, Gatch asked over the crowd noise, "Where's the crystal?"

Gable laughed. "When you show me the palace, I'll show you the crystal." He led them to a place at the bar amid the crowd, called for bottles of beer and launched into a monologue about his first job as a roughneck. "Meanest man I ever worked for. I was so scared I dropped my tongs down the well the first time we went to add a length of pipe. Driller got madder'n a stallion locked in a stall next to a ready mare. Took us half the shift to fish 'em out. Pulled 'em up, shoved 'em at me and told me not to let it happen again. Ever. Well sir, they was real greasy and I was twice as scared so when I next went to work with 'em, dropped 'em again. Driller come at me cussin' like I'd never heard in all my boyish years. B'time we fished 'em out the second time, the tour was over an' so was my employment. He shoved 'em at me and told me to get off the platform, I was fired. That's when I finally got my nerve. 'The hell I'm fired! I quit!' I yelled, throwing them tongs back down in the well." He threw back his head and bellowed out laughter. "That was Ohio and I never stopped running 'til I got to Oklahoma."

He went on laughing while Jacques and Gatch drank and smiled. Jacques drained his bottle and set it on the bar among the many, many empties. "Must see the man about the dog," he announced. As Jacques left the barroom for the urinal behind the building, the brassy blond madam climbed up on the bar and announced, in a throaty howl, a new entertainment. As Jacques returned, he heard a clunky piano tune and a very familiar voice.

As he neared the bar, Katie Marie was standing on it over Gatch and Gable, finishing her song with a flourish. "Toot, Toot, Tootsie don't cry, Toot, Toot, Tootsie GOODBYE!"

The room went wild with applause and cheering. Reveling in it, Katie Marie called out that she'd be back to sing another one as soon as the madam knew the customers were drinking up. The crowd cheered again. Grinning happily, she leaned on Gatch's shoulder and jumped down from the bar. Landing, she lost her balance and fell into the leering Gable's all-too-ready arms.

By the time Jacques pushed his way through the boisterous barroom to them, Gable was all over Katie Marie and she was using all her strength to keep him at arm's length while Gatch tried to mediate. "I'm not that kind of entertainer, you oaf!" she yelled.

"Hey! Hey! Hey!" Jacques screamed at Gable over the turmoil. "That is my WIFE you're manhandling!"

Suddenly Gable let Katie Marie go. "What?"

"Break the bastard's head!" Katie Marie screamed at Jacques. Jacques laughed at Gable's discomfort, not appreciating his wife's rage. "What the hell are you laughing at, you son-of-a-bitch! I'm you're son's MOTHER!" She grabbed a beer bottle from the bar and started to swing at Gable.

"Whoa! Whoa!" Gatch exhorted, grabbing her arm.

She glared at Jacques. "Beat this bastard!" she demanded.

"This is Clark Gable, your husband's new boss," Jacques replied. "He had no idea who you were!"

"That's right, little lady!" Gable chimed in, grinning. "Most of the gals here like my attentions."

"Who you calling little?" she challenged, though she only stood to Gable's chest.

"Settle down, Katie Marie!" Gatch told her. "How did you wind up here, anyway?"

"Good question," Jacques agreed.

"DeGolyer sent me. Said the madam would give me a job singing."

"You do not need to work," said Jacques.

"What am I supposed to do while you two are drilling out and blowing up the countryside?"

"This isn't the kind of place for you," Gable told her.

She glared at him. "I'll ask you the same thing I asked DeGolyer: You got a music hall in this town?"

"A music hall? No."

"That's why I'm here."

The madam leaned over the bar. "Alright, honey," she told Katie Marie. "Let's give 'em an encore to get 'em thirsty again."

"Yes!" Katie Marie exclaimed. She pointed across the room to the piano player, wiggled two fingers for song number two and circled toward the stepladder to climb up on the bar again. "You might want to find a companion for the big galoot," she called back to the madam. "A girl who likes hands with a life of their own."

"Never mind, Mooch," Gable told the madam. "I'll take care of myself."

The madam looked at Gatch. "You're sweet-looking. I've got a girl for you who's never been away from her mama."

"Yeah," Gable said, reaching for another bottle of beer. "But her mama ran a house."

*****

They took up long-term residence at the Broadway Hotel and settled into their work. Time passed. Summer waned. The autumn chill came. In the living room of their hotel suite, Katie Marie hung a painting of the sun setting over the Pacific Ocean at Malibu and kept herself happy singing at The Crystal Palace. Just like in Chicago, she became a local celebrity. She ended every night's performance in a joyous rendition of "California Here I Come" and, for her encore, a heartbreakingly melancholy "Indian Love Song." She reveled in her nights as a singing star and, invigorated by the intense Oklahoma seasons and the hilarious night-by-night vulgarities of The Crystal Palace, she also found unexpected joy in the day-by-day surprises in being Monty's mother.

Monty was as happy as a pre-schooler could be who was the center of the universe to every adult in sight. Gatch fell in love with working on the drilling machinery. Gable trained Jacques, who showed an amazing aptitude for the oil business, considering how much he detested it. He quickly grasped the basics, and then the intricacies, of drilling. Gable took him to other wells

141

around the region, pointing out things about well location and drilling operations only a veteran of the fields would see. Jacques assimilated the information quickly and easily and soon was a truly astute oilman.

But before Jacques could move to the geophysical field research team, the well they were working came in. Gable got drunk that night at The Crystal Palace and the next day he left for Hollywood. DeGolyer asked Jacques and Gatch to take over management duties at the well. The Canadian winds blew in. The prairie turned bitterly cold. Blizzards followed. Bartle City's oil boom hibernated.

Due to the huge expansion in the California petroleum industry, Bennett—according to word from inside the 77 refinery—was temporarily headquartered in Los Angeles. "Running lease hounds in Long Beach and playing thoroughbreds in Mexico," an insider at 77 told them. Just as Gatch and Jacques began discussing the possibility of following Gable west, they heard rumors Bennett would be making an inspection in Bartle City between Thanksgiving and Christmas. He did not. New rumors put the inspection between Christmas and New Year's Day. It was not. The inspection was then said to be coming in the spring. They decided to wait. When drenching March did not bring Bennett and neither did fickle April, they started talking again about going to California. Gatch also raised the possibility of a trip to New York to find out what he could at Wade Automotive. But, at the end of April when local Indians started turning up dead, Gatch's attention shifted dramatically.

*****

Osage tribal leader Wah Ti An Kah advised his people, in 1872, to relocate in the rugged, hilly northeast of the Oklahoma territory rather than the tamer prairie lands to the west. Wah Ti An Kah warned them white men would want the farmable prairie lands but not the hill country. He was right about the topography but he did not know about mineral rights.

Neither did the territorial men who made the land deals with the tribe, so they did not withhold rights to what was below the surface when they deeded the lands to the Osage. Imagine the white man's rage when he discovered HIS oil was under THEIR land, Native American-owned land, Native Americans the U.S. government now promised to protect as best it could from exploitation as penance for centuries of previous abuses. Oil lease negotiations by tribal leaders and their advisors made the Osage the richest Native Americans anywhere.

The wealth was widely distributed, whether the newly rich were ready for it or not. The "oil curse" afflicted 1920s Oklahoma as it would the 1970s Middle East and 1990s Africa. The first "Coal Oil Johnny"— a character who fritters away fortuitous wealth – was a white male protestant Pennsylvanian profligate with unexpected petroleum riches. Perhaps the last will be western Canadian or Venezuelan or Nigerian. But in 1920s Oklahoma, somebody suddenly started killing the newly rich Osage. Some turned up shot. One or two were hung. Then, a farmhouse was burned. A cabin was dynamited. Local law enforcement, overburdened by the lawlessness of the boomtowns, was slow to respond. State officers finally arrived. No perpetrator was brought to justice and no satisfactory explanation except hate and resentment was ever offered, but the killing slowly dissipated as the Osage community united in vigilance under the stern guardianship of the Oklahoma Rangers.

*****

During the time of the killing spree, Gatch could have chosen to remain incognito as the Frenchman's New York-Italian partner. Instead, in his wrath at the brutal, senseless injustice, he revealed his Huron roots and joined with the Osage leaders. He and Jacques helped organize against the killing. They set up guard posts, patrols and schedules. When the state peace officers moved in, their vigilance waned but the bond between Gatch and the Osage people remained. He began regular visits with a particular elder's family. Now, instead of making plans with Jacques, he was sharing intimacies of another sort with the elder's adult daughter.

As the spring turned into summer, the mood of an Indian love song played over the Oklahoma hills. By the dog days of August, Gatch often mentioned to Jacques and Katie Marie, on his infrequent visits with them, "life among his own kind." He seemed to forget about Bennett. He thought instead about Rosa, the elder's daughter, about a life with her, a home, a family. He developed a new perspective, a longer view. Suddenly, he needed a goal more concrete than "waiting for Bennett." One day, without talking to Rosa or Jacques or Katie Marie or the Osage elder, he impulsively withdrew most of the money in the savings account he shared with Jacques and Katie Marie and purchased an oil lease on a tract of land Crystal Palace Madam Mooch told him was even more promising than the one she had sold DeGolyer.

Jubilant with anticipation, he immediately went to their hotel room to deliver the "good news" to Jacques and Katie Marie. After hearing him out, Jacques slowly fumed while Katie Marie began screaming. She called him names she had only recently learned on her job and proclaimed that he had squandered the money they were saving for their escape to Hollywood. He assured her he

143

had done the right thing because the oil wealth would fund his life here with Rosa as well as Katie Marie's escape. She asked him with brutal sarcasm why he did not get investment money from Rosa's oil-rich Osage father. Gatch just looked at her like she was crazy. To go to Rosa's father, he told Katie Marie, would be humiliating himself. Through a face frozen in rage, Katie Marie forced herself to stay calm and sympathetic long enough to quietly affirm the importance of his love for Rosa. Then she exploded in fury, screaming curses and grabbing a baseball bat. Swinging at him viciously, she raged that humiliation would seem like heaven to him before she was through beating him. She destroyed two lamps and a vase before Jacques could calm her. Her violent outburst seemed to finally dissipate their raw emotions, bringing on quiet.

Gatch sat in a chair in the middle of the room, his head hung down, his hands covering his face. Once again, he told them he could not go to the Osage for support but must earn his way to where he was Rosa's equal. Katie Marie, her back to him, stared at her painting of the sun setting over the Pacific Ocean at Malibu, too angry to care what he was saying. Jacques stood between them facing away, staring across the room, at the wide empty gray-blue sky out the window. Finally, he turned and spoke. "There is really nothing we can do except find oil." Gatch raised his head, joy flooding his face. He was about to exclaim enthusiastically when Jacques silenced him with a sharp shake of a finger. They both watched Katie Marie, waiting for her to react. There was only silence.

Finally, she turned to them. "One: From now on, I keep my own earnings in my own bank account. Two: If you don't find oil before you go broke, Monty and me are going to Hollywood without you. Now get out of here and start raising the money to drill."

After explaining their move to DeGolyer and promising to train replacements to work his well, he gave their project his blessing. So they set out to locate their own well. Rejecting out of hand Gable's method involving the drunken Indian's silver dollar throw and the dog with the tin can tied to its tail chasing the bone, they were left to choose between the costly, unproven DeGolyer geophysics and other as yet unidentified though less expensive methods. Inclined to avoid expenses, they began with the second option.

Glass Ball Gertie, a woman in a tent near The Crystal Palace renowned for her ability to foresee brawls in the local saloons, accepted a fee, looked at a map of the tract under lease and picked a spot for the well. A man in a fine suit accepted a fee and escorted a little African-American boy, who the man said had x-ray vision, in a hike over the tract. They picked a spot near Glass

144

Ball Gertie's where the man said the boy's nonsensical babbling was the indication of where he saw oil deep in the earth.

An ancient miner walked the leased tract with a magic Y-shaped stick, a divining rod. After several days of ritualistically pointing the stick up and down, he settled on a "certain gusher" location but would not accept a fee "...until I do further testing." The next day, the old miner returned with a rod attached by string to a receptacle filled with a potion, the ingredients of which the old miner would not reveal. When the receptacle started spinning, the old man announced the site "must" be drilled and demanded his fee. The site was within a stone's throw of the other two spots. When Jacques asked about the wrist-flicking action associated with the receptacle's spinning, the old man looked deeply offended and told Gatch his partner was a foreign fool. "Pay me my fee and drill where you want, dammit!"

The next afternoon, Gatch came into the hotel room in a huff and insisted Jacques must hurry out to the land with him. Arriving, they stood by the Model T and watched Dr. P. S. Griffith, a small, lean, clean-shaven man in an 1890s-style suit and hat with wide, narrow blue eyes, heavy brows and a deeply wrinkled face, stomp the grounds.

"Is that something in his MOUTH?" Jacques asked.

"A wiggle stick."

"A what?" Jacques studied the device. Two silver, pencil-sized lugs hung from a plate in his mouth. From the lugs hung small, 6-inch long spring coils. At the end of each spring was a tiny silver plate the size of a quarter.

"The silver plates are for oil," Gatch explained. "Iron would find gas but I told him to look for oil."

"Good," said Jacques with more than a hint of irony.

They continued watching while Dr. Griffith worked. Every few minutes his body jerked, as if he had been shocked or startled. Each time, he marked the site with a wood stake. This activity went on through the afternoon. Near sunset, Dr. Griffith came toward them, reached into the back of the car, lifted out a log book, turned toward the field where had he been working and began drawing a map of the sites staked.

"What do you think, Doctor?" asked Gatch.

"Too soon to tell!" Griffith snapped back.

Griffith continued mapping the terrain. When they drove out to meet him on the evening on the third day, he demanded three days' pay and delivered several pages of mathematical equations that made no sense to Jacques, along with a recommendation to drill in almost the same place the others had indicated. After they paid him and delivered him back to Bartle City, they parked the car near The Crystal Palace for Katie Marie to drive home when she finished singing, and walked to the hotel together.

"Looks like we know where to drill," Gatch announced, grinning. He looked at Jacques' skeptical expression. "They all agree!" Gatch beamed. "You don't think they're all wrong, do you?"

"I don't," grunted Jacques with a grimace. "It is where anybody would drill."

"How do you know that?" Gatch asked in wonderment. "Some kind of technical assessment?"

"A little bird told me," Jacques answered disdainfully.

"What?"

"All you have to do is look at the lay of the land, Gatch."

"Well," grinned Gatch. "I guess that makes it unanimous. Let's hire a crew."

Oil leases were time limited. If the investor did not produce oil revenue in the specified time period, the land owner had the right to lease to someone else. To produce results, Gatch and Jacques had to drill. To drill, they had to spend money. They could get drilling equipment and supplies on credit. But bills and salaries had to be paid regularly. As time passed, expenses grew and debts mounted. Soon they resorted to the oil business's most familiar tactic, selling shares. Since they estimated that $50,000 would bring the well home, they planned to sell $1/100^{th}$ of the project for $1,000 to fifty investors, retaining one-half of the project for themselves, minus the $1/8^{th}$ they had promised to the land owner.

With the raising of $50,000 as their goal, Gatch and Jacques set out to find investors, meanwhile continuing to use credit with their suppliers and persuasion with their crew to keep the drilling going. Initially, share sales were to people they had come to know in Bartle City. Soon, they ran through such people. Referrals kept investments coming in but soon enthusiasm for the location waned and they realized they would have to find some way to stimulate it. But how? They had no credentials to recommend them.

"We brought in the DeGolyer well," Gatch pointed out.

"Gable brought that in," Jacques reminded him. "And DeGolyer spotted it."

"But we were there. I'll talk to people, convince them we had a part in it."

"How?"

"Leave that to me. You keep the drilling going."

"Without money?"

"I'll get you the money."

A month passed, and then another, and another. Gatch raised money, only to find out the well required more, and then more. When he raged about it, Jacques only laughed and reminded him who got them into this dilemma. So Gatch returned to Main Street, trolling for yet more investors. Nearing the collection of the whole $50,000, Gatch stopped by the well. There was a fully constructed derrick and platform, a smooth running engine and boiler and a steadily turning drill. He found Jacques standing away from the derrick and platform, next to the shack they used for their office, worry on his face.

"What is it?" Gatch asked.

"Nothing," Jacques said, staring at the drill.

"It's something!" Gatch said angrily. "I can tell by that look."

"There is something worse than running out of money," Jacques said.

"You think this is a dry hole?"

Jacques shook his head like he was trying to wake himself up from a bad dream. "It is down there," Jacques finally said.

"How can you be so sure?"

"All we have to do is keep drilling."

"For how long?"

Jacques said nothing, just stared at the drill.

"For how long?" Gatch repeated.

Jacques remained silent, staring at the drill.

"FOR HOW LONG?" Gatch yelled.

"Until we get oil," Jacques said quietly.

In light of this heightened commitment to persist, they agreed to sacrifice 25 more shares of the lease, retaining a controlling twenty-five per cent of the company against any other investor's one or two per cent. Therefore, after $50,000 in shares was sold, Gatch kept selling. On the day he reached $75,000 in sales, he proudly returned to the drill site to announce the news. He found the drill silent. The crew was huddled gloomily at one end of the platform, grousing. Jacques was inside the shack, on a stool in a corner, his head back against the wall, his eyes shut.

"What the hell is going on?"

"The hole caved in," Jacques said quietly without raising his head or opening his eyes, defeat in his voice.

"Well, what do you DO about it?" Gatch asked, not ready for defeat.

"Casing. But that takes time. And money."

"I've got money," Gatch told him excitedly. "We hit seventy-five thou today!"

"When the hole caved," Jacques said tiredly, "the drill bit the sand hard and bent and stuck."

"Can you fix it?"

"With time," answered Jacques quietly, his head still back, his eyes still shut. "And more money."

"More money?"

"More money."

"What do we do?" Gatch asked, his enthusiasm waning like air from a balloon. "Sell our own shares?"

148

"We would be working for nothing."

"No! We'll sell shares until we raise the money we need."

"We will spend more than our $100,000 before this well comes in."

"I'll raise it!"

His head still back, his eyes still shut, Jacques waited before he answered. "If we sell more than 100% of the company, we become con men."

"We can't finish the well?"

"Our only choices are crime or ruin."

"But you said there is oil down there!"

"If I could prove it, we could get loans to keep us going. But I cannot prove it so it is irrelevant," Jacques answered quietly.

Gatch did not reply but just stared at Jacques, who still sat against the corner, his head back and eyes shut. "Irrelevant?" Gatch finally asked.

"Yes."

"With big ears?"

Jacques' head came forward and his eyes popped open. "What?"

"Irr—ELEPHANT: Big ears. A trunk." He galumphed around the tiny shack, his gestures mimicking an elephant.

Jacques began laughing. His stool slipped out from under him. He crashed back against the wall and went down. This fueled their hysterical laughter. The crew heard and looked over quizzically. Jacques and Gatch were now bellowing laughter and the crewmen began to smile and chuckle, without knowing why. At the sound of an approaching car, they all looked toward it. A worn Model T rumbled to a stop beside the shack, DeGolyer behind the wheel.

"Doesn't look like you've hit oil," DeGolyer grinned, seeing them laughing. "So what's the joke?"

Gatch and Jacques glanced at each other, remembered they didn't really have much to laugh about, and calmed. "No joke," Gatch said, looking at DeGolyer. "Just something that seemed funny at the time."

"What brings you here?" Jacques asked.

"Yeah," said Gatch. "We heard you were blowing up Texas. They send you home?"

"No, no," smiled DeGolyer, shaking his head. "But we need some results. I was wonderin' if you boys would do me a favor?"

Gatch and Jacques glanced again at each other, both thinking how bad a time it was to be asked to repay past favors.

"If we can," said Jacques.

"I want you to let me map your lease before you get any result so I can prove the method's accuracy."

"That's it?" Gatch asked in surprise.

"You want me to pay you?" DeGolyer asked defensively. "I have funding from Lord Cowdry. I will pay a fair fee."

"No! No!" Both shouted at once.

"Then you'll help me out?" he asked grinning.

"If we must," Jacques replied with a relaxed smile Gatch had never seen before. DeGolyer's grin widened. He stepped forward, extending a handshake. "But," continued Jacques, his own smile widening. "Perhaps there is a way we can help one another."

*****

It is a modern myth, perhaps THE modern myth. A disrespected man, or a man who becomes disrespected in the process, sets out to find oil. The best science cannot tell him where to drill. He must trust his own heart and mind. Often, the geologists oppose or criticize him. Finally, drilling begins. He finds no oil. Trouble develops. He must improvise new techniques, make risky decisions. Still there is no oil. Money is running out. He finagles, cajoles and cons. But it seems useless. His supporters withdraw, his financing fails. Yet he gathers his resources, makes one last desperate

150

effort—and it produces no results. He must go to the well, discontinue the drilling and stop the pain. He sleeps one more night, perhaps at the drill team's encampment, intending to cease operations in the morning. And in the stillness of the end, at the very brink of failure, the earth suddenly rumbles and spews forth black-green fortune. "Redemption is mine," sayeth the driller. Somebody always tells him along the way, "If there's oil there, I'll drink every drop!" If all these promises had been kept, oil would be a beverage instead of a fuel.

It happened to Colonel Drake in Titusville, Pennsylvania, at the very first commercial American well. It was probably the same in Baku, before Drake. The story of Patillo Huggins and Colonel Lucas at Spindletop, the first Texas giant, conforms. As does the story of the first oil explorations in Persia (later Iran) on behalf of the British by Australian gold miner William Knox D'Arcy. It is the shape of the story told about Lyman Stewart in California, Benedum and Trees in Colombia and E.W. Marland (later the state's Governor) in Oklahoma. The tale of Dad Joiner, who brought in the Daisy Bradford #3 and opened the humongous East Texas giant field, begins with a stint as a gigolo, succeeds by the nickel and dime contributions of the small farmers and working folks in the region and ends with a famous poker game involving H.L. Hunt.

This is the story they always tell, the one about the man and his well. But these men's names are on no oil companies. At best, they were names only for a while. It was the powerbrokers, the men who turned success in one aspect of the oil business into an integrated corporate entity, who learned to move the commodity from the well to the tank, whose living monuments still stand.

*****

When DeGolyer's seismographic data revealed they were almost down to the producing sands, he unhesitatingly arranged a loan from Lord Cowdry. The well came in a gusher. Gatch named the well Rosa Number One. It became the cornerstone of their company, which they call the Monty-G Oil Company and, despite fluctuations in oil prices, Rosa Number One soon brought in enough cash to pay off the loan. This gave them access to credit. They quickly began drilling other sites on their leasehold.

Despite deficit financing, they charged forward. For Gatch's marriage to Rosa, Jacques and Katie Marie threw them the biggest wedding celebration the Bartle City corner of Oklahoma had ever seen. After the honeymoon, each couple bought a home on the affluent west side of town. Rosa began her new life as Gatch's wife, away from her family for the first time. Katie Marie enrolled Monty in the local school and reveled in her roll as the singing star of The Crystal Palace. Gatch and Jacques focused on growing the business. Thanks to the richness of the sands beneath their lease, they became the biggest oil producers in the region. When their production exceeded the capacity of all the local refineries and pipelines, yet they needed to sell still more oil to cover their costs, they decided it was time to consult a financial advisor. They arranged an appointment at the Bartle City First National Bank.

"After a careful and thorough analysis of your situation, there is one thing I can say with absolute certainty," Frank Bartle, the tall, lean, genial founder, president and chief financial officer of the bank, a son of the town's first family and a good man equally at home in an oil field, at a dinner party or behind a desk, told them. "To make more money, you need more money."

Gatch looked at the man in surprise. "I could've told YOU that." He looked over at Jacques. "This meeting was your idea," he said impatiently.

Jacques looked at Bartle. "While you have been studying Monty-G Oil, I have been studying your bank."

"Our records are public."

"You are the largest shareholder in the 77 Refinery, yes?"

"That's right. But it is working at full capacity."

"Capacity can be expanded."

"With investment."

"We will restructure our cash flow. We will redirect expenditures now in drilling to provide capital to expand the 77 refinery capacity."

"77 will not let you invest."

"We will invest in the bank. You represent the bank on the 77 Board of Directors, yes?"

Bartle nodded 'yes.'

"The 77 Board can be convinced to expand refinery capacity. It is a good move for them."

152

Both Bartle and Gatch looked at Jacques in astonishment.

"It is," Bartle finally replied hesitantly, "a very complicated plan."

"Yes," smiled Jacques. "But it profits all participants, does it not?"

Bartle studied Jacques without saying anything. Jacques simply sat quietly, watching Bartle and waiting. Gatch held his breath. "You know what, Mr. Livingstone?" Bartle finally said, breaking into a smile. "We are going to make a lot of money together!" He stood and extended a handshake. Jacques stood and took it.

"And we wind up in business with 77," said Gatch, grinning as he stood to join in the deal-making handshakes.

"Yes," smiled Jacques, glancing at Gatch with the twinkle in his eye of a man with a plan.

The restructuring of Monty-G Oil's finances was completely successful. Soon, in silent partnership with Bartle City First National Bank, it began expanding its production again, opening new fields and new pipelines as well as new refining capacity through the Bartle City 77 plant. From the oil in the ground to refined material for manufactured products as diverse as automobile fuel, Bakelite plastics and celluloid film, Jacques and Gatch became major forces in Oklahoma oil. From their Monty-G Company offices, now located in the 77 refinery complex, to the drilling platforms and pumping stations all across the Osage, they came to know virtually every boiler, derrick, driller, roughneck, pipe tong and pipeline in the region. They often heard the name Bennett, yet they never encountered him. Discreet inquiries through the bank revealed that 77 corporate officers thought it best to leave the refinery in the hands of local management as long as it continued to run successfully and cause no trouble. Bennett, they learned, was now spending time buying and raising Derby thoroughbreds for 77 corporate officers. It was therefore without trepidation about an encounter with him that Gatch and Jacques accepted Bartle's invitation to join him, with their wives and Monty, on the dignitaries' platform for festivities to celebrate the opening of the refinery's newest operation, something the company scientists called a "cracking" tower.

The celebration was a day-long festival like only Oklahoma could put on. An Osage Corn Dance kicked off the morning. A company picnic followed, featuring an Indian stick ball game between a refinery team and tribal players. In the afternoon, townsfolk, refinery workers and their families gathered in bleachers on a field behind the plant to watch rodeo events starring local cowboys. Bartle, Gatch, Rosa, Jacques, Katie Marie and Monty had front row seats. When the horses and riders and clowns and bulls finished their show, the crowd stood for the singing of *My Country 'Tis of Thee* (led by Katie Marie) and, finally, it sat one last time for speeches from Frank Bartle and the 77 refinery manager.

Bartle's speech, from the podium facing the crowd on the platform in front of the bleachers, was brief and jesting. The sated crowd was more than ready to go home for supper when, concluding his remarks, Bartle said, "And now, Ladies and Gentlemen, to finish off the day, we have a special treat. Here from Tulsa, to tell us about blessings the 77 Corporation has in store for our fair city, is 77 Vice President Harry Bennett. And with him comes a special guest, a pioneer in America's great auto industry, Harry Wade! Let's give them a loud and warm Bartle City welcome!"

From a Pierce-Arrow limousine behind the cheering and applauding bleachers, walking side by side and sharing jovial private exchanges, came Gatch's former boss and Jacques' former nemesis. But it was not just Jacques and Gatch who stood and stared in astonishment while Wade and Bennett made their way to the podium. As the two men came up the steps of the platform, waving to the yelling, clapping crowd, a third face stared at them, its expression of stony amazement turned to raging agony. Jacques and Gatch were so focused on Wade and Bennett they did not notice the third person until they heard, as the crowd quieted to hear Bennett speak, Rosa suddenly exclaim, "Katie-Marie! Are you all right?" They turned to where their wives sat. Katie Marie's face was twisted in fury and hatred. Her eyes seemed to glow with a red fierceness. Dramatically, she raised her arm, pointed toward Bennett and screamed, "KILL HIM!"

Suddenly, a hush fell over the crowd. Bennett looked at Katie Marie with slight irritation and no recognition, as if he was seeing her from high above. Wade felt the shock of the moment without understanding it. Seeing his former assistant, he exclaimed, "Gatch! What's this all about?"

As if in a trance, Katie Marie continued pointing at Bennett and drew all attention back to herself when she again shouted, "KILL HIM—OR I WILL!" She suddenly leapt across the platform toward the man at the podium.

Jacques grabbed her and held her back. While he wrestled with her, he looked at Rosa. "Take Monty home!"

Rosa grabbed Monty, who was terrified at the sight of his mother raging. With some difficulty, Rosa managed to get the boy off the podium and moving away.

Meanwhile, Bartle stepped back to the podium. "Ladies and Gentlemen, let's wrap it up for this afternoon and you keep an eye on the Bartle City Bugle for news of the big changes coming our way thanks to the 77 Corporation and Wade Automotive." He tried to lead them into conclusive applause but nobody was about to interrupt the potential drama unfolding.

Even before Bartle finished talking, Katie Marie—unable to wrestle from Jacques' grasp—began screaming again. "He turned me into a slave and a whore! Kill him! He's an animal! Kill him! KILL HIM!"

Wade again looked at Gatch, still trying to understand. When he saw Gatch did not understand either, he turned to Bennett. Bennett remained aloof, looking from Katie Marie to Jacques with irritation, as if looking at mosquitoes buzzing around him. He turned to Bartle. "Let's go back to town and have dinner," he said. Next, he turned to Wade. "I'll give you one more chance to deal with this French trouble-maker." He started to walk away, expecting Bartle to follow.

"No, Bennett," Jacques suddenly said, harshness coming into his voice. "It is time to answer."

Bennett looked at Bartle expectantly.

"NO!" Katie Marie shrieked. "KILL HIM! KILL HIM OR I WILL!" She struggled with Jacques, trying to get at Bennett.

Bartle hesitated. "Let me disperse this crowd," he told Bennett. "Then we can get this settled." Before Bennett could reply, Bartle turned to back to the crowd. "OK, folks, the show's over." He clapped his hands twice. "Come on, come on!" He pointed at familiar faces in the crowd. "You managers. Let's get these people moving! We've got to get this place closed and cleaned up so we can get you back to work tomorrow!" He left the platform and went down into the crowd, clapping and calling out at them, "Come on, come on!"

While Bartle worked the crowd, Jacques handed Katie Marie off to Gatch and Wade, who together restrained her, though she went on wailing "No-no-no! Kill him! He doesn't deserve to live!"

Jacques stepped intimately close to Bennett and spoke quietly yet fiercely through a clenched jaw. "It is time to face your guilt."

"I don't even know who she is," Bennett muttered impatiently.

There was a riveting intimacy in this muted confrontation between Jacques and Bennett while Bartle's calls, the chatter of the crowd and Katie Marie's wailing surrounded them.

"You are guilty of many things," Jacques answered Bennett.

"Aren't we all," Bennett smiled.

"The death of the American journalist in Paris."

"Or did you do that?" Bennett asked, still smiling.

"The British diplomat."

"Suicide."

"Really?"

"We met, discussed his position. He made his choice."

"You had nothing to do with the position he found himself in?"

"Mr. Brown of Chicago is presently managing rather crudely some young women whose positions YOU had something to do with."

"It is not the same!" Jacques snapped back.

"No?" By now the crowd diffused, its chatter fading away in twilight shadows. Katie Marie's rage had exhausted her and her wails turned into sobbing against Gatch's shoulder. Bennett's voice suddenly seemed louder. "And now we are partners in the oil business. So what am I guilty of that you are not?"

"You blackmail Wade," Jacques blurted.

"No!" Wade interrupted. He released Katie Marie, still sobbing but now compliant, to Gatch, and stepped to Jacques. "At first he needed money to suppress a memo my son wrote."

"I read Sam's memo."

156

"You know my son?"

"We met in Paris at the start of the war."

"How did you read the memo?" Wade asked.

"I discovered it while working for Colonel House in Paris. Bennett is the man who leaked it!"

"I know," Wade replied.

"You know?"

"He came to me. He did not know who Sam was when he gave the information to the British delegation. I funded his people in Mesopotamia protecting Sam."

"That is blackmail!" Jacques protested.

"Son," Wade said quietly, sadness in his voice. "That is business."

"Speaking of business," Bennett interrupted, smiling broadly. "How about this? Did you know we're all working together now? Wade Automotive is putting up an airplane engine plant to burn that high-octane fuel your refinery's new cracking tower is going to be pumping out. And I'm running security for both of you."

Without a reply, Jacques simply looked from Wade to Bennett and back to Wade. The grounds were nearly empty and very quiet now. The only sound was Katie Marie's sobbing into Gatch's shoulder. Bartle came back up the steps of the platform. Jacques looked at Gatch. With a flick of his wrist, he signaled for Gatch to take Katie Marie home. Gatch nodded and walked her off the platform, still sobbing.

Seeing Bennett, Wade and Jacques standing alone and silent, Bartle smiled. "What say we walk across to the Broadway Hotel for steaks and scotch?"

"Finally!" exclaimed Bennett, breaking into a grin. "I'm starving. What about you, Frenchie?"

Jacques stared at Bennett and Bennett stared back with an "I-dare-you" grin on his face. Unsure whether the dare was to come to supper or attack, Wade broke the silence. "Mr. Livingstone?"

"I have no appetite," Jacques finally said.

"Can I have my driver take you home?" Bartle asked.

"I will walk," Jacques replied abruptly, pivoting and striding away. Bennett's loud voice, telling Bartle about a prize thoroughbred, echoed in the evening.

Jacques walked south through the noise and bustle of Main Street. At The Crystal Palace, he looked in, wishing he could find Katie Marie gaily singing but knowing he would not. He kept walking south until he was out of town and across the railroad tracks, walking into a deepening darkness on a hard dirt road.

Long after dark, his thoughts flowing on and making no sense, his walking brought him, he did not know how much later, to nothing but weariness. For a reason he did not know, he decided to turn back. Finally beginning to feel tired, he started stopping at boulders or logs beside the road to sit and rest and look up into the Oklahoma stars and think about things he did not know anything about. He wondered many things and had no answers. Not since the war had he walked for so long.

Near gray-blue dawn, he walked up to his silent house with a strange feeling of finality. Wearily, he pushed open the heavy door and entered without noticing his Model T was not there. He slowly lifted his heavy feet up the stairs to his bedroom, looking forward to seeing the peaceful beauty of Katie Marie sleeping. He found to his surprise the bed empty, unslept in.

With a rising feeling of panic, he hurried across the hall to Monty's room. His son's bed was also empty and unslept in. Now his sleepless, numb, exhausted mind was screaming. Where were they? With Gatch and Rosa! Of course! He raced back out the front door. The Model T? She drove it there! Before he began walking the country road to his friends' house, he found himself running but could not catch up with his racing mind. She drove to Gatch's? But Gatch would drive her and Monty in his Cadillac...His mind offered explanations, scenarios, unlikelihoods, impossibilities...It would not quiet. Memories of despondence and rage and terror in Paris and Chicago flashed through his mind, always with the name Bennett attached, each awful memory and possibility culminating with Bennett smiling and saying, "We're all working together now..."

Breathing heavily, he came in sight of his friends' still sleeping home. The Cadillac was there. Where was the Model T? Though he was not aware of deciding to do so, he was suddenly pounding on the front door. Lights came on upstairs. He was calling their names. "Gatch! Rosa!" They were answering sleepily from upstairs, coming down gathering their dressing gowns to themselves, opening the door to him without answers to where Katie Marie and Monty were, only groggy nonsense about where they were not.

"I took her home from the plant," Gatch told him. "She had quieted, said she would be all right."

"Were they taken?" Rosa exclaimed, asking one of the questions Jacques did not want to think about. Both men looked at her without replying.

Gatch turned to Jacques. "Let's go."

After Gatch quickly threw on pants, they drove back to Jacques' house. "They probably weren't in the bedrooms because she fell asleep with Monty on the sofa in the living room, or in the library, waiting for you to come home," Gatch told him on the drive.

They went into the big silent house together, Jacques numbly going back up the stairs to look again, as if he had not been there before, Gatch switching on lights and looking everywhere downstairs. A few minutes later, Jacques stood at the top of the stairs, still numb and blank and fearing the worst, not wanting to go downstairs and find out what it might be. He looked down and saw Gatch come out of the kitchen reading a sheet of paper. Gatch looked up at Jacques, his eyes welling up with tears. He held out the sheet of paper. Jacques looked at it, then at Gatch.

"You have read it?" Jacques asked from the top of the stairs.

Gatch nodded 'yes.'

Jacques read Gatch. "They have not been taken."

Tears rolled down Gatch's face as he shook his head 'no.'

Jacques stared blankly at Gatch for a long, silent moment. Finally, he turned away from the stairs. "I will read it another time," he said quietly. "Now I am tired. I am going to sleep."

Just before Jacques disappeared down the upstairs hallway, Gatch found his voice. "I will be in the kitchen or the living room, O.K.?"

"Of course," Jacques replied without looking back, disappearing into the guest bedroom at the end of the hall.

159

Gatch went back into the kitchen to make coffee for himself, leaving the letter on a small table at the foot of the stairs, its words still reverberating in his mind:

"The HELL with him because I cannot KILL him and the HELL with you because you WILL NOT!!! I am going to California. DO NOT FOLLOW ME."

*****

Plodding, one foot in front of the other, and going on. Plodding, one foot in front of the other, going on. Walking from the entry hall of his house where Katie Marie's painting of the sun setting over the Pacific Ocean at Malibu still hung, to his office at the oil company where there were only oilfield charts and maps. Sitting at his desk answering questions about the business from Gatch while others kept it brief and pleasant or avoided him altogether. Walking with Gatch across to the Broadway Hotel at lunch, watched by nervous and artificially pleasant or suddenly elsewhere attentive eyes. Walking back in silence or giving silent nodding assent to Gatch's endless questions. Where to drill? Should we take a well to 3000 feet or cap it and cut our loss? The gas lines with the red dust problem: Bartle wants to lease the gas to a company with a materials-and-celluloid processing scheme, but who needs such stuff? Do we back a pipeline going east to the Mississippi River or another going south to the Gulf of Mexico? Not caring about the company but caring about Gatch, Jacques just listened.

Empty afternoons of agonizing minute by agonizing minute until Gatch came in to announce quitting time. He always turned down the never failing offer of a ride home. The evening prison march down Main Street, where the emptiness in him screamed loudest but was heard least amid the everyday anonymity and tumult. Arriving at the always unrealized wish to hear her song once again coming out of The Crystal Palace. The emptiness at the south end of town. The railroad crossing where the westbound slowed cautiously and then grunted, picking up speed, the roaring noise feeling good against his empty feeling inside. And then the train disappeared beyond the western horizon and the emptiness hurt again. The slow walk back with numbness and regrets and a thousand thoughts yet none specific, no understanding, no answer, no plan.

The entry hall and the painting of the sun setting over the Pacific Ocean at Malibu. The empty house. The food Rosa always left in the cooler. The eating, without appetite. Falling asleep over a book he had little interest in or while the radio played something he only half heard. Half waking in the

160

middle of the silent night thinking he heard Monty crying, Katie Marie must be seeing to him. And then coming fully awake and aware. Tossing. Rolling over and over. The damned pillows. The tight muscles in his legs and hips and back. The air: Too hot, too cold, too still, too humid. The buzzing flies. The chirping crickets.

The gray-blue dawn. Ablutions. And once again plodding one foot in front of the other.

As minutes turning into hours got him through days and nights, so days turning into weeks wasted away his months and seasons. The empty place in him did not fill but healed over. He began to find the strength to talk to people again. Just little chats. A smile now and then when he heard about a winning bet or an engagement or a well coming in. A yes or no response to the unending questions from Gatch about where to drill, where to run pipelines, the gas lines with the red dust, new refinery schemes, artificial nylon and celluloid. One afternoon, during lunch in the hotel, someone mentioned something new in Bartle City, a movie house. Walking south on Main Street that evening, he saw it and, out of curiosity, bought a ticket.

Inside, he found the seats comfortable and the darkness comforting. The movie was Charlie Chaplin's "The Gold Rush." It made him laugh and it made him feel for the tramp and the dance hall girl and, in the end, he wept for joy when the tramp found her. Suddenly unaware of time or place, lost in emotion, he could not stop the tears. When the lights in the theater came up, he remembered where he was, covered his face and scrambled out the rear door. In the alley behind the theater, he tried to get hold of himself but remembered the exquisite expressions of love and confusion and joy on the faces of the dance hall girl and the tramp at the movie's climax, slumped to the foot of a brick wall and began crying uncontrollably again.

After he had no idea how long, he began to calm. Attaining quietness, he suddenly felt hungry and remembered the food Rosa always left in his kitchen. He stood and walked up out of the alley. At Main Street, instead of turning south and passing The Crystal Palace, he turned toward his house, thinking about eating. He walked quickly, laughingly remembering the tramp's journey up the Chilkoot Pass and his potato dance. Reaching the house, he walked purposefully into the kitchen, past the painting of sunset in Malibu without noticing it, hungrily gobbled a hearty indulgence of Rosa's chicken and potatoes, fell into his bed and slept an exhausted sleep.

The next morning, while walking into town, he came to a decision. A decision. He went on with the routine he had numbly been following but he was no longer numb. Excitement was growing in him. He had a direction. At the end of the day, walking out, he left a note on Gatch's desk: "When you see the world with your head OR your heart, everything is positive OR negative, good OR bad, happy OR sad. When you see it with your head AND your heart, everything is positive AND negative, good AND bad, happy AND sad. I will be halfway to California by the time you read this. Take care of the company for all of us."

As the westbound slowed at the south end of Bartle City, Jacques hopped into an open, almost empty boxcar. A half-dozen motley scruffy men sat around the perimeter, backs against the walls. He settled down across from a hard looking one with dirty eyes and greasy hair. The man yelled at him. "Purty nice suit for a 'bo!"

Jacques grinned and replied loudly in French. Dirty Eyes stared at him and shouted back over the rattling of the car and the roar of the train picking up speed, "Say WHAT?"

Jacques laughed and answered again in French. The man's eyes narrowed meanly. "You French?" he yelled.

Noticing they now had the attention of the other men in the car, Jacques yelled back. "Francais! Oui!"

Dirty Eyes stood and walked across the car to Jacques. "I ate a lot o' yer mud and lost a good friend savin' you lacey creeps an' I could sure use me a new suit coat," he said, smiling as he stood over Jacques. He grabbed the coat's lapels. With his outstretched legs, Jacques scissored the man's legs out from under him and flipped him, slamming him against the floor. Without pause, Jacques leapt to his haunches and pounced on the man, hitting him hard several times in the face with his fist while the others around the car watched without response. When the man's face was a bloody pulp and he was unconscious, Jacques grabbed him by the lapels of his scruffy suit coat, dragged him to the open door and tumbled him from the car. He watched the man fall for a moment, catching his breath, and then suddenly snapped his attention back to the car. He glanced around.

The other men just watched, not moving. Finally, an older man with a gray beard and a bald head in an overcoat extended an arm palm up toward Jacques' previous place against the wall. "Welcome aboard, Frenchie."

"Thanks," Jacques replied without expression, settling back down.

"You speak English?" the man asked in surprise.

Jacques was licking the blood away from the scrapes on his knuckles, examining them. "And I speak fist," Jacques answered angrily, then looked up at the man. "You want to chat?"

"Take it easy, pal. You just got rid of the troublemaker."

Jacques relaxed, put his hands into the warmth of his coat pockets, rested his head back and let the train rattle them west. It felt good. All of it.

Hours later, they sat on a siding while an eastbound train took the tracks. "Why is this car empty?" Jacques suddenly asked Overcoat.

"That's a good one," Overcoat smiled. "Some oil company guy's got his private car hitched on. Goin' to California to buy a race horse."

"How do you know this?"

"That's the best part," Overcoat grinned. "I was just about to get tossed off in the Chi yards. But one o'th'bulls stopped the other'n before he come on lookin' fer 'bos. Says the oil guy runs his own security and don't want no bulls messin' with his cars!" Overcoat read the incredulity on Jacques' face. "That's right, Frenchy. So start singin' *California Here I Come* and wake me up when you see orange trees!"

When the train pulled into Los Angeles, six rough looking men in suits came at the boxcar from either side and before the hobos could flee, they were in custody. The leader of the suits, a heavyset man with slicked back hair and a pencil thin mustache, had five of his men sit the hobos in the dirt beside the tracks and stand guard while another was sent for the L.A. police. "Tell 'em we've got a bunch of vagrants they can escort out of the city!" he yelled after the messenger, laughing. Slick Hair turned back to inspect the boxcar.

While the hobos waited to be arrested, Jacques sat among them. All were sullen and silent but Overcoat, who muttered furiously. "What's the big idea? They said back in Chi they was layin' off this car!"

Slick Hair turned and looked hard at Overcoat. "Shut up." He went on inspecting the car. A work crew arrived. After identifying themselves to Slick Hair, they hauled a ramp to one of the boxcar doors, laid it out, and began installing pre-made sections of fencing inside, creating a makeshift horse stable. As they worked, Slick Hair supervised from outside the car. "Mr. Bennett likes this work done just so," he told them, beaming. "Mr. Bennett treats his race horses better than he treats his women."

"Is that right?" The carpentry crew supervisor replied snidely, not looking up from his hammering.

"That's right," Slick hair snapped back. "An' sees his horses don't git rid so hard nor put away so wet! Hah! Hah!" He roared at his own humor.

The hobos and security men waited in the hot California morning, railroad yard sounds and smoky, dusty air surrounding them. The workmen finished the horse corral alterations to the boxcar and stowed their tools. Bennett made ridiculing observations about the work crew and his men dutifully laughed.

As the work crew drove off, a two-vehicle convoy drove up. The lead vehicle was a Rolls Royce limousine. It stopped at the tracks beside the boxcar. The driver got out, opened the rear door and Bennett emerged, laughing genially. He took no notice of the hobos or Jacques among them. Behind Bennett came a buxom, laughing, middle-aged woman in riding jacket and blouse, jodhpurs and boots of shining leather. Behind her came an elderly man in a suit as elegant and expensive as Bennett's, also laughing. Once on her feet, the woman looked back, past the pickup truck behind the limousine to the horse trailer it pulled. A small old man, a former jockey, came out of the trailer holding a riding crop, stood behind it, spit tobacco juice and waited, chewing. Two Latino boys jumped out of the pick-up truck's bed, scurried into the trailer and began unloading the horse there while the small, wizened old jockey slapped the crop against his thigh, spit tobacco juice and supervised with sharp admonitions. "Careful. Careful." When the horse stopped backing, stomped and neighed angrily, the jockey exclaimed, "Cuidado, dammit!"

Bennett and his companions, watching, stopped laughing.

The boys got the horse backing again. Just as they got the big, black shiny-coated stallion to the ground, two motorcycles came roaring up and stopped, one carrying a uniformed police officer and Slick Hair's messenger, the other carrying two officers. Seeing the officers approach to arrest the hobos, Overcoat angered again. "This ain't right, I tell you. I'da got out if I'da knowed!"

Slick Hair looked at Overcoat, his hand going to a three-foot length of hardwood dowel left against the boxcar wheel by the carpenters. "One more crack outta you…" He wielded the dowel threateningly.

Bennett's head snapped away from the horse toward Slick Hair. "Is there a problem?"

"No, SIR, Mr. Bennett," Slick Hair answered quickly.

The police got off their motorcycles and came forward toward the hobos as the two boys walked the horse toward the boxcar, one holding the lead line and one at its flank, the old jockey following.

"There IS a problem, Mr. Bennett!" Overcoat suddenly exclaimed. "This ain't right! I can't go to jail!"

Slick Hair swung the dowel hard and fast against the side of Overcoat's head. It landed with a dull thud.

The buxom lady screamed as blood spurted from Overcoat's ear.

The boys with the horse froze in fear and stepped back. The one dropped the horse's lead line.

The old man saw him drop the line and shouted, "HERE!" He grabbed for the line but missed.

The horse spooked at the shout, reared, neighed, and came down. Bennett grabbed for the lead line but missed, spooking the horse further. Frightened to be blamed, the boys turned and ran. The horse reared again and squealed in terror. Bennett grabbed again for the line as the horse came down. It cow kicked viciously with its foreleg and hit Bennett square in the left chest as he was lunging forward, penetrating deep into his thorax, inevitably crushing his heart. He fell inert at the horse's feet and the terrified animal stomped at his head, smashing it bloodily.

"Holy shit!" Slick Hair exclaimed.

The hobos and their guards sat frozen with astonishment, staring.

Bennett lay unmoving, unbreathing. The horse seemed to calm. Overcoat, dazed, came to one knee, his head down, bleeding profusely from the ear. Next to him, Jacques quietly rose, walked a few steps forward, took the horse's hanging lead line and handed it to the old jockey, who had come up quietly from the rear.

Seeing Bennett laying motionless and bloody, the woman started screaming again and crying and fell against the elderly man. The horse started to spook again but the jockey quickly calmed him. The elderly man wrapped the woman in his arms and eased her back into the limousine. With a swift, angry snap of his head he communicated his order to the driver to get them away from the scene. As he closed the limousine door behind himself and the woman, the elderly man spoke one last time to Slick Hair. "Clean this mess up!" He slammed the door and the Rolls Royce sped away.

Suddenly, Slick Hair took over. He ordered one of the policemen and three of his men to lift Bennett's body into the pick-up's bed for transport. He sent the other two policemen on their motorcycles to prepare the way. He ordered the remaining men to unhitch the horse trailer.

As soon as they were left unguarded, the hobos scattered, running.

As soon as the pickup was unhitched from the trailer, its driver, at Slick Hair's orders, wheeled around in a tight circle and drove off, Slick Hair in the passenger seat shouting directions and the rest of his men in the back, holding Bennett's body.

Finally, only Jacques, the old jockey and the horse remained beside the boxcar.

The old man spit. "He's dead sure."

"Yes," said Jacques.

"Whattaya suppose we oughtta do now?"

"That is always a good question," Jacques replied, looking at the horse.

"This horse has gotta go to Oklahoma. Them boys was gonna ride with it."

"Oklahoma?" asked Jacques.

"Yep," said the old man, spitting tobacco juice. "That fella Bennett bought it for one o'them 77 Company brothers in Tulsa."

"Tulsa?"

"There they are now." The old man nodded up the tracks to where some rail yard men were backing an engine toward the boxcar. "Comin' to hitch up. Hell," he spit. "I can't ride with him. Bones're too old." He looked at Jacques. "You interested in work?"

"Ride with the horse? To Tulsa?"

166

"Somebody's got to. Plenty o' food and water in the trailer. Blankets. You'll be fine. They'll load hay and oats for the horse at the main yard. Water him at the stops."

Now, as if for the first time, Jacques began thinking. In flashing images and disjointed, half-remembered phrases, he assembled things that had happened to him and things he had done, trying to understand in them the answer to the old jockey's question. He realized he had jumped aboard the boxcar in a fantasy of imitating Charlie Chaplin's tramp and finding his way to Katie Marie and Monty. And then what? He had not thought of that.

The old jockey stood in front of him, offering the horse's lead line. Suddenly, Jacques saw that finding Katie Marie and Monty meant bringing them back into his life, back into the oil business. The oil business that created and resolved his conflicts but never let him go. He suddenly saw in his mind's eye an image from his boyhood: The Caspian Sea. The stinking, smoky, foggy docks at Baku. The sea disappearing into the haze of the east. The muddy, oily beach running to the Aspheron Peninsula and its gas-fire-sprinkled hulk in the haze to the north. The muddy, oily beach disappearing into the hazy marshes in the south. Huge old dirty rusty tankers filling the near distance with industrial stench and pounding and clanging and grinding. An old weary-eyed fisherman in dirty clothes hauling a half-empty net of fish from the oily deck of his dilapidated trawler to the oily surface of the worn and splintery dock.

The racehorse's whine startled Jacques from his reverie. He looked at the sleek horse. Suddenly he remembered Katie Marie's painting of the sun setting over the Pacific Ocean at Malibu, the clean sand, the palm trees, the glistening blue-golden colors. Now he knew. He will not drag them back into it. He will not go looking for them. He will have them found, yes, and they will have everything the wealth of the Monty-G Company can provide. But it will come to Monty through Katie Marie, somehow. He will work that out. He looked up at the old jockey. "Ride with the horse to Tulsa? I can do that," he shrugged.

Gatch and Rosa were overjoyed to have him back in Bartle City, more so when they saw his quiet attentiveness restored. He never anymore seemed to them a happy man but now he once again seemed to have found his inner peace. Even with his wife and son, he had always seemed alone. Now he again seemed inside his aloneness rather than outside it and lost.

Once again, his day began with the walk from his house to the Monty-G Company offices on the 77 refinery grounds, but now he accepted the ride home Gatch offered daily. During this ride, Gatch went over the company's developments and tribulations. They had changed little: Where to drill, when to keep at a well and when to call it a dry hole—in short, when to persist and when to cut losses; whether to finance pipelines to the northeast for domestic consumption or to the south for overseas shipping—in short, seeing into the future; and, finally, how best to use the refinery—pump out more automobile fuel or reinvest in infrastructure to make airplane fuel and petroleum products. Jacques noticed that now Gatch was almost obsessed with a process by which a 77 scientist insisted he could turn the red dust-polluted byproduct of pumping natural gas through pipelines into marketable commodities like artificial nylons, fertilizers and photographic film. These conversations were especially important in Jacques' new role at the company because he now refused to accompany Gatch to the Broadway Hotel for "big business" lunches where such decisions were often made but where Jacques would have to encounter the movers and shakers of the region, like banker Bartle.

Instead, Jacques went daily, alone, to a lunch counter on South Main Street, across from The Crystal Palace. Most days, he had a bowl of soup and laughed with the regular customers and the waitress-owners, a pair of stout oil-heiress Osage battle-axe grandmothers who ran the place for their own entertainment. They took no interest in cost control and their only interest in customer service was overfeeding their favorites. Jacques also enjoyed trading oil field gossip with the grandmothers' grill man, an old African-American roughneck too arthritic for the drilling platform who knew all the same stories Gable had told.

Most days, Jacques simply sat at the counter, sipping soup and listening to the chatter. Once or twice a month, however, a heavyset man with slicked back hair and a pencil thin mustache walked in. Jacques moved with him to the lunch counter's corner booth. The man was Slick Hair, from the train yard, now working for Jacques. Slick Hair showed Jacques reports. Everyone in the lunch counter assumed the reports were oil field findings. None suspected they were detailed reports on the progress of a single mother and her son in Pasadena, California. The mother liked her airplane factory front office day job as well as her happy weekend life as a jazz club singer, Slick Hair reported, and she had a growing real estate and investment portfolio. The boy, Slick Hair reported, was in an excellent school, getting good grades and excelling at athletics, particularly baseball and boxing. Slick Hair's visits were always brief.

One average day, as Jacques sat alone at the counter, sipping and listening, a rattletrap Model T that looked like it might have come off Henry Ford's first production line parked on the street. A man of middle height, medium build and high brow, with a small, comic mustache and twinkling eyes behind

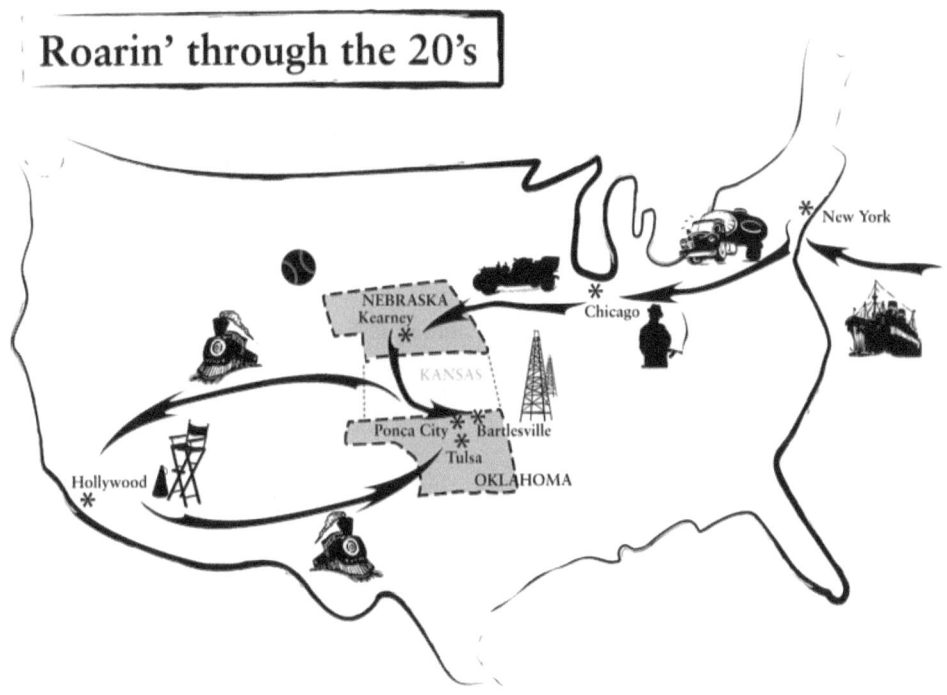

heavy glasses, got out of the car carrying a very large, flat leather satchel. He walked in with a gentle smile, immediately fixed on the battle-axes, took a large pad from the leather satchel and asked, in a jovial, gravelly voice, if they would trade sketch portraits of themselves and the cook for a meal. In Paris, Jacques knew, this would be a tedious proposition. But in Bartle City, he saw immediately, it was big stuff.

Soon, lunchtime was at a standstill as customers watched images of the grandmothers appear on the artist's sketchpad. As he held up the second sketch, grinning, his eyes twinkling, he asked, "Think I've earned some soup?"

Delighted with this doodling stranger, the battle-axes flurried to feed him, calling forth a feast from the roughneck in the kitchen. Soon the artist was hungrily gobbling from bowls and plates set before him. Jacques moved over and started a quiet, friendly conversation and quickly discovered the man was on his way to Hollywood.

"There's this thing they're doing with cartoons," he told Jacques. "They put them on celluloid and make them move."

"I have seen that," Jacques smiled. "It is delightful."

"Exactly," said the artist, setting down his fork and knife. "Look at this. He opened the leather satchel and pulled out a large pad. In it were drawings in black and white, simple lines and shapes formed like everyday creatures and then magically anthropomorphized into charming critters inhabiting a reality of their own. There was a big-eyed happy mouse, a portly struggling duck and a gangly, floppy-eared hound. The drawings told stories about the silly critters. Quickly, the artist had Jacques and a gathering crowd around the counter innocently smiling.

As his show ended, the waitresses demanded everyone scatter and let the artist eat so they could clean up. As the artist finished eating and settled back with a last cup of coffee, Jacques stood, intending to head back to his office. "You'll do well," he told the man.

"If I get a chance to show them what I can do," the man replied, setting the cup down.

Just then a gaggle of 8 to 12 year olds, the battle-axes' and roughneck's grandchildren and their schoolmates, came in off the street. The battle-axes shooed the kids to the rear booths. Jacques and the artist watched, smiling, as the grandmothers brought the children cold carbonated beverages and got them busy with homework.

"Those kids will do well, too," Jacques observed. "They've got adults who love them enough to make them do their homework."

"True," said the artist. "But all work and no play?" He looked at Jacques and grinned. "Watch this." He dashed out to the dilapidated Model T, grabbed an armful of large sketch tablets, came back in and walked over to the kids. They looked up at the approaching stranger. He smiled, picked up one of the large pads and said, with a hint of mystery and promise, "Watch!"

He displayed a tablet and opened it. "Meet Mortie Mouse." He flipped a page. "And his sister, Mary Lou Mouse." He flipped another page. "Here's the house where their mouse hole is..."

Jacques watched the children watching. Galvanized and enthralled by the images, they became enraptured and delighted as the artist told stories about Mortie and Mary Lou and their nemesis Crabby the Cat. He flipped through the pads of images so quickly the figures' actions came to life. The children, enthralled, forgot about their cola drinks and homework and sat on the edges of their seats in fascination, oohing in delight and giggling with hilarity as the artist took them through adventures and escapes to the end of his sketchpads. When the grandmothers, finished cleaning in the kitchen, came out and saw the children laughing with the artist instead of doing homework, they threw a fit, sending him packing and setting the children back at their own tablets.

The smiling artist had packed his sketchpad away into the leather satchel and was reorganizing his tablets when Jacques stepped over to say goodbye. All over the counter, Jacques saw endearing sketches, images as everyday as household and barnyard critters and as exotic and enchanting as princesses and witches. "You'll do well in Hollywood," Jacques repeated.

Without looking up, the artist repeated his deepest doubts. "If I get a chance to show what I can do. But how do you get their attention?"

"Make your own cartoon movie."

"I can just about buy a second hand camera," the man said, continuing to arrange the sketches. "But it takes a lot of film to make a cartoon. You know what celluloid costs?"

Jacques looked at the dozens of delightful drawings all over the countertop: Kings and queens, horses and coaches, castles and thatched-roof huts, farmers and milkmaids, cows and goats and deer and squirrels and chipmunks, witches and dwarves and giants. He looked up at the man. "What if I told you I could get you all the celluloid you want?"

"How could I pay you?" the man said without interrupting his organizing.

Jacques smiled. "I could take the cost out of the profits of the films."

The man looked up and stared at Jacques. He reached to his black-rimmed glasses and reset them on his nose, studying Jacques. Finally deciding Jacques was sincere, he spoke. "I'm gonna go out to Hollywood and buy a camera and rent a garage. You draw up the papers and start shipping the celluloid."

"When I see the cartoons in the picture theaters, I'll start sending the bills," Jacques grinned.

"Deal," said the artist, holding out his hand.

"Deal," smiled Jacques, shaking it.

End of Part I

So he found a way *to make oil into a good thing?*

For him, she said. Not for all of them.

Part II: The Woman Everybody Loved
1938: Prelude

Victoria studied her gleaming green eyes in the candle-lit mirror and worked around them with her eyebrow and eyelash make-up. Finishing, she turned to the barefoot Arab girl in the loose black gown holding the mirror. "Now," she said, gesturing toward a scarf and veil.

The girl set down the mirror, picked up a strand of gauzy black cloth and gently placed the heavy black scarf over Victoria's elegant brunette coiffure, smoothing the garment down her back, around her shoulders and over the scooped bodice of her chic gown. She then took the silky black veil and attached it to the scarf and hung it over Victoria's nose and mouth. Waiting for the girl to finish the damage, Victoria thought back to the D.C. dinner party and the intelligent-eyed handsome young man who asked her to dance. She always enjoyed dancing with that kind.

*****

"My boss said I'd be the one to get to you," he said as he whirled her through a full turn in waltz time.

She smiled. He was so good-looking, so sure of himself. His gleaming brown eyes were so innocent yet mischievous, his skin looked so creamy, his lips so soft, his muscles under her hands so toned as he held her in dance frame. "Who is your boss?"

"That unnamed State Department official you always read about."

"And what—whee!" she exclaimed as he whirled her through another turn.

"Can you do for your country?" he finished her question.

She smiled up at him. "The hell with the country, sweetie, what can I do for you?"

He fell into a steady straightforward rhythmic rolling around the dance floor and talked.

"You're going abroad with your husband."

"No secrets in this town," she shrugged without missing a beat of the waltz time.

"Put in a good word for America."

"With the sheik of the burning sands? What's the worry?"

"Someday soon he's going to be very oil rich."

"The oil men haven't found anything in Arabia but sand."

"That's why we need you to put in a good word."

"The Mexicans are so mad at my husband's country they're taking their oilfields back. The Shah of Persia already threw the Brits out once. What good can I do?"

"The wrong move in Mexico or Persia and we push them toward Hitler."

"So you have to hang on in Arabia."

"Saudi Arabia."

"Right. And Ibn Saud is getting impatient with your oil men."

The music rose to a climax. He whirled her around again and brought her to the edge of the dance floor as the music fell away.

"What can I do about it?" she smiled, shrugging helplessly.

"They'll let us dig holes in the desert but they don't trust us enough to explore in Riyadh."

"You have my permission."

He smiled and his face tightened. He glanced around the room. "You are going to have an audience with the King. He quit listening to our guys. We think he might listen to you."

"My husband will get an official audience, out of respect for the British government."

He interrupted her. "Our people out there got you invited along," he paused. "Your brother arranged it."

"Sam?"

174

He nodded.

"I didn't know he was in Arabia. I thought he was in Mesopotamia."

He smiled. "Lets walk toward your table."

"But nobody's there. Lord North is in the study with father. What about Sam?"

"Your brother did us a favor."

She smiled at the handsome young State Department man. "I'd do you a favor."

"You're a married woman, Lady North."

She grinned. "I never let that get in my way."

"Send a little of that Ibn Saud's way."

She pouted. "You don't want any?"

"Just enough to open up Riyadh to our geologists," he smiled that charming, threatening smile. "You're our last best chance, Lady North."

*****

Back in the shadowy tent, the girl completed her work at the scarf and veil. Victoria stood and gestured toward the mirror. The girl again held it up. The scarf covered all her face but her eyes and fell over the bare bodice of her stylish gown. "Let me just touch up my eyes," she said to the uncomprehending girl, who got the message when Victoria again reached for her mascara. As she did the finishing touches on those slightly aging but still extraordinary green eyes, her mind drifted back to the young man and the D.C. dinner party.

*****

She was mock pouting. "You don't want any?"

"We'll talk about that at your debriefing. Adults defer gratification."

175

"My mother said I never grew up, that I'm still Father's little girl." She glanced toward a doorway at the rear of the room. "But I suppose we will have to defer. Here comes Phillip with Father."

The young man's alert brown eyes darted. Lord North, the British Ambassador, and Harry Wade walked toward them. "Father, huh?"

"What about him?"

"Nothing," he grinned. "But you can call me Daddy." He took her hand.

She smiled back, deeply engaged and fully excited. "Call me Victoria."

"I will," he said quietly, promisingly. "Thank you for the dance, Lady North," he then said more loudly so the men approaching could hear. "You are an elegant waltz partner."

"Try me some time at the fox trot, dear," she said quietly, grinning, squeezing his hand. She turned to the men approaching.

"Father, Phillip..." She took her hand from the young man. "Mr..." She looked at the young man quizzically.

"LeClaire Harold of the State Department, sir." He extended his arm toward the older man for a handshake.

"His waltzing was worthy of an introduction," she smiled at her father and her husband.

"Watch out, Mr. Harold. No man adores my daughter like her father does," said the older man, smiling broadly, leaning forward, politely extending his hand. "Harry Wade."

Harold first glanced at Phillip, or Lord North, the Lady's husband. He was studying his wife as she stood so vivaciously among them, smiling with perfect social poise and aplomb. When Harold saw Lord North's attention on Victoria, he turned calmly to Harry Wade and changed the subject. "We met briefly when you visited Secretary Hull about the factories you are planning in Germany, sir," smiled Harold.

"Yes, well, those factories are as forgotten as that visit."

"So we hear, sir," replied Harold, turning and extending a handshake to Victoria's husband, a tired looking man near Victoria's age and yet seeming more elderly than her father.

"Phillip Bridger, Lord North, British Ambassador," the man said, reluctantly turning his attention away from Victoria and introducing himself with a weak handshake. "Good to meet you. Don't you wish we could only convince old man Ford to follow Harry's example and stop selling his trucks to Hitler?"

"Some businessmen can't see the difference between a customer and a dangerous country," Harold answered.

*****

"Aren't we all having a gay old time now," Victoria remembered muttering to herself at the turn of the conversation to business.

The shadow of a man fell on the flap over the tent's entryway. He muttered in Arabic.

Victoria looked at the girl. The girl nodded and gestured outwards. Victoria gestured for her to hold up the mirror again.

One last time, she studied her flowing gown and then her hair and her face beneath and behind the scarf and veil Wahabbi Saudi custom required of her. She studied the gleaming green eyes and smiled to herself the smile of a woman who knew she still had tools at hand. "Fine," Victoria said, turning away from the mirror. Glancing from herself to the girl's shapeless black gown, she added, "I'll bet you're a hell of a lot more comfortable in your outfit than I am in mine."

Victoria put her make-up kit into her bag, turned to the young Arab girl in the loose black gown and handed over the bag. She glanced at the choices of eye makeup on the table by the lantern. "Take it back to my tent," she told the girl, adding emphatic gestures. The girl nodded, understanding, and slipped through the tent flap, which the swarthy Bedouin soldier in the uniform of the king's guard, held open for Victoria. "I'd hate to lose that bag and be stuck with your roaring twenties supply of female magic," Victoria muttered to herself as she stepped outside the tent.

She followed the Bedouin soldier across the carpet-covered sands of the royal encampment toward the King's sprawling tent. Muffled voices and

177

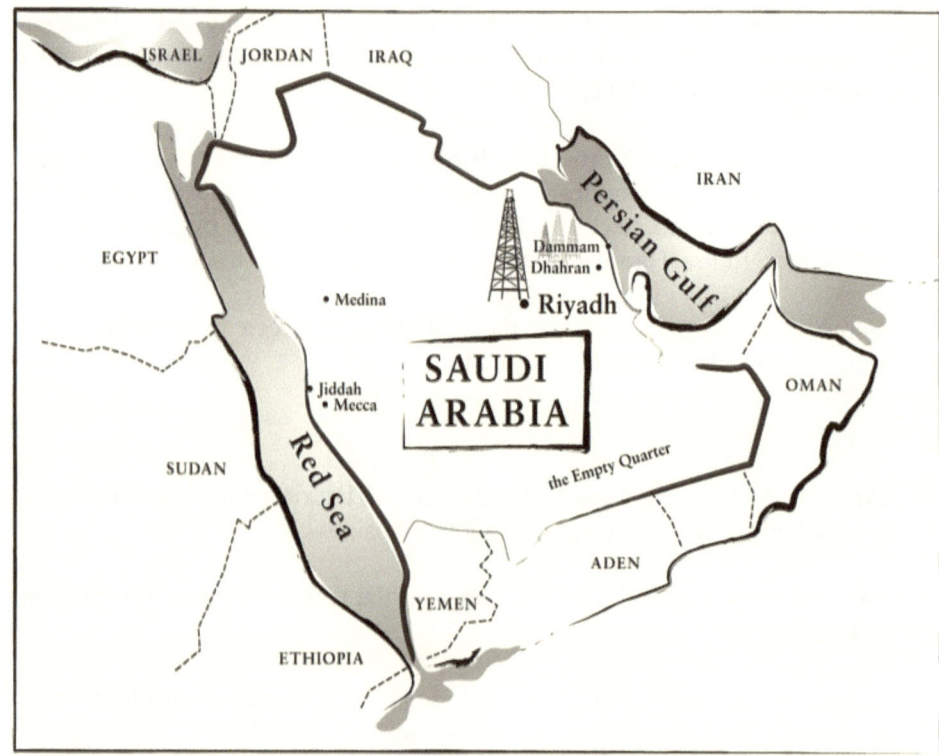

distant howls filled the distant desert night. Firelight flickered behind tent fabric under a black night sky filled with stars. Imaginings of her mother's nineteenth century childhood in western Pennsylvania and early California flashed through her mind until the smell of cardamom seed-flavored coffee coming from the king's tent shook her into thoughts of the mud-walled palace in Riyahd.

"Three small cups, more is an insult," her husband had reminded her. She shuddered at the thought of the palace's long narrow hallways, dark shadowy closed dens, threatening low noises and musty odors. She thought of the tiny cubicle flickering with lantern light where she had listened to interminable pointless explication as Sulaiman, Ibn Saud's most trusted advisor, prattled on to her husband about the forces of liberal Salafi tribesmen and literal Khalafi tribesmen the king was trapped between.

Voices inside the king's tent harshly shouting in Arabic interrupted her thoughts. Victoria nervously cleared her throat.

"Huna!"

"La La La! Fiha!"

178

A small, balding man in ceremonial Bedouin robes with thick glasses and heavy facial hair stepped through the tent flap. Stepping too near her, his body odor filling her senses too sharply, he whispered. "Sulaiman sent me. I am to translate for you.

From inside the tent came more shouts. "Uskuf!"

"La! La! Fiha!"

"Don't worry," whispered the translator, seeing her anxiety, smiling a cruel smile. "It has been many years since the King slit a throat."

Victoria glanced a 'gee, thanks' expression but said nothing.

The men were still shouting harshly in Arabic.

"La! La!"

"Uskuf!"

"Just avoid angering him," the translator added quickly.

Victoria glanced dubiously at him again. "Sounds like the opening act took care of that."

Silently, she was wondering if she had already angered him, just the day before.

*****

A troop of camel riders in Bedouin robes, scarves across their faces against the windblown sand, followed King Ibn Saud across the desert. Sporting spirits were high for the ritual hunt, the last reliving of Ibn Saud's desert warrior youth. Two generations of Bedouin majlis members, carrying the finest western carbines, joined in the ritual pursuit of desert gazelle. To those devout old Wahhabis who objected to his introduction of radio and telephones into the kingdom, Ibn Saud offered to dispense with the radio and telephones when the tribesmen gave up their modern carbines. This ended the debate.

At the rear of the troop, the foreign guests wrestled with the unfamiliar indignities of their desert mounts. After a few moments, the Arab camel wranglers were laughing at the foreigners' frustration.

179

"Bloody hell," Lord North cried in self-effacing hilarity. "I'm a cryptographer, not a cavalryman!"

American engineer Karl Twitchell flopped and bounced even more comically at the camel's uncooperative antics. "I'm an engineer, dammit. I don't ride anything without a motor!"

At the margin of the scene, Victoria quietly worked her camel, studying the reins, the balance of the seat, the camel's mouth and head, its ears and gait. Suddenly, she laughed, and gave the familiar Arab "Yalla!" She wheeled her camel and galloped after the hunt. She weaved at full gallop through the pack and soon emerged near the head of the chase on the king's left.

He glanced toward her in surprise. Not because she was female. He could not tell that with the robes and scarf covering her. His surprise was because his people did not usually pursue him so closely. But a desert gazelle darted across the horizon to the right, seizing his attention. He angled his camel toward it. Unaware of the unspoken taboo against riding too near the King, Victoria stayed at his flank.

Nearing his prey, Ibn Saud lifted his rifle and shot while at the gallop but missed. Without hesitation, he rode after the gazelle. Galloping at his side, Victoria raised her rifle, shot and missed. Enjoying the unexpected competition in the heat of the moment, Ibn Saud glanced back and then urged his camel on. Skillfully, she kept her camel at the king's flank. Both readied their rifles again quickly. He raised his a beat ahead of her. Suddenly, his camel stumbled. He lowered his rifle while regaining his balance. Seeing this out of the corner of her eye, she sportingly lowered her rifle. When he regained his seat, he glanced at her and saw she had held her shot.

Looking more closely at him, her gleaming green eyes met a vicious brown-eyed glower. He grunted a command in Arabic. Understanding his fierce will, she dared not disobey but looked toward the gazelle, raised her rifle and fired. She missed. His shot was in her shot's echo. The gazelle fell. He whooped with the joy of a hunter and circled his camel right, toward where the gazelle had emerged on the horizon, pursuing other prey, leaving the carcass to his followers. Uncertain how this strange, brutal melodrama would play in the Majlis, she fell off and into the anonymity of the pack.

*****

The tent flap before them opened. Men emerged muttering the usual "Allah Akbar" and "Aleichem Salam" formalities to the guards and officials inside.

180

"Now," said her translator to her, leading through the tent flap. With a deep breath, she marched through behind him.

It was a huge, torch- and lantern-lit, shadowy tent with carpets decorating the sides and hanging above. On the far side from the opening was a wide arc of armchairs where men sat muttering Arabic in low tones. She saw her husband and Sulaiman among them.

The translator kept his eyes slightly down as he led her just into the tent and stepped aside. "Walk to the king, eyes down," he instructed. She walked forward and he followed.

She walked across the wide expanse of carpet-covered sands. Men of the Majlis sat in the semi-circle of chairs flanking the king. Eyes still down, she walked forward toward him, cadences of Arabic announcing her.

Sulaiman and Lord North rose from carved wooden armchairs, approached her in the bright flickering light of torches, lanterns and candles around the room, and led her to the king. Her eyes down, she noticed the king's heavy, colorful robes and his large feet in worn sandals. Ibn Saud's cushioned armchair was surprisingly low to the ground and unlike a throne, the same as the chairs of those to either side, with delicate craftsmanly carvings in heavy wooden arms and legs and thick cushions at the seat and back. At Sulaiman's indication, she knelt before Ibn Saud, a charade she simultaneously found exciting and absurd. She kept her eyes diverted downward, seeing only the king's great ugly hairy feet in his thick dirty worn desert sandals on worn carpets of intricate and colorful but fading weavings. She heard an exchange of Arabic between the harsh voices of Sulaiman and other men around the throne. Suddenly, it became silent.

In a deep tone tinged with boredom, the king spoke Arabic with disinterest and authority. In response, she began to raise her eyes but heard the translator mutter, "no, no, no." Sulaiman stepped forward beside the king and she noticed how much smaller and cleaner his feet were and how much newer his sandals were as he made the formal introduction of her in Arabic. She heard the king clicking prayer beads with a steady tap-tap, tap-tap of impatient disinterest. Sulaiman's introduction ended. There was silence but for the steady, emotionless tap-tap, tap-tap of the prayer beads.

"Rise, approach and look up," she heard the translator whisper behind her.

She did. King Ibn Saud was a big, heavyset man with a long lean face, a salt and pepper black beard, a great nose, dark brown skin and deep dark eyes holding lightning and weariness. When she met those eyes with her luminous green ones, she saw the familiar and sudden flicker of male interest and an almost recognition. The king shifted his prayer beads to his left hand and reached out his right hand, palm up. He spoke again in that deep, commanding voice, but quietly, intimately, so that only she and the translator could hear clearly.

"Give him your right hand, palm down," the translator whispered.

She laid her hand in the king's. He spoke.

"Even with your charms concealed as our Holy Qu'ran requires, you are beautiful, madam," the translator repeated.

She smiled gracefully and answered. "A wise woman has much to say, yet remains silent." The translator repeated.

The king smiled, recognizing the Arab verse, and commented with interest.

"Rarely do the British take an interest in our culture." Translation.

"I am an American married to a British subject." Translation.

"You have divided allegiances?" The king asked in Arabic. While she took the translation, she noticed he still held her hand.

She took a deep breath, breathed out and inhaled his attention. "A woman's allegiance is to the man," she said, squeezing and caressing his hand during translation. "A man like you knows that."

At her hand's work, his eyes lit up with genuine interest. When he heard the translation, he answered with an Arabic proverb, shaking his head with a gentle smile. "Woman is a calamity."

At the translation she smiled to herself and completed the proverb. "Necessary in every tent. Is that not how the verse ends?"

On hearing this from the translator, the king smiled with deep genuineness. "We have another proverb: Three things drive away sorrow: water, green trees and a beautiful woman."

Sulaiman came forward during the translation, sensing a breach of the intimacy he alone had with the king in this public setting. She realized her

182

audience was about to come to an abrupt end. "To each hunter a shot!" she said quickly to the king, pulling gently on his hand.

Making no sense of this, Sulaiman disdainfully waved the translator off as he finished translating this strange remark. Announcing in Arabic that the Majlis had pressing businesss, as he lifted Victoria to her feet and gently began pushing her back, away from the king. Urgently, she repeated, "To each hunter a shot!" She looked at the bewildered translator and repeated the line again, gesturing desperately for him to translate. Bewildered, he repeated the line to the king as Sulaiman pushed both Victoria and the translator across the tent.

The king stood and spoke loudly and harshly. Sulaiman stopped, hung his head and turned to the king. The king waved him off with a brutal harshness and ordered Victoria and the translator back to him with commanding tone and gesture. When she again stood near him, he looked hard into her green eyes and in a sudden flash recognized her from the hunt.

"You!" he exclaimed in English.

She nodded 'yes.'

Now Ibn Saud was truly interested. Sulaiman approached again, muttering insistently in Arabic but Ibn Saud angrily waved him off and called Victoria and the translator closer. No others could hear them as Ibn Saud began whispering to the translator. Sulaiman's angry, suspicious glances made the translator tense and guarded but Victoria was excited by the turn of events and Ibn Saud's sudden attention. As he stood near her and towered over her, the translator repeated the king's compliment. "You ride the camel well." She smiled with her eyes as the King studied her.

"I know horses," she answered, enjoying the familiarity of subtle flirtation. The translator, a half step away and seeing an opportunity for a bond with the king, protected their intimacy.

"Many horsemen fail to adjust," said Ibn Saud, smiling with his profound brown eyes while he waited for the translation.

"It is a woman's skill, appreciating differences, adapting." She waited, wondering if the translation would carry the seductiveness she intended.

"A ruler, like a lion, makes others adapt to him."

At the translation, she smiled, seeing her opportunity. "The whisper of a beautiful woman can be heard further than the roar of a lion." She paused, waited for translation, saw Ibn Saud recognize the Arabic proverb, saw him realize she had something she wanted to tell him.

He gestured for her to go on.

She leaned close to him. "The American government knows you are uneasy with the oil exploration."

He shrugged, glanced at some of the men of the Majlis who were straining forward, trying desperately to hear what the King and the brazen British woman were saying. "An ass is but an ass, though laden with gold," he smiled.

"The oil explorers are not beasts of burden," she said. "They are hunters."

"Of wealth in the desert," he said with a wave of his hand, a gesture that said he believed "wealth in the desert" is a myth.

She nodded at the translation. "A wise ruler allows the hunters who know the prey to pursue it where they must."

His eyes opened wide when he heard the translation. "Even into his own city?"

When the translator repeated the question, she nodded 'yes' very seriously. "The hand you cannot bite, kiss," she told him.

Recognizing one of his favorite Arabic proverbs, he smiled, stepped back and sat in his chair. He thought a moment, then looked up at her, laughed out loud and, finally, waved her off with a few final Arabic remarks and commands.

With a big smile, the translator took her arm, eased her back and then quickly away. Knowing the king had ended the audience, she did not resist though she did not know if she had swayed the king. After the translator led her through the tent's flap and out into the desert night she stopped on the carpet on the desert floor outside and demanded the translator tell her if the king's last, laughing remarks were meaningful.

"Meaningful?" asked the translator, smiling broadly. "I think yes. You tell me. He said, "For every look back, look ahead twice. I will remember you, your husband and your country." What do you think?"

She smiled at him. "I'm done here."

The next morning Lord and Lady North returned with the foreign delegation to Riyadh where Lord North would pursue the details of the British delegation's negotiations with Sulaiman. Before the afternoon meetings began, Phillip reminded Victoria he adored her and sent her off on an overdue social call.

*****

The sky over the eastern Saudi Arabian plateau was clear blue and cloudless, the kind of perfect blue emptiness that begged the questions of infinity and forever, yet the roar of the Aeronca Model K Scout engine shut out sound and abstraction, forcing Victoria's eyes to the endless plane of rolling desert below. Brown earth raced by under the plane, emphasizing the desert's apparent emptiness. Soon, she noticed the flat placidity was punctuated by occasional huge abrupt up thrusts of jagged rock.

"What's that about?" she yelled over the engine roar, pointing at one of the columnar rocky peaks.

"Jebels," the wiry young pilot sitting beside her yelled back.

"Some kind of earthquake deformity?" She asked, staring at the dramatically isolated sandstone looming over the featureless desert floor.

He shook his shaggy, brown-haired head 'no.' "Everything around them washed away." He waved a hand quickly over the scene out the plane's windshield. "Water and wind and time."

She stared at the rocky towers in wonder. "A lot of time."

"A lot of time," he agreed.

She continued to stare at the desert immenseness. "Anybody search out here for Amelia Earhart?" she yelled. He did not look away from piloting or answer.

She glanced at him. His axe-blade profile did not waver toward a smile as his keen brown eyes shifted carefully between the distant horizon and the instrument panel. He wore the leather flight jacket well as he carefully worked the steering stick and foot rudder pedals, banking the plane into a wide arc. She looked out at the desert, following the direction of his eyes.

Across the desert floor, at the far edge of what she saw as nothingness, her eyes fixed on a tiny huddle of small dark shapes. As the plane's wide arc took them nearer, she realized she was looking at the focus of all the diplomatic to-do.

"That's what its all about?" she yelled, pointing.

He glanced at her and grinned, then quickly attended again to the instrument panel. She studied the scattering of seven derricks, the huddle of small wood slat buildings, worn canvas tents, steel pipe stock pens, sand-blown pick-up trucks and handful of busy men moving back and forth below.

"It's nothing!" she yelled.

"Not yet," he yelled back as he started to bring the plane out of its banking arc into a southwesterly return heading. "Have you ever seen the Anglo-Persian operations? Abadan or Mosul?"

She shook her head 'no.' "Lord North only takes me to civilized places," she yelled. "This trip is special, just to see your father." She studied her nephew's profile and family emotions roiled up, reminding her to add, "And you!"

"Well, then," he yelled, grinning. Reversing his previous course correction, he rocked the plane back into its circular arc. "You should see Abadan!"

Victoria's eyes widened at the seemingly precarious motion of the small aircraft in the enormous blue sky over the immensity of desert. But he quickly brought them back to a smooth northeasterly heading and then took them upward. Just as she relaxed and began looking out again, the lift incurred some turbulence, the plane lurched and she looked over at him again with wide eyes.

"Normal lift bumps," he laughed.

"Is it safe to go so far?"

'We've got plenty of gas," he smiled. "What else is there to worry about?"

Almost immediately she saw sunlight glint off water on the northeast horizon.

"The Arabian Gulf," he yelled. "Pull up the collar of that travel coat! It gets chilly over the water."

186

She stared out at the golden light reflecting off the sea. Minutes later, she noted something on the coast and stared. She pointed at the huddle of mud adobe buildings on the point of a bay. "What's that?"

"Kuwait City," he told her. "A trading port for centuries. They had a pearl diving industry there until the Japs figured out how to farm them."

"Cultured pearls," she smiled. "Love those little Japs."

She glanced at her nephew, expecting to see him smile at her joke but instead saw his eyes narrow and worry crease his brow as he studied the horizon ahead.

"What?" she demanded.

"Look."

She studied the distance. "I don't see anything," she reported.

"That's right," he answered grimly. "The sky's coming down."

"What?"

Suddenly the plane started bouncing. Victoria gripped her seat and looked at Hank but said nothing. His eyes darted from the horizon ahead to the instrument panel. He pushed the throttle lever hard forward, pulled the stick forward and toward himself and thrust down hard with his left leg against the rudder pedal.

"Winds," he said, thinking aloud. "Shamal winds." He banked the plane into a wide, upward heading arc. "I've got to get up above them," he told her, a hint of panic in his young voice.

The plane continued to bounce through air pockets.

"Shamal winds?" she asked.

"Sandstorm winds..." he began to explain, when the engine suddenly coughed.

"Up too fast," he thought aloud, pulling the stick toward himself and easing off the throttle. The engine coughed again, and then again, and the plane started slowing.

She watched him but said nothing, knowing he had to act, not explain.

He let his foot off the rudder pedal, eased the stick over toward center and brought the throttle lever slowly back. The plane leveled and the nose fell. He glanced at her. The strain of withholding pestering questions showed on her face.

"I've got to drop the nose or we'll fall out of the sky," he said quickly.

She nodded and watched him. The plane began to glide down, its engine still intermittently misfiring. He listened intently and prepared for the right moment to reaccelerate. As the plane glided forward and downward, buffeted hard by the wind, Victoria gripped her seat and focused her attention on the desert floor. To her surprise, she saw an automobile. Wondering why she hadn't seen it before, she realized their acceleration and wide arc had now taken them miles away from their outbound flight path.

The plane dropped fast and bumped hard. As it neared the ground, she struggled with the fear of a crash. Unable to keep watching the earth come up at her, she closed her eyes. An image of her husband and her brother walking through the plane's wreckage flashed in her mind. Her grip tightened on the seat. Suddenly, she thought how irritated an expedition to such wreckage would make her husband and she could not help but smile. She opened her eyes and looked again at the automobile, now so near. It was a fine new open-topped Cadillac. Like the plane, it was turned away from the storm. One man sat at the wheel and four others hovered at the fenders, trying to lift it from a sand drift. The men hid their heads and faces from the burning blowing sands with keffiyah and scarf. They were protected over their bodies, arms and legs by the long flowing Bedouin robes. In a flash, she understood the practicality of Arab dress.

The plane swooped down right over the Arabs. Hank slid the throttle lever forward and the engine roar came back. Hearing the motor noise over the din of the windstorm, the Arab men looked up. There was calm in their deep dark eyes as they took in the harmlessness of this odd intrusion. Victoria saw that they instantly recognized the plane as no threat, no aid and no obligation. They observed it as merely another phenomenon of the desert.

"Yes!" Hank exclaimed beside her with a quick thrust of his fist. He looked at her, his eyes wide with thrill. "You hear it?"

She listened. The engine hummed steadily, powerfully, and the plane was now moving forward instead of drifting down, though still low to the ground and bouncing forcefully in the windstorm.

Hank put his full concentration back on the plane. "I've got to ease back up out of the storm, this time slowly, so I don't stall out," he told her.

He nudged the throttle lever forward and gently pulled the nose up. The plane raced across the desert floor with just a hint of ascent, leaving the Cadillac and its Arabs behind. Hank studied the instrument panel, continuing to ease their pitch upward as they jostled and bumped through the harsh windstorm.

Victoria took a deep breath, waited for the plane to rise and watched the barren terrain fly by. Suddenly she saw what at first appeared to be an illusion coming at her out of a sand-cloud. In another moment, she saw it was a caravan of Bedouin marching, heads down, away from the Shamal. As the caravaners heard the plane's engine roaring at them, so near to the desert floor, they turned and reacted. The camels and mules neighed and bellowed and bolted. Women shook their fists in outrage and then ran to shelter their children. Some of the kids laughed and pointed while others screamed in terror. Some men chased after their families and livestock while others ululated in bold defiance and raised their rifles.

Seeing all this, Victoria screamed. "Pull away, Hank!"

Still intently watching his instruments, he replied calmly. "Easy, Aunt Vic. We'll get above it soon."

A bullet tore through the thin fabric wing-covering on Victoria's side. Seeing it, she screamed "No!" and turned to him. "Now!"

He looked up from the panel and glanced out the windshield in time to see two more bullets tear through the wing and one come through Victoria's door, just missing her. Without hesitation, he hit the rudder pedal hard with his foot and sticked left, away from the caravan.

Their pitch remained a mild ascent but the yaw left took them across the wind's force. The ride became drastically more turbulent. They bumped violently until, leaving the caravan behind, Hank steered them back into the wind's flow. Soon after, the plane finally gained enough altitude to rise up into smooth blue open sky above the storm.

Hank checked his compass and set a course for the U.S. compound at Dammam Camp, his father's home. His job more routine now, he glanced at Victoria. She was sitting back in her seat, still holding tightly underneath the cushion, eyes shut, waiting.

"We'll be home soon."

"I know," she said without opening her eyes. "But what will I do for fun tomorrow?"

He laughed loudly. "Don't count on my father to think of anything!"

"Is he going to be worried because we're so late?"

Hank laughed again, this time with a hint of meanness he had not previously revealed. "Just irritated with us for keeping him waiting."

Because she did not want to find herself caught emotionally between her brother and his son, she changed the subject. "Do you fly a lot?"

"As often as possible. Its what I love."

"Maybe when you finish college…"

He threw a hand up in a quick 'halt' sign. "I've heard it."

"From your father."

"I'm going to be a pilot. I'd like to find a training program in the Far East because I've always wanted to see the South Seas," he paused and gathered some inner anger. "But the R.A.F. and the Luftwaffe are recruiting, too."

She quietly studied him as he barked passionately at her. She decided not to reply.

"Look," he suddenly said, nodding ahead.

Two neat rows of houses with picket fences lay along a wide dusty street in a dusty plain.

"Dammam Camp," he said. "There's father."

Even at a distance they could see Sam, in khaki shirt, sleeves rolled up, work slacks and boots, standing beside the dusty landing strip, hands on hips in an impatient posture, scanning the sky.

"Irritated," Hank observed. "As predicted."

Victoria saw Sam's familiar axe-blade profile, now set in a tight grimace. As they taxied toward him, she could see the familiar studious brown eyes, though darker and deeper with age and thoughtfulness and pain. "He looks more worried than irritated to me," she said as the plane came to a standstill and Hank flicked off the magneto switches.

As they stepped from the plane, Sam walked toward them, staring at Hank but saying nothing.

Hank turned to Victoria. "I'll get your gear from the plane and take it home in the truck. Go visit with Father." Before she could reply, he glanced at Sam, said nothing and disappeared around the other side of the plane.

Sam walked up to her, his eyes following Hank. When he knew Hank would not reappear, he looked at Victoria and sighed.

"Quite a young man," she smiled warmly. "Reminds me of a brother of mine at that age."

"I was NEVER like THAT." Looking at her, he finally met her smile with a big grin and then wrapped her in a warm hug. Still holding her, he added, "But I had a big sister to keep me in line."

"You needed it."

He broke the hug and stepped back. "Its good to see you, Vic."

"Looks like I got here just in time to stop a father-son feud."

He looked at her with a hint of defensiveness and a hint of pleading but said nothing.

"But before I go to work," she smiled, "I need a bath and a meal."

"This way," he said, pointing at the rows of houses beyond the landing strip. "And speaking of work," he added, grinning, "this cable came in for you." He took a folded sheet of paper from his shirt pocket and handed it to her as he led her toward a sprawling bungalow.

"Fine," she said. "But carry this coat for me, will you. It's HOT here."

He took the coat and she read the cable as they walked in silence.

YOUR COUNTRY ADORES YOU AND I CANT WAIT UNTIL YOU COME HOME SO I CAN SHOW YOU HOW MUCH I ADORE YOU STOP DADDY END

Sam was still grinning when she finished reading it and looked up at him. "You read this didn't you?

"You call Harry 'Daddy' now?"

Slightly embarrassed, she flipped her hand, dismissing the subject. "It's a long story."

"Mother still says you'll never grow up."

"I suppose I'll always be Father's little girl."

"He was just the first in the long line of men who adore you."

"I know what men adore."

As they neared the bungalow, the pickup drove around them and pulled up at the front door. Hank jumped out of the cab and took an armload of Victoria's luggage inside. As Hank re-emerged for more luggage, Victoria saw Sam tighten and become silent.

"He's a fine young man," she whispered to her brother.

Sam took a deep breath and his face relaxed. He looked over at Hank. "How did your aunt take to flying?" he asked lightheartedly.

Holding an armful of luggage, Hank looked across the truck's bed. "Like a hawk," he grinned.

"She comes from pioneer stock," Sam replied, smiling.

"I had a good pilot," Victoria said.

"This is the last of your stuff," Hank told her, hurrying past them and into the house.

Sam and Victoria followed. "I hope I'm not crowding you," she said, going through the screen door he held open.

"Plenty of room," he smiled. "We opened up her bedroom and bath for you."

"You don't mind?" she asked, studying him.

A calm certainty came into his voice and expression. "She'd be pleased."

"She'd be pleased at how Hank has come along, too."

"I just don't want him to grow up so fast."

"Like you?" she asked, smiling. "You want him to be like me and never grow up?"

He stopped in the living room, looked at Victoria and then looked around until his eyes fell on a big painting across from the front window.

"She loved those mad Europeans," Victoria said quietly.

"She loved Mondrian especially," Sam said. "There was something about the straight lines, the big blocks of color. I love to look at the paintings and think about her and try to imagine what she loved about them." He turned to Victoria. "She wanted him to get an education."

"But he wants to fly. And he's going to run off to those mad Europeans to do it if you keep fighting him."

He looked at her, a tightness gripping his face. "Sometimes you have to fight."

She smiled sympathetically. "Looks like you need me now like you never did before."

He looked at her and his face relaxed. "You've got some work to do."

"Mind if I take a bath first?"

*****

That evening, over a feast of lamb and rice prepared by Sam's Saudi cook, they ate quietly while an unspoken tension between Sam and Hank filled the

193

room. To get Sam talking, Victoria asked why the oil companies thought there was oil in the desert.

"The Brits have a character named Philby who came in as a trader and got close to the king."

"I've heard about him. Philby. A Foreign Service man out of India."

"That's him."

"He keeps orangutans for pets," Hank threw in. "Takes them for walks on the streets of Riyadh."

Victoria smiled, not as amused at Philby's eccentricities as she was pleased at the developing conversation.

"Philby started taking Ibn Saud for long drives in the desert in his Rolls Royce. Convinced him there was water under the desert. Brought in an American engineer who says there's no water but it looks just like Bahrain." Sam waved toward the Arabian Gulf island kingdom just off Saudi Arabia's east coast. "So there's bound to be oil."

Hank interrupted. "Why doesn't Mr. Philby do the drilling?" he asked Sam.

Sam's brow furrowed. "Good question."

"I can tell you that," Victoria interrupted, pleased about the development of conversation and anxious to keep it going. "It was the talk of the Foreign Office. Philby set himself up as the king's negotiator and then stabbed Anglo-Persian…"

"Anglo-Iranian."

"Yes, that's right, Anglo-Iranian now, thank you, Sam. Philby stabbed Anglo-Iranian in the back by pushing the leases to the Standard."

"The American consortium."

"The Standard consortium," she smiled. "Philby probably took cash from both before he closed the deal."

As they finished eating, a Saudi maid took their dishes from the table and brought them yogurt, fruit and tea. Sam sat back, glanced at Hank and then at

Victoria. "Tell us about Harry and Maria and the family. The aunts and uncles in Ohio. The cousins in California. It's been a long time."

Victoria looked from him to Hank. "Do you remember them, Hank?"

"I was just a little kid the last time we were in Pittsburgh."

"Always meant to go back," said Sam. "Never got to it. Too busy. Then she got sick and, well, you know how it goes."

"They're thriving," Victoria answered with a bright, if forced, smile. "They hardly even know there's a depression. Harry is so busy building airplanes in Oklahoma and California he barely has time for cars and trucks. Maria never leaves Pittsburgh and her beloved study."

"Still churning out letters to every strand of the bloodline and cataloguing the answers," Sam laughed.

"Which is why I never write," Victoria laughed with him.

"Airplanes?" Hank asked.

Victoria and Sam just looked at each other and grinned, remembering how everybody always said they were just like their grandfather, Barrett Lithachik. And now both were thinking how like Harry Wade his grandson Hank seemed to them.

"Did Harry get into Oklahoma oil?"

"Harry?" Victoria asked. She shook her head 'no.' "The motor, not the fuel, that's Harry."

"Too much pride to go into his wife's father's business," said Sam.

She smiled at him. "Runs in the family, doesn't it?" Victoria watched both Hank and Sam blanch but before either could become defensive, she went on. "The oil business crashed. There was a glut."

"And Mother wrote that somehow the glut led to her finding one of her brother's sons?"

Victoria grinned, warming up to her story. "That's a good one. You remember old Chinga's son, Gatch? He worked for Grandpa Barrett down in South America before the war?"

195

"Good man. Got sick and then worked for Father in New York City."

"That's right," nodded Victoria. "His godson, Monty, wanted to work the oil fields the summer before his last year of high school. So Gatch brought him out to Oklahoma from L.A."

"How's that boy's father?" Sam asked nonchalantly, unconsciously massaging the muscles of his hip and leg.

"You knew Monty's father?"

Because Sam rarely said anything about his past, Hank listened intently.

"I met Jacques in Paris during the war," Sam replied. "By coincidence, he went to New York and worked for Harry when the war was over. Then he and Gatch went into the oil business in Oklahoma. That's how Gatch wound up so close to Jacques' son Monty."

"Jacques is good," Victoria said quickly, watching Sam massage the leg he broke when he was with Jacques, during the first year of The Great War. "Busy. Really wrapped up in the movie business. Cartoons. He was supplying celluloid. One thing led to another and he became a big producer. Spends his time riding trains between Bartle City and L.A."

"Did he remarry?"

"No. Gatch says he's not interested."

"I can understand that," Sam shrugged, glancing at a Mondrian painting on the dining room wall.

"He keeps in touch with his ex-wife. She never remarried either. A nightclub singer, I understand."

"So what's this about his son Monty?"

"Can I tell the story?"

"You better," Hank said.

"The boy was living in Los Angeles with his mother when he told her he wanted to spend a high school summer working the Oklahoma oil fields. She was thrilled because it meant she could tour with a band for a couple of

196

months. She wired Gatch, who got him a job in one of the camps, running errands for the roughnecks. They expected him to be howling for a hot bath and a train ticket back to L.A. in a week."

"But he didn't, did he?" Hank gloated. "He knew what he wanted."

Victoria glanced at Hank with an expression that silenced him and went on quickly. "Monty fell in with the boys in the fields like he was coming home, which he sort-of was, since he had spent part of his boyhood in Bartle City when it was a boom town. An older roughneck named Jimmy took Monty under his wing, showed him the ropes, even gave Monty a room in the shack he lived in with his common-law wife and kids. Taught him the roughneck rules. Showed Monty a life he never saw at home."

"I doubt that's what Jacques wanted," Sam remarked, still massaging the old war wound.

"Still," Victoria went on, "that's the way it worked out. Anyway, late one Friday afternoon Monty and Jimmy were at the local bank, depositing their pay, when guess who came in?"

"Grandpa Harry?" asked Hank.

Victoria smiled. "Grandpa Harry only does business in New York banks, Hank."

"Why?"

"Well, I guess partly because of who walked into that Oklahoma bank: Pretty Boy Floyd."

"The bank robber?"

"Yep."

"What happened?"

"Just when the money was bagged and the robbery was almost done, one of the tellers decided to be a hero and pulled a pistol from under the counter. Monty could see Floyd would shoot the fool dead so he grabbed the teller's gun arm and started wrestling him."

"Did Monty get hurt?" Sam asked anxiously.

"Just the opposite," Victoria answered. "The teller was shouting for Monty to get out of the way so he could shoot Floyd and Floyd raised his Tommy gun and was shouting for Monty to get out of the way so he could shoot the teller. And Monty started shouting for them both to shut up because nobody needed to get shot. He stayed between them and kept shouting. He shamed the teller for risking everybody in the bank over a bag of money. And he convinced Floyd he didn't want to add murder to armed robbery. When they finally started listening to him, he told Floyd to take the money and get out."

She paused and smiled at Sam and Hank, pleased she had a captivated audience.

"What happened?" Hank demanded.

"Floyd was so impressed with Monty's nerve he tried to get him to go along down the robber's highway as a partner," Victoria told them. "Apparently old Jimmy liked the idea but Monty said he was in Oklahoma to work the oil fields. Floyd didn't want Jimmy without Monty. He told Monty he'd started out in the oil fields and maybe it would've been better in the big picture if he'd stayed, so he took off alone."

"The FBI caught Floyd and killed him, didn't they?" Sam asked.

"So they say. But the incident gave Jimmy and Monty doubts about putting their money in a bank. They decided to take a lease on a piece of oil land and drill for themselves."

"Very enterprising," Sam muttered.

"Maybe so," Victoria replied. "But the glut was coming on and oil prices started dropping right after they used up all their savings, all their credit and all their good faith to get the well in."

"Isn't that what happened to Grandpa Barrett in Pennsylvania?" Sam asked.

"Something like," Victoria nodded. "And just when they were almost broke and it looked completely hopeless, their well came in."

"Hot damn!" Hank grinned.

Victoria and Sam grinned at each other but both sent half-serious glances of rebuke for foul language at Hank.

"So they got rich?" Hank asked, ignoring the glances.

"Hardly," Victoria snapped back. "There was the glut. Before they could even begin to get out of debt, the government put a limit on how much they could sell."

"I don't understand," Hank snapped angrily. "They hit oil!"

"Those were the darkest days of the American depression, Hank," Sam said. "There was a lot of oil and not enough business to burn it."

"Suppose," Victoria explained, "they found so much oil out here in Arabia it would cost more to get water to the drillers than they could sell the oil for."

"Ibn Saud wouldn't let that happen," Sam remarked offhandedly. "He'd control the amount of oil going out." He sat up and looked at his sister. "The oil men were fighting the quota system in the courts, weren't they?"

"Some of them were fighting the legal battle. But some were running oil out of the state like bootleggers, selling it "hot." Apparently Monty was an idealistic kid and believed in the lawsuit. Jimmy was mad. He'd started life as an oil camp gopher and lived long enough and tough enough to become a roughneck. Now he'd hit his own well but because of the government he was still stuck in his shotgun shack on the wrong side of the tracks. He was ready to hit the outlaw trail."

"What happened?"

"Monty went to Gatch. Gatch was having his own business troubles but he made sure Monty got a good lawyer. Then the New Dealers extended the Connelly Hot Oil Act, making the quotas the law."

"Just like Pennsylvania in the 80's."

"Just like. The little producers were upstream without a market. Big Oil just waited for the banks to foreclose and then bought the little guys' assests for pennies on the dollar."

"Some rob with guns, some with fountain pens," Sam said quietly, remembering one of Grandpa Barrett's favorite expressions.

"What did Monty do?" Hank asked.

"He and Jimmy turned into oil field outlaws. They got a big truck, mounted a giant tank in the bed with rail fences around it, covered it over with hay bales and ran hot oil out of state from their well-head."

"Whoa," muttered Hank. "That's bold."

"Too bold. There were spies all over, roughnecks with the big oil companies who got bonuses for naming the hot oil runners to law enforcement. One night some Oklahoma Rangers trailed them to the state line and tried to stop them before they could cross. Jimmy was driving. He lost his head and made a run for it across country."

"Just like a movie!" Hank exclaimed.

"Just like. The chase ended when the truck rolled. Monty was thrown clear. He was bashed up pretty bad and broke his arm. Jimmy was trapped inside the cab. The tank split open and spilled oil all over the hay and the dry Oklahoma underbrush. The engine sparked and set off a huge fire. The truck's gas tanks blew. The Rangers pulled Monty clear, arrested him, took him to get his arm set and put him in jail. They didn't ever find much of Jimmy, just charred remains."

"Did Monty go to prison?" Hank asked.

"Gatch took him to see the Governor in Oklahoma City. He's an old oil man. Went partners with Gatch and Jacques on the wells drilled outside the Oklahoma State House before he was elected. He gave the boy a pardon on the basis of youth and extenuating circumstances, on the conditions that Monty would make amends with Jimmy's common-law wife and sons and go back to school."

"I thought you said this story was about finding mother's long lost brother!" Sam suddenly remembered.

"That's just it. When Monty went to see Jimmy's wife and set her up with a job in Gatch's company and see to the boys, he started asking about Jimmy's family. He found out Jimmy's father was a no-good roughneck from Pennsylvania named James Baxter who ran off on Jimmy's mother and died in an Oklahoma blizzard a few years after the first Spindletop strike."

"Uncle James!"

"No doubt."

"I'll be damned."

They sat and stared at each other and thought about the long road from a Pennsylvania farm to an Oklahoma blizzard and about their own half-finished roads.

"Where is Monty now?" Hank suddenly asked, breaking the reverie.

Victoria looked hard at him. "You really want to know?"

"Why wouldn't I?"

"He finished high school this spring. Your Grandpa Harry is helping get him into Harvard. He'll start next fall."

Sam looked at Hank and smiled. "You see?"

Rage inflamed Hank's expression and he rose. "I'm going to be a pilot, not a student!" He stormed from the room, Sam's reprimand and Victoria's plaintive pleas lost at his stomping feet.

Sam looked at Victoria. "You see? No way out."

"Maybe there is," she smiled. "I know where he can get some business education and fly everyday. And it's a long way from the madness that's coming in Europe."

"What are you talking about?"

"He wants to see the South Seas. Phillip can arrange a training post in Borneo with Royal Dutch/Shell."

"Flying?" asked Sam.

"We've been there. They need pilots. And he'll learn the oil business."

He looked at her with wide eyes. "Yes!"

She smiled. "Consider it done."

*****

The nightclub was nearly empty, the room shadowy in dim lighting, the candles at the many customerless tables unlit. The small pop orchestra on the bandstand huddled together over their instruments, muttering indistinctly about their next number. Behind the bar, the tender rattled a few bottles as he inventoried the ample stocks, nobody on the stools to interrupt him.

Victoria sat alone in a booth along the far wall of the club, a choice table on a busier night during a happier day. She smoked a cigarette and watched the doorway at the far end of the bar. She was waiting for someone to come through it.

From a different direction, a svelte woman of middle years and still lovely walked into the room from kitchen doors behind the bar. Her golden hair was stylish and glistening, her blue eyes were bright and alert, her face was as pretty as Victoria's, if more petite and vivacious against Victoria's auburn-haired, green-eyed sultry undeniability. As the petite blond rounded the bandstand end of the bar, she glanced at the conferring players and then across the room. Seeing only three men, heads down, whispering over a whiskey bottle in a corner and two couples laughing over a pitcher of beer in a far booth, she walked to Victoria, who held up her freshly lit cigarette in a gesture of familiarity. The blond woman unhesitatingly took the cigarette, inhaled deeply and did not return it. The two women's eyes met. Neither smiled.

Victoria shrugged. "Still waiting."

The blond woman's obviously sympathetic expression was her only reply. A man on the bandstand with a coronet turned away from the other players to the room, stepped to the singer's mic and looked out at the blond woman. "You ready, Katie Marie?"

The blond woman glanced at him, then at Victoria's strained face, finally back at him and called, "Play us a foxtrot, Benny. Something upbeat." He nodded, turned to the players and said a song title. While the man with the coronet counted the players in, Katie Marie looked at Victoria. "Get up, girl. All the good dancers are shipping out. You need to practice leading or you'll spend the whole war crying in your whiskey."

Victoria's head dropped but her face turned, she looked up at Katie Marie, her expression softened and she smiled sadly. "Brandy," she corrected, standing up.

"When I'm in town, you don't cry into brandy or whiskey or a lace hanky," Katie Marie snapped back, taking Victoria's arm and pulling her onto the small dance floor. She put the taller woman's hand around her back, lifted her left arm, stepped into dance frame and pulled Victoria into the dance. As

202

Victoria picked up the tempo, Katie Marie followed her, eyes darting around the club.

"You used to turn this into one of the most crowded dance floors in D.C.," Victoria said as they danced.

"That was before…" Katie Marie began, "before…" The words caught in her throat.

"Pearl Harbor," Victoria finished the sentence, grimness once again freezing her face.

"Yeah." Katie Marie took in Victoria's hard face.

"Fucking Japs."

"Turn me," Katie Marie suddenly told her.

After the turn, Katie Marie stepped back into dance frame and saw Victoria's expression was still stony. "Gutless Washington politicians," Victoria muttered. "They ought to show their defiance, get out and party."

"I wouldn't be here if it wasn't my job," Katie Marie replied quietly. "People are still trying to deal with it."

"Deal with it?" Victoria answered angrily. "Drop me into Tokyo with a butcher knife and I'll show you how to deal with it. I'll turn that little asshole Tojo into a choirboy!"

Katie Marie looked up at Victoria and giggled. This drew a smile onto Victoria's hard face.

There was a movement at the bar's front door. Both women looked. LeClaire Harold, the young State Department man who had sent Victoria to Ibn Saud, shed his overcoat as he came into the room.

"Your boyfriend," Katie Marie smiled.

"Lover," Victoria corrected her, dropping her arms from dance frame and turning toward Harold.

"Time for me to go to work anyway," Katie Marie said, turning toward the bandstand.

203

"Play us a slow one," Victoria said over her shoulder as she walked to Harold.

The band brought the foxtrot to its end as Katie Marie stepped up to the mic and told the man with the coronet what she wanted to sing. Meanwhile, Victoria walked her young man to the booth as they reconnoitered. The band began playing. Harold dropped his overcoat into the booth, gulped down the glass of brandy on the table and shook his head 'no.' Katie Marie read "no word yet" on his lips as she began singing and watched him pull a crestfallen Victoria back onto the dance floor.

I'll be seeing you
In all the old familiar places...

Katie Marie saw Victoria grit her teeth against the song's sadness and follow Harold's   lead.

That this heart of mine embraces
All day through

Victoria asked another question. He shook his head 'no.' She asked something else. He made a gesture with his head and shoulders that said 'there just is not any information.'

In that small café
The park across the way
The children's carousel
The chestnut tree
The wishing well

As they went on dancing, Katie Marie saw Victoria's face drop to Harold's shoulder and her eyes close. Katie Marie went on singing.

I'll be seeing you
In every lovely summer's day
In everything that's light and gay
I'll always think of you that way

I'll find you in the morning sun
And when the night is new
I'll be looking at the moon
But I'll be seeing you

As the song ended, the man with the coronet looked at Katie Marie. "Another ballad?"

She glanced at the room. The two couples in back were looking up at the bandstand, waiting to see what the next selection would be. She saw Victoria leading Harold back to their booth. She thought, then smiled at the bandleader. "No, let's swing."

*****

At the end of the set, Katie Marie eased herself into the booth next to Victoria, with Harold across the table. The singer sipped a coca cola while Harold and Victoria smoked over brandies. Seizing a pause in the chat, Harold asked Katie Marie about herself. "Victoria tells me you have family in Romania."

"Not anymore."

"All moved to Chicago?"

"All slaughtered by the Nazis."

"Bucharest?"

Katie Marie nodded. "I was born there. In 1925, the Black Guard told my father—he's a doctor—they'd make him a citizen even though he was a Jew. For a fee."

"He didn't pay?"

"He knew it was only a matter of time until they asked him for another fee. So he took a teaching position in Paris and when the year was up he got us on a steamer to Quebec and then smuggled us into Chicago."

"You remember Bucharest?" Harold casually asked.

"Sure. You want to hear a Romanian love song?"

Harold seemed very interested. "You speak Romanian?"

Katie Marie grinned. "My parents spoke it to each other so me and my brothers wouldn't know what they were talking about. Good reason to learn a language, eh?"

"I have a little German and I speak French but I didn't learn either like that," smiled Victoria.

Suddenly two men in military uniform pushed open the door of the room and stepped inside. One, carrying a large manila envelope, looked around the room for someone while the man beside him, carrying a carbine in the ready position, looked around the room for anyone threatening. Harold waved to the man with the envelope, who walked briskly to Harold, his armed escort following. Others in the room, seeing this represented no immediate threat and unsurprised by military urgencies in these suddenly dark, paranoid days, turned away, keeping watch at the periphery of their socializing for news of a new horror.

Harold identified himself and took the envelope, telling the soldiers to stand at ease and wait. He studied the cables in the envelope while Victoria and Katie Marie held hands, watched and waited.

*****

Many remember that Japan destroyed the Pearl Harbor naval base on December 7, 1941; fewer remember why.

Japan was a proud, intelligent and industrious nation on an island of sharply limited natural resources. It had been expanding its sphere of influence and dominance since it rediscovered its modern muscle by defeating Russia in 1904. It gained greater resources from control of German holdings in China awarded to it by the Allied Powers at the Paris Peace Conference for remaining neutral in the 1914-1918 Great War. But to fulfill its technological, industrial and spiritual potential for greatness, Japan needed an energy supply. In the first half of the twentieth century, that meant one thing: Oil.

Japan set its sights on the Western-controlled international oil companies' vast Indonesian and Malaysian reserves. From the Harding administration (1920-23) on, this ambition created political conflict with the United States. President Roosevelt, in the mid-1930s, more or less invented the concept of trade sanctions by attempting to curb Japanese aggression by limiting its access to certain U.S. produced and refined petroleum products, especially high octane airplane fuel. This only made Japan more determined to obtain its own oil resource.

Continuing its diplomatic posturing, Japan surreptitiously stockpiled adequate oil supplies for a short naval war. While the world's attention was turned to the horrors unfolding in Europe, Japan's air force struck at Pearl

Harbor. It crippled the U.S. fleet. Meanwhile, its army and navy invaded and occupied Indonesia and Malaysia, taking control of the precious oil resources. The intention was to secure this sphere of resources Japan believed was its due and dare any other nation to challenge it.

The U.S. was enraged by the devastating sneak attack. It was completely unwilling to forego the territory and vast oil resources Japan had captured. It was also sympathetic to the many nations, nation states and protectorates overrun by Japanese aggression, like China, French Indochina, the Dutch East Indies, the British colonial outposts of Singapore and Hong Kong, and several South Pacific countries. But the U.S. Pacific fleet and air force were in ruin. Unable to respond to the provocation immediately, it declared its intentions and quietly, firmly, prepared itself for cold, hard, unrelenting vengeance. Meanwhile, Japan ran rampant in the South Pacific, leaving horror and ruin in its wake.

*****

After reading the cables, Harold folded them, put them back into the envelope, resealed it and handed it back to the courier. "Thank you, Sergeant. You are dismissed."

The soldier snapped off a salute, stepped back, pivoted and marched out of the club, his escort following, Harold watching. Only then did Harold look across the table at Victoria. She read his expression and hung her head. "The Royal Dutch Shell facility on Borneo is in ruins, burned to the ground and spewing toxic clouds of black smoke for a month. The Japanese are in full possession of the island. All personnel are accounted for. Hank is not listed among the survivors."

Tears streamed from Victoria's eyes, falling from her cheeks to the table over which her head hung. The three sat in silence until, finally, Harold whispered, "I will have more details sooner or later."

Victoria continued sitting silently, motionless, her head hanging down. Harold and Katie Marie sat with her, saying nothing, watching her, waiting.

"He wouldn't be there if it wasn't for me," Victoria finally muttered with intense anger, her head still hanging over her brandy.

"You couldn't know," Harold told her while Katie Marie sat quietly, still holding her hand, watching, unable to find words.

Victoria suddenly lifted her head. Her hand came free from Katie Marie's grasp and both fists came to the table. There was cold, red fury in her green eyes. "I want back at the bastards."

Harold stared at the fierceness he was facing but said nothing. He thought. Victoria's intensity was unremitting, her clenched fists on the table a sign. Katie Marie was speechless in the face of this seething and calculating silence.

"We've got to take out Hitler first," Harold said.

Katie Marie gravely nodded her head in agreement. "That's what the papers say: Hitler's got to go first."

"Fuck Hitler," Victoria whispered. "I want at the Japs!"

Harold leaned across the table, very near her, and grabbed her chin between his thumb and forefinger. He leaned in and looked hard into her eyes. "There IS something you'd be damn good at," he said. "but its not killing."

She pulled her head away and sat back.

Her fists unclenched and she laid her hands firmly on the table, palms down. "What?"

"You know the Vichy diplomats, don't you?"

"You mean the Nazi France Ambassador and his stooges?"

"Yes."

"I gave them a dinner when they took over the embassy. I wanted to invite the gutsy Frenchmen who turned in their credentials, but they had already left to join the Free French in London."

"Perfect," Harold smiled.

"Why?"

"Make any conquests?"

Victoria shrugged, momentarily distracted. "They're Frenchmen. Fools for lace. Easy pickings. What does this have to do with anything?"

"We're landing our navy in North Africa in the spring. It would save a lot of lives, a lot of lives, if what's left of the French navy was somewhere else in the Mediterranean when we do it. We could plan that if we knew their codes."

"And the codes are in the embassy."

He smiled. "You could only get to those codes if you had the trust of somebody inside."

She stared at him and, finally, replied. "Somebody who likes lace."

He nodded.

"They're in French," Victoria said.

"They're codebooks," Harold answered. "You don't have to read the language to recognize them."

"So steal the codebooks," Katie Marie said quietly.

Victoria looked at her. "They would change the codes." She looked at Harold. "Right?"

He nodded grimly.

"So it has to be done without anybody knowing," Victoria said. "Right?"

He nodded again, his jaw tightening.

"And it would save lives?"

"Young sailors and marines. Boys like Hank."

She stared at him, thinking.

"I guess I ought to warn you," he said quietly. "It's a crime against the Vichy government, not ours. They catch you, you're theirs."

She continued to stare at him. Finally, she turned to Katie Marie. "How would you like to meet an Ambassador?"

Harold turned to Katie Marie so she looked from him to Victoria. Both awaited her answer. She thought. Emotions rippled across her face. Finally, she smiled. "Love to."

*****

Determined to win a State Department assignment to the Far East where she could avenge Hank, Victoria set out to prove her value to Harold by obtaining the Vichy codebooks. She quickly developed a plan of seduction and intrigue. But Harold demanded she work methodically. He suggested she start by returning her prey, the Vichy Ambassador, to her A-list of dinner party guests. Once he was back in her social circle, she gave him only formal attention in public but subtly initiated a flirtation. As she had predicted, he proved easy to win over. Slowly, over the late winter and early spring, she wove her web.

On a hot, muggy, D.C. midspring midday, Victoria—finally ready to pounce—walked with Katie Marie across the bridge over Rock Creek Park between the Wardman Park Hotel and the Vichy Embassy. Both wore striking, tailored linen day suits over bright white blouses with lace trim and sharply plunging décolletages. As they walked, they traded deep background information in anticipation of the timeless espionage of seduction for which every woman knows the preparation.

"How well do you know this guy?" Katie Marie asked casually.

"He's a fop. A flirt. But charming. Very useful at dinner parties."

"You know him well?"

"I know him."

"In the biblical sense."

Victoria gave an annoyed glance. Katie Marie studied it.

"You're really in love with Harold!" Katie Marie exclaimed in surprise.

Victoria's annoyance grew more visible as they walked.

"All this 'he's my lover' is poop," Katie Marie went on. "You don't want to brag about the ambassador and you don't want to take him on again. You're not doing this to save those boys, you're doing this for Harold!"

210

At the corner of Connecticut and Wyoming, Victoria grabbed Katie Marie's arm and stopped her on the sidewalk just around the corner from the Vichy Embassy, a three-story house on Wyoming Avenue with a wide, columned porch and a layered, many-windowed heaviness.

"This is serious work," Victoria said earnestly. "You expect me to laugh and tell you I'll take any excuse to get some French nookie?"

Katie Marie studied her friend's too-earnest expression. "It's harder to cheat on somebody you really love, even for a good cause, even with his permission, than it is to cheat on a husband you stopped loving a long time ago."

A sadness fell over Victoria's earnestness. "You're pretty smart for a girl singer."

"I have a doctorate degree from the University of the Chicago Streets."

"Well, doctor," Victoria replied, taking a deep breath and setting her face, "Let's go do our country proud."

With glowing smiles, girlish giggles, womanly charm and strategic name dropping, Victoria led the charge through the embassy's male clerical staff to the private office of Auguste-Petain de la Grandville, Ambassador Emeritus. He was an older man, portly and genial, perhaps less genial due to the impromptu nap their call interrupted, but still genial. His geniality became almost comic conviviality when they announced they were there to take him to a lunch where he could help them plan Victoria's next soirée.

They satiated de la Grandville with veal and heavy sauces while distracting him with light-hearted chatter about a supposed dinner gala "to celebrate life in the face of tragedy" at which Katie Marie would supposedly entertain. After they dipped strawberries in chocolate and heavy cream, Victoria invited him to her Georgetown home "to help me lay out the seating arrangements, so to speak."

Two hours later, the gentle old man awakened. He and Victoria lay naked beneath cool sheets in a shady guestroom at the back of her house. She was wide-awake, thinking, and immediately noticed his stirring. "Did you enjoy your nap?" she asked, sitting up in bed as—in all his naked, obese splendor—he padded heavily across the room to the toilet and peed. She watched him waddle, then turned her head and looked at a small model of an Aeronca Model K Scout sitting on the dressing table beside a decorative hairbrush and hand mirror.

After a pause accompanied by the sound of a stream of water, he sighed with satisfaction, grinned and answered her question about the nap. "Indeed I did." He walked toward his clothes, draped over a chair beside the bed. "Did you?"

"I did not sleep," she replied with a polite smile. "I have much on my mind."

He turned, looked down at her sitting naked on the edge of the bed. "Perhaps if I had been able to perform."

"It was wonderful," she interrupted, smiling more sincerely.

"Yes," he nodded. "The actual joining of genitals is over-rated, isn't it?"

"Companionship," she smiled.

"Only young men swollen with ego and raging hormones require the battering deed."

"I remember it well," she smiled again, thinking about the ecstasy of being lost in Harold's passion. He turned to her, half-dressed. She saw an inclination toward renewal emerging in his lustful eyes. She needed to head that idea off. "Do you have to get back to the embassy?"

"Yes," he sighed, turning toward his shirt and tie. "But they will not miss me."

This caught her attention. "Surely you have responsibilities."

"I am but a figurehead," he sighed, grunting with the effort of leaning down, pulling on his shoes and tying them. "It is the German attaché who is really in charge."

"You must have responsibility for the building, its security, at least."

He laughed. "I have access to nothing but my office. And I must obtain the guard's cooperation when I come and go from there."

She stared at him in chagrin, saying nothing.

He went on, confessionally. "I do treasure the office as a refuge when that Nazi bastard and my whore of a wife entertain their American fascist friends in my home."

"Your wife and the attaché?" She thrust an extended finger into a closed fist to suggest intercourse. He nodded 'yes.' She stared at him, concealing frustration beneath a sympathetic expression, thinking hard and fast. "So," she concluded, suddenly smiling. "There is another place for us to meet when my husband is in the house."

Putting the last touches to his tie, he suddenly started and looked around. "I thought Lord North was in London."

She walked to the dressing table and picked up the brush beside the model airplane. "He is," she answered, staring into the mirror and brushing her hair. "But he is in and out of the country and I do not want to miss my time with you."

"Ah," he smiled, watching her. "I had forgotten how deliciously sweet you could be."

"Yes," she nodded, absently brushing her hair, watching his reflection as he finished dressing, thinking. "Yes."

*****

A vacant hotel room was rare in wartime Washington. And married diplomats could not be seen out together frequently without starting detrimental gossip. And Victoria arranged obstacles to prevent further assignations at her house. So if De la Grandville wanted to be with Victoria – and she made sure that he did – he had no other option than to accept her suggestion they obtain the embassy security guard's blessing for late night tête-à-têtes. The night guard, a sturdy man named Paul with a simple if sharp face who made regular nightly rounds inside the embassy armed with a pistol and accompanied by a vicious Alsatian attack dog, was uncomfortable with the arrangement. He became even more uneasy when Victoria began bringing Katie Marie along. He informed the Nazi attaché overseeing the embassy.

The stern attaché's initial impulse was to squelch the little "parties" – until he realized they would facilitate his own assignations with Madam de la Grandville at the ambassador's house. He made inquiries into Victoria's background and found nothing but "social frivolousness." Katie Marie's background revealed "degradation" but no apparent danger to Vichy. So the attaché told the guard to ignore de la Grandville's affair.

213

But Paul was French and, therefore, desirous of and amenable to both personal gain and feminine charms. Rather than ignore the partiers, he let the ladies know he wished to be "noticed" in return for his courtesy. Ambassador de la Grandeville gladly saw that there was a regular "overpayment" for the taxi that always awaited Katie Marie when she left and always returned later to take Victoria home. The "overpayment" was split between the taxi driver and Paul. And both women regularly asked Paul to signal for the taxi, carefully remembering to reward his loyalty with a flirtatious goodnight peck on the cheek and caress just before they hopped into the taxi.

Soon both women were regular uninterrupted late night visitors at the embassy, Katie Marie offering the ambassador song and laughter, Victoria enticing him afterwards with rare brandy, expensive silk and mature flesh. Following these late night visits, Harold held regular afternoon reconnoiterings in suite 215B of the Wardman Park Hotel. There he asked the women questions and gave directions, developing their information. Together, they put together a floor plan of the house and identified the codebook room.

Based on what they knew and still needed to know, Harold helped them plan a surprise afternoon sortie into the embassy to obtain more information. On that outing, they identified the brands and types of locks on the doors to the codebook room. During the visit, Victoria made a pre-planned pause in the codebook room doorway and bent forward "to wipe something from her shoe," revealing leg and lace. While the men in the room stared at Victoria, Katie Marie, from a pre-designated position, studied the open closet inside the room holding the safe where the codebooks were kept, noting the types of locks on the closets and the brand and model of the safe.

Further consultation at the Wardman Park with Harold filled out their plan. Within days, sooner than either Victoria or Katie Marie expected, he announced they must act.

"We're not ready," Victoria told him.

"You are," he insisted.

"You aren't going to wind up in a French prison if this goes wrong," she argued.

"The North Africa invasion is imminent," he told her. "Boys lives are at stake."

"Our lives are at stake!" Katie Marie protested.

He looked from one to the other, saying nothing, and then finally spoke. "I think you're ready. You don't have to do this," he pronounced. "But if it's going to be worth anything, you have to do it now."

That night, Victoria and Katie Marie arrived together at the embassy with carafes of champagne, their gowns displaying feminine bounty and their manners displaying joy and giddiness, all to mask their anxiety. Seductively, they confessed to their friend Paul, the security guard, that this night was special.

"A birthday?" he asked with a leering smile.

"Tonight," Victoria told him, looking with sauciness at Katie Marie, "is the night I will share my special friend with my special lover!"

He looked from Victoria to Katie Marie, confused. Then, realizing what Victoria meant, he could barely contain himself. "You mean you will, I mean she will, I mean the old man and the mademoiselle will..." He simply could not overcome his excitement to finish his sentence.

"It is the deepest love a woman can express, don't you think?" Victoria asked him seductively, putting an arm around Katie Marie.

"Ooh, oui. It is, it is," he stammered.

"You will protect our privacy, won't you?"

"Oui oui oui, indeed, oui! I will guard your privacy with intense caution. You shall not be disturbed!"

De la Grandville arrived. The women greeted him in the entryway with fondling exuberanance. Glancing at Paul, the flabby, sad-faced ambassador took Victoria's hands in his and shrugged. "I adore this woman."

"Zee othair one is not so bad, too," Paul replied with a lecherous grin and a glance at Katie Marie.

The women retreated with de la Grandville to his office. Paul watched, leering. Through the interior windows of the Ambassador's office he saw them pop champagne corks and watched Katie Marie go to the Victrola, put on a record and dance back, singing, toward the other two. Victoria held out a flute of bubbly to her. Even after de la Grandville walked to the window and drew the curtains, the guard listened to the muffled music and laughter, his imaginings running wild. Finally, certain the revelers were settling in for their private festivities, he sighed and led the dog out on a lonely patrol of the building.

A while later, Paul sat at the reception desk opposite the front door and across from the Ambassador's office. The Alsatian slept peacefully at his feet. The inner office was quiet, though Paul heard muffled romantic music still playing on the Victrola. Suddenly, the door opened and out danced Victoria, slowly and sinuously, wearing only a lacey chemise and an inebriated smile, holding out a flute of champagne to him. It was almost too exciting and titillating for him to believe and yet here in this remarkable land of impossible dreams called America it was happening to him.

A few minutes later, however, he was in another dreamland, the crushed Nembutal-laced champagne having done to him the same thing it did to de la Grandville moments before. Quickly, Victoria completed phase one of the taking of the codebooks by stirring an ample dosage of the crushed Nembutal into the watchdog's water, putting the sweet beast into a harmless deep sleep like Paul's. Meanwhile, Katie Marie initiated phase two by hurrying to a predetermined rear window and sliding it open. When the window opened, the man who had been posing as the women's taxi driver while studying the building came up over the sill and into the room.

"Where's da locks?" he asked loudly and gruffly into the darkness of the rear hallway, his heavy harshness an exact opposite to his small, wiry frame and almost intellectual face framed by heavy glasses.

"Shshsh!" both women cautioned. He stared at them in their lacey slips and licked his lips. "Put your eyes back in your head and get to work on those locks," Victoria snapped at him, pointing at the double doors leading into the codebook room. He swallowed hard, turned away muttering, and shuffled toward the codebook room carrying his heavy black duffle bag of lock picking and safecracking tools.

"I didn't owe da government dese years, I'd smack you bot' around an' show you what a woman's for."

"Harold calls this guy the Georgia Cracker?" Katie Marie asked Victoria.

"If he gets us in and and out of those safes before that Nembutal wears off the Frenchmen and the dog, I'll call him the Georgia Peach," Victoria whispered back.

The Georgia Cracker quickly, easily opened the double doors into the codebook room. They followed him in, snapped on a lamp and pointed out the closet housing the safe. He quickly opened its door, too. Both women breathed a deep sigh of relief and smiled at one another. Obviously, the Cracker knew his work.

He settled in front of the safe, studying its row of four combination dials, each with a short, solid handle above it. "Bring dat lamp," he ordered. Victoria lifted the small lamp from a nearby table and walked it into the closet. "Dere," he grunted, nodding toward the top of the safe, which he still had not touched. He looked up. His eyes devoured her and she felt it. She said nothing, waiting him out. When she did not respond to his provocative stare, he barked. "Write dis down, dese numbers. When we close her up and wipe her down, ya put dese dials back where dey was, got it?"

"You can open it?"

Lustfully, he looked her up and down again. "Ain't no box I can't get into, lady. Not even yours. Just takes time."

Victoria struggled to restrain her response until Katie Marie came up behind her and handed over a pencil and note pad. "The pencil's not too sharp," she smiled. "Just write with it, no stabbing."

The Cracker dictated numbers from the four dials on the safe, took a stethoscope from his bag, placed it on the safe above the first dial and began turning, listening for the tumblers to fall. Once he was at work, Victoria and Katie Marie excused themselves to check on their drugged hosts. Finding the Nembutal to be acting as predicted, inducing numbed sleep of up to six hours with little more than a champagne-drunk headache in its wake, they returned to find the cracker staring at the safe and frowning.

"What?" demanded Victoria in an anxious whisper.

"Ain't woikin'. Should." He grasped the handle above the first dial and pulled up and down on it. It did not budge. "Ain't."

"What do you do now?"

He looked up at her. "Got any dynamite?"

Terror froze both women, their eyes opening wide. "You've got to be kidding!" Victoria whispered.

217

He looked up again, grinning. "Sure am." He looked back at the safe. "I'll figure it, sooner or later. Lemme try another dial."

Victoria and Katie Marie dropped to their knees and rested on their haunches, watching over his shoulder with growing fear as he worked and worked at the second lock, listening carefully with the stethoscope. After an eternity of a few minutes, he let the stethoscope's bell drop to his chest, reached for the handle and cranked. The handle did not move. He cranked harder, up and down, without any response. Behind him, Victoria and Katie Marie groaned.

"Fuck!" grunted the Cracker with a last futile pull at the handle. He glanced back at the two women, a glance that wordlessly told them something was not right. He looked back at the safe. "Lemme try dis one," he said, placing the stethoscope bell above the third lock.

More precious minutes stolen from de la Grandville, Paul and the guard dog ticked away. The Cracker seemed to work more slowly but the final result with the third dial and handle was the same. Shaking his head, he moved to the last dial, muttering curses under his breath about what should have been a simple, if slow and repetitive, job.

Victoria and Katie Marie watched helplessly. Victoria glanced at her watch and then to a clock on the wall to confirm. Katie Marie saw concern tighten her friend's face. She met Victoria's eyes. It was almost time for phase three to begin: Harold would be at the rear window to receive the books and hurry them to the Wardman Park suite, where a huge photocopying setup was waiting. Both women knew he might very well cancel the operation if the safe was not even open when he arrived. Each saw in the other's eyes the questions such a reversal raised: Would they have to continue the masquerade? Repeat this night's charade? Could they hope to go on getting away with it or would pushing too far get them arrested and shuttled to a French prison? And even if they dared to try again, would they get another chance?

"Lemme try dis last sucka," the Cracker muttered, breaking into their thoughts.

"If you can't get the first three, why should you be able to get the fourth?" Katie Marie hissed.

"If I'd-a took dat attitude wit' da babes, I'd still be a virgin, honey," he said over his shoulder as he lifted the stethoscope bell to the last dial. He then turned and gave her his leer. "An' if ya ever wanna treat yerself and give me a try, you'll know I ain't a virgin."

"I'll give it a pass," Katie Marie smiled tightly. He started to reply but she cut him off. "But if I'm ever so inclined, I'll just stick my head up a pig's ass and get the same thrill."

"Funny," he muttered, turning back to the safe. "Funny."

As they watched intently, barely daring to breathe, he began slowly turning the dial and listening. After agonizing minutes of waiting, he reversed, turned slowly, reversed again, turned slowly again and repeated. Just as he raised his hand toward the handle, Katie Marie startled and her eyes snapped to the room's door. Sensing her movement, the Cracker's hand froze.

Victoria looked at her. "What?" she whispered.

Katie Marie pointed toward the hallway and swept her left hand in an arc, indicating she had heard something down the hall near the open rear window. Victoria nodded. They rose, closed the closet door to conceal the Cracker and the lamp, and peeked into the hallway. It was Harold. He came toward them in the hall's moonlit darkness.

"Time for the handoff!" he whispered angrily. "What's the problem?"

"You were supposed to wait outside!" Victoria protested, snapping her head back toward the codebook room, sending Katie Marie to set the Cracker back at work.

"You're late!" He looked at Victoria disapprovingly. "And skulking around in your lingerie!"

"We're overdressed for the job and YOU planned it!" Victoria answered defensively, pivoting away and moving back into the codebook room. Harold followed. Katie Marie met them in the room's doorway but said nothing, seeing them fuming at the verge of a full-fledged lovers' quarrel, overtly about the moment but actually about his concern for her danger and her realization that by coming inside he had become an American spy on foreign territory, subject to a firing squad.

The quarrel was averted when the Cracker walked up behind and startled all three. "I got it."

"What?" they all exclaimed in whispers too loud and excited.

219

"Shshsh!" the Cracker cautioned them. "C'mere!" He led them to the closet and opened the door. The fourth handle was perpendicular to the others.

"You got it!" Victoria exclaimed in a jubilant whisper.

"Only one?" Harold asked angrily.

"He has a problem," Katie Marie explained, attempting to cut off bickering between Victoria and Harold.

"Had," the Cracker smiled. "You solved it," he said to Harold.

With no idea there was a problem or what it was, Harold's expression showed he could not imagine how he solved it.

"Its old, the safe," the Cracker grinned. "Like me. You gotta wait for da tumblers t'fall." He leered at Katie Marie. "Like me."

Victoria interrupted. "So when we heard the noise, you stopped, and the tumblers fell."

"You got it."

"So now you can open the other three?" Victoria concluded.

He smiled. "Just like I told you."

When the safe was open, Harold took the books and the Cracker out the back window. The women straightened out and wiped down the codebook room, preparing it for a quick, undiscoverable retreat once Harold brought the codebooks back so they could be tracelessly restored to the safe. They then settled down on the carpet at the rear of the hallway by the open window in the moonlight.

"What the hell do we do now?" Katie Marie asked.

"Wait."

"Easier said than done. Got any cigs?"

"In the front. Might as well check on the boys."

They tiptoed up the hall. In the ambassador's office and at the front reception desk outside it, everything was dulcet. Their subjects, including the dog,

220

were somnolent, breathing evenly and deeply, occasionally snoring. Victoria grabbed cigarettes, a lighter, an ashtray and a deck of playing cards from the front office and they settled again at the back window. Soon they were smoking and playing gin rummy, saying nothing, trying not to think, especially about time.

Eventually, time became an unbearable burden. Right after Katie Marie laid down a hand full of gin, Victoria threw in her cards. "So here we sit," she said, whispering bitterly.

"At least we get a little insight into what it's like in the army. Don't they all complain about wasting time sitting around in their underwear smoking and playing cards?"

"Sorry I dragged you into this."

"Hey!" Katie Marie hushedly protested as she scooped up the cards. "I volunteered."

"Well, not exactly," Victoria tossed off, lifting herself up to the sill and looking out the window yet again. "Where IS he?"

"Looking out the window won't do any good."

"Really?" Victoria exclaimed. "Look!"

Just as Katie Marie was about to sit up on her knees and look out the window, she heard something at the reception desk up front, across from the office.

"Harold!" Victoria called in a happy whisper out the window.

"Shshsh!" Katie Marie warned her.

Victoria jerked back down. "What!?!" she whispered. Katie Marie nodded. Victoria looked. The Alsatian was stirring, licking Paul's face.

The codebooks appeared on the windowsill. Having seen Victoria's head appear and then suddenly disappear at the window, Harold was cautiously anticipating the need for stealth. Seeing the books, Victoria grabbed them. "Get rid of him and wait here!" Victoria exclaimed. She dashed for the codebook room.

Katie Marie rose up on her knees, looked out the window, waved Harold off and slumped back to the floor, watching the front desk. An instant later, Victoria was back. By this time, the dog was alert and Paul was about to be.

"What do we do!?!" Katie Marie asked in panic.

"Strip!" She commanded, pulling her own slip over her head.

"What are you talking about? This is not a game!" Katie Marie hissed in confusion and fear, watching Victoria unhook and slough off her brassiere and quickly step out of her lacey chem-pants.

"Strip, dammit!" Victoria ordered desperately, glancing over her shoulder to the front where Paul was sitting up. She pulled Katie Marie's slip off and pushed her brassiere over her small plump breasts as Katie Marie uncomprehendingly cooperated by tossing off the brassiere and pulling down and kicking off her own panties. "Good," Victoria finally grunted. "Now come here!" She pulled Katie Marie, naked but for an elegant strand of pearls, into her arms. "Get ready..." she told the smaller woman, watching over her shoulder as Paul stood, looked around, picked up his flashlight and the dog's leash, all the while muttering to the dog. Suddenly, to Katie Marie's astonishment, Victoria moaned.

Paul heard this and his head snapped toward them. The dog growled. Peering into the dark, Paul shone his flashlight at them.

"Kiss me like your life depends on it!" Victoria whispered and met her friend's lips with a desperation and fear that looked very like sexual passion. In terror, Katie Marie responded, finally understanding the ploy.

They lit up, naked, in the flashlight's harsh beam. Victoria screamed and coyly covered Katie Marie's naked buttocks with her hands, pulling the smaller woman harder against herself and staring into the light. "Who's there?"

"Lady North?" Paul asked in confusion. "Mrs. Livingstone?"

"Paul?"

"What are you ladies doing back there?"

"You and the Ambassador were asleep. We wanted a little time, just ourselves and the moon." She nodded to the window. "Do you mind?"

222

"No, madam, mademoiselle, I am so sorry to intrude," he answered, not lowering the flashlight, still staring and grinning lecherously. "It's a beautiful night!"

"Don't you have rounds or something, Paul?"

"So sorry, Lady North," he replied, noting her impatient tone. He turned and led the dog away. "Lovely pearls, Mrs. Livingstone," he called back with a snide smile in his voice as he disappeared into the building.

"Yeah, I'm sure he was admiring my pearls," Katie Marie muttered.

"Don't worry," Victoria chuckled, slapping her palms lightly on Katie Marie's butt cheeks. "I had your assets covered."

"Yeah," Katie Marie smiled, pushing away from her friend and getting back into her panties and brassiere. "And I could go for you if you had a little more hair on your chest." She pulled her slip over her head while Victoria giggled. "But I think you saved both our assets."

"I think so," Victoria agreed, also dressing again in her underthings. "But lets go wake up the old goat and get out of here before Paul starts wondering why he got such a long nap and heavy hangover from a couple of glasses of champagne."

"Right," Katie Marie agreed, hurling the ashtray contents into the early morning breeze where the evidence of their extensive smoking would blow into Washington's hot air gusts and across the city.

Victoria picked up the deck of cards. "Ready?' Katie Marie smiled and nodded. "Remember: we answer any questions about the naps and hangovers with gentle reassurances that we'll never let anybody know they left us running around here alone half the night.'

"Got it."

They smiled at each other. "Good. Let's go."

*****

As Victoria regained energy drained by the intensity of the spy mission, her life began going through what seemed like inescapable changes. First, the State Department was overjoyed with the codebook material. Not realizing the embarrassment it would cause, Harold happily told her his report on the operation was best-seller reading among those with Top Secret clearance and she had a whole new crowd of adorers in the government.

"Those are people I know socially! My uncle drinks with FDR!"

"Its mostly need-to-know, Victoria," he back-pedaled. "Intelligence services, diplomatic corps."

"It will go across Lord North's desk!"

"The report is entirely professional. Nothing lurid."

"Except for the parts where I seduce and party with the French Ambassador Emeritus and have a threesome with him and a girl singer!"

Harold studied her. He thought about reminding her she was a volunteer and had planned much of it herself, but decided she would know this when she thought it all through. Perhaps if there was not a war on he could make his own pledge to her and hope to keep it. But that all blew up at Pearl Harbor.

"Nevermind," she finally said. "It was bound to happen. At least this way it was for a good cause. I will make a separate peace with him."

Simpler to accept, but more immediately painful, was the news that Katie Marie would be leaving town with her band on a tour of the Midwest.

"I'll miss you like hell," she told her friend as they sat together in Victoria's favorite booth on the band's last night at the club.

Katie Marie took the cigarette Victoria had just lit. "Me, too." She took a long drag on the smoke. "I don't think I've ever had a girlfriend like you."

"Me, either. It's always men."

Katie Marie glanced at the band. "Exactly."

"Heard anything about Monty?" Victoria asked.

"Training," Katie Marie replied. "They expect to ship for Europe sooner or later."

They sat silently. "Did you settle with the old goat?"

Victoria laughed. "Poor old fool. He was so in love."

224

"You were probably the sweetest thing he's ever known."

"Knowing that Nazi-fucker he's married to, I'd say you're right."

"You're going to go on with it?"

"Can't. Couldn't. I'm not that sweet."

"What, then?"

"We had lunch. I cried." She acted it out, crying crocodile tears. "I can't wreck your home, your life. I can't live with the responsibility. You'll lose your marriage, your family. They'll send you back. It's horrible there." She paused and wiped away the tears while Katie Marie grinned and shook her head. "I'm going to be the brave one. I'm going to sacrifice myself. I'm leaving now. Don't follow. Don't phone. Don't write. It's over."

"So melodramatic," laughed Katie Marie. "Did it work?"

"He phoned so many times I had to get an unlisted phone. Then he wrote. Every day. But he only came around once."

"You must've been cruel."

"Actually, I was kind."

"Wait, let me guess—he had to tell you how much he adored you."

"And I assured him I cared for him, too. Then I told him it was impossible and sent him off."

"And he didn't come back around?"

"Seems there was a State Department memo to the FBI that the Vichy embassy may have 'accidentally' picked up."

Katie laughed. "Harold?"

Victoria nodded, smiling broadly. "Something about a possible improper arrangement between 'a Vichy ambassador and an American socialite.' Haven't seen him since."

They laughed together.

"I'm going to miss you, Katie Marie."

The singer nodded, fighting back tears.

Behind her, on the bandstand, the coronet-playing bandleader stepped to the singer's microphone. "You about ready, Katie Marie?"

Fighting back emotion, Katie Marie quickly stood, stubbed out the cigarette and dashed across the empty dance floor to the bandstand. She listened to the bandleader call the selection, nodded, took the microphone in hand and turned back to the room. Victoria was walking across the room toward the door, waving and smiling. The coronet player hit a sweet and longing note and held it. As Victoria walked out the club's door, she heard Katie Marie say, "Let's swing it, boys."

When Lord North was next in D.C. on British diplomatic business, there was the inevitable necessary confrontation. But the emotion was truncated. Soon after he endured the private embarrassment and rage of reading the State Department report, Lord North suffered through the humiliation it brought down on him in the Foreign Service. His peers were inclined to look the other way, given the mission's military value (not to mention the report's salacious delight). But his political enemies seized the opportunity.
The most embarrassing details of Victoria's adventure, without mention of the mission's value, were whispered to the most prudish of the wives in the diplomatic community. Quickly, the self-righteous women demanded moral redress from Lord Halifax, Lord North's superior in the U.S. delegation. After a hasty consultation with Deputy Prime Minister Attlee, Lord Halifax gave Lord North lunch but it did not stimulate his appetite to hear the blunt decision: "There is a war on. I cannot reveal the Top Secret purpose of Lady North's mission in her defense. I have no choice but to limit your responsibilities if you remain married to her. Perhaps," he concluded with a smile, tossing down his napkin, "an out of the way posting in South America can be arranged."

By the time they met, Lord and Lady North were ready for a quick dispassionate settlement. Sadly, he acknowledged that he adored her but could not allow his career to be tainted by such scandal with the British Empire at stake. Secretly pleased, she sadly acknowledged his position but confessed she could not apologize for doing what was necessary to aid her own country's cause. In the end, they quietly agreed to a formal separation. She would remain in the Georgetown house her father had given them as a wedding present while he would change his U.S. residence to the Mayflower

Hotel. Both agreed to the simple stipulation of further legal arrangements after the war.

During her next tryst with Harold in the Georgetown house's guest bedroom (still her choice for afternoon callers), they were cuddling naked and amiable in post-coital leisure under a sweaty bed sheet and sharing a cigarette when she requested a State Department assignment working undercover in the Far East.

"No can do."

"I can make you a eunuch," she half-jovially threatened.

"Or you can make me proud by volunteering to help take Hitler down."

"I want Japs!"

"You'll never pass the physical."

"For Hank!" she grunted angrily, wrapping herself in the sheet and rolling from the bed. She stomped to the toilet, leaving him naked and coverless in the rumpled bed, smoking. He waited. When she finished at the toilet, she returned to the bedroom but sat in a chair, the sheet still tight around her. He handed her the cigarette and padded barefoot and naked to the toilet.

"Hitler's out of control," he said as he finished. "Taking down the Japs means nothing if Hitler is still left when we finish."

"Fuck Hitler," she said with quiet rage, crushing out the cigarette. "Somebody's got to get back at the Japs for Hank."

Harold turned, walked to the dresser, took a thick file folder from his briefcase, walked to her, handed her the file and stood naked in front of her.

She took the file, looked up at him, looked down at the quarter-inch thick file and studied it. TOP SECRET was stamped in two-inch letters across the front. She turned back the cover. It was a stack of cablegram typescripts, hole-punched and clipped together by brass fasteners. She paged through. In chronological order, the cablegrams all originated at the same place.

"GHQ is General Headquarters. What's SWPA?"

"Southwest Pacific Area. You're looking at reports from the Melbourne office of the Commander-in-Chief of Allied Forces. MacArthur. What's really happening there. Events."

"I'm supposed to read it?"

"January 24, 1942."

She flipped the pages to a cablegram with that date.

"Last paragraph."

She read for a moment and, suddenly, looked up.

"Balikpapan!" she said with a gasp.

"Keep reading."

She looked down, read intently and muttered parts aloud. "Commencing December 8, blah blah, destroyers, transports, destruction of all facilities, wells, tanks, pumping stations, evacuation of personnel…"

"Hank had been flying the families out since before Pearl."

"I know that," she cut in. "Let me read." A moment later she looked up. "Some of these stubborn bastards tried to fight the Japs off!"

"Buying time." He saw terror on her face as she lowered her head and began reading again until she looked up at him again with amazement on her face.

"The worst disaster since Krakatoa?"

"They were trying to blow up and burn it all. So the Japs couldn't use it."

"Finally retreat, blah blah, the jungle…insects…" She was skimming the text. "Hunger…seaplane!" She looked up. Expressionless, he said nothing. She looked down and continued reading. A moment later, she excitedly read aloud. "Novice pilot Henry Wade was making the last runs between Java and the oil workers trapped upriver in the Borneo jungles. Despite reports it was too dangerous to go on, he refused to be grounded." She looked up, a few involuntary tears on her cheek. "He was the last pilot," she told Harold. "He wouldn't leave his companions behind."

"There was a question of adequate fuel. And then the Jap navy opened up on the plane with anti-aircraft fire. Apparently, those oil field men spent a lot of nervous empty time speculating on where an X-32 would have to hit a destroyer to sink it."

She lowered her head and, reading through eyes now flooding with tears, she began mumbling the last paragraphs in the cablegram transcript.

"Without fuel, burning oil and dragging an aileron, he dropped his passengers with rubber rafts and emergency supplies in the South China Sea and swooped back toward the destroyer. He reportedly planned to aim the plane and jump but the survivors on the rafts report he was taking heavy anti-aircraft fire. Most agreed Wade must have been shot. One said he was determined to place the plane's hit on the destroyer precisely."

She looked up at Harold, her eyes streaming with tears.

"Hank got his," Harold said quietly.

She looked at the model airplane on the dressing table across from the bed.

"I can't get you a mission to the Japs," he said. "It won't happen." He waited.

Finally, she looked up at him again with a new grimness in her expression. "Time to talk about Hitler."

*****

"This is ridiculous," Victoria protested as she strode beside Harold along a concrete walkway through streaming throngs of excited baseball fans and patriots. The pale pink brick walls of Cleveland's Municipal Stadium loomed over them and the stirring military march coming from inside set Harold's upbeat pace. He turned into a tunnel marked "Authorized Personnel" and flashed credentials from the inside pocket of his suit coat. When the uniformed guard there eyed Victoria, Harold simply said, "She's with me. Official business." The guard waved them through.

"Ridiculous?" he asked her as they made their way through the mob hurrying to its seats from the refreshment stands. The background was noisy with the chatter of 60,000 fans, the last strains of the military band leaving the field and the public address system announcer asking for the crowd's attention. "Ladies and Gentlemen, the Mickey Cochrane Service All-Stars!"

The stadium throng roared as today's home team took the field.

229

"Ridiculous," she affirmed, walking a step off his shoulder and following his lead around the home plate end of the cavernous stadium walkway and up the third base side.

"Maybe," he said as he noted a specific aisle, walked to the top of it and started down, scanning the fans in the seats below. "But it's the only way you'll be able to get through what you have to get through to do what you have to do."

A young girl in a red, white and blue dancer's leotard and tights approached. "Ticket?" she smiled.

Without a word, he again flashed his credentials and muttered, "Official business." The girl smiled seductively and pressed herself perhaps a little too close to him as she slipped by and up the aisle.

Victoria gave the girl a passing catty glare but turned back to Harold. "How do you even know where she is?" Victoria asked, but Harold was already walking down the aisle toward the field. At the third row, he stopped and tapped the man in the end seat on the shoulder. The man looked up.

"Of course," Victoria muttered as Harold and the coronet-playing leader of Katie Marie's band greeted each other and shook hands.

As Katie Marie looked up, the public address announcer's voice blared.

"Ladies and Gentlemen! Today's starting pitcher for the Service All-Stars, Bob 'Rapid Robert' Feller!"

Katie Marie's attention turned back to the field and she joined in as the crowd set the stadium rolling with a thunderous ovation for Cleveland's young pitching hero, among the first Major Leaguers to join the service after December 7th. On the field, Feller trotted out and began taking his final warm-up pitches while the players around him prepared to do their work.

Katie Marie looked up again, then jumped up and, leaning across the bandleader and Harold, hugged Victoria. "Hellfire and damnation!" She said loudly. "It looks like a GREAT day for baseball!"

"Down in front!" Someone behind them protested. A chorus of agreement followed.

Katie Marie sat down. Seeing no empty seats among the overflowing stadium's boxes, Harold squatted between Katie Marie and the bandleader. "Can you go get some hotdogs and beer?" He asked the bandleader.

With a deference indicating he knew his role in this operation, the man immediately vacated his seat. Harold waved for Victoria to sit as the bandleader disappeared up the aisle.

As Victoria plopped down, she looked at Katie Marie and grunted, "I didn't have anything to do with this."

Katie Marie looked from Victoria to Harold. She did not try to reply to Victoria over the noise of the public address system but simply studied Harold. He looked back at her with calm serious eyes.

"LADIES AND GENTLEMEN!" bellowed the announcer, "leading off for the American League All-Stars, the hero of yesterday's victory over the National League in the Polo Grounds, the manager and shortstop of YOUR Cleveland Indians, Lou Boudreau!"

Another thunderous ovation filled the stadium. Katie Marie looked again toward the field and she cheered vehemently.

Boudreau stepped in and Feller began working to his teammate for the last four years, now his opponent due to Feller's enlistment.

"You must be surprised to see us," Harold said to her.

"Let's just watch the game," she said without turning to him.

"You expected us?"

She glanced at him. "I should have." She turned back to the game, but looked away again between pitches. "We got this Cleveland gig awful easy after that fire in Boston."

There was a groan from the crowd and Katie Marie looked toward the field in time to see Boudreau disappearing into the dugout while the Service All-Stars tossed the ball around the infield. First baseman Johnny Sturm walked it back to Feller.

"Missed it, dammit," Katie Marie muttered. She looked again at Harold as Tommy Heinrich stepped in to hit. As Feller worked, Katie Marie continued to split her attention between the game and Harold. "You could work through my bandleader but not through me?"

"I wasn't sure how it would go," Harold said. "I just wanted to know where you would be. The bandleader thinks he got the Cleveland gig himself. I got him some tickets to an exhibition game, told him I wanted to talk to you about entertaining the troops."

Suddenly there was a crack of bat on ball. Katie Marie pivoted her attention back to the action. Players were moving on the field as Heinrich raced up the first base line. By the time Katie Marie picked up the action, second baseman Benny McCoy was taking the throw from the outfield and Heinrich was trotting back to first base with a single.

"Looks like Feller's wild with the heater," Katie Marie told Harold. "He'll have to work harder to Williams."

She focused on the game. Harold watched her. Victoria, confused, uneasy and disinterested, watched all of it like a farce she did not want tickets to. "I didn't know you were such a big baseball fan," she said disinterestedly to Katie Marie. "I'll have to introduce you to Judge Landis sometime. He and my grandfather became friends during the disputes about the Standard Oil Trust."

Feller was taking time working to Ted Williams, missing with his best pitches to the famously disciplined hitter.

Katie Marie looked at Victoria. "Do you know DiMaggio?"

Victoria looked back hard at her friend, knowing she was being teased. Then she smiled. "No, but give me a few days. I'm sure I can arrange an introduction."

Katie Marie smiled and there was now warmth between them again. They heard a loud "Ball Four!" from the umpire and Katie Marie looked back at the field to see Williams tossing away his bat and trotting up the first base line.

A murmur rolled through the crowd as the New York Yankee in the on-deck circle stood from his kneeling position and swung three bats around and around. "Now batting for the American League," blared the loudspeaker, "the Yankee Clipper, centerfielder 'Joltin' Joe DiMaggio!" The crowd's murmur broke into a huge roar that broke into an ovation for the man who just the year before had set a major league record by hitting in 56 consecutive games, only to be stopped in this very stadium game in front of these very fans who now, as then, honored him with their resounding applause. He stepped to the plate.

"That's DiMaggio!" exclaimed Katie Marie. "This is what I came to see!"

"He's handsome," Victoria remarked.

Katie Marie turned to Victoria. "Did you know that after they broke his streak he came back the next day and started another one that went on 15 MORE games?" she proudly asked.

"That must be good," Victoria smiled.

DiMaggio, not as patient a hitter as Williams, quickly lashed at a poorly placed fastball. At the crack of the bat, the crowd came to its feet with a roar and the outfielders were on the run. By the time the dust settled, Heinrich was home with the All-Stars' first run, Williams was standing on third and DiMaggio was returning to first after rounding the bag.

"Alright!" Katie Marie exclaimed gleefully, not sitting as the other fans did but turning to pick up her handbag. She looked at Harold, who had returned to his squat, and Victoria, who was again in the bandleader's seat. She turned to them, ready to leave. They looked up at her quizzically. "What?" She asked. "That's what I came to see. You know as well as I do that Joltin' Joe and the Splinter will be in the service, playing on the same side as Feller by next season. I just wanted to see them hit against him one more time before the war ends it all. Now come on." With that, she pushed past them and started up the aisle. "There's a war on!"

As they stood to follow her, Victoria looked at Harold, who was grinning an I-told-you-so. "You talked to her already!" she protested. He shook his head 'no' with a grimmer, more serious smile.

"Come on," he said, following Katie Marie up the aisle.

Victoria shook her head and followed, muttering to herself. "The ballplayers want at him. Katie Marie wants at him. This guy Hitler has no idea what he's got himself into."

*****

On Janurary 14, 1942, Kenesaw Mountain Landis wrote to President Roosevelt, addressing the question of baseball's place in a war-torn world.

233

As a federal judge he had in 1911 fearlessly ruled against John D. Rockefeller and the Standard Oil monopoly. As the newly appointed Commissioner of Baseball he had in 1920 unhesitatingly restored the game's integrity in the wake of the Black Sox scandal, dealing quickly and harshly with the taint of gambling. On this question, he was equally forthright:

...inasmuch as these are not ordinary times, I venture to ask what you have in
  mind as to whether professional baseball should continue to operate...

...Health and strength to you--and whatever it takes to do this job...Very truly
  yours...

The next day, President Roosevelt replied with what has since become known as the "Green Light Letter:"

...I honestly feel that it would be best for the country to keep baseball going.
  There will be fewer people unemployed and everybody will work longer
  hours and harder than ever before...And that means that they ought to have a
  chance for recreation and for taking their minds off their work...Baseball
  provides a recreation which does not last over two hours or two hours and a
  half and which can be got for very little cost. And, incidentally, I hope that
  night games can be extended because it gives an opportunity to the day shift
  to see a game occasionally...individual players who are of active military or
  naval age should go, without question, into the services...Very sincerely yours...

To the joy of those driving the prodigious effort on the home front, anything the game lost in quality during the war years it more than made up for with zest and inventiveness. Reports in newspapers and newsreels about their favorite athletes and entertainers going into service both comforted and sobered the public. 'There's a war on' suddenly became a phrase as ubiquitous in America as it had been for two years in Europe. Meanwhile, the game brought distraction, rest and recuperation, buoying spirits on the war-weary home front. Watching it and playing it truly became a more national pastime. Both players and fans became newly diverse.

With the innovation of a women's professional league, females newly liberated by their dominating numbers and vital roles in the workforce took a new, enthusiastic interest in seeing their sisters compete. Male civilians and soldiers on leave did not strongly object to watching women compete in short skirts and knee socks. Perhaps the highest quality baseball available during the early war years was found in the Negro big leagues, which reached the pinnacle of their success thanks to the discriminatory practices of the United States military and the absence of top talent in the still segregated Majors.

Even Major League Baseball became innovative and more diverse. Teams played patriotic fund-raising exhibition games against Service All-Star teams and hosted bond drive entertainments, raising impressive amounts for war bonds, for war-related charities and for the Ball and Bat Fund to provide baseball equipment to soldiers across the globe. The Leagues also expanded the night game schedule, as the President had suggested, making the games more available to war-workers. And the St. Louis Browns inspired the country's handicapped and war-wounded when they played Pete Gray, a one-armed outfielder who could hit major league pitching. Perhaps even more inspiring was the perennial ner-do-well Browns' astonishing American League championship season of 1944, proving to fans everywhere that in this war literally anything was possible.

*****

On a northbound train, Victoria and Katie Marie sat in the lounge car, nursing brandies and sharing a cigarette. Victoria stared out the window as the train passed through dense green summer forest. Katie Marie read a newspaper.

"They keep talking about North Africa but they still haven't done anything about it," Katie Marie said.

"What are you reading?"

"The Trib."

"You expect to find anything out from the Chicago Daily Tribune? They barely know who's President."

"Sorry," Katie Marie laughed. "I couldn't get the society page of the Washington Post."

"You wouldn't look for war news on the society page," Victoria snapped back lightly. "Just the important news."

"Starring you, of course."

"Of course."

"You think we did any good?" She glanced around the car. Nobody was sitting nearby or paying attention to them. "With that, uh, job we did for them."

Victoria double-checked for listeners. An elderly couple was in a pair of observation seats at the other end of the bar, he sleeping and she watching the forest go by. A bartender was restocking behind the bar near the elderly couple. Two grandmothers sat in a window booth nearer, both with martini glasses and knitting on the table between them, chatting. There was a kindness and calmness in the older women's demeanor, an acceptance of time and travel, that Victoria—facing an immediate challenging unknown and a dangerous unknown beyond that—did not feel.

Getting no reply, Katie Marie looked up. "Vic?"

"Time will tell," Victoria finally answered without looking away from the older women.

Katie Marie followed her gaze. "You think that will ever be us?"

"Time will tell."

"And war."

"That too."

At a middle-of-nowhere station in hot, sweaty farmland, they climbed down from the train and looked around.

"Are you sure?" Katie Marie asked. Victoria set down her suitcase and makeup case and looked around without answering while Katie Marie watched her. Inside the one-room, one-bench station, the pale wrinkled clerk behind the ticket window stopped his paper shuffling and stared at them without saying a word. Victoria finally turned to Katie Marie, who repeated her question. "Are you sure?"

Victoria frowned at her, still not answering.

"They're testing us," Katie Marie finally suggested. "What if this was the middle of nowhere in the middle of a war and we were on assignment to someplace strange where we'd never been?"

Victoria stared at her. "That's exactly what this is."

"True," Katie Marie shrugged.

At the sound of an approaching vehicle, both turned toward the far end of the platform. A rusty, dented Ford pick-up truck drove down the barely paved country road to the station and stopped, its engine still running. Both women cautiously approached it, leaned and peered through the passenger window. A sturdy, barrel-chested, middle-aged man with thin, graying, closely cropped hair in a plaid shirt and a worn corduroy jacket sat behind the wheel. He bent his head and looked out at them. "Lady North and Mrs. Livingstone?" he asked in a gravelly voice.

"Us," Katie Marie affirmed while Victoria eyed him dubiously.

"Good," he smiled toothily, a gold front tooth gleaming conspicuously. "I'm Colonel Williams, your commanding officer and training instructor. Stow your suitcases in back and climb in. This is your limousine."

An hour-long torment of a bumpy, dusty, sweaty ride on a rundown highway crowded into the pickup's cab followed. Colonel Williams briefly explained he was their commanding officer in a conditioning and training program that included two other pairs of women a few days ahead of them in preparation for other European missions. The women would be introduced to them only by codenames and they would be known to the other women the same way, Victoria as Ladyleader and Katie Marie as Songbird. They would train and condition together but have separate planning sessions.

He turned onto a worse gravel road and, out of sight of the highway, he turned into a dirt driveway, passed through an open rusty gateway opening in an ancient, falling down fence and drove up to a cluster of unpainted wood structures. After he stopped the truck and climbed out, he stood by the cab and waited for them. Once again, he warned them against discussing their mission with the other groups during training.

So busy looking around at the dilapidated buildings and other structures, Katie Marie paid him no attention. "What the hell is this place?"

"We call it Camp X," Williams said.

"If I didn't know we were in the-middle-of-nowhere Ontario, I'd say it was an old oil refinery."

"You would be right," Colonel Williams told her. "You can get your baggage out of the back of the truck and take it in there," he told them.

"In Canada?" Katie Marie asked.

"One of the first big places for oil," Williams said. "Back in the 1840s and '50s."

"And you're using it for a training camp?" Katie Marie asked.

He looked at her. "YOU'RE using it for a training camp."

"What exactly does Secretary Harold think we need to learn here?" Victoria asked with a bemused sneer as she lifted her suitcase and makeup kit from the truck's bed.

Colonel Williams walked around the front of the truck and stood one step up on the splintery front porch at the front of the house. He stared at Victoria intimidatingly, not answering. Victoria turned toward the house, saw the Colonel staring at her, stood and returned his stare.

After getting her bags, Katie Marie turned and saw the face-off. "Come on, Ladyleader," she urged in an attempt to break the intensity. "There's always something to learn."

Before she finished the sentence, Williams spoke out as if she was not talking. "You're insubordinate," he told Victoria, his gold front tooth flashing. "We'll start you on the endurance course."

He pivoted and walked into the house. They followed Williams inside, through a big front sitting room and down a hallway. Katie Marie angrily whispered to Victoria to be polite and keep her mouth closed until they knew more. Meanwhile, the Colonel explained the house was once living quarters for men who ran the refinery. Williams stopped halfway down the hall, turned to them and pointed to a door. "That's your room."

"Both of us?" Victoria asked irritably.

Once again, he just stared at her, without answering, until finally he stated his reply as if it was a considered and definite conclusion. "You'll get used to

238

it." He immediately pivoted and disappeared into a doorway at the end of the hall. "Supper in 30 minutes," he called back.

Over a hot meal of simple food, they met the other four women in the program and exchanged codenames. Colonel Williams allowed little other conversation. They were younger women, in their twenties and early thirties. A shaggy-haired, bright-eyed, smiling blond named Playrunner and a small, wiry, blue-eyed, thoughtful-looking, raven-haired girl named Bluestar made up one team. The other pair, Typewriter and Farmgirl, were taller brunettes, heavier in the chest and buttocks, who looked like sturdy girls accustomed to office or indoor work, Typewriter with a slightly blank expression and Farmgirl with a permanent scowl. Williams' restriction on conversation did not stop them from moaning about their soreness from training or groaning when they were told the next day's training would begin with the endurance course.

After kitchen cleanup, the work weary women retired in teams into the two other bedrooms along the hall. Travel weary, Ladyleader and Songbird seized the opportunity to fall onto thin twin-bed mattresses and wrap themselves in rough army sleeping bags. They slept soundly.

Williams roused them at sunrise, moving up and down the hall pounding on the three bedroom doors, chanting gleefully. "WHEN I'M UP, EVERYBODY'S UP!" On his second round of the rooms, he added "SUMMER FATIGUES AND HIKING BOOTS!" to the chant. He allowed them toilet and ablution time while he doled out daywear to Katie Marie and Victoria in prearranged sizes. After a communal breakfast, he had the six trainees line up in early morning 80 degree, 90 percent humidity heat. He handed out twenty pound canvas knapsacks and canteens and set them marching.

They started with a brisk loop around the cluster of broken down refinery buildings. Katie Marie studied them as they walked. "What the hell?" she exclaimed at the sight of huge cylindrical structures.

"Old style storage tanks," Victoria told her, walking easily.

Katie Marie pointed at a long low building with tall metal tanks poking up through the shingle roof from inside and pipes running into it at both ends. "Some kind of factory?"

"That's where they did the cooking," Victoria told her. "They turned the raw crude into different grades of oil and then made everything from lubrication to airplane fuel, depending on the grade they used. Even vaseline."

"And chewing gum," Williams curtly interrupted. "You're quite the expert, aren't you Ladyleader?" he asked snidely.

"My family," she began to explain.

"Save your wind for walking," he cut her off.

He led them out the dirt driveway and up the rutted gravel farm road through lush green pastureland.

"Hey, Colonel," Katie Marie grunted an hour later, sweating and breathing hard as the road went up over a rise. "How 'bout we stop for a smoke?" Next in line behind her, Victoria laughed.

"Keep moving!" yelled the sturdy Colonel from the head of the column where he was leading at a vigorous pace. "Move. Move. Move," he called, keeping the trainees moving as he dropped back to Katie Marie and Victoria at the end of the line. "Anybody else makes a suggestion," he yelled as they passed, "and we go double time!" He drew even with Katie Marie and Victoria. "You're trainin'!" He said threateningly.

"We're going in under diplomatic cover," Victoria protested with frank disrespect. "Not on foot."

"You don't pass my endurance course, you're goin' home!"

"Colonel, you're killin' me," Katie Marie interrupted. "You're makin' me carry a full canteen, the least you could do is let me stop for a little water."

"Drink on the march!"

"And a smoke," Katie Marie added with a mischievous grin.

"Smoking ruins your wind!" He started to walk off.

"But sweat ruins my make-up," Victoria remarked dryly.

He turned to her. "You may go in as a diplomat's girlfriend," he said moving closer to her. "But you may not get out unless you master what I'm here to teach you. Men I trained may have to go in to get you." He stepped very near her and talked right into her face, his gold tooth gleaming. "AND I'M NOT LOSIN' THEM BECAUSE YOU THINK YOU'RE TOO GOOD TO TRAIN. DO YOU HEAR ME?"

Unfazed, Victoria smiled. "So you want me in the same condition as you and the men you train?"

"That's right."

"I'll race you back to the bunkhouse. Winner decides what we do the rest of the day."

Groans came from Typewriter and Farmgirl, marching in the middle of the line behind Bluestar and Playrunner. "Keep your pace!" Williams ordered them, then turned to Victoria and smiled. "You're givin' me nothin' for winnin' – I already decide what we do around here."

"No more questions from me if you win. How's that?"

"Hard way or easy way, you're going to learn not to mess with me."

"Why?"

From in front of her, Typewriter groaned again. "Just shut up!"

"This training is tough enough," a scowling Farmgirl blurted out, "without you making trouble."

"All the more reason for me to win us an afternoon off," grinned Victoria.

"Keep your mouth shut and march," Farmgirl snapped back angrily.

"Farmgirl's right," grinned Colonel Williams, stepping nearer Victoria. "I'm liable to get really nasty if you push me." He continued to march near her and stared at her challengingly.

"Just ignore her," Katie Marie interrupted. "You're gonna really like her when you get to know her."

"Race me, Williams," Victoria smiled, returning the challenge.

"You really want to do this?" Katie Marie asked Victoria.

"Don't you want the afternoon off?" Victoria answered, returning Williams' stare.

"You make me beat you, I make you pay," Williams said to Victoria quietly.

"You afraid, Williams?"

He gritted his teeth, stared at her, then suddenly exploded. "Go!" He pivoted and burst into a run. Caught off guard, Victoria nevertheless quickly hit her stride and stayed just behind him as they disappeared up over the rise, heading for the house.

With groans and whining, the other two teams turned and followed, walking. Katie Marie started with them but, spotting a stump near a pair of small boulders, she walked to it and sat with a grunt, dropped her knapsack at her feet and started to open her canteen.

"Hey!" she called to the others. They stopped and turned to her. "What's your hurry?" She took a gulp from the canteen, looked at them and smiled grimly. "This may be our best chance for downtime the rest of the day."

They stared at her in silence until Playrunner shrugged. "Right." She and Bluestar plopped down on the stump with her and reached for their canteens. Typewriter and Farmgirl exchanged questioning expressions, shrugged and plopped down on the boulders. Soon, they were chatting about the day, the hike, the weather, still avoiding the secrets they had been ordered to keep. But a scowling Farmgirl said little and watched Katie Marie too vigilantly. Finally, Katie Marie tired of it.

"Clearly you are furious with my partner."

"What is wrong with her?" Farmgirl finally blurted out.

"Yeah," agreed Typewriter. "You seem OK. But she's got a real chip on her shoulder."

"It's like she's so desperate to prove herself she's trying to do the impossible," said Bluestar.

Katie Marie watched them watch her as she tried to figure out how to explain Victoria without revealing the secrets she had been ordered to keep. "She lost somebody in the Pacific," Katie Marie finally said.

"So did I," said Playrunner.

"I've got somebody there now," Farmgirl chimed in, her scowl deepening. "Nobody knows if he's alive or not."

"I've got two in Iceland, training to go into Europe," said Bluestar.

"Look," Typewriter said to Katie Marie. "Everybody's in this together and we all know the only way out is winning it. That's what makes your partner's attitude so hard to take."

Katie Marie looked around at them. "I know," she finally said. "But Ladyleader is just a different kind of a girl. Give her a chance."

"Yeah, well," said Farmgirl after downing a swallow from her canteen and standing up. "First she's going to have to give me a chance to get through this training."

Bluestar stood up beside her. "Let's get back to the house and see how she takes getting left in the dust of an old man."

"Yeah," said Playrunner after a long swallow from her canteen. "Maybe she'll surprise us and eat crow."

"Well," shrugged Katie Marie, standing up with them. "I guarantee you she's always good for a surprise."

When they got back to the house, the pickup truck was gone and Victoria, gleaming from the bath, was lounging on the porch with a pitcher of iced tea and five extra glasses.

"See what I mean about surprises," Katie Marie told them as they gathered around Victoria, gulped the ice tea and learned she had won them the afternoon off. With grudging respect, they congratulated her while Katie Marie sat by, grinning and silently gloating. Soon, warming to the reward Victoria had won them, the other two teams scurried into the house to indulge in baths, a big lunch and an afternoon of catnapping. Victoria and Katie Marie sat in the shade together and quietly sipped ice tea until Katie Marie decided to go in and clean up.

"Did you eat?" she asked Victoria.

Victoria shook her head 'no.'

"Not hungry?"

"Got overheated," Victoria said. "Threw everything up. Waiting for my stomach to settle."

Katie Marie stepped to her and stroked her still damp hair. "You make it look easy."

"Don't let them see you sweat."

"But it's not easy."

"No," said Victoria, looking up at her. "But you know what? I like making my way on something besides whose wife I am."

"I know the feeling," agreed Katie Marie.

 Williams did not return until after the six women ate supper and turned in that night. But the next morning, he waked them again with loud knocking and an even more obnoxiously cocky "WHEN I'M UP, EVERYBODY'S UP!" chant, as if he had a new and more delightful plan.

After breakfast he announced they would be doing firearms training. Carrying a pistol and a knapsack, he led them beyond the dilapidated refinery buildings and splintery holding tanks to a makeshift firing range. A bullet-riddled paper bull's-eye target was tied to hay bales across twenty paces of dust and weed. Victoria showed disdainful disinterest as he explained the mechanics of the .38 revolver to the trainees. He demonstrated how to open and load the cylinder and how to aim. Finally, he took a new target from the knapsack, had Farmgirl tie it to the hay bales and, aiming carefully, he emptied the gun into the target, the loud cracks of the weapon announcing hits just above and outside the center ring six straight times.

The other women were impressed. "You make it look easy," Typewriter told him as he reloaded the pistol.

Victoria laughed. "I can do more harm with my lipstick."

The women laughed but Williams did not. "So you want to challenge me again?"

"I don't want to hurt your feelings."

"You know how to shoot?"

"It doesn't look too hard."

He reloaded the pistol and held it out to her, butt first. "Want to show us how it's done?" He turned to the other women. "Always hand over a pistol like this," he lectured. "Never like this." He flipped it around on his finger and pointed it at Victoria. "It might be loaded." He raised it and fired a loud "crack" over her shoulder, into an empty field. The women beside and behind him recoiled at the noise and the intimidation. "Accidents can happen." The other four trainees watched in silent anticipation of more trouble. Katie Marie muttered "Son of a bitch" in almost silent fury. Williams snapped back the catch and flipped open the .38's chamber, replaced the fired cartridge, firmly closed it and snapped the catch, rolled the cylinder, again spun the pistol around his finger and held it out to Victoria butt first. "Show us."

Showing no nervousness, she stared at him and smiled. "You're the trainer."

His return smile was unflinching. "I insist."

She looked at the trainees, who watched with trepidation. She finally took the pistol. She weighed it in her hand, looked toward the target, hestitated, then quickly raised the gun and shot once. At the loud crack, everyone looked to the target. From their distance, they could see a new bullet hole near the centerline but at the very top edge of the target.

"I guess it's not as easy as it looks," Katie Marie blurted out nervously.

"No," Williams smiled gloatingly. "But that's not bad shooting." He reached for the gun.

"Yes it is!" Victoria grunted, snatching the gun away from him and studying it. "Oh," she said quickly. "I see." She looked at Williams. "It's off line high." She raised it again and shot again at the target, five rapid, resounding cracks without pauses, then turned to him, spun the gun on her finger and handed it to him butt first.

The trainees studied the target. "Four, Five!" exclaimed Bluestar. "Five holes inside the bull's-eye at the top!"

As he snatched the pistol away, Victoria added, "It fires high and you're used to it."

Their eyes met and, once again, held. "Good," he finally concluded without resentment. He turned, picked up the knapsack and handed it to Victoria. "Divvie up the rounds in here," he said to her. "I want each one," he nodded toward the other trainees, "to know the weapon." He turned and started to walk away as the women watched him in astonishment. "When you finish," he called back over his shoulder, "take the rest of the afternoon off." He did not stop walking until he disappeared beyond the refinery and tanks. While the six women were looking around at one another, trying to grasp the new pecking order, they heard the pick-up truck start up and drive away.

"Well," said Victoria, seeing the others' surprise, "You heard the man. Who's first?"

She told Bluestar to divide the rounds in the knapsack and, meanwhile, began coaching each of the women through some work with the pistol. She explained her knowledge and skill by talking about experience with hunting and range weapons, but she was careful not to reveal personal information. She was a good trainer and they picked up the rudiments of shooting quickly. When they expended their rounds, they broke for lunch, then spent the afternoon in their familiar pairs. It was quiet and restful. Once again Williams did not return until they had eaten supper and gone to bed.

He roused them the next morning with the familiar loud knocking and "When I'm up, everybody's up" chant, but as they finished eating breakfast he made an announcement. "From now on," he told them," "your mornings will be routine: a training hike and a session at the shooting range. Then you will return here for lunch. After lunch, you'll clean up and take a rest. At 1500 hours everyday, we sit again, here in the kitchen, for table work."

"Table work?" Katie Marie asked.

He frowned at her. "1500 hours," he repeated. "You're going to learn what you need to know to do your jobs and stay alive." He stood, put his plate and coffee cup in the sink, started out of the kitchen toward the front of the house but stopped in the doorway and turned to them. "One more thing: Ladyleader is in charge." He pivoted and, in the shocked silence of the kitchen, they heard his footsteps down the hall and out the door, they heard the screen door slam behind him, his steps on the gravel out front, the truck start and drive away.

In tense silence, the women finished their breakfast or did their cleanup. All stole secretive glances at their partners and Victoria, wondering what would come next. Victoria, staring into her coffee cup, finally broke the silence. "I'm going to count on you." Now they all stared at her. She looked up, from face to face. "You heard me."

"What are you talking about?" Farmgirl, scowling, asked angrily. "You can't turn this on us. He just put you in the hot seat."

Victoria looked squarely at her. "That's just it. I'm not on the hot seat any more than you are."

"Tell them what you want them to do," Katie Marie suggested.

"No," Victoria replied. "They know what to do. They do it because their country is counting on them or there's no point."

"She's right," Bluestar interrupted. "That's the difference between this country and the ones we're fighting."

"Yeah," agreed Playrunner. "Fascists order their people around. The whole idea of this country is that we do for ourselves."

"I got you," said Typewriter. "First things first. Clean up the kitchen. Then line up for the hike." She looked at Victoria. "Right?"

Victoria smiled. "You got it." She looked at Farmgirl.

Without a hint of change to her scowl, Farmgirl looked back at her and finally said, "How long 'til you want us lined up out front?"

Victoria looked squarely at her. "How long will it take you?"

Farmgirl looked out a kitchen window and thought, scowling. Finally, she looked back at Victoria, a hint of a grim smile breaking into her scowl. "Ten minutes?"

Victoria smiled. "Ten minutes sounds right to me."

From that afternoon, Williams gave daily two-hour instruction sessions covering a wide range of subjects. He taught them how to pick locks and how to piece together bits of paper from trash cans and how to interpret what they found. He introduced them to a small camera and discussed how to take pictures without being noticed, describing tricks like posing as tourists or snapping a picture of something important as the camera was being put away after clicking an irrelevant photo. One afternoon, Williams brought in train schedule pamphlets from cities all over the world and they spent the time comparing and interpreting them, readying themselves to grab a train quickly anywhere. He used an afternoon to talk about improvising weapons, discussing the rolling of a knife from newspaper, the filing of a toothbrush into a shiv and using a cake of soap in a sock as a club. He discussed bomb making with them, and pointed out things they could buy in grocery stores or drug stores or feed stores that could be combined into potent explosives. He talked about foreign languages, how to pick them up, how to fake them, how to avoid using them by acting unconscious or shell-shocked or just by tying your head up in a scarf like you had a terrible toothache and it hurt too much to talk.

For several days, he showed them photos of factories and explained how to identify what they manufactured, regardless of what the sign in front said. He taught them how to evaluate a factory's level of productivity by studying the traffic and trash. At the conclusion of this part of the training, he walked them through the grounds of their camp and discussed oil refinery structures in detail. Pointing out an old fashioned cooking tower, he elaborated on modern cracking towers and the flares that burned atop them.

None of the women except Victoria showed any interest in the oil refinery but at the mention of flares, Bluestar interrupted him.

"I heard the underground movements use flares as signals," she said. "Can we contact them?"

He shrugged. "It depends," he said. "Let me show you what the most vulnerable part of a cracking tower is." He glanced around and saw by their expressions they were suddenly dubious because he was avoiding the question about underground contacts. "You'll know what you need to know when you need to know it," he told them with grim honesty. They groaned in unison. "And if you're wondering how I know so much about the oil industry," he went on, smiling as he again obviously changed the subject, his gold tooth shining in the sun, "it's because I grew up in California's central valley, one of the biggest oil fields in the world."

"Do we really need to know that?" Katie Marie asked.

"You never know," he grinned. "Now about this tower."

They showed more interest when, during the next few afternoons, he went over short wave radios in detail. With a standard suitcase-size kit, he showed them how to operate the radio, discussed circuitry and showed them how to replace fuses and wiring. He talked about operating schedules and placement for optimum signal reception. He showed them how to send and receive in Morse code. He spent an entire session on codes and, finally, he conducted a series of hands-on sessions in which he had them work extensively with the radio, sending, receiving and translating coded messages.

Williams regularly ended the afternoon sessions between 1700 and 1800 hours and asked them to rehash the material covered while preparing and

248

eating the evening meal. This led to lively discussions and wild speculations among the trainees. After supper and cleanup, they were free. They shared the few newspapers and periodicals around the house and chatted about the (mostly grim) world events of the day. They also had access to the house radio in the evenings and often gathered around it for programs from Chicago, Detroit, Cleveland or Buffalo that offered primarily audience-soothing big band music, serialized melodrama and silly episodic comedy. They fell into an early-to-bed, early-to-rise, hard working, wearying routine.

Five weeks into the training, as they settled down to a table session one afternoon, Williams noticed more whining and griping than usual. First, Typewriter nagged at Farmgirl about hair in the bathtub drain, then Farmgirl complained about the loudness of Katie Marie's big band music on the radio. That set Katie Marie off on Playrunner for breadcrumbs in the toaster. "What the hell is going on?" he whispered to Victoria as he sat at the kitchen table.

"There you go with your damn secrets!" Bluestar exploded.

He turned to her. "What?"

Sensing an important confrontation, Farmgirl snapped the radio off with a sidewise triumphant glance at Katie Marie, who looked away. She saw Playrunner watching them and angrily swept breadcrumbs near the toaster off the kitchen counter onto the floor.

"Here's a secret for you," Bluestar went on loudly and angrily at Williams. "Time is slipping by, the war is not going well and we aren't in it!"

He stared at her for a moment without replying until, suddenly, he dropped a heavy hand flat and hard on the table with a loud thwack. They all now stared at him. "Time for hand-to-hand combat training. Outside, let's go!"

Without waiting for a response, he was up and out the backdoor. Shrugging at one another, they followed, Typewriter reminding Farmgirl in an angry whisper "for the last time" to clear her hair from the bathtub drain.

He led them to a small yard on the shady side of the house, walked to the middle of the grassy patch and, with a sweep of his arm, gathered them around him. "Nobody expects you to go toe to toe with a soldier or a cop," he began. "But there are things you can do, no matter the difference in size and strength, to get yourself out of a fix. First, some basics." He worked them through stance and hand/arm positions, then talked about body position and movement. Next, he showed them how to fall, with a roll, and put them to work doing somersaults onto the grass from a moving start.

After a while, he stood them up, introduced basic punching and kicking techniques and started drilling them. Katie Marie and Bluestar, the two smallest in the group, felt graceless making the unaccustomedly aggressive movements. They started to giggle with each other and clown. He stopped and looked sternly at them but spoke quietly and sincerely. "This is serious. You've got to learn these basics before you can learn the variations that will work on somebody much bigger than you. Do you understand?" They nodded 'yes' at his unusual frankness and the session went on with quiet purposefulness. As evening came, he announced they would end by beginning Fairburn judo.

"That Jap stuff?" Farmgirl asked.

"A system designed by a military trainer from Oriental martial arts," he said. "It's a combination of wrestling and self-defense designed for easy mastery of survival street fighting."

"Dirty tricks?" Katie Marie asked.

"Exactly," he smiled. "First, elbows and knees."

He showed them a series of knee and elbow close-quarters blows and had them practice each one repeatedly. When they were sweating from concentrated effort, he called a halt to the session. Having released some of their pent-up aggression, the bickering diminished and they settled into their normal evening. They continued to train, the afternoon sessions now split between table work and fighting drills.

Late one afternoon a week later, as they were about to leave the table session in the kitchen at the rear of the house for the fighting drill in the side yard, they heard someone come in at the front door. Steps came down the hallway toward them.

"Who could that be?" Bluestar began to ask, looking at Williams, but he slashed a finger across his throat to cut her off and raised his hands up, palms outward, in a sign of 'stop' to all of them, then waved them into their seats. All looked to the hall doorway. LeClair Harold walked in, wearing a wrinkled summer suit and tie.

Before Katie Marie or Victoria could greet him, they heard the women around them exclaim.

250

First, Farmgirl. "Mr. Assistant Secretary!" And Typewriter. "Mr. Harold!" Then, Bluestar. "Sir!" And, finally, Playrunner. "Harold!" The four women immediately turned to one another in surprise and began discussing the fact that they all knew him and then suddenly stopped talking, realizing they might be revealing something they should not. During this chatter, Williams watched Victoria and Katie Marie sit silently, suppressing quizzical expressions not only about Harold's arrival but about the obvious fact that he had recruited the others as well as themselves.

Harold stood before them, expressionless. When the room fell silent, he spoke through a restrained, impatient smile. "That you all eventually realized you must restrain yourselves suggests you MIGHT survive a similar but more dangerous situation. What do you think, Williams?"

"I think these four are dead," Williams grunted with a wave of his hand at the four women who spoke. "And probably took the other two with them," he concluded, standing.

The women were now somber.

"We're about to move to the Fairburn training," Williams told Harold. "Want to watch?"

"I am here to observe," Harold nodded.

Harold following, Williams led the chastened trainees into the grassy side yard. "Now pay attention," Williams began. "This is the heart of Fairburn's technique." They gathered around him, nervously glancing at Harold, who stood off to the side, silently watching, arms folded over his chest. "Most hand-to-hand breaks down into grappling and wrestling pretty fast," Williams lectured. "Here, Farmgirl. C'mere. You're on assignment. I'm a cop. I grab you. You can't let me take you."

He grabbed her arm. She pulled away. "No!" he grunted. He easily pulled her back to himself, grabbed her with both hands and pulled her down onto his up thrusting knee.

"Oof!" She ejaculated as his knee hit her gut. "Hey!" she protested.

He let her go. "Mistake number one and you won't make it again," he said to her. He looked at the rest of them. "You don't pull away. That's what he's expecting. You come in. Hard. Use your knee before he uses his."

Farmgirl backed away, rubbing her cramped gut.

"Once you are on the offensive," Williams went on, pursuing her, grabbing her and delivering mock blows, "you've got your elbow, another knee, another elbow, a kick to the shin or the thigh. You don't stop coming until he can't fight back!"

"O.K., I got it!" Farmgirl said angrily.

He let her go and smiled as she backed away toward the group. "Good. Break up into pairs and go over that response. One grabs, the other comes in, attacking. Then trade off. Everybody does it twice. Let's go." They did as told and practiced while he walked over to Harold and talked with him quietly. A few minutes later, he went back to the center of the yard and called the trainees together again.

"O.K., another one. Ladyleader." Looking at him suspiciously, Victoria stepped forward. "A cop grabs you," he began, walking around behind her. With a sudden lurch, he wrapped both arms around her, bear hugged her and lifted her off the ground. "Now what?"

She wriggled and twisted. He squeezed harder. In helpless frustration, she writhed frantically. He laughed. "No!" She screamed in rage and lifted a foot back hard, heel up, into his groin.

"Ugh!" he groaned, going to one knee in pain.

Her feet hit the ground and she was about to pull away from his reach when, from behind her, he grabbed her crotch and pulled up and back violently. She screamed, whirled and lashed out at his face with her fingernails. It was now a sudden, brutal, vicious and very real fight, all the smoldering hostility between them exploding in hand-to-hand violence. She swung her other hand at his face, going across his face for his eyes with her fingers and nails. Still on his knees, he roared in pain, pulled up on her crotch harder, then drove the heel of his other hand into her lower abdomen. She folded and fell to the ground.

He came up over her, ready to fall on her with blows as she curled defensively, screamed again and rolled, attempting to get away. As he came down on her, she raised a knee and fended him off to the side. As he regained his balance and advanced again, the other women came alive, attacking Williams almost as one, screaming epithets and reigning down a furious flurry of raging fists and kicks, allowing Victoria to roll away.

At that, Harold stepped in, shouting "Stand down! Stand down!" He pulled the women away from Williams, who was curled into a self-protective ball. Harold was finally able to stop their attack, though the women continued shouting both at him and Williams. Stepping between the trainees and Williams, he shouted for the women to see to Victoria, quieting them.

As the women gathered around her, Victoria rose to a seated postion and looked at Harold, fire in her eyes. "What kind of animal do you have training us!?!" She demanded.

Standing over Williams, Harold studied Victoria without replying until he finally said enigmatically, "What kind?" He then looked down at the trainer, who now sat up.

All eyes fell on Williams and there was an intent silence. He wiped blood from the scratches on his cheek, looked at it on his hand, and then looked at Victoria as he rubbed the blood between his fingertips. Finally, he looked up at Harold. "Yes," he said with a smile. "They're ready."

*****

The Naval convoy from South Street to Southhampton, exotic to Katie Marie and others in the party, was nothing new to the well-traveled Victoria. Despite the eminent threat of German U-boat attacks attendant to North Atlantic crossings in December 1942, they arrived without incident in the usual week's time. They sailed to Cairo as part of a military supply flotilla. It might have been dangerous even two months before but the success of the early November Allied assault on North Africa, in which the codes obtained by Victoria and Katie Marie played a central role, had restored any threat to British Naval dominance in the Mediterranean. While Katie Marie was exhilarated by the freedom of the sea, Victoria remained in her cabin, oblivious, studying details pertaining to their mission.

Even the passage through Suez and the final leg of the trip down the Red Sea and around the Arabian Peninsula did not distract Victoria. But as their Naval transport steamed north along the coast of Arabia, Victoria began remembering Hank, remembering the view of the Gulf she had seen from his airplane in 1938. They had set out for Basra that day. He did not get there. She would.

Sam met them at the Basra docks. It was the first time they had seen each other since Hank's death. Wordlessly, they embraced, oblivious to the bustling dock world around them. For a long time, they could only hug and weep together. When that wave of emotion passed, they pulled themselves together. Sam drove them the short distance to Khorramshar, telling them about the reception he had arranged for them at the Anglo Iranian Oil Company's elegant country club. He also informed them that, though he kept a comfortable house in the small oil-shipping port, they—along with the many local and foreign dignitaries invited to the reception—would, according to the State Department's orders, have elegant accommodations at the British-run country club.

As they drove through the club's elegant wrought-iron gates and along the circular driveway through lush, tropical gardens, Sam looked at Victoria. "This Operation Tidal Wave."

"We are not allowed to discuss it," Katie Marie interrupted from the car's back seat.

"Thank you, Mrs. Livingstone," he said, glancing back. "You and I will talk later." He turned back to Victoria. "You don't even speak Romanian."

"That's what Katie Marie's here for," Victoria said, admiring the fecundity of the British club's gardens.

"What if you need German?" he asked angrily, frustrated with her nonchalance.

"I know a little from school. I can't speak it very well, but I understand some of what is said and I can read a newspaper or a letter."

"Or a secret file," Katie Marie added.

"I thought you weren't supposed to talk about the mission!" he exclaimed with another glance back at her.

He glanced again at Victoria. "Is it worth your lives?"

Victoria studied him as he pulled up at the portico outside the club's main entrance. Uniformed Indian porters moved to the car but when its doors did not open, they stepped back. "The Germans can't fight long without oil," Victoria said. "You know that."

He turned from her and stared out the windshield, his hands remaining on the steering wheel. The porters moved to other arriving cars, which dropped off passengers and departed around Sam's car. Katie Marie and Victoria watched him. In the silence of the car, in the heat of the day, perspiring, they waited.

Finally, he turned back to her. "Fine," he said. "But you stay alert. Get out when the time is right or you are lost."

She smiled and opened the door. "First we've got to get in."

*****

During The Great War, the Anglo-Persian Oil Company matured from a desert outpost into an industrial cog of the British Empire. In the 1920s, Britain aggressively expanded the oil regions it called Arabistan, in the west of Persia, while simultaneously developing the refining center on Abadan Island at the mouth of the Tigris-Euphrates estuary south of Basra. Its thousands of Indian and Persian workers lived in working-class quarters on the island, while the British elite developed its own enclaves on the island and in Khorramshar, across the river.

Despite a slowdown associated with the worldwide economic depression at the end of the decade, the 1920s had been a time of enormous expansion for Anglo-Persian. By 1930, Reza Shah had taken control in Tehran and Anglo-Persian had taken control of the oil. Reza Shah, on dominating the Bakhtiari tribes, had changed the oil region's name from Arabistan to Khuzistan. Abadan became one of the largest, most modern refineries in the world.

Through the 1930s, oil deposits were identified throughout the Middle East from North Africa to Central Asia but the only ones both proven and open to exploration were in the Gulf region known to western nations as the Persian Gulf and to local people as the Arabian Gulf. In 1935, Reza Shah, Shah of Shahs, asserted his presence by restoring the name Iran to his country. The British investment there was by now enormous and, perhaps remembering the Bard's observation that a rose by any name smells as sweet, the company was respectfully rechristened Anglo-Iranian. The National Socialist Party in Germany was worrisomely expanding its economy during the 1930s by feeding its war machine and its war machine was hungry for oil. If a name change would keep the Hun at bay, the British would not object.

Oil grew increasingly important to European nations like Britain and Germany that, unlike the United States and Russia, had no domestic supplies in a world of growing hostilities. With Germany's September 1, 1939, invasion of Poland, the hostilities became a death knell. As the war enlarged, the hunger for oil increased. Exploration of the Gulf region gave way to a heightened focus on development and production. Incipient and potential fields like those in Ibn Saud's Saudi Arabia were set aside for times of less urgency.

255

The proven oil wealth of Iran and associated state-of-the-art refining capacity at Abadan, by 1938 the largest refinery in the world, became strategic lynch pins. Even as its military drove west, Germany began wooing Reza Shah's government. Hitler sought not only Iran's oil wealth, but a southern attack route into the Soviet Union's Caspian oil region as well.

Both Britain's Churchill and Russia's Stalin were extremely uneasy with the flirtation between Hitler and Reza Shah, especially when his Royal Highness expressed admiration for German efficiency and his government stubbornly asserted its neutrality. Britain demanded that Iran expel German nationals. Neutrality was acceptable for Turkey; it had no significant oil. Neutrality was out of the question for Iran.

When Germany invaded the Soviet Union through Eastern Europe in June 1941, the British and Soviets decided to act. August 25, 1941, was the date Iran would forever after refer to as its Pearl Harbor. The British Navy and a British Expeditionary Force from India took control of the Abadan refinery, the port region and Khuzistan. Soviet forces occupied the northern border areas. Reza Shah was invited by British and Soviet representatives in Tehran to abdicate in favor of his Oxbridge-educated twenty-one-year-old son. With a government unequivocally sympathetic (if not dependent) on the west restored, the Allies withdrew to advisory positions. (This was a pattern repeated in Cairo and Baghdad during the early years of World War II, where leaders inclined toward the Axis were also unseated by western military force and replaced by governments sympathetic to the Allies.)

The Soviets turned their attention to Hitler's assault on their European frontier, the British to the cross-channel Battle of Britain. The Anglo-Iranian Oil Company geared up to maximize capacity and production. Within months, Pearl Harbor brought the United States into the war and brought American troops and advisors to Abadan. Aside from its service as a petroleum pump, Iran was now a back door by which Stalin's stand against Hitler could be supplied and supported while the Allies prepared to strike back in Europe.

*****

"He was as good to me as a man can be," Katie Marie quietly told Sam as the reception swirled around them. "But I wanted to sing." Sam nodded, his expression distant. She guessed he was remembering the Jacques he knew twenty-odd years ago and trying to understand.

The party at the Anglo Iranian Oil Company Khorramshahr country club buzzed with excitement, a rare social treat in a war-torn acetic outpost. A jazz combo of American GI's stationed at the nearby docks played by the front window. Indian waiters carried trays of canapés and glasses of champagne to a room full of diplomatic dignitaries. A grinning young prince from Ibn Saud's royal house trailing his white linen robes followed a heavily made up blond stenographer in a stunning, low-cut cocktail dress across the room. Near the band, a pair of Russians in extraordinarily ostentatious uniforms stood around the fleshy American wife of an absent diplomat, staring with uninhibited, wide-eyed anticipation at the soft hillocks of flesh barely concealed by her plunging décolletage. Across the room, in an alcove, Victoria was whispering with the Romanian Foreign Minister, flirting.

"Sam," Katie Marie said, awakening him from his revery. "That was then." She smiled and shrugged. "This is now. You're hosting a very important party."

He stared at her, thinking again. "Right," he finally said. "Nothing I can do about it now." Suddenly he looked harder at her. "Your son."

"He tried to enlist after Pearl Harbor. Jacques convinced him to finish school and go in as an officer. He's training now."

He looked down. "It's taking everything we have left."

She studied him, seeing the grief etched into his face by the deaths in recent years of his wife and his son. Perhaps Victoria was all he had left. Her vigilance returning, she glanced across the reception room at her friend, her partner and—for the sake of this mission—the woman to whom she was personal secretary and assistant.

Looking up, Sam followed her eyes but looked back quickly.

"She need you?"

Surreptitiously watching Victoria operate on the Romanian diplomat, Katie Marie laughed. "Victoria? Are you kidding? He's eating out of her palm."

"You think she can get an invitation to Bucharest?" He asked her.

"At the very least, this sets up another encounter. Sooner or later, he's hers."

"It would have been a little easier if the British hadn't pushed all the Germans out of Persia last year," he muttered, shaking his head.

"Easier one way, harder another," she said. "Take it from me, Romanians are romantics. Easier than Germans to seduce and maneuver."

"Maneuver," Sam said. "A military tactic."

"No two ways about it," Katie Marie told him, watching the Romanian diplomat and Victoria across the room. "Your sister and I are on a military maneuver, nothing more. And from your report on this character, I'd say we'll be taking this beachhead tonight."

Sam glanced across the room, then back to Katie-Marie. "Deputy Prime Minister Antonescu does love the ladies."

Across the room in the alcove, standing very close to Victoria, was a lean, pale man with a thin, perfect mustache and large, weepy brown eyes in an elegant black dinner jacket and white ruffled shirt. His languorous gaze drifted unselfconsciously between her luminous green eyes and her deeply cut bodice.

"But why are you not sympathetic to your own country?" the Romanian asked Victoria with more apparent interest in her cleavage than in her politics.

"Mr. Deputy Prime Minister," Victoria began.

"Perhaps when we are alone," he interrupted her, "you should call me Mihai."

She smiled at him coyly. "It does feel more intimate."

He returned her smile, falling further into the hypnosis of her glamorous artifices, hints of lace and compelling roundnesses. "But you were going to tell me why you are alienated."

"The pre-historic morality, the scandals that ruined my marriage, the infantile dread of divorce. I hate the hypocritical prudes."

"But there is the ideological divide." He looked up at her. "The political issues."

"I am more interested in the man than the politics. I have known capitalists and fascists and even communists who were charming men, fabulous lovers."

He smiled hungrily. "And what kind of a lover do you think I might be?"

She met his smile with a quiet, sure hunger of her own. "Do you think a woman like me would bring such a thing up if she was not wondering about it?"

His smile turned to a lecherous grin. "And you have brought it up?"

Her smile was ingratiatingly complicit. "Have I?" She waited for him to make the suggestion.

"A private dessert in my rooms?"

"My rooms," she told him. She glanced across at Katie Marie and Sam. "I will arrange for my secretary to stay at my brother's house."

"Even better," he smiled lustfully.

On the other side of the room, Katie Marie, still standing with Sam, saw Victoria roll her left palm up and then down and then up, as if she was playing with her bracelet.

"Your sister is in need of an excuse," Katie Marie told Sam quietly.

"Good," he said, pointing toward the rear of the room. "I am pointing so that it will look like I am sending you to take care of something." Katie Marie smiled, nodded and walked purposefully in the direction he was pointing. Meanwhile, Sam walked across the room toward Victoria.

After exchanging cursory familiarities with Deputy Prime Minister Antonescu, Sam looked at Victoria. "I'm sorry to intrude," he said. "But I'm going to need you at my house tonight. I just sent your secretary to pack for you."

"Really, Sam," she replied irritably. "I'm not your housekeeper."

Antonescu, also irritated, interrupted. "Do what you would do if she was not here."

"But she is!" Sam snapped bluntly. "I opened my home to her. Just like you opened Romania to the Nazi fascists!"

"You can be sure, Mr. Wade," the Romanian snapped back, "we will never open our country to YOU again."

"I assure you I have no desire to ever see Romania again," Sam smiled meanly.

"But Sam," Victoria interrupted, seeming to want to make peace. "You told us Romania was magnificent: Towering mountains, green river valleys, quaint farms, charming old world cities."

"Oil!" Sam interrupted her, his World War I memories of Romania rushing back to him. "Smelly greasy oil. That's what I will always remember about Romania. Oil turning into fiery flames and stinking choking smoke like the deepest pits of hell."

"Sir!" exclaimed Antonescu, drawing himself up to full attention, clicking his heels together in loud protest, his face tightly clenched in rage. "I will not stand here and listen to you insult my country by describing the horror YOU brought on it!" He turned to Victoria. "Perhaps you will someday do me the honor of allowing me to show you my country."

"I would like nothing more, Mr. Deputy Prime Minister," Victoria smiled, flaunting the man's title for his own benefit.

"Then come back with me tomorrow," he said excitedly.

"That would be grand but I don't think the necessary diplomatic arrangements, the papers, are possible," she smiled sadly.

Antonescu looked fiercely at Sam. Sam smiled triumphantly. "Ridiculous," the diplomat said suddenly, waving his hand in a dismissive way. "I will handle the arrangements myself. Please let me know when you are ready to travel."

"I am overwhelmed, Mr. Deputy Prime Minister," she said with graceful surprise.

"Nonsense," he said, smiling leeringly at her. "It is the kind of attention a great lady like you deserves." He snapped his heels again, took her hand for a quick if courtly kiss accompanied by a bowing gesture, and then looked up, meanly, at Sam. "And with that, I will take my leave before I am forced to defend my country's honor by more violent action." Satisfied that he had dominated the encounter, he pivoted and walked away.

Sam stared at the Romanian but did not speak until the man was out of the room. "That went well." He looked at Victoria.

She smiled. "It couldn't have gone more perfectly if we had planned it." They exchanged furtive eye-twinklings and turned back to the party.

*****

By the winter of 1942-43, the Allies had finally begun to effectively challenge the Third Reich's war machine. The Russian winters (1941-42 and 1942-43) and the literally millions of gravely under-equipped Russian soldier-martyrs were first among the heroes of the challenge. Slowed first by walls of Soviet troops dying for their country and then by unpassable roads in unbearable weather, Hitler's proud Wehrmacht could capture neither Stalingrad (which would have given Germany control of Russia) nor the Russian Caucasus (where it could have obtained the Russian oil that would have sustained its drive). Therefore, the Wehrmacht retreated.

Second on the roll call of heroes in the renewed challenge to the Reich were the British forces under General Montgomery in North Africa. Though out-soldiered, they fought and ran from German General Rommel until the German hero extended his supply lines too far. At El Alamein, Montgomery's British forces turned and made their stand. Rommel's forces did not have the fuel to maneuver or retreat. The U.S.-led Allied invasion of French Northwest Africa followed immediately and Rommel's army was helpless to respond. Soon the vaunted Africa Korps, its last hope of fuel resupply cut off by British naval resurgence in the Mediterranean, was crushed from both flanks.

Now, both the Allies and the Axis knew, the ultimate battle, for Europe, would be joined.

*****

The day after Victoria informed Deputy Prime Minister Antonescu she and her secretary were ready to travel, they took off in a private diplomatic air transport, arranged through the young Shah of Iran. They flew to Ankara, the new center of Turkish life in the Attaturk (post-Ottoman) era. Flying out of Khorramshar, Victoria was barely able to choke back the emotion she felt when she saw the desert roll below the plane and remembered too vividly her air adventure with Hank. She remembered his youth and poise, and how his courage and concentration almost masked the fear she saw in his youthful eyes as he flew their plane over the Arabian desert in that windstorm. She knew it must have been the same that horrible day in the South Pacific: Courage and concentration surely once again beat back the fear as he took his

261

vengeance on the Japanese battleship and protected his co-workers. Good for you, Hank, she thought to herself, calming.

She turned from the window to Katie Marie, who sat beside her. Victoria smiled. Katie Marie saw what Victoria felt. It was a deep, deep smile. Courage and concentration beating back fear. They had a job to do. For Hank.

Turkey's precarious neutrality allowed, even in late 1942, for international air traffic. A private German diplomatic plane met the Romanian diplomat and his party in Ankara and ferried them to Romania. As the plane's pilot initiated procedures for landing in Bucharest, Deputy Prime Minister Antonescu countermanded the flight plan and ordered the pilot to land at Mizil, the new military base north of Bucharest, just east of the city of Ploiesti. Despite the pilot's protest that this was against standing rules, Antonescu asserted his political authority. As the pilot approached the Mizil airfield, the military commander on the ground also objected, but Antonescu insisted, despite the ground commander's warning that he must notify "the Protector."

"Notify whoever your small, enchained bureaucratic mind must but to get this plane down! And send for a car and driver. And arrange accommodations for my party at the Hotel Europa in Ploiesti."

The Deputy Prime Minister led his party down the gangway from the plane, his four civilian assistants in rumpled suits following and making notes on the clipboards they carried to record his instructions. Victoria and Katie-Marie brought up the rear of the entourage, at a distance. The plane's crew came down last. At the sight of a small red-haired man in a formal green Waffen SS Luftwaffe uniform bearing a chest full of decorations and shoulders full of rank storming at them across the tarmac trailing a retinue of German and Romanian officers, Victoria pulled Katie Marie back. They paused at the foot of the gangway, letting the plane's crew pass. The approaching German wore an expression of fury.

Antonescu continued walking forward, elaborating instructions and dictations to the assistants at his heels in Romanian, emphasizing with flicks of his fingers. When he noticed his attendants' hesitant glances at the oncoming German officer, Antonescu paused in the middle of the tarmac, looked at the man approaching and awaited the confrontation. As the German neared, the Romanian took a bold stance and began speaking loudly and angrily in Romanian. At this, the German abruptly stopped. He stood silently for a moment, staring with a cold deadliness that froze the Deputy Prime Minister's assistants and sent chills through Victoria and Katie Marie.

Sensing only dominance and triumph, the Romanian began walking toward the German again, yelling more loudly, more aggressively.

The German's expression turned even darker and more furious. Without taking another step, he made a short, intense forward snap of his head in a 'yes' nod of tremendous fury, accompanying it with a vicious snap forward of a fisted wrist at the end of the rigid arm held tightly to his right side. Instantly, four officers behind him, two German and two Romanian, moved forward.

The Deputy Prime Minister's bombastic attitude suddenly shattered and he froze in his steps. Terror overwhelmed him as the four officers seized him, lifted him off the ground and carried him, wriggling and protesting powerlessly, toward a nearby hangar. He began babbling in Romanian but soon stopped, repeating pleas of "Gerstenberg! General Gerstenberg!" over and over until the officers carried him into the hanger, beyond earshot.

Antonescu's four assistants stood and watched in helpless astonishment, their faces twisted with terror. The German General walked to the first of them, took his clipboard and studied it while the man stood trembling. The German handed back the clipboard and dismissed the man, who moved quickly off and away with obsequious expressions of gratitude in German and Romanian. After Gerstenberg repeated this intimidation with each of the other three assistants, he looked at the plane's crew. Without a word, he made graceful "carry on" gestures with his wrist, sending them on to their next flight duties. Finally, he turned to Victoria and Katie Marie.

By now, it was clear to Victoria she must seize this moment and, if possible, this man. As he approached, she watched him carefully. He looked at her. She saw the male hunger flash in his eyes but then something else. It was not something she recognized.

Katie Marie, to give Victoria more time to study the General and think, quickly stepped between them and began speaking to him in Romanian, introducing Victoria and explaining their presence.

He raised a rigid left hand with sudden violence and once again his face clinched in fury. "I speak English, Mrs. Livingstone. Please step back or I will be forced to have you put with the Romanian."

Katie Marie looked at Victoria, who nodded.

He stepped forward. "Lady North, I am Generalmajor Alfred Gerstenberg, air attaché to Romania for the Reich."

"You know me, General?" She asked as she shook his hand.

He smiled an enigmatic smile. "Your reputation precedes you, Lady North."

She smiled invitingly. "I hope you find it appealing."

His enigmatic smile glimmered with a bit of desire and then closed abruptly. "You are the guest of the Romanian government. As such, you are innocent of wrongdoing. But you are where you should not be. I must therefore detain you in Ploiesti." He noticed a limousine arrive at the airfield and roll slowly toward them. "Walk with me, Lady North." He abruptly pivoted and started toward the limousine. She followed. "I will have the car take you to the Hotel Europa as planned but the Deputy Prime Minister will not be able to host you as he must return immediately to Bucharest." As they reached the car, he opened the door and stepped aside for her. "You will be my guest for a small dinner party tonight at my house here."

"In my honor?" she asked, starting to get into the car.

"Already planned," he answered quickly.

Instead of sitting down into the car, she stopped, looked up at him and unhesitatingly met his gaze. "Is that an invitation or an order?"

"An invitation, by all means." He smiled the enigmatic smile. "But I am anxious to hear you in conversation."

Halfway into the car, she looked up with a knowing smile, ready to finally hear what was really on his mind. "Really?" She self-consciously leaned forward on the car's door, one leg in the car and one leg, bared of skirt, still on the ground, her coat and blouse gapping in front to display more than a glimpse of lace at her bodice.

"There is a question about your morality. If you are the whore the SS reports you are, you will not be welcome in the Sudostraum."

"The Sudostraum?" she asked without reacting to his verbal slap in the face.

"The Balkan Empire the Reich is rebuilding."

"Is there not," she smiled, leaning toward him, "a place in the Empire for a courtesan?"

His enigmatic smile opened a bit. "That is possible, depending on politics."

She leaned farther toward him and smiled, revealing yet more lace and promise. "I have always been more interested in love than in politics."

He studied her without reacting. "Your secretary."

She glanced at Katie Marie. "What about her?"

"She is Romanian?"

"She is from a Romanian-American family."

"Is she Jewish?"

"Do you think I would employ a Jew as my personal secretary?"

"One never knows."

"As a matter of fact, I favor keeping the Jews in their place. And before you ask, I don't like it a bit that my country is going to bomb yours."

"What? You have knowledge of a bombing attack?"

"Of course," she dangled, now seducing him with hints of lace and information. And then she pulled back. "Sooner or later, don't you think it must happen?"

"Ah, yes, I see what you mean," he smiled.

"Is that all?" she asked innocently, though both now knew he could no longer be sure if he did know what she meant.

"Yes," he smiled, the full enigma returning as he realized he might need to know more about what she knew. "I will see you tonight."

"Good." She waved to Katie Marie to come to the car. "I would like to get settled in the hotel. I hope it is a place with standards."

"I think you will find it satisfactory." He studied Katie Marie as she walked toward them, as if trying to discern Jewishness or deceit in her.

"What time?" Victoria interrupted his concentration.

Startled, he looked again at Victoria, who was now sitting inside the car. "I beg your pardon?" he asked.

"The dinner party. What time will you send your car for me?"

"Ah," he said, remembering the dinner obligation. "Seven."

"Perfect," she smiled as Katie Marie got into the car beside her. "Have your driver call for me at the hotel desk and wait until I come down. Now close the door. We must get settled so I have time to dress." As he closed the door of the car, she removed a compact from her purse. Completely satisfied that she had achieved some parity with this bullying Nazi, she ignored him and began studying herself in the compact's mirror while giving orders for Katie Marie to convey to the driver.

*****

Following the "Casablanca Conference" of January 1943, Roosevelt, Churchill and de Gaulle announced their non-negotiable demand for unconditional surrender by the Axis powers. The German Wehrmacht was retreating into Eastern Europe with the Russian army at its heels. The Allies, victorious in North Africa, were preparing to invade Italy and planning an ultimate assault on France. To the Allied surrender demand, Third Reich Propagandaminister Joseph Goebbels responded on behalf of Hitler with his "Sportpalast" speech, calling for "Total War" and ending with the dramatic declaration, "And storm, break loose!"

*****

The dinner party was at Gerstenberg's elegant but unpretentious house in the countryside between Ploiesti and Mizil. "It made the Romanian collaborators from whom it was seized happy," he told the guests who complimented him on the house. The fare was far better than wartime shortages should allow, owing to Gerstenberg's privileges. Katie-Marie assisted Gerstenberg's maid and butler in pampering the six diners. Aside from the host and Victoria, there was an officious, high-ranking Romanian military officer and his obsequious wife, as well as a 60-ish Countess who reveled in telling stories of pre-war days when she chaperoned Romania's now 23-year-old figure-head King Mihai. The other guest was a handsome, 50-ish, red-haired, genial Swedish oil man named Erickson.

Victoria cautiously, quietly, charmed the guests without interrupting Gerstenberg's dominance of the conversation. Both the Countess and the oil man made this very easy, seeming to share her own sense of social rhythms and moods. To Victoria, it almost seemed they shared her distaste for their host and might be happier but less alert at a British or American General's dinner party. Nor did the Romanian officer and his wife prevent Victoria from displaying for Gerstenberg's benefit her social grace, except that they were so deferential she could never be sure how they would react until Gerstenberg reacted.

To Victoria's relief, Gerstenberg's conversation steered away from the war. With Erickson's energetic help and the Countess's excited interest, Victoria entertained the General and his guests with descriptions of current fashion and popular culture. She was careful about Third Reich prudishness, despite the fear of and disdain for it she saw in the eyes of the others. To Victoria's surprise, the Romanian officer's obsequious wife piped up, in response to a remark about British Prime Minister Churchill's filthy cigars.

"He seems so common," the woman remarked disdainfully. "I just heard an astrologer on the radio say our Fuhrer's Saturn position in his natal chart is the same as Napoleon's!"

Surprised the woman took astrology so seriously, Victoria was about to remark sarcastically when Gerstenberg interrupted. "Reichsfuhrer Himmler's personal astrologer, Herr Wulff, is at this moment preparing my chart."

Victoria paused, smiled graciously, and asked if the General might introduce her to Herr Wulff.

"You have an interest in the stars, Lady North?" Gerstenberg asked.

"I am especially interested in star-crossed love, General."

The other dinner guests laughed lightly but Victoria was pleased to see a sparkle in Gerstenberg's eyes. With such winning conversation, she offset Gerstenberg's aloof seriousness with ease and delight. As the evening went on and the flesh above her low cut gown's bodice flushed pink and glistened with the warmth she created around herself, she watched the desire she intended to provoke in him rise.

Then a phone deep in the house rang, and Gerstenberg's expression immediately revealed intense irritation. His guests watched him, waiting to see what he would do. After three rings, the butler stepped into the room, looked at the General and waited. The phone rang again. Gerstenberg nodded once and the butler disappeared into the house. Victoria recognized the intense nod of the head. She had seen it that afternoon at the airport when he was ordering his officers to carry away the Deputy Prime Minister.

A moment later, the phone stopped ringing. All waited, listening expectantly, watching Gerstenberg. They heard nothing. The butler returned. At the entrance to the dining room, he stopped. "Sprecht!" Gerstenberg grunted.

"Prime Minister Antonescu will be arriving for a private conference with you and Lady North in five minutes. He requests the house be cleared of other guests."

"What? Did he ask to speak with me?"

"No."

"Ach!" Gerstenberg exploded, slamming his fist against the table and bursting from his seat with a raging stomp of his boot. He spun around to the rear wall of the dining room on which a large mirror hung, saw his own furious expression in the mirror, froze, took a deep breath and turned again to his guests. "My friends, you must excuse me."

The other four guests were polite. The Countess told Gerstenberg she would save him the trouble of sending his car and driver with the other guests by having her own chauffer drop the Romanian couple at their house and Erickson at the Europa Hotel on her way back to her estate. Gerstenberg studied her suspiciously for a moment, then shook his head back and forth as if realizing he was being a bit too paranoid. He grunted his acceptance of the offer with a "fine" and a wave of his hand.

In the large, high-ceiled foyer near the front door, the Romanian officer's wife said goodnight to her host and turned to offer a word of encouragement to Victoria before following her husband out. "You needn't be afraid of meeting the Prime Minister. He is a charming man."

"Of course he is," Victoria smiled, without mention of Antonescu's rise to power by the brutal aggression of the violently fascistic Iron Guard.

"Ion is hard, but reasonable," the Countess said of the Prime Minister as she said good night to Victoria. "I have known him since he was a young cavalry officer before the Great War."

"The Deputy Prime Minister probably told him about my arrival," Victoria smiled at the Countess, glancing conspiratorially at Gerstenberg. "And he simply wants to greet me. I'm sure he is coming mainly to see the General."

The last to leave was Erickson. The tall, heavyset Swede shook hands with Gerstenberg and then bent his freckled face to affectionately kiss Victoria on the cheek. At the same time, he whispered to her. "Think very thoroughly. Do what the innocent would do. You will be fine."

His insight astonished her as much as his encouragement and she flushed with emotion. He saw her involuntary response and laughed to cover for her. She laughed with him, perhaps as much from the absurdity of their encounter as from her own nervous terror.
They regained their composure and looked toward Gerstenberg, smiling with embarrassment.

"What, may I ask, is so hilarious?" the small General asked impatiently of the big, red-haired oil man.

"I was whispering to Lady North," Erickson said quickly, "that even when the food is unexpectedly plentiful and delicious one can't seem to eat one's fill all the way to dessert these days."

"Another time," Gerstenberg snapped back angrily.

A black Mercedes pulled up on the country road outside the house. It stopped and waited, its motor running. Taking this cue, the guests hurried to the Countess's touring car. Meanwhile, Katie-Marie came into the foyer, stood to one side and waited, in service to Victoria.

As soon as the guests drove away, a small, dark-featured, man with a high forehead and a stern expression got out of the Mercedes and marched angrily past Gerstenberg and Victoria into the house. He wore a natty green Romanian military uniform with heavy metal insignias of supreme authority on the shoulders and carried himself with intensity, walking through the door into the foyer without a word of invitation or greeting. The four armed, uniformed bodyguards who trailed him from the car stopped outside the house and closed the front door behind him.

Before the Prime Minister could get out of the foyer and into Gerstenberg's living room, the General bellowed at his back in Romanian.

At the sound of Romanian, Katie Marie stepped near Victoria and pulled her back from the confrontation between the two men.

The Prime Minister pivoted and glared at Gerstenberg. "You will speak English in the presence of our guest!"

269

"OUR guest?" Gerstenberg exploded in Romanian. "You mean MY guest!"

"She was a guest of Romania before she was your guest!" Prime Minister Antonescu shouted back in English.

"She arrived at a MILITARY facility, Antonescu! That makes her MINE!"

Victoria leaned toward Katie Marie. "The Deputy Prime Minister, the Prime Minister," she whispered. "Is everybody in Romania named Antonescu?"

"She is a GUEST of this country!" The Prime Minister shouted at the German General. "And you have illegally detained a Romanian official! My own DEPUTY!"

"Coincidence," Katie Marie whispered back. "No relation."

"Except through me," Victoria answered.

"A lot of men seem to have that gene," Katie Marie muttered to herself as Victoria walked away from her.

"Gentlemen," Victoria interrupted.

Gerstenberg and Antonescu turned suddenly to her as if they did not remember she was present.

She smiled. "It is late. I am tired. You both know this is really a power struggle about something you must settle between yourselves." She turned to Antonescu. "Prime Minister, please drive my assistant and myself to our hotel." She glanced at Gerstenberg and then back to Antonescu. "Perhaps the General will follow and obtain a conference room at the Europa, where you can continue this, ahem, diplomatic negotiation, on neutral ground."

Both of the men stared at her. Antonescu spoke first. "My sincerest apologies, Lady North. We have not formally met, but your reputation precedes you."

Gerstenberg snorted cynically.

Antonescu's head snapped toward the German. "Will you deny your guest her request to retire to her hotel?"

Gerstenberg glared at the Prime Minister. "It will be a pleasure to get you out of my house."

Antonescu turned to Victoria. "It is settled then." In his smile, everyone in the room could see the lust of a man with a sudden, unexpected opportunity.

"I WILL follow in my own car," Gerstenberg interrupted, almost sadistically. "So that we may do as Lady North suggests, have a chat at the hotel."

Antonescu turned quickly back to Gerstenberg and found the German smiling.

"Fine," Victoria said happily, knowing she was interrupting Gerstenberg's moment of satisfaction. "Get my things, Katie-Marie."

"Yes, mam."

A little later, two elegant Mercedes limousines drove up and parked, one right after the other, beside the curb in front of the Europa Hotel. While the Prime Minister's uniformed bodyguards quickly secured the street around the building, his chauffeur/bodyguard scurried to open the passenger door onto the sidewalk beside the still, quiet, black-out-dark, empty Strada Greceanu where the handsome concrete, brick and wrought-iron Europa sat across from and among some of Ploiesti's finest shops and shopping.

While Katie Marie stepped onto the sidewalk from the front passenger seat, the Prime Minister stepped out of the back door, turned and, with a slightly excessive show of manners, extended his hand into the car for Victoria.

Gerstenberg emerged from his own car, walked over in time to see Antonescu's courtly display toward Victoria and turned away in irritation. Through the hotel's brightly lit front windows, he saw Erickson in the lobby, chatting with another patron. Intending to have a word with the oil man, he started for the hotel's entrance. But there were gunshots—pop! pop! pop!— in the distance up the street. He pivoted toward the sound.

The sound of running footsteps echoed off the walls of the silent street's buildings. All eyes turned north, up Strada Greceanu. Around the corner from Strada Degherea came two shadowy figures running. From the loose skirts at their legs, it appeared they were women. One carried something bulky and lagged behind. A moment later, men in uniforms brandishing pistols came around the corner, running. The men shouted. The women kept running. The men shot. All kept running, now nearing the hotel.

While the four armed guards converged around him, the Prime Minister's driver/bodyguard grabbed him around the chest and drove him toward the safer shadows of the hotel's walls. Held by Antonescu's grip on her wrist, Victoria was pulled along. The momentum carried her to the wall nearby, where Antonescu's grip released. Katie Marie quickly came to Victoria and they huddled together in the shadows, watching the street. The chauffeur/bodyguard shielded Antonescu with his own body, rolled around to face the street and pulled a pistol from inside his jacket. "Still!" he ordered.

At the hotel entrance, Gerstenberg pivoted and looked up the street intently, studying the situation as he drew a Luger from his belt's holster.

Still in running pursuit, the uniformed men in the street, now discernible in the moonlight as Romanian police, shouted at the fleeing women again.

From the hotel entrance, Gerstenberg calmly walked into the street.

Seeing movement on the hotel side of the street in front of them, the fleeing women cut toward the far side. The officers shouted and shot again.

One of the women was almost across the street and into the shadows on the far side. The other, carrying the bulky object, lagged behind, in the open. Gerstenberg raised his pistol and shot the first woman near the far curb. She grunted, started to take one more step, failed and fell, tumbling until she thudded against a parked car. The second woman cut hard, desperately making for the shadows. Gerstenberg shot again. There was another grunt. The woman tried to stride again but could not, and fell. The bulky object in her arms dropped, cracked against the pavement, and clattered along the street into pieces.

Gerstenberg kept walking toward the women, both still writhing and groaning.

Behind him, Victoria pulled away from Katie Marie and followed Gerstenberg. Katie Marie followed at a distance.

The Prime Minister's bodyguards checked him and, though he protested, rushed him into the car. Quickly, the driver jumped behind the driver's wheel and the car screeched away into the night.

Gerstenberg now stood over the second woman, looking down at her.

Victoria walked near, Katie Marie stepping to her side.

The pursuing officers came huffing up, saw Gerstenberg's superior rank and stepped back. In Romanian, Gerstenberg exchanged curt questions with their deferential answers while Katie Marie whispered translation for Victoria.

"The cops say the girls are partisans. They were caught stealing a radio."

Gerstenberg looked down at the girl again and used his foot to roll her downturned face upward.

"The cops don't recognize..." Katie Marie began as the wounded girl on the ground moaned. Katie Marie stopped mid-sentence as she recognized the girl on the ground as Farmgirl.

Farmgirl moaned as Gerstenberg's foot at her head brought her back to her world of wound and pain.

Katie Marie looked desperately at Victoria, whose face was an emotionless mask.

Gerstenberg bent to Farmgirl and studied her while he gave orders to the officers, who walked to the other girl, grabbed her by her legs and dragged her across the pavement to the middle of the street, beside Farmgirl. Victoria and Katie Marie immediately saw it was Typewriter. Both girls were bleeding freely from gunshot wounds to their torsos and from cuts, scrapes and likely fractures from their falls. Typewriter also bled from a deep gash her face and was not conscious, though there was perceivable breathing.

"You've got to do something," Katie Marie whispered in desperation, horror and terror twisting her face.

Victoria looked from the wounded girls to Katie Marie. Suddenly, she slapped Katie Marie hard across the face, then grabbed her shoulder and spun her away, toward the hotel. "Get out of here!" she shouted.

Katie Marie turned back. "What?" she demanded angrily.

"You question me?" Victoria challenged her. "Get out of here." She stared at Katie Marie until her companion, reaching the conclusion that Victoria knew what she was doing, decided to follow the orders, turned and walked slowly away.

As Katie Marie reached the shadows of the sidewalk in front of the hotel, Red Erickson stepped up beside her. "Wait here with me," he said reassuringly. She stopped beside him and turned back to watch.

"What do you know?" She whispered to him.

"You do not need or want to know," he whispered back. "Just stay here with me."

Gerstenberg, standing over the girls in the street, looked up. "You should not be here, Lady North. This will become uglier."

"Proceed, General," Victoria told him, reading immense, controlled rage in his face and eyes. "My assistant was begging me to intercede on behalf of the traitors. I cannot tolerate that kind of misplaced emotion."

"Ah," he said, looking down at the barely conscious Farmgirl who was not alert enough to discern Victoria's presence. He spoke to her in Romanian, an obvious demand for information. Farmgirl grunted an obviously contemptuous answer.

The rage on Gerstenberg's face emerged now as a sadistic smile. He thrust a gloved thumb into the wound on Farmgirl's chest and lifted her upper body off the street. She screamed in agony. He repeated his question. Her eyes opened. She groaned a horrible 'no' in throbbing pain and contempt.

He dropped her to the pavement, eliciting another grunt of animal agony. He twisted to the unconscious girl, lifted his gun, held it at Typewriter's bloody head and screamed at Farmgirl. Farmgirl struggled to raise her head, took in Typewriter's condition and Gerstenberg's threat, dropped her head back to the pavement and said nothing, staring at the stars high above in the nighttime sky.

Gerstenberg screamed at her again. Farmgirl's screaming eyes stared silently at the stars. Gerstenberg fired point blank into Typewriter's head. Blood spurted out on his pants legs and on Farmgirl's face. Farmgirl tried to raise an arm to her face but groaned at the pain of movement. Her tongue swiped from between her lips and tasted the blood dripping, perhaps Typewriter's, perhaps her own, it did not matter anymore.

Gerstenberg leaned to her, repeated the question and then said something more soothingly, obviously offering her life in exchange for something less valuable to her but more valuable to him.

Refusing to allow herself the luxury of turning away from the horrible scene, Victoria saw doubt and terror flash in Farmgirl's eyes. She stepped forward. "Kill her," she whispered to Gerstenberg. He looked at her. There was lust and fury in his eyes but it was tempered by a calculating coldness. "Kill her," Victoria repeated with a hint of ultimate, insane intimacy. She saw a greater excitement rise up in him.

At the next instant, Victoria saw Farmgirl's head turn toward her and a dull awareness replace the doubt and terror. Grimly, Victoria smiled and flicked her head in a minute suggestion of a 'yes' nod. She saw understanding and courage come into Farmgirl's eyes.

In the next instant, Gerstenberg thrust his entire gloved hand into the gapping, oozing wound where he had previously put his thumb. Again he raised Farmgirl's torso and now shouted his question. She screamed an agonized "NO!" in intolerable pain. Gerstenberg raised his pistol, held it between her eyes and shouted his question again. From an animal place deep inside her, Farmgirl emitted a passionate grunting Romanian epithet but before she could finish, Gerstenberg fired the Luger. After the loud boom and echo of the gunshot, there was a splat of blood and then silence.

Gerstenberg dropped the body, stood upright, turned and smiled at Victoria. "It was the humane thing to do, was it not?"

"Yes," she said.

He holstered the Luger, removed the bloody gloves, tossed them on top of the bodies and walked away. Victoria followed.

At the curb, Katie Marie stood staring beside Erickson. He glanced at her as Gerstenberg and Victoria walked toward him. Reading Katie Marie's mounting verbal explosion, he grabbed her and held her face to his big broad chest. Katie Marie submitted to this, allowing her outrage to express itself as sobbing grief, which avoided compromising Victoria's act.

Victoria followed Gerstenberg to his car. Watching his body language as he walked away from her, she saw hesitation in his attitude toward her, an awkwardness not previously revealed. It was like they had been too intimate and he was recoiling. "You will want to clean up," she commented lightly to his back.

He turned to her, suddenly comfortable with the slight distancing in this personal yet innocuous remark. "Yes," he said, looking down at the blood on his uniform.

Seeing his comfort return, she stepped nearer to him and wiped a bit of blood from his shoulder with her fingers, then held her hand between them and rubbed the blood between her fingertips. The emotion of what she had just been forced by circumstance to do and say began to overwhelm her. She looked at Gerstenberg, allowed herself to reveal this powerful feeling to him, and then looked down.

He smiled, reached to her and pulled her chin up. He looked into her eyes. "Perhaps you and I should have another dinner tomorrow night."

"You have another dinner party planned?" she asked with mock derision.

"I am planning it at this very moment," he said quietly. "You and I will be the only guests."

"Will we get to dessert?" she asked, intending the double meaning.

"Yes," he said confidently. "Most certainly."

*****

A month later, in the closed, cluttered garage of a small house on the outskirts of Ploiesti between the center of the town and Gerstenberg's house, Katie Marie and Victoria sat in dirty overalls, wearing work gloves, and shuffling through bags and boxes of detritus. Both silently studied bits of trash as if it might offer a clue to life's plan.

Finally, Katie Marie dropped a used wine bottle into a cardboard box and sighed. "We have studied this man from his pubic hair to his used tissue and we still don't have any better idea of what kind of defenses he's set up than when we got here!"

"We know they call him 'The Protector' because the defenses are elaborate," Victoria said, pulling a sheaf of typing paper from a bag of trash in front of her and studying it. "It is only a matter of time."

"Dammit, Victoria, grow up. This could take a lot of time—too much time!" Katie Marie sniffed at papers she pulled from the trash in front of her. "Uch. Getting nothing here but stink."

"You should smell the goats."

"So why do you waste your time? You like getting dressed up like an old peasant?"

"Well, it's not what I find out about the oil facility defenses," Victoria answered, still studying the trash. "I've learned exactly nothing for a month of herding those goats. But I like it."

Katie Marie laughed. "You've finally found yourself. You're not really a queen of high society, you're an old peasant crone goat herder."

"Laugh if you like, but the men don't stare at me. They don't even LOOK at me. It's like when we were training. I feel kind of free."

"So you're having fun play-acting. But you're getting nothing on the defenses."

"Nothing important."

Katie Marie turned to her. "We're running out of time and you know it!"

"Tidal Wave is still a few weeks off."

"But can you keep his interest? And what will he do if he loses interest? The man is a cold-blooded murderer!"

"This is the mission. You knew what it was."

"But I didn't know who he was. He's not some fat old cuddly Ambassador."

"You know what knocking out these oil facilities means."

"Do you remember what your brother told you?"

"I will know when it is time to get out."

Katie Marie did not answer but just stared at Victoria. After a few silent seconds, Victoria felt the stare and looked at her companion. "What?"

"You might know," Katie Marie said. "But will you get out?"

Victoria looked at her. "There's still one thing we haven't tried."

Immediately agitated, Katie Marie jumped to her feet. "Oh, no. No, no no." She walked across the concrete garage floor toward Victoria.

Victoria ignored her and went back to sifting through the trash. "We can do it."

"No, Vic, no. It's too dangerous."

Victoria looked up again. "He's just like the Nazi who ran the Vichy Embassy. He's going to have it all organized and filed away in a safe in the office."

"But we're not talking about prison or deportation for getting caught now. This bastard will torture us and then shoot us dead."

"If we don't find out how those oil facilities are protected, he's going to shoot down hundreds of Air Force boys."

"Boys just like Hank?" Katie Marie asked.

Victoria did not reply, just sat with her hands motionless inside a trash bag and looked at Katie Marie firmly.

"If we get caught, it won't do Hank OR those boys any good," Katie Marie argued back at Victoria's silence.

"Well," Victoria finally said, looking again at her share of the trash. "We'd better get something out of this crap."

"Unless you can make some extremely strategic pillow talk," Katie Marie shrugged, returning to her box.

They both resumed working, the silence of rustling papers the only sound in the garage.

"It must be pretty awful," Katie Marie said.

"He is surprisingly gentle," Victoria replied, as if reading her companion's thoughts.

"Huh," Katie Marie answered, studying the trash.

"Yes," Victoria said, doing the same.

*****

The April 1942 Doolittle Raid on Japan, in retribution for the attack on Pearl Harbor, has been celebrated in books, movies, legend and lore. Led by American aviation pioneer James Harold "Jimmy" Doolittle, sixteen modified B-25B Mitchell bombers flew off of the aircraft carrier USS Hornet on April 18. They dropped 500-pound high explosive and incendiary bombs on Tokyo, Yokohama, Kobe, Osaka and Nagoya.

Fifteen of the crews crash-landed on the China coast and one landed safely near Vladivostak, Russia, and was taken prisoner. Most of the crews in China got home safely thanks to help from the Chinese. The crew in Russia eventually escaped and got home. Two five-man crews were captured and taken to Japan where six of the men died.

The raid inflicted little material damage on the Japanese war effort but dramatically boosted American morale and diminished Japan's air defenses on the Pacific front because aircraft were called back from places like Wake Island and Midway Island to protect the homeland. Following the mission, Doolittle was boosted two ranks, to Brigadier General, and awarded the Medal of Honor.

In contrast, the June 1942 Halverson Project, America's first bombing raid into World War II Europe, is barely known or remembered. Overnight on June 11-12, Harry A. "Hurry-up" Halverson led twenty-three crews in B-24D Liberator bombers, a plane never before flown in combat by Americans, from a desert base in Egypt. The planes crossed the Mediterranean, Turkey and the Black Sea to drop an indeterminate amount of ordnance imprecisely into the Ploiesti region of Romania and then scattered.

Twelve of the twenty-three bombers made Romania and returned to base. Nine others landed safely in Iraq and Syria. Four crews landed and were interned in neutral Turkey. Most of the latter eventually escaped or were safely returned.

Like the desperate Doolittle raid, the "Hail, Mary" Halverson Project did little actual war-related damage. And like the Japan raid, the first Ploiesti raid was a stern signal to the Germans, who depended on Romanian oil supplies and refineries for the bulk of their high-octane tank and airplane fuels. Resources which might otherwise have been extremely useful against Russia on the torturous Eastern Front were pulled back to supplement Romanian defenses. Unlike Doolittle, Colonel Halverson won no promotion. He remained in command of his bomber group, which saw action against Rommel in Egypt and then was shifted to quieter duty in Palestine, through the summer of 1942.

Hitler's ambitious 1941 "Operation Barbarossa" assault on Stalingrad failed. His mad 1942 "Operation Blau" assault on Russia and its Caspian oil resources broke on Russian military masses, the vicious streets of Stalingrad and the brutal Russian winter of 1942-43. As Germany pulled back, Nazi strategists became deadly serious about protecting Ploiesti. The Luftwaffe's Alfred Gerstenberg, a veteran of German aviation from World War I, was named Romanian air attaché. He developed oil facility defenses with a thoroughness that can only be described as "German" and thereby won from the Romanian people his nickname, "The Protector."

*****

In a dark rear hallway of Gerstenberg's house outside Ploiesti, Victoria and Katie Marie moved stealthily toward the locked back office. As they passed an open door, they saw him on a massage table. A fat, round-faced man in a necktie and shirtsleeves was bent over him. They heard Gerstenberg laugh. "The partisans in the mountains?" Gerstenberg asked in German. He laughed again. "They are too little and too late." He groaned at the doctor's aggressive massaging.

"The magic word is stop," the doctor, also speaking German, reminded him.

Gerstenberg groaned again. "No, no, it is good. It hurts good." The doctor and Gerstenberg laughed.

"What are they talking about?" Katie Marie whispered.

"If I understand," Victoria whispered back, "Gerstenberg likes his massages rougher than he likes his sex."

"I'm just glad he's so distracted," Katie Marie replied.

"Right," Victoria agreed, continuing down the hallway. At the office door, Victoria took a sharp, thin blade from her dress pocket and slipped it between the lock's tongue and the doorpost sleeve. "It's amazing what you can do with a good nail file," she whispered to Katie Marie, grinning.

"How long do his sessions with Doctor Magic-Hands usually last?" Katie Marie asked as Victoria worked at the lock.

"An hour. Maybe a little longer, but we can't count on it," Victoria answered as she opened the door and led into the office. "In here." Victoria crossed the moonlit room to the open window, pulled the curtains across it and snapped on a lamp. "Watch the door," she said to Katie Marie as she began studying walls and furniture. "I'm sure the safe is here, somewhere."

"Just like you were sure it was at the airport and his downtown office."

280

"But I've watched him more carefully since we searched those places."

"We're not going to keep getting away with this, Vic."

"You want to give up?" Victoria asked, studying the walls and furniture, trying to figure out where Gerstenberg's safe was hidden. "Go back to the States and tell Harold the Air Force will just have to send those boys in blind and hope for the best?"

"There's a reason you do this and I'm sick of putting up with it!"

"Well whatever you think the reason is, it's not because I don't know what I'm talking about," Victoria announced with quiet pride. "Look."

Katie Marie glanced away from the door. Victoria stood grinning, open arm and palm indicating a safe hidden behind a portrait of Wagner. Katie Marie looked.from Victoria to the safe and back. "You going to try to get into it or just stand there and gloat?"

Victoria stepped to the safe and went to work with a stethoscope and delicate turns of the tumblers, the same way "The Cracker" had worked at the Vichy embassy safe in D.C.

Katie Marie watched. After a few minutes Victoria paused, removed the stethoscope, sighed with frustration and stared at the safe.

"We only have about a half hour left," Katie Marie said.

Victoria glanced at a wall clock. "More like forty minutes."

"You always push it to the absolute limit."

Victoria smiled and put the stethoscope back into her ears.

"Why do you do it?"

"Patriotism?" Victoria asked dismissively.

"Getting us caught and blowing the whole mission is patriotic?"

Victoria turned the safe's dial one turn, there was the distinct sound of a click, Victoria smiled, turned the handle on the safe's door and her proud

281

smile widened as she opened it. "Just like The Cracker said." She looked at Katie Marie. "You have a point?"

"Yes."

Victoria began rifling the files inside the safe. "Make it. Meanwhile, I'm going to find out if my boarding school German really is good enough to do this job."

"Typical."

Victoria looked up from the files. "What?"

"You're always at the edge of disaster. You can't get past the guilt."

Victoria picked up a file, scanned it, put it aside and picked up another. "Hank?"

Katie Marie divided her attention between attending to sounds outside the door and watching Victoria. "We both know it's not guilt for all the men you screwed."

"I'm punishing myself?" Continuing to scan a file, her next remark was blunt. "I killed Hank."

"No, you didn't. The Japs killed Hank. But you won't let yourself believe that."

"I killed Hank," Victoria repeated as she read another file.

"I'm no psychologist," Katie Marie said, "but I had a teenage son who was guilty because he believed he had caused his mother's and father's divorce. So he took off on his own and got himself in trouble and got himself caught and got himself punished."

Victoria was still reading the same file. "The hot oil thing."

"But you're not just putting yourself at risk, you're putting Operation Tidal Wave at risk."

Victoria looked up at Katie Marie. "It doesn't matter anymore," she shrugged.

"What? Why?"

"Operation Tidal Wave is impossible." Victoria held open the file she was reading for Katie Marie to see.

"Apparently your German IS good enough," Katie Marie shrugged. "What does it say?"

Victoria looked again at the file and summarized its contents. "The oilfields have the best defenses anywhere outside Germany. 'Fortress Ploiesti,' he calls it here. There's no way in." She pointed at diagrams in the file. "He has rings of anti-aircraft all around the city and he repositions them so we can't pre-spot them. He's even got auxillary pipelines above ground for easy access to connect refineries if we get to anything! Our bombers will never get through and they can't stop the oil operations even if they do."

"Do you hear something?" Katie Marie asked, turning toward the door.

Victoria, still scanning the file, went on describing the defenses. "He's got a special set of trains positioned on north and south lines with rolling artillery positions to track incoming bomber squadrons. There's no way..." She suddenly stopped reading. "Wait a minute!"

"I tell you I hear something!" Katie Marie insisted, putting her ear to the door.

"This is it!" Victoria exclaimed.

At Victoria's excitement, Katie Marie forgot for a moment what might be outside the door and turned to her. "What?"

"Our bombers can come in low. Very low. He's planned everything on how they came in last year, high. He admits, here..." she pointed at a page of the report, "... he can't quickly or easily adjust the range settings on his anti-aircraft batteries!"

Suddenly, both heard heavy footsteps and voices speaking German. "Staff!" Victoria whispered through clinched teeth.

"That's what I heard!"

A uniformed man carrying a Thompson submachine gun walked through the door, saw the women, stopped in astonishment and processed the meaning of them standing in front of the open safe with open files. Suddenly, he realized what they were doing and raised his weapon. Frozen for a moment with surprise, Victoria now struck without hesitation, sticking the sharp metal nail file deeply into the man's neck and pulling hard at it, killing and silencing him to an impotent gurgle instantly. As he fell, Victoria followed him down, grabbing him and breaking his fall to prevent noise. Katie Marie stepped out of the way. In this murderous dance, Victoria ended up with her back to the door and Katie Marie ended up facing it.

"Just like Williams taught," said Victoria, letting go of the body. "Amazing what you can do with a nail file."

"Cold-blooded murder," Katie Marie said quietly, staring at the dead soldier. She looked up at Victoria with a slightly crazed expression, her emotions rushing upon her.

"War," Victoria replied.

Another guard came to the door. Victoria did not see him. Katie Marie grabbed the dead soldier's machine gun by its barrel and swung it like a club into the second man's face, smashing his face open. He groaned and fell to the floor on top of the man killed by Victoria, then groaned again. In a sudden frenzy, Katie Marie pounced on him with a knee in his chest and beat him at the head with the butt of the gun until he was silent, his face a bloody pulp. After a final blow, she dropped the gun to the floor and looked up at Victoria.

"War?" Victoria asked.

"And murder," Katie Marie moaned, hanging her head.

In the next moment's silence, they heard more footsteps at the far end of hallway.

"Listen to me!" Victoria whispered desperately. "We've got to make our move now!"

"First we've got to get out of here," Katie Marie whispered back with the same desperation. "Through the house or out the window?"

"Both," Victoria answered. "We've got to separate." She quickly returned the files to where she got them. "We both know the secret to getting our planes in and out safely and they have no idea we know it. One of us has got to get that out."

"Both of us!"

"Shut up. If you get caught, remember: All we know is that they are coming to bomb. We don't know when, just soon. And we haven't learned ANYTHING, do you understand? Tell them everything you know, and you haven't learned ANYTHING."

Katie Marie did not answer for a moment but just looked at her companion. Finally, she said very quietly and calmly, "This is what we came for."

Tears welled up in Victoria's eyes and she nodded 'yes.' There was a moment while they simply looked at one another. "O.K.," Victoria finally said. She pointed to the window. "Go." She watched Katie Marie climb to the desk chair and onto the desk. As Katie Marie parted the curtains, Victoria clicked off the lamp. "When you get beyond the estate, make your way to the woman who keeps the goats. She will see you to the underground."

As Katie Marie climbed through the window, Victoria opened the door and stepped into the hall. Although Katie Marie did not see Gerstenberg come striding angrily down the hallway barefoot, wrapping a bathrobe around him, she heard him bellow at Victoria, "WHAT ARE YOU DOING IN THERE?"

"Alfred, darling, I was looking for a bottle of ink," Victoria replied.

It was the last thing she heard Victoria say before she dropped to the ground below the window and started running.

Knowing nothing of Victoria's fate, she could only assume, though she dared not think it, that Victoria would not be able to get the precious secret about Ploiesti's defenses—that they could be penetrated by bombers coming in very low instead of, like the 1942 raid, very high—out to their allies. It was, therefore, up to her to complete the mission. She stayed some distance from the road and stealthily followed it from Gertenberg's side of Ploiesti, through the darkest back streets of the town, toward the goat farm in the rural foothill region to the northeast. Haunted by the terror of being caught, she barely managed to hide from the Gerstenberg-alerted military and police truck, car and foot patrols everywhere on the highways, town streets and dirt roads. Just after dawn the next morning, when Williams would have been shaking them out for the training she was at this moment remembering with deep gratitude, she knocked on the farmhouse door.

A lean 60-ish woman wearing a tattered dress over trousers tucked into boots with a wrinkled freckled face, few teeth, thin gray-blond hair and big blue serious eyes opened the door.

Katie Marie identified herself in Romanian and mentioned Victoria's name. The woman studied her. Katie Marie glanced nervously over her shoulder to the dirt road that led to the highway to town. "It would be better to send me away or invite me in," Katie Marie told the woman. "You don't want anybody to see you talking to me."

The woman grinned and stepped aside, inviting Katie Marie in. Instantly, Katie Marie's hope was renewed. The woman introduced herself as Ionela, fed Katie Marie and told her to sleep, pointing her to the only bed in the two-room farmhouse.

"But we've got to get on with things quickly," Katie Marie told her.

"Yes," Ionela grinned. "But carefully. You rest one or two hours. I will take the goats out and bring back a plan."

Katie Marie laid her weary head down. "I like the way you think," she said, and fell into an exhausted sleep.

Late that morning, Ionela returned, woke and fed Katie Marie and got her into worn Romanian farmgirl clothing similar to her own. "We will take the goats out now," she told Katie Marie. "No matter who we meet, you say nothing."

"But I speak Romanian. You know that."

"The patrols are everywhere, looking for a woman who speaks Romanian like an American," the woman laughed. "You speak anything else?"

"Isn't two languages enough?"

Ionela laughed again. "I am a peasant farmer, I don't know how many is enough. I only speak Romanian and Russian and Polish. And my parents' language, Bessarabian. And my husband's parents' language, Slovak. It is enough for me."

"Well," shrugged Katie Marie. "I can keep my mouth shut."

"You better," the woman said, looking deadly serious. "If we meet anybody I don't know, which I doubt, I will tell them you are my stupid cousin from Targoviste and you have an earache and can't hear."

They set out across the Carpathian foothills, following the goats, Katie Marie pondering the old woman's mysterious strategy of avoiding speaking with the excuse of an earache. Fortunately, she did not have to test it. At an outcropping of the dense pine forest running up the mountainside to the Carpathian peaks, the old woman waved to a man standing inside the tree line holding a submachine gun. He nodded and pointed at Katie Marie. Ionela nodded 'yes' and soon a group of men came to the edge of the forest outcropping. The two women approached them. Katie Marie saw immediately they were on high alert, scanning the hillsides to make sure this was not a trap. One, a small muscular man with a dirty beard and deep brown eyes, stepped forward and talked with the old woman, who explained Katie Marie's presence.

He looked at her. "I am Dumitru. Do you want me to get you out of the country?" He asked in Romanian.

"Not yet," Katie Marie said firmly. "Get me to somebody in radio communication with the Western Allies."

"Why?"

"I have information. You don't need to know anything else."

Dumitru frowned. "I can't take you anywhere. Patrols. Your Romanian accent stinks."

"That's why I have been working as an American."

"Yes," he went on frowning. "But for radio communication I must take you back into Ploiesti." He studied her. She waited. He sighed. "Very well." He sent a man to tend the old woman's goats, turned to another and told him to bring a horse cart, then turned back to Katie Marie. "Step forward and open your mouth." Katie Marie looked dubious but did as she was told. "Do you have a handkerchief?" he asked her.

Her mouth still open, Katie Marie nodded 'yes.' It was one of the few things of her own the old woman allowed her to keep when she changed clothes.

"Give it to me."

She reached inside the old dress and handed him her clean handkerchief. He took it with one hand.

"Open your mouth."

She looked at him questioningly.

287

"Open your mouth," he demanded.

She did. He used the handkerchief to grip her lower teeth, brought a penknife up with his other hand and stuck her shallowly in the gums.

"AH!" Katie Marie screeched, pulling away from the man. She felt blood running in her mouth. "What the hell do you think you are doing?"

"Put the handkerchief against the cut," he ordered. "Quickly, while it is bloody."

Katie Marie did as she was told. "Shit!" she exclaimed. "That hurts."

"Yes," he said. He stepped toward her and she instantly backed away. He smiled. "That is all the cutting," he said, studying her. He took the bandana from around his own neck. "I must wrap this around your head. Will you let me?"

She looked back, still stuffing her white handkerchief into her mouth against the cut. When she finished, she stepped toward him and stood quietly while he wrapped the bandana below her jaw. "This will prevent you from giving yourself away with your accent, it will alter your appearance and it will make it necessary for us to take you where you need to go." He tied the bandana in a knot at the top of her head, effectively tying her mouth closed. While he did this, the man returned with a cart drawn by a sway-backed, sad-eyed old horse.

Dumitru looked at the old woman. "We must take your stupid cousin Doina from Targoviste to the dentist."

Ionela smiled her toothless grin and nodded 'yes.' Dumitru, Ionela and Katie Marie all climbed into the horse cart.

Late that afternoon, after being stopped twice by Romanian police patrols, the horse cart clopped to a halt in front of a two-story building in the low rent district of Ploiesti, far from the Hotel Europa. "Take her in," Dumitru told the old woman.

Inside was a dentist's waiting room where several people sat reading magazines, including a man in a German officer's uniform. Ionela led her to the receptionist's station. The frosted glass partition separating the front office from the waiting area slid back and Katie Marie and Bluestar stared in astonishment at each other, an astonishment that froze both.

"My stupid cousin from Targoviste has a toothache," Ionela said tiredly. "Can the dentist see her?"

Bluestar regained her composure. "The dentist is too busy," Bluestar said officiously, in an authentic, unaccented Romanian. "You need an appointment."

"She is bleeding. Look!" Ionela grabbed Katie Marie's lower lip and pulled down, revealing the bloody handkerchief. Katie Marie moaned.

"I will have the assistant take care of her," Bluestar said, grimacing for Katie Marie. She rang a small bell twice. Behind her, a door to the treating area opened and Playrunner appeared. When she recognized Katie Marie, she, too, froze in surprise.

"Emergency toothache," Bluestar reported nonchalantly.

"Ah," Playrunner replied. "Bring her through. I'll take a look."

Bluestar opened a door in the partition and let Katie Marie through. "Wait here," she said to the old woman and pointed Katie Marie through the door to the treating area.

Soon, Katie Marie was in a private cubicle, in a dentist's chair. "Open wide," Playrunner told her, looking into her mouth and leaning close to whisper. "Say nothing." Katie Marie nodded. "This is going to take some work," Playrunner went on. She turned away, walked to a table and rang a bell like the one in front. Bluestar reappeared. "Tell her cousin to come back tomorrow morning," she instructed Bluestar in her own flawless Romanian. "We will need to do a minor surgery and keep her overnight for observation."

"Very good," Bluestar nodded, without reaction, and disappeared back to the front office. They barely heard the muffled sound of Bluestar's instructions to the old woman and the slamming of the front door.

Playrunner again bent over Katie Marie, pulled the bloody handkerchief from her mouth and studied her cut gum. Katie Marie looked up dubiously.

"Don't worry, this was my real work," she said. "Bluestar, too. And we are both first generation so we grew up speaking the language. We were placed here when you and Ladyleader left for Basra. The demand for dentistry is so great nobody questioned our arrival."

"What about the dentist?" Katie Marie mumbled through a mouth full of Playrunner's hands.

"He's no hero," she smiled. "He doesn't ask, he doesn't tell and he doesn't tolerate risk. He gets a little grabby sometimes. It just gives us some extra leverage."

"You're not really going to operate on me, are you?"

Playrunner grinned. "Let's clean your teeth and make it look like surgery," she said.

"But..."

"Shsh. You don't know how dangerous it is for you. They caught Ladyleader last night."

The expression on Katie Marie's face showed her pain at the news. "Is she..."

"She is in the women's prison downtown. You are wanted dead or alive." She removed her fingers from Katie Marie's mouth. "What the hell happened?"

"You don't need to know. Do you have radio contact? Farmgirl and Typewriter..."

"We know," Playrunner interrupted her. "They came in after us with the radio but the tubes were no good. They were trying to steal a table model for the tubes but got caught."

"No radio contact?" Katie Marie asked with obvious chagrin.

"We got hold of their short wave kit and got tubes through the underground."

"Great," Katie Marie breathed out. "I've got to get something out with your next report."

"Tonight."

"Perfect."

"Then we'll figure out how to get you out of the country."

"Oh no you don't. Once we get this report in, we'll start working on how to get Ladyleader out of that prison. Then you can get BOTH of us out of Romania."

Playrunner stood back, her expression deeply troubled.

Katie Marie saw she was dubious about being able to get Victoria out of prison but looked back challengingly. "What?"

Playrunner smiled. "Let's get started cleaning your teeth before the dentist gets nervous. Then we'll work on getting your radio report out tonight. If we wake up free women tomorrow, we'll talk about what comes next, OK?"

"Nothing to talk about," Katie Marie said, leaning her head back. "Clean my teeth."

After Playrunner finished with Katie Marie, Bluestar put her into a small, hospital-like one-bed room the dentist kept for overnight oral surgery patients. Katie Marie lay down to wait, restlessly asking herself endless questions without answers. She finally fell into an uneasy sleep by quietly singing her favorite lullabye to herself, delighting in the memory of the words and melody.

There's a saying old says that love is blind
Still we're often told "seek and ye shall find"
So I'm going to seek a certain lad I've had in mind
Looking everywhere, haven't found him yet
He's the big affair I cannot forget
Only man I ever think of with regret

I'd like to add his initial to my monogram
Tell me where's the shepherd for this lost lamb

There's a somebody I'm longing to see
I hope that he turns out to be
Someone who'll watch over me

I'm a little lamb who's lost in a wood
I know I could always be good
To one who'll watch over me

Although he may not be the man some girls think of
As handsome to my heart

He carries the key

Won't you tell him please to put on some speed
Follow my lead, oh how I need
Someone to watch over me
Someone to watch over me

Won't you tell him please to put on some speed
Follow my lead, oh how I need
Someone to watch over me
Someone to watch over me

A little later, the dentist went home. Playrunner and Bluestar closed up and took Katie Marie upstairs to the apartment above the office where they lived.

After some soup and bread, Katie Marie was ready for another night of work. When Bluestar asked her for the message so she could pre-code it for transmission, Katie Marie refused. "Give me tonight's code. I'll code and send it. Nobody else needs to know this."

Both Bluestar and Playrunner studied Katie Marie for a tense moment, then looked at one another. "She's right," Playrunner finally said. "If they'd have wanted us sharing like a bunch of girls at a tea party, they'd have set it up like that."

"OK," Bluestar agreed. "And we scratch this code after tonight."

When the coding was done, Katie Marie announced she was ready.

"Not quite," Playrunner told her. "First we've got to change how you look. This is a small town. We don't want you getting recognized."

"Nobody ever noticed me," Katie Marie told them. "I was always with Victoria."

"Still," Playrunner said. "Try those." Bluestar handed Katie Marie a pair of wire-rimmed glasses and a head scarf.

When she got them on, Playrunner held up a hand mirror. "Glasses, no hair, no makeup, shapeless clothes," Katie Marie said. "Nobody's going to be making a pass at me."

"That's just how we want it," Playrunner smiled.

They set out into the hot summer night on foot, dodging patrols twice reaching the countryside. They then followed a dirt road southeast into a farming region. It was too dangerous for chitchat. After an hour of silent walking in the tall brush at the edge of the dirt road, Bluestar led them into and across a cornfield. Amid the tall stalks, they came upon the wreckage of a bomber. While Katie Marie stared in astonishment at the blackened metal skeleton, Bluestar looked up at the sky. "The stars, the stars, a million and three stars," she said in Romanian.

"A million and five," a voice inside the airplane replied.

A lean young man with big eyes in worn farmer's clothing came out carrying a small suitcase. Katie Marie immediately recognized it: The short wave radio they studied in training. The young man handed it to Bluestar, turned and ran into the night.

Bluestar stepped into the shadows of the burned out bomber, knelt over the suitcase, opened it, took out a flashlight and handed it up to Playrunner, who snapped it on. In the flashlight's dim glow, Bluestar began setting up the radio.

In a moment, Bluestar had the headset over her ears and was testing the battery-powered signal. Katie Marie watched for a moment in amazement, then turned and looked into the cornfield.

"Good idea," Playrunner whispered. "Keep watch."

"This is your regular broadcasting post?" Katie Marie whispered.

Playrunner laughed brusquely. "Can't risk anything regular. We'll hand the kit off to another runner in ten minutes. Similar passwords. The underground will set up another site when we signal for a 'send.' All new every time. Nothing lost when somebody goes down."

When the radio was ready, Bluestar made contact, Katie Marie took the headphones, tapped out the vital information in code and returned the headphones to Bluestar, who signed off. They quickly packed the radio kit. As they finished, a teenage boy with messy hair, acne and luminous eyes and a barely adolescent girl with long blond hair and smooth white skin appeared. The girl traded passwords with Bluestar, took the kit, handed it to the boy and they ran into the cornfield.

The three women turned back toward Ploiesti but took a different, more circuitous route. They wound up on the far side of the town. When they came to a small public house, Playrunner and Bluestar had Katie Marie wait in the hayloft of a nearby barn while they stopped in for a drink of apricot brandy and a few folksongs, a way to explain their absence from their apartment if anyone asked. Before they went in, Katie Marie stopped them.

"Give me your cover names, just in case."

"Right," smiled Bluestar. "I'm Rahela. Your dental hygienist is Bogdana."

"And I, as you know, I am Doina, the stupid cousin from Targoviste."

A couple of hours later, they came out of the pub, relaxed and happy, provided "Doina" with a secreted shot of brandy and strolled back to the dentist's office with her, chatting. Tipsily giggling, "Rahela" and "Bogdana" shared stories in Romanian about their over-sexed dentist.

"At least he hasn't fallen in love with either of us yet," Bluestar whispered.

"But he keeps giving me those somber eyes," said Playrunner.

Katie Marie laughed. "Let me give you some expert advice on how to handle a married man in love," she said, and proceeded to tell them how Victoria fended off the Vichy ambassador with crocodile tears and melodramatic self-sacrifice. By the end of her story, the three young women were laughing and crying. After she told it, a silence fell over them as they reached the dentistry.

"We'll tuck you away in the post-surgery recovery room again," Bluestar told Katie Marie. "Tomorrow, Ionela will get you back to Dumitru, and he'll get you out of Romania."

"I'm not leaving this country without Victoria," Katie Marie replied quietly, firmly.

"I thought that's what you'd say," Bluestar smiled. She looked at Playrunner.

Playrunner seemed to come to a decision. "Go back out to the farm with Ionela tommorrow," Playrunner said. "Herd the goats. Watch the town. We'll see what we can find out about the prison. We'll see you again on market day."

"Perfect," Katie Marie agreed.

The next day, a visitor to a petty thief in the Ploiesti women's prison passed a message that eventually made its way to Victoria. She was to complain of a toothache. A day later, in a filthy, smelly room on the third floor of the prison, Playrunner was bent over Victoria, peering into Victoria's mouth while Bluestar stood nearby, holding a kit of dental instruments and supplies. Bluestar watched for guards and cleverly made covering chit-chat with Playrunner in Romanian while Playrunner pantomimed a dental procedure across the language barrier while whispering English with Victoria.

Observing that Victoria seemed safe and sound but bruised and beaten, Playrunner first asked about her status.

"They did what they did," Victoria whispered slowly. "It's over. I gave them everything but…"

"But Katie Marie's secret about the defenses."

"Did she get it out?" Victoria asked anxiously.

Playrunner smiled and nodded 'yes.'

"Then it was worth it," sighed Victoria.

"What are they going to do with you?"

"Right now they seem to be ignoring me. I guess they'll shoot me sooner or later."

"Maybe Antonescu will do something," Playrunner suggested hopefully. "Or exchange you with the Russians."

"Gerstenberg won't let him," Victoria said. "He hates me. Hell hath no fury like a Nazi dupe."

"What is this strange effect you have on men?" Playrunner smiled gently.

Victoria looked away. "At least Katie Marie got out."

"Well, actually," Playrunner whispered.

"You said…"

"She got the information out by short wave. She refuses to leave Romania without you."

"Tell her to get out!" Victoria whispered through clinched teeth.

Playrunner leaned back and studied Victoria. "Would you leave without her?"

Victoria looked back, then down again. "What's the plan?" she asked reluctantly.

"Whatever it is, our best chance will be in the middle of the bombing raid."

"Sounds right. But dangerous."

Playrunner shrugged. "We got what we came for." She stood up, turned to Bluestar and said something in Romanian.

Victoria looked up at her and whispered. "Can you make up an excuse to treat me one more time?"

"A follow-up? Yeah, sure."

"Thank you."

"Don't thank me," Playrunner smiled. "I'm about to drill out a filling with a hand drill."

The follow-up visit two days later was routine except Victoria slipped an envelope into the lining of the dental kit as Bluestar was packing up. "Give it to Katie Marie," Victoria whispered. "But tell her not to read it unless..." Victoria hesitated.

"I understand," Bluestar whispered quickly.

"I never thought it would play out like this," Victoria said quietly, staring at the floor.

"Nobody ever expects a toothache," Playrunner said. "And there's nothing you can do about it but endure it – or pull it."

With surreptitious smiles and hugs, they took their leave, reminding her to be ready when the bombing started.

Eight days later, Sunday, August 1, 1943, Ionela, the goat herder, and Katie Marie rode the cart drawn by the sad-eyed, sway-backed horse into town with cans of goats' milk to sell at the Ploiesti market. The market place was buzzing with activity. The German occupation made Ploiesti one of the few well-supplied towns in all Europe. The square was picturesque with heaps of corn and beans and tomatoes and apples at farmers' stands. Chickens in coops squawked; fat goats baa'ed; plump corn-fed pigs bleated. Cheeses and salamis lined cubicle countertops and hung from tent rafters in the stalls lining the white-tiled market square where women in brightly embroidered skirts and men in white tunics and black hats chattered and hawked wares.

As Katie Marie helped the old woman unload the cans of goat milk at Ionela's stall, Playrunner and Bluestar wandered up the aisle, shopping for a chance to confer with Katie Marie. Seeing them come, Katie Marie nodded to Ionela and walked back to the cart. The other two women stood by the horse.

"Any progress?" Katie Marie asked.

"Romanian," Playrunner demanded in a whisper.

"Right," Katie Marie answered in Romanian.

"We saw the patient," Bluestar replied in Romanian.

"And we have a treatment plan," Playrunner added. "But it isn't much."

Katie Marie lifted a can of goat's milk and walked from the cart toward her two companions beside the horse. "Tell me," she smiled through clinched teeth, angry that they had an inadequate plan.

"We're going to wait until the chaos of the bombing raid," Playrunner told her.

"That I like," Katie Marie smiled.

"Ladyleader likes it, too. She will be ready."

"We bribed a man on the inside. It was expensive."

"Don't worry about that," Katie Marie told them. "We'll make sure you get it back."

"When the bombing starts," Bluestar concluded, "he will make his move."

"I'll find some way to get into town," Katie Marie said with a nod, still holding the milk can. "We can meet at the dentist's office."

"Good," said Playrunner.

"When do you think it will be?" Bluestar asked.

"Any day now," Katie Marie smiled, leaning against the old sway-backed horse.

"As far as I'm concerned, it can't be too soon," Bluestar said. "This waiting is…"

"What's that?" Katie Marie interrupted, suddenly standing upright and shifting the weight of the milk can.

"What?" Bluestar asked.

"That," Katie Marie replied, looking south. "There."

"What do you mean?" Playrunner asked, looking south with her.

"Wait," Katie Marie said, her head snapping to the west. "There."

"What do you mean?" Bluestar asked, following Katie Marie's eyes across the horizon. Her eyes widened. "LOOK!" She pointed to the west. A huge plume of black smoke rose from the western edge of the town.

Distant explosions sounded from that direction an instant later. In the next instant, explosions sounded from the south. Playrunner pointed there. "Look!" More huge, dense thick columns of smoke rose above the horizon and a swarm of distant airplanes came into sight above the town.

"This is it!" Katie Marie exclaimed, dropping the bottle. "They're coming in low on the oil facilities! Look at the anti-aircraft fire – it's going over the bombers just like Victoria said it would!"

"Victoria!" Bluestar and Playrunner exclaimed at the same moment.

There was a terrific roaring noise above and beyond the rooftops to the south and coming toward them. Air raid sirens started blaring. The three women stood transfixed as everything began shaking, the walls of the buildings around them and the street below their feet. They looked back. A monstrous green airplane, its engines groaning deafeningly and its propellers blowing a windstorm, came up the boulevard, its wings barely missing the apartment windows on either side.

A small black fighter jet roared in from the east, swooped up over the rooftops and bore down on the big bomber, its nose gun raining down a volley of deadly fire. One of the bomber's engines exploded into flames. The fighter swooped under the bomber, then up and over the buildings across the street. It happened so fast few people even took cover from the hail of fire. A man across the street lay dead on the pavement in the fighter's wake.

As the fighter disappeared, the bomber suddenly dipped its wing on the side of the burning engine, like it was losing its balance. Its nose dropped, then dropped further and it was too low to keep flying. In the next instant, it crashed with a terrific explosion into a three-story brick building at the end of the boulevard on Strada Carpati.

"That's the women's prison!" Bluestar screamed.

"Victoria!" Katie Marie yelled, and started running toward the crash. Bluestar and Playrunner were at her heels as they ploughed through a wave of people running away from it.

At the jail, great flames leapt from the wood frame brick building's top two floors. On the street, Katie Marie, Bluestar and Playrunner slipped past seared and blistered women prisoners and prison guards strewn on the ground. Kindly people from the market gently stripped smoldering rags of uniforms and prison dresses from them and bathed horribly disfigured swaths of face and body with what cold water was available.

Struggling past this heart-wrenching sight, the three women looked up at the burning jail and saw the tail section of the bomber protruding from what was left of the top of the building, its fuselage streaming a waterfall of highly explosive gasoline into the burning ruins, feeding the flames. Amid the moans of people on the pavement and the screams of those still trapped inside, someone hurried by shouting for the jailer. "There are women locked in!" he screamed. "Find the jailer! He has the keys!"

"The jailer is our man!" Playrunner said desperately to Katie Marie. "He said he would take her down the back stairs when he heard the bombers coming."

They all three pivoted and dashed around the fire to the building's rear. The nose of the bomber stuck through the back wall. The building's bricks, the plane's plexiglass cockpit and the wood of the rear stairs were an almost indistinguishable wreckage. Adjacent to the jail's second-floor rear-door, the blackened body of a portly man hung, tenuously impaled on the one remaining vertical beam of the staircase.

"Look!" Bluestar yelled, pointing. "Ladyleader!"

Atop a charred, smoldering window frame on the crumbling jail's first floor was a woman's burnt, bleeding body. On seeing it, none of the three women could move until, horrifyingly, it raised its head a tiny bit and opened eyes in a black and bloody face. It was Victoria.

Katie Marie started for her but as she neared, the gasoline-fed flames exploded at the foot of the staircase and drove her back. Victoria seemed to see this and tried to speak. Katie Marie started forward again despite the fire. Her companions held her back, but they were near enough to hear Victoria's weakened, dying voice. Katie Marie struggled against her companions, then stopped and looked at Victoria.

"No," Victoria groaned.

"She wants you to stay back!" Playrunner told Katie Marie.

"But I can't!" Katie Marie protested desperately. She looked again at Victoria.

"They came in low," Victoria said with enormous effort and what she had left of a smile.

Katie Marie again struggled against the women holding her and looked up desperately until, unable to get away from them, looked toward Victoria.

"No," Victoria said again, more weakly.

Their eyes met. Katie Marie looked at Victoria plaintively, words utterly failing her. The last gasps of life ebbed from Victoria. "I will always adore you, Vic," Katie Marie finally said.

"Everybody does," Victoria replied. Her eyes closed and life went mercifully out of her just before the last remnants of the flaming building crashed in on her.

Katie Marie fell to her knees, her body folding in agony as she wailed "NO!" She wretched thin green goo and sputum onto the filthy concrete and her eyes flooded with tears that cascaded down her face. "Noooo!"

Through their own pain, Playrunner and Bluestar came to their senses, realized Nazis and Nazi collaborators were everywhere around them and quickly acted. Each lifted one of Katie Marie's arms and they dragged her, still bent and curled into an agonized, weeping fetal position, from the scene.

Playrunner and Bluestar partly carried and partly dragged Katie Marie back from the burning, exploding building just as German military fire trucks and crews arrived. In the garden of the cathedral across the boulevard, they cooled her face with holy water and whispered calm reassurances in Romanian. A priest hurrying from the cathedral toward the burning prison stopped when he saw them. "Can I help?" All three looked up at him.

"It's all right, Father," Bluestar told him. "Her sister was in the prison."

"It's not all right, Father," Katie Marie wept. "Not all right."

He stooped to her. "You are not from Ploiesti, are you?"

"She is the cousin of Ionela, the goatherd," Playrunner said quickly. "She is visiting from Targoviste for dental care."

"And she has a sister in the women's prison here?"

"Had," Bluestar corrected him.

"She is dead, Father," Katie Marie moaned, hanging her head. "Dead."

The priest looked at the back of her head. "I must go to the others, child. But remember this:" He stands. "Your sister is with her Lord now, who will forgive and adore her."

Katie Marie looked up suddenly. "Of course he will," she said, rage in her eyes. "Of course he will."

The priest smiled uncomprehendingly, turned and walked away. Katie Marie looked at Bluestar and Playrunner. "He's crazier than the one who expelled me from confirmation class when I slapped him for feeling me up," she told them, standing up.

"Looks like he brought you around, though," Playrunner said, looking Katie Marie over.

"I doubt Vic would want me laying here slobbering," she replied.

"Let's get back to our apartment for the night," Bluestar said, leading the way. "We'll get something to eat and figure out what comes next."

"What comes next..." Katie Marie replied, following, as they walked quickly through the Piata and up Strada Vasile Lupu avoiding the many other pedestrians hurrying to and away from the fire, "...is we get the hell out of Romania."

"I'm not so sure about that," said Bluestar. She looked at her partner. "What do you think?"

"Katie Marie can't stay," Playrunner said. "And we can't go. It would blow our cover. They'd pick us up immediately." They reached the dental office and went up the outside stairs to the apartment. "The whole region is going to be crazy with police and military patrols."

"You're right, I guess," Katie Marie said. "And I guess I've got to go fast or it makes it more dangerous for you."

"That's what I'm thinking," Playrunner said, leading the way into the apartment. Katie Marie and Playrunner sat at the kitchen table and continued talking while Bluestar laid out food and wine and listened.

"How do I go? They will be watching the trains and the roads. I'd never get on a plane."

"Ionela?" Katie Marie asked.

"She could take you in but your Romanian isn't good enough. She can't keep you and she doesn't dare contact the underground for a long time."

"In other words, I'm a problem for everybody."

"She didn't say that," Bluestar smiled, sitting down with them and pouring wine. "Let's just eat and relax. We'll put you in post-surgery downstairs tonight. If anybody asks, your toothache came back. Tomorrow, we'll see how things look."

Playrunner smiled. "Best plan yet."

Katie Marie looked from one to the other. "It will have to do."

Late that night, hours after Playrunner and Bluestar had settled her, Katie Marie rose, took what she could find for her purposes in the dentist's office and slipped out the back door into the night. Playrunner and Bluestar, safer for her leaving, would understand.

She made her way north through Ploiesti. It was a completely different town than it had been the night she ran from Gerstenberg's house when Victoria was captured. People wandered the streets, worriedly asking one another if they were all right. Military and police vehicles and foot units moved back and forth in every block. By the middle of the night she reached the foothills north of town. Behind her in the west, ahead of her in the east and far to the south, fires glowed on the horizon. A heavy blanket of smoke hung over the entire town. Wrecked buildings and crashed airplanes intruded weirdly into the skyline.

In the still familiarly bucolic nighttime countryside, Katie Marie relaxed. Walking alone at the edge of the road, she felt confident of reaching Ionela's farmhouse by morning. There, she knew she could obtain provisions. After that, there was only a very long journey into the unknown.

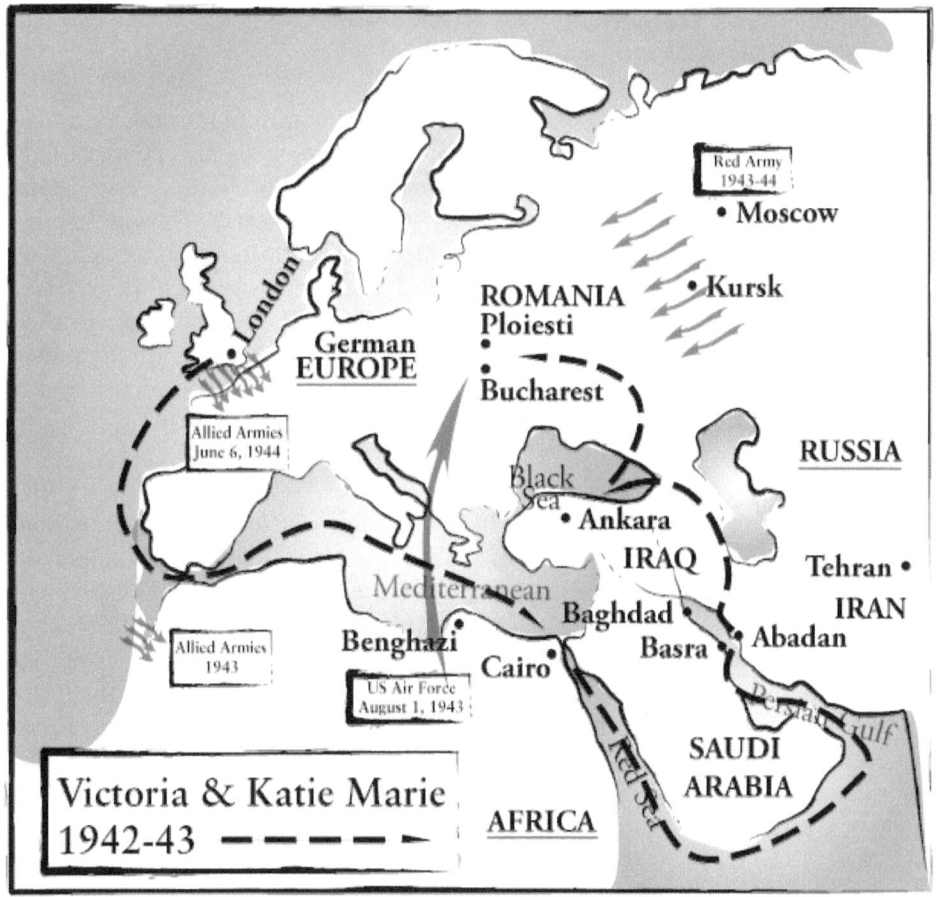

Once again, she reached Ionela's farmhouse as the sun was rising. The old woman opened the door with a worried expression. When she saw Katie Marie, she simply grunted and stared at her.

"I will leave tonight," Katie Marie said, marching inside.

The old woman turned to her guest. "You will make for the Russian lines?"

"Have you got a better idea?"

"No," Ionela said tiredly, "but that is not a very good one either. Make for Kursk."

Katie Marie slept through the day while Ionela was out with the goats. She set out again after darkness fell. There was a new moon and the dense smoke of the oil refinery fires had now spread across the region so it was deeply dark and quiet. Katie Marie trudged northeast across farm fields. The land was full of desperate people and enemies.

Staying near but off the road, away from German military and Romanian police patrols, she walked through the night, following the course of the foothills. Her eyes became accustomed to the darkness. She rested frequently, knowing the distance was too great to rush. Saving Ionela's cheese and salami and bread for need, she watched for farms along her route where, though she dared not approach the occupants, she could help herself to water from the well and fruits of their fields if she could get to them without setting the dogs howling. When the sky turned blue-gray, she moved up the nearest hillside, found a culvert into which she could curl, pulled fallen pine branches over herself and rested, sleeping fitfully and waiting for nightfall to move on.

After walking cautiously and watchfully through a second long night, gaining confidence and hope with her slow, steady progress, she was in the process of falling asleep under pine branches when she heard heavy footfalls, labored breathing, moans and the sound of something being dragged. She was too afraid to try to peer out between the pine needles, fearing even the slightest noise might be her ruin. She lay still and silent, like a terrified rabbit, and listened. At what she heard, she was overjoyed: American English! "Looks pretty safe up in here," the one breathing hard said. She heard him lay something heavy down. "Lay back." A man groaned. "Talk to me." There was a pause.

For a long moment, she stopped breathing, terrified the man had seen her, was talking to her. She could not make herself reply. The only sound was the man's continued hard breathing. Finally, another man spoke.

"I'm hurtin', Darryl," the other voice moaned quietly.

"Yeah, an' still bleeding."

She could hear the pain in their voices.

"Leave me here."

Darryl sat on the dirt beside his friend. "What?"

"You heard me."

"You know I cain't hear when you say things like that."

"Darryl…"

"Shut up and save your strength. I need to figure how to get you some medical supplies."

She heard no reply. There was a short silence. Then she heard Darryl's voice again.

"Randy?" No answer. "Randy!" She heard rustling in the dirt and brush as Darryl became excited about Randy and attended to him. "Don't you die and leave me out here, you son of a bitch! We left Memphis together and we're going back together, damn you!"

Though mortally fearing, Katie Marie threw back the pine branches that concealed her. Darryl, big brown eyes wide beneath a shock of curly dark hair, stumbled clumsily over big feet but quickly drew his gangly six-foot frame up and pointed a .38 revolver at her.

Tremblingly, she held out her bag of medical supplies stolen from the dentistry. "There's medicine and bandages in here," she said. "I think all three of us could use a new friend right about now."

"Who the hell ARE you lady?" Darryl barked, right at the edge of panic.

She looked up at him. "I…" She stopped. "It would take too long to explain how a Chicago nightclub singer and a couple of Tennessee boys could wind up in a ditch in Romanian farm country surrounded by people who want to capture, torture and kill them. Why don't we see if we can help Randy first?"

Darryl stared at her, and then finally smiled and dropped the pistol to his side. "For somebody who makes no sense, you sound pretty smart."

As he turned back to his friend, she stepped next to him. "I don't know much about doctorin'," Darryl said sadly.

"I had a son," she said, taking the bag of medical supplies back from him and kneeling to Randy, who was almost Darryl's size, with the same dark hair and eyes, but rounder in face and body. "Just about the same age as the two of you."

"It's my foot," Randy moaned as she lifted his foreleg.

"It's your heel," She corrected him. The rear of the boy's boot was in shreds, the sock was gone and the flesh of his heel was not much better. Dried blood covered his boot and pants leg.

"Somethin' hit me in the foot as we was comin' down," Randy told her weakly.

"Wanna wash it?" Darryl asked, handing her a canteen. While she washed and probed the wound, Darryl told her what she had already guessed, that they had been in one of the bombers shot down in the raid on Ploiesti.

"And you're making for the Russian lines."

"Yes'm," Darryl said.

"Well, I took advantage of the chaos you caused to steal some medical supplies from a dentist and some food from a farmer. I'm trying to make the Russian lines, too."

"Maybe we can help each other."

Something about these boys reminded her not of her own son but of a boy she never met, Victoria's nephew Hank. Maybe this was her opportunity to do something for Victoria by giving these boys the help Hank never got.

Randy moaned at her probe into his wound. "Good news. The bone and muscle seem intact. Now if we can keep it clean and keep you off it, you should recover."

She doctored Randy, fed them both and showed them how to settle under pine branch cover to sleep. They rested all day. Periodically, she washed Randy's wound and gave him pain medication.

At dusk, she used his belt for a sling to keep the foot off the ground, had him wrap one arm around her and the other around Darryl, and they again started across country. Hobbling like this through the night, with frequent rests, they made slow progress toward the distant allure of safety. Two or three times they ducked into the underbrush when they spotted vehicles, probably German military patrols, traveling the road along the base of the foothills. At dawn they stopped again, sheltering in a gully.

When Katie Marie checked Randy's foot, her findings were not happy. "He's losing a lot blood and it's getting dirtier," she replied to Darryl's impatient questioning as she again bathed the wound.

"Change the bandage," he impatiently told her.

"I will," she snapped back. "But I don't have much more gauze or tape. And he needs to be flat on his back with that foot elevated for a long time."

"How do we do that and travel?"

"We could make a litter," Katie Marie thought aloud. "But I doubt we'd get all the way to Russia like that."

"Darryl could steal a car," Randy suggested.

"Shut up and lay still," Katie Marie cut him off. "They'd run us down right away."

"Any chance of finding the underground?" Darryl asked her.

"They might find us," she told him, thinking about Dumitru. "But we'd never find them."

"Well," said Darryl.

"Yeah," replied Katie Marie. She finished re-bandaging the foot. "Let's get some rest and just try to get through another night."

"Yeah," grinned Darryl. "You never know WHAT might happen."

"That's what worries me," Katie Marie replied, rolling under a pine branch to sleep.

By dusk, Randy's foot seemed a little better and they set out with renewed hope. But after they walked a couple of hours, a summer rainstorm blew up. The ground below them turned muddy and the footing was treacherous. They fell once, then again, and then again. Each time, Randy's foot banged into the mud and the dressing got dirtier. Their determination eroding, they nevertheless plodded on, until the path they chose led them down a ravine and into the face of a cliff. All three looked up desperately and realized it was too high and vertical to climb. They then peered into the rain-drenched darkness as far as they could along the cliff's face in both directions, seeing no way around.

Katie Marie groaned, left Randy leaning against Darryl, turned her back to the cliff and slid down into a sitting position at its base, slightly out of the rain. "Looks like we'll have to go back," she said.

Darryl turned to his friend, eased him down beside Katie Marie and stood over them, leaning against the rock, sheltering from the rain and sheltering Randy. "Prob'ly two or three miles," he said quietly.

Randy moaned. "Leave me here," he said.

"Shut up," Darryl snapped.

"You've got to!"

"Ain't gonna happen."

Katie Marie remained silent.

The two boys lapsed into the same exhausted silence, devoid of options. In the silence, there was a faint, distant sound.

"What's that?" Katie Marie wondered aloud.

"Train whistle," Darryl said disinterestedly, staring into the night.

"Heard 'em all the time back home," Randy added with equal disinterest. Suddenly, he turned to Katie Marie. "Maybe we could ride the rails to Russia!"

"The trains would be watched," Katie Marie told him.

"Sure they would!" exclaimed Darryl excitedly. "But me'n'Randy've rid 'em all over the U.S. of A.! We know the tricks 'bos use to beat the bulls! We can do it, cain't we Randy?"

Randy looked from Katie Marie to Darryl and back to Katie Marie, then leaned his head back against the cliff. "It's worth a try."

Concluding that further travel in the rain and wind and mud with Randy in his present condition was more dangerous than staying where they were, they sheltered under branches and brush against the cliff face. Later in the night, when the rain stopped, Darryl went out alone to locate the train tracks and follow them to a jumping off point.

Katie Marie spent the two following, tense nights and days nursing Randy on thin rations and dwindling medical supplies. She kept the wound clean and kept him on his back. He seemed to heal with the rest, though his pain was worryingly worse. As she used the last of her sulfa powder to prevent infection, she assured him the pain would soon dissipate. He shivered at her touch. She shivered with the fear that her therapeutic lie would be revealed.

In the middle of the third night, a frightening sound turned out to be Darryl returning with good news. There was a switching yard outside Bacau, a nearby town.

"Isn't that dangerous?" Katie Marie asked dubiously. "A switching yard's busy. It's going to be heavily guarded."

Darryl grinned at Randy. "Explain it to your nurse."

"Just beyond the yard is the 'bos train station, past the bulls but still goin' slow enough to board," Randy explained happily. "All you've got to do is bandage me up so I can sprint to that open boxcar and jump on."

"We've done it a dozen times out west," Darryl told her. "Nothin' to it."

"Pick us a car with a pile o' stuff we can hide up behind."

"Ride east all the way to Russia."

"Sounds like a plan!" Randy exclaimed.

Yeah, Katie Marie's expression read, one of those best-laid plans. The two happy country boys did not notice and would not understand her expression or the thought that went with it: Only a couple of hillbillies could be optimistic about such a crackpot scheme.

But two days later, without a hitch in the plan, they were hidden away behind big rolls of military canvas in the boxcar of an eastbound freight train, watching through worn slats in the walls as the verdant countryside rolled by. Randy's pain was even diminishing. Provisioned by Darryl's deft thievery from pre-spotted farms along their route to the switching yard, the two boys settled back for the train ride with new confidence. Katie Marie, however, could not relax. Later in the day, her anxiety was rewarded when, at a stop on a siding, the boxcar door slid open and they heard the desperate grunts and gasping of someone jumping aboard and pulling the door shut.

Darryl reached for his pistol. Beside him, Katie Marie stayed his hand and signaled to let the train start up again before making his move. They heard the intruder fall to a roll of canvas in front of them. The breathing evened. The train began moving northeast again. Darryl crept around the rolls of canvas, Katie Marie following. Both relaxed appreciably when they discovered a lone, unarmed woman sprawled before them, her eyes closed.

Darryl put the pistol's barrel to her temple and cocked the hammer. She started alert but immediately felt the pistol barrel, saw her captor and laid still. A haggard, weary-looking mid-thirtyish pale blond with colorless eyes, she began speaking German.

Katie Marie shook her head 'no' and said "Romanian."

The woman shook her head 'no' and said "Ruski." Katie Marie shook her head 'no.'

Angrily, Darryl shouted "English!"

Tentatively, the woman again shook her head 'no' and asked "Francais?"

Katie Marie was just about to again shake her head 'no' when, from behind the rolls of canvas, Randy yelled "Oui! Oui!"

"How the hell does a Tennessee hick speak French?" Katie Marie asked loudly in surprise.

"My momma was French 'til she married daddy when he was in Paris in the last war," Randy called.

"Well," said Darryl. "Our hideout ain't no secret now." Katie Marie glanced at the woman and saw an ironic, almost cruel smile flit across her face but before she could say anything about it, Darryl continued talking. "Let's bring her back to where we got Randy laid out and see what he can get out of her."

"Fine," Katie Marie agreed curtly, turning away from the woman's cold eyes, hoping the German woman did not realize Katie Marie now suspected the woman probably understood their English.

As they rode east, with all the translating left to Randy, Katie Marie was helpless to prevent the two innocent boys from revealing far more information than they obtained. Like them, the woman, who gave her name as Kockava, was bound for the Russian lines. Kockava explained that her mother was a Russian captive of the first war and she had always been sympathetic to the Russian rather than the German cause but it was only recently, when her mother died, that she had fled the Nazis.

Revealing they were American Air Force men, the boys told her of their bombing raid on Ploiesti and their escape. Kockava applauded them, calling them heroes. Katie Marie stuck with her cover story, explaining she had been the private secretary to a rich American woman who was a guest of the Romanian government until captured by the Nazi occupiers and killed, while she herself was lucky enough to escape and was now on the run.

Neither Katie Marie nor the German woman questioned the other's story but each was clearly skeptical. The boys did not notice the tension. They rode for two more days and nights, through endless starts and stops on sidings. They cautiously doled out their food and water, not daring to leave the boxcar to replenish their supplies for fear of being left behind. Randy's foot benefited greatly from the rest. The wound closed, making the bandaging easier and eliminating his need for aspirin.

On the second day, they began hearing artillery, mile-by-mile nearer, louder and more incessant. By midday, they heard rifle and pistol fire and exploding hand grenades in the distance. Early in the afternoon, there were fighter planes streaking back and forth above, and intermittent dog fights. Then the train came to a stop in nondescript farm fields, the middle of western Russia's vast nowhere.

They heard men moving all around the train. Through the slats, they saw it was the Russian military. A commanding officer, who looked to Katie Marie like Dumitru in a dirty uniform, issued orders and the men scattered along the train's cars.

"He tells them to search the train and see what they have," Kockava whispered to Randy, who translated.

"Now what?" Darryl asked Katie Marie.

"Brutal men," Kockava, through Randy, warned them.

"But they're Russian," Katie Marie whispered to Darryl. "They might get us home." She moved to where she could see the boxcar door. Pulling his pistol, Darryl crawled over behind her. Kockava was at his shoulder. "If they don't find us," Katie Marie said, "we'll keep riding east. If they find us, we'll tell them the truth."

" 'Bout all we can do," Darryl agreed.

The boxcar door slid open. Sunlight fell brightly on the car's interior, illuminating the occupants before they could duck behind the rolls of canvas. The soldiers at the door shot into the canvas with sub-machine guns and backed away. Footsteps outside the car came running from all directions.

Once again they heard the commanding officer's voice, yelling in Russian.

"We're Americans," Darryl yelled back, holstering his pistol.

"We're looking for asylum!" Katie Marie added.

"American?" the Russian officer asked.

"We want to come out!" Darryl yelled. "We've got a wounded man in here."

"Dah. Dah," The Russian yelled. "Good, good. Come out!"

They heard him give orders to his men. Darryl and Katie Marie looked at each other. "We were trying to get to the Russian lines," Katie Marie shrugged.

He studied her for a moment, then decided she was right. "Help me get Randy out."

Together, he and Katie Marie slid Randy around the rolls of canvas and to the door of the boxcar. They then jumped down and lifted him to the ground. He draped one arm around each, in their by-now standard hobbling posture. Kockava jumped out of the boxcar last and followed.

The Russian officer ordered men to enter the car cautiously and search for others. Meanwhile, he studied these ragged stowaways. "American?" he repeated.

"English?" Katie Marie asked.

"A little," the officer smiled.

"More'n my Russian," Darryl grinned.

Suddenly, from behind Darryl, Kockava grabbed his pistol from the holster on his belt and barked shrilly in Russian, pointing the pistol at the three Americans.

"She's a liar and a German!" Katie Marie yelled quickly. "I don't know what she's saying but don't believe her!"

All around them, Russian soldiers leveled weapons on the four train riders.

"She is telling us she is a German communist party member," the officer sighed with melancholy as he pulled his own pistol from its holster. "You, she says, are American spies," the officer explained to Katie Marie.

"It's a lie!" Darryl protested and started to turn on Kockava until the click of several instantly readied weapons froze him.

Kockava spoke in Russian. The officer nodded.

"Don't believe her!" Katie Marie protested without knowing what Kockava was saying. "Look at these boys!" She argued. "Spies don't sneak around wearing uniforms. We took this woman in because she said she wanted to get to you for asylum, just like us."

The Russian officer sighed, began speaking in a friendly tone to Kockava in Russian and stepped forward. Suddenly, he raised his pistol and shot her straight between the eyes at short range, knocking her backwards. Before she hit the ground, the officer was speaking to the three Americans in English. "You maybe are spies. I will leave it to the NKVD in Kursk. She is maybe a comrade, but she turns on you like a German dog so she dies like a German dog." He bent, took Darryl's pistol from Kockova's dead hand, stuck it in his belt, turned and barked orders at his soldiers.

Moments later two soldiers approached, marched the three Americans slowly to a canvas-covered military transport truck, Katie Marie and Darryl still

313

helping Randy. The soldiers loaded them in and sat them on bench seats along the truckbed's sides, Katie across from the two boys. The soldiers took seats behind them, nearer the open air at the back of the truckbed. Soon, the truck was rumbling and bumping northeast. For a while, Katie Marie, Darryl and Randy stared at the floor without talking, still trying to grasp what had happened. Occasionally, at the booming and roaring sounds of battle going on all around them and in the sky above them, one or the other would look out the open back, though nothing was there except dust. Soon, Randy laid his head back against the frame of the truck's canvas cover and closed his eyes.

Darryl looked up and caught Katie Marie's eye. "They're our allies?"

"The Germans are worse," she said quietly.

One of the guards snapped at them in Russian. Both understood he was telling them to shut up. They hung their heads again and resumed their careful study of the truckbed's floor.

Katie Marie looked up again and turned to the guard who had reprimanded them a moment before. "Where are we going?" she asked.

The guard stared at her in silence. She asked again in Romanian. She got the same stare. She dropped her head again.

Hours later, the truck came to a stop at a farm. The guards unloaded them and allowed them to walk, Randy limping, behind bushes to toilet themselves. They were led to an outdoor table and handed bread, dry salami and a canteen of water. While they ate, another soldier marched a young black-haired, brown-eyed, round-faced woman in a long, loose gypsy dress from the farmhouse and sat her at the same table. She eyed the three Americans coldly, almost contemptuously. The guard doled her salami, bread and water, which she consumed ravenously. Katie Marie, Darryl and Randy ate sullenly. Soon, the three guards marched the four prisoners, Randy leaning on Darryl, to the truck, loaded them and climbed in after. Once again, the truck rumbled on.

As they climbed back into the truck, Darryl whispered to Katie Marie. "Tell me again they're our allies."

"Yeah," she grunted back before the guard again snapped at them.

The soldier from the farmhouse became a third guard and sat with the other two near the open end of the canvas-covered bed while the prisoners resumed their previous seats, the black-haired woman sitting down next to Katie Marie, ignoring her and assuming the forearms-on-knees, head-hung posture.

The new guard was chatty and began questioning the other two, ignoring the prisoners. Katie Marie leaned to the woman. "English?" The woman shook her head 'no.' "Romanian?"

Recognition flitted through the young woman's passionate brown eyes.

"Are you Romanian?" Katie Marie asked in their common language.

"I am Russian from Bessarabia but my husband is..." She paused. "...Was from a Moldavian family," she whispered in Romanian.

"Do you know where they are taking us?"

"East."

"What for?"

"Questioning."

"Questioning?"

"That is all I know."

"We are Americans," Katie Marie told her, changing her approach slightly. 'My family is from Bucharest. You are with child?"

The woman put her hands around her belly protectively. "It shows?"

"Only in your face and your appetite," Katie Marie smiled. "Why are you a prisoner?"

"They caught me with a German officer."

"Your lover?"

"My captor."

"Where is he?"

"Dead."

"He is the father?"

"Or the Russian officer who he killed and took me from." Katie Marie just stared at her. The woman read the wordless confusion of horror and sympathy in Katie Marie's eyes. Her expression took on a deep seriousness. "I have a juice between my legs that keeps me alive. All the men who use it are dead. Now I have a child."

Katie Marie smiled. "You are brave."

"Not really."

"What is your name?"

"Violeta."

"Perhaps you will have a son, Violeta, and you can teach him to hate killing."

"I doubt it. Both of the men who raped me had fine blond hair and bright blue eyes. If he is like them, he will love to kill."

"And if he is like you?"

"He will have hate in his heart."

"Maybe you will have a girl," Katie Marie told her.

"I think I would drown her," the woman said, without a hint of irony or dark humor.

Late in the night, the truck arrived in the small city.

"Kursk," Violeta whispered.

The guards unloaded the prisoners, one marching the two women toward the town's jail, the other marching the boys, Randy leaning on Darryl, in another direction. "Tell the truth. Hold back nothing," Katie Marie called to the two air force men as the guard led her away from them.

In the foul-smelling, dark jail, the two women were led past a row of large cells crowded with female prisoners. Violeta was put into one of these. But the guard marched Katie Marie on, to a small, empty, windowless cell at the end of the building with nothing but a stinking hole in the far corner for human waste. The guard pushed her in and the door clanged shut heavily behind her. Katie Marie felt terror and desperation welling up as the sound of the guard's footsteps grew distant.

She walked to the wall beside the door and slumped to the floor, curled into a protective ball and closed her eyes. Her imagination began to run away. She shook her head to force herself to think. She opened her eyes. She began to see in the dim almost-darkness of the cell. She saw it was at least safe. The air was still and foul. Her weariness began finally to take hold. Her head fell to her knees and she slept.

She snapped awake at the sound of the door opening. She had no idea how long she had slept. A flashlight beamed into the darkness. The same guard grabbed her arm and pulled her to her feet. A few minutes later, she was sitting in an empty room with windows open to the summer night, drinking a glass of water and answering questions in English and Romanian from three men in shabby suits. She stayed with her truth: She and Victoria were guests of the Romanian Deputy Prime Minister until taken into custody by General Gerstenberg. Victoria was accused unjustly and imprisoned. She ran away. She never said anything about the Ploiesti defenses or about her Jewish father and they never asked. After repeating the same questions over and over, the men left her alone in the room. A moment later, the guard returned and marched her out of the building and back to the truck. Darryl, Randy and Violeta were sitting inside it.

"What took you so long?" Randy asked tiredly as the guard loaded her in and again began chattering with the same two other guards at the rear of the truck.

As she sat down next to Violeta, she glanced around and saw they were all unharmed.

"Our allies, huh?" smiled Darryl tiredly.

"I'm not sure we have any allies but each other anymore," Katie Marie told him.

"They're motherfuckers," Randy muttered, eyeing the guards with contempt.

One of the stern guards made the usual grunt to stop the chatter. The truck got under way again and her guard—Katie Marie had come to think of the chatty one who marched her in and out of the Kursk prison as hers—distracted the other two with chatter.

She leaned to Violeta. "You have any idea where they're taking us?" she whispered.

"East."

"For questioning?"

Violeta looked up into an almost smile in Katie Marie's eyes and almost smiled back but remembered where she was. "Yes."

As the truck bumped along blown out, torn up back roads through the night, both guards and prisoners slept restlessly, sitting up, slumping over and startling awake in unpredictable turns. Near dawn, as the sky outside the canvas cover turned from black to gray-blue, the truck pulled up at a vast military encampment, a hive of activity despite the early hour. The passengers roused themselves. The guards jumped down, urinated at the side of the truck and disappeared into the camp.

"What is this place?" Katie Marie wondered aloud.

"Looks like some kind of central base or general headquarters," Darryl said, nodding at a dense web of communications lines and the multiple train tracks running in and out. As they watched, a column of men marched west and a line of trucks drove past them in the same direction.

"Yeah," said Randy. "Must be brass around. Smell that chow?"

"Mmm," Darryl replied.

"How was your interrogation?" Katie Marie interrupted.

"Peachy," Randy smiled.

"No torture yet," Darryl agreed. " 'Less you count askin' me the same questions a hundred times."

"No way to catch us up as long as we keep tellin' the truth," Randy agreed. "But that don't stop 'em from tryin'. How 'bout you?"

"Same." She turned to Violeta. "Did they question you?" she asked in Romanian.

"Weeks ago," Violeta answered disinterestedly. "They just keep me to fuck. My juices."

"Right," said Katie Marie quietly.

"She know anything?" Darryl asked Katie Marie.

"Way too much," Katie Marie answered.

The guards returned. Two unloaded the three Americans and the third climbed into the truck with Violeta. The two women exchanged poignant glances of reassurance but said nothing as Katie Marie and the boys were marched off, Rnady hobbling with Darryl's help.

In a nearby tent, they were seated at a table. Three men in shabby suits entered and left the tent flaps pulled back for air circulation in the muggy heat of the August morning. Randy glanced up. "You must buy your suits the same place as those NKVD guys back in Kursk."

"Shut up," one of the men snapped.

"We're your allies!" Katie Marie snapped back. "Where's the Red Cross?"

Another of the men, remaining calm, looked at her. "The Soviet Union has no allies. When the workers of the world are liberated, it will have no enemies."

"Looks like we got us a true believer here, D," Randy said quietly.

"Yep," agreed Darryl.

"Do not complain. Millions are starving. You are fed," the third suit interrupted. "You will see the Red Cross people when we decide you need to see them. Now explain to us again how you came to be in a German supply train going into the war zone."

Outside the open tent flaps, the business of running a war went on, drilling in the distance, people on urgent errands passing by. In the distance, Katie Marie could see the glowing red-yellow sun coming up over the long, flat horizon. After her agonizing night, she enjoyed the feeling of the bright, warm, almost blinding light in her eyes until a hulking dark shadow stepped between it and herself and stopped. She startled and looked away, afraid she was in trouble with one of the suits.

"Mrs. Livingstone?" The voice asked.

Where did she know that voice from? Ploiesti. Erickson? Erickson! "Erickson?"

He stepped into the tent and her eyes adjusted. "What is this woman doing here?" Red Erickson asked angrily of the suits, taking in her ragged, weary, hungry appearance. "She is an American citizen. And..." he noticed Darryl and Randy. "Are these men American military personnel?" He took in their worn appearance, then looked at the three suits. "Is this how you treat your allies?" He turned to the Russian General who had walked into the tent with him and his voice became louder. "If this is how you treat allies, I am in the wrong place!"

A few minutes later, Erickson and the General with him were walking Katie Marie and the two boys, Randy limping and leaning, past the truck they came in on toward the cafeteria tent.

"We'll get you fed and cleaned up," the big, red-headed, Swedish oil man told her. "And then we'll get you on a train to Stalingrad, where they can put you on a State Department plane for home."

"Are you sure you can make all that happen?" Katie Marie asked, glancing cautiously at the Russian General.

"If they want me to do what I'm here to do, that will happen."

"What are you here for?" She asked. "You buy and sell oil with both sides?"

"I do business with the Nazis so I can pass on information to the Allies."

"Isn't it dangerous for you to be here?"

"Yes," Red Erickson shrugged. "I do a lot of dangerous things. Uncle Joe is nervous about how good his friends in the west really are, so the Brits arranged to send me on a quick trip to evaluate his defenses in Baku as a little bit of reassurance."

As they came to the cafeteria tent, Katie Marie stopped outside.

"Come on!" Darryl and Randy urged her. "Let's eat!"

"You boys go on in," Katie Marie told them. "I want to talk with Mr. Erickson." As they disappeared inside, she turned to her rescuer.

"Does Lady North need help?"

"Lady North is dead."

"I'm sorry to hear that. She was a magnificent woman."

"Yes."

"What is it, then?"

"Come with me." She led him to the truck. Inside it, Violeta was laying across the bench seats, staring at the canvas over the top. Others, haggard and starved looking, sat farther back in the truck, hunched on the benches. When Katie Marie and Erickson approached, Violeta sat up.

Katie Marie stared hard at her for a moment and then, nodding toward the other prisoners, spoke to her in Romanian. "They are being taken east?"

"Yes."

"For questioning?"

"Yes."

"Do you want to go to America to have your baby?"

Violeta just stared at Katie Marie.

"Answer me!"

"Yes."

Katie Marie turned to Erickson. "This is Victoria Wade Bridger."

He turned his head back and forth, evaluating the two women. "Can she keep her mouth shut?" he finally asked.

Katie Marie looked up at Violeta. "He wants to know if you will remain silent and do as I say until we get to America."

"And after we get there," Violeta said.

Katie Marie turned back to Red Erickson. "The answer is 'yes.'"

*****

321

Operation Tidal Wave was at best a partial victory. The tactical decision to attack low and avoid the worst of the German defenses, which was based on several intelligence sources, was the right one. But navigational mistakes cost the U.S. Air Force planes and crewman. The Germans, however, lost invaluable oil supplies and facilities to the bombing. The USAF proved its courage and commitment and laid the groundwork for the complete crippling of the Romanian fields, right after D-Day in June 1944.

The most important outcome of the heroic August 1, 1943, raid on Ploiesti was not easily quantifiable and therefore often forgotten: Gerstenberg's defenses had been penetrated. The Protector's elaborate scheme to create Fortress Ploiesti had only been partially successful. More resources would be necessary to defend the precious oil region. More of Germany's precious and dwindling resources were assigned.

After Operation Tidal Wave, General Carl A. Spaatz (U.S. Strategic Air Force Chief) argued for repeated bombing, contending that continued pressure on Ploiesti kept the Luftwaffe from defending against other offensive operations. Due to political infighting and objections from Britain's Royal Air Force, Supreme Allied Commander Dwight D. Eisenhower rejected Spaatz's strategy.

When the Allies gained footholds in Italy, Spaatz – still determined to go after the oil region – found a loophole in his battle orders permitting another raid in the guise of bombing Ploiesti rail yards. Spaatz's belief in the value of the operation was justified on May 12-13, 1944. The Luftwaffe, which had been avoiding other fights and marshalling its strength against the imminent Allied final assault on France, came out and fought over Romania and its precious oil. On seeing this, Eisenhower gave Spaatz a tentative go-ahead for stepped-up pressure. Consequently, the Luftwaffe grew weaker on the western front than it had been at any time since the war began. June 6, 1944, at Normandy, could have been much worse.

On June 8, 1944, General Spaatz announced (with Eisenhower's approval) that denying oil to the enemy was now the primary aim of the Air Force. It would remain so until the German surrender. With invaluable intelligence supplied by Erick "Red" Erickson, the Allies knew precisely where and how to locate their strikes. They were enormously successful. In Germany's last desperate offensive, the Battle of the Bulge, the Wehrmacht lost its initial destructive momentum when it ran hopelessly short of airplane, tank and truck fuel as well as oil-derived explosives and synthetic rubber for tires. With the German army reduced to retreating on foot and in horse- and ox-

drawn tanks and trucks, the Allies motored all the way to Berlin on Hitler's Autobahn in 1944-45.

In February, 1945, as President Franklin Delano Roosevelt was returning from the Yalta summit with Churchill and Stalin, he invited Ibn Saud, King of Saudi Arabia, to meet with him aboard the U.S. Navy heavy cruiser USS Quincy at the Great Bitter Lake in Egypt. Roosevelt's plane, The Sacred Cow, brought him to Egypt. The Naval destroyer USS Murphy brought Ibn Saud from Jidda, providing space for the King's forty-eight person contingent to pitch royal tents and carpets in its forecastle.

The two leaders discussed much and it is generally agreed by historians that Ibn Saud came away from the meeting with a trust of FDR that cemented the "special relationship" between their two nations. It was a relationship that guaranteed U.S. access to Saudi oil supplies for the foreseeable future.

*****

The President and the King sat in the sun on the deck of the Quincy in matching wheelchairs, laughing and talking, while near the ship's rail, watching, were Assistant Secretary of State LeClaire Harold and British Special Envoy to the United States Phillip Bridger, Lord North.

"She demanded the mission," Harold told Lord North, keeping an eye on FDR.

"I know," Lord North replied, staring out to sea.

"You still miss her," Harold said.

"I adored her," Lord North admitted.

"Most men did," said Harold. "But she wanted respect."

They remained silent, both remembering her.

"I suppose Churchill is going to have to meet with the King now," Harold said, changing the subject.

"I am already making the preliminary arrangements," Lord North replied.

"With the oil under his sand, he's going to have them all coming to see him."

323

Suddenly, the President and the King burst out laughing and Ibn Saud stood up. The King turned away and rolled the wheelchair he had been sitting in before him as he walked slowly, limpingly, back toward the stairs down to the launch that would take him to his encampment on the Murphy.

Harold, Lord North at his heels, moved quickly to Roosevelt and grabbed the handles on the president's wheelchair.

"Give me a cigarette!" the President demanded as Harold rolled him toward the temporary Presidential quarters on the Quincy. Harold and Lord North silently watched the President light up and draw deeply through his cherished ivory cigarette holder. After he inhaled the calming nicotine, Harold dared to speak.

"Did he go for the Jewish homeland idea, Mr. President?"

"Hah!" FDR exploded. "He says give the Jews part of Germany!"

"But it looked like the two of you got along."

"He's quite a man," FDR laughed. "I hope we always have Arab kings with his combination of wisdom and humanity."

"You liked him?"

"A cleansing of the palate, after that butcher Stalin."

"What was all the friendly gab about? Oil?" Lord North asked.

Roosevelt glanced suspiciously at Lord North and smiled. "Didn't say a word about oil," Roosevelt smiled. "Either of you know anything about an American woman we sent to meet with the King in 1938?"

Harold and Lord North glanced at each other nervously. "I'm surprised the King remembered her, sir," North said. "It was a brief mission, a long time ago."

"You know her?"

"Knew her, sir. She was killed in the 1943 bombing raid on Ploiesti. She was the one who got the word out about how to penetrate the Nazi defenses."

"The King asked about her. Apparently he really adored her. Said she was a remarkable woman. Said I reminded him of her. Think that was an insult?"

324

Harold and Lord North glanced at one another again. "No, sir," Harold finally replied. "I adored her myself," he added, wheeling the president on.

End of Part II

She wept silently, the pain of memory written across her face.

It had to be done, I shrugged, making my best effort toward solace. It's always about oil, isn't it?

She looked at me through tear-streaked eyes. Is it? Let me tell you a story about power.

Part III: Where Oil Is Power
August 1953

"Can't anybody here play this game?" …Casey Stengel

"Are you ready?" Irdeshar asked Monty Livingstone. They stood facing one another over a small table in a bungalow behind the walls of the British embassy compound in Tehran.

Monty Livingstone looked back at the lean handsome young man wearing open-collared military fatigues and boots, his thick black hair swept back. The nose and chin jutted angrily but the brown eyes were open and calm. He waited for Livingstone's answer.

Here, at the brink of pandemonium, Monty Livingstone – now a sturdy, broad-shouldered, thick-chested full-grown man – could not answer. The question was impossible: Was he ready? The only answer now was the unspoken question in his thoughtful blue eyes: Did it matter?

A soldier burst through the front door, sweating profusely and breathing hard. Both Livingstone and Irdeshar turned. The soldier immediately crossed the small room to them and began reporting in Farsi, a language Monty now knew, with desperation and urgency. "General Riahi was not at his house so Colonel Nassiri led us on to Prime Minister Mossadeq's residence to serve the firmans."

"No!" Irdeshar sat down hard, his lean shoulders slumping forward. He banged his fist against the table. "The fool!" He looked up at the soldier. "He was met with stronger forces and arrested at Mossadeq's residence?"

The soldier stared back, still breathing hard and sweating but now wide-eyed at Irdeshar's insight. "Yes."

"Of course," Irdeshar said grimly.

Monty sat back down, laid heavily muscled forearms and fisted hands on the table, leaned his broad shoulders forward, his round face intent, his blue, intelligent eyes now burning. He spoke quietly to Irdeshar in English. "They must have had inside information."

"Yes," Irdeshar agreed. He looked up at the soldier. "Does Roosevelt know?"

"He sent me to you."

"With orders?"

"He has sent out other runners, calling in his people," reported the soldier. "I am to await your instructions."

Irdeshar looked back at Monty, the question of readiness still unanswered.

"What should I do?" the soldier asked urgently.

Irdeshar thought, then abruptly stood. "Come with me."

Monty Livingstone looked up and, anticipating where Irdeshar was going, spoke again in English. "It's not safe. They will arrest you. Or shoot you."

"I've got to know what's going on in the street."

"Fine," Livingstone groaned, standing. "Let's go see." Irdeshar looked across the table at him. Livingstone smiled tightly. "Are we stupid or crazy?"

"Probably both," Irdeshar smiled, his tone grim. "But if we make this happen, history will call us heroes." He turned to the soldier and switched to Farsi. "Lead us back to the Prime Minister's house exactly the way you came. I want to know what has changed."

"I can tell you the route," the soldier said tentatively. It was clear he was afraid to go back out.

Irdeshar reached to the Luger 9mm holstered on his belt, pulled it, checked the automatic slide mechanism and said, without looking at the soldier, "You will lead us."

"Yes, sir."

Irdeshar replaced the weapon in its holster and looked up at Livingstone. "Are you ready?" Without waiting, he turned and walked toward the bungalow door. The soldier followed.

Monty Livingstone followed them into the dangerously revolutionary Iranian August night. That question again. Why, he wondered, did they always ask if you were ready as they led you into something you couldn't possibly know you were ready for until it was too late?

*****

328

"There comes a time in every man's life and I've had plenty of them."
…Casey Stengel

Two years earlier, in the spring of 1951, it was what Rhoades had asked Monty: "Are you ready to be a spy?"

Spring 1951 was the third time he had met Rhoades. He was in Tehran, working for Socony-Vacuum. He had been sent to Abadan to inspect the world's finest refinery, just ahead of the trouble everybody in the world knew was coming. The British owned and operated Anglo-Iranian Oil Company was playing financial and political hardball with Iran, the country whose oil the company owned and operated.

The British had discovered and developed the immensely rich Iranian oil fields in the first decade of the twentieth century. In 1910, they had founded and built Abadan on an island near the mouth of the Tigris-Euphrates-Karun estuary. By 1930, it was one of the biggest refineries in the world. In 1951, Iran's budding nationalist democratic movement, led by Prime Minister Mohammed Mossadeq, was demanding its fair share of the wealth produced by the British oil fields and the world's finest refining complex.

Livingstone's job at Socony-Vacuum was not exciting, but he knew the oil business from the hole in the ground up so he was good at it and it paid good money, which he needed for the mortgage and the alimony. During the inspection of Abadan, he had been invited to tour Tehran by the refinery's British management. Late on the second day of the tour, he was walking across the British embassy compound, headed for a late afternoon retreat-from-the-heat bath and nap before dressing for dinner. He was relishing his first moment of solitude in several days when Rhoades walked up alongside him.

"Distinctly American stride, that."

Livingstone turned to the remotely familiar voice and immediately placed the face. "Hardy Rhoades!"

"Our paths cross again," the big-bodied Brit smiled, genially shaking Livingstone's hand in his big fist, his tiny eyes beaming in his soft, round, wrinkled, leathery face, looking especially ex-patriot in his white tropical suit and wide-brimmed white hat. "What the hell brings you to bloody Persia?"

"Iran," Livingstone corrected Rhoades' intentional anachronism with a grin. "I'm in the oil business now. Socony-Vacuum."

"Is that right?" Livingstone noticed immediately the Brit's reply was not one of surprise but was almost suggestive. Rhoades opened his arm and hand outward in an 'after you' gesture. "I'll walk with you." As they continued toward Livingstone's bungalow in the embassy guest quarters, Rhoades chatted amiably. "When was the last time we ran into each other?"

"The last time? 1948. At that Israel rally outside the Lake Success UN headquarters."

"That's right. You were with the wife?"

"Ex-wife."

"What happened?"

"Israel."

"I told you those Jews would make trouble," laughed Rhoades. He studied Livingstone. "A painful parting, then?"

Walking, thinking, Monty suddenly started talking. "I was eating at a delicatessen on Fifth Avenue when a snappily dressed, dark-haired, dark-eyed, obviously no-nonsense, obviously upper-Westside Jewess asked me if I liked her shade of neon red lipstick. Rachel. Not observant but very ethnic. Her father was an inventor of artificial aromas. Her mother was the Girl-Friday to one of the most successful men on Broadway."

"Producer?"

"That's right."

"Who?"

"I can never remember his name. He has some kind of nickname."

"Ah, sweet love."

"It was a very fashionable wedding—though not pretentiously large. Her gown was specially-designed by a friend of her mother's boss. Another catered. Prominent people at the reception. Fine gifts from her mother's guests and her mother's boss's clients. I wore my dress uniform. Rachel thought I looked dashing."

"Nice honeymoon?" Rhoades asked facetiously.

"She had her period. Bad cramps. I took a job as a suit at Socony-Vacuum. She kept her job at NBC Radio. We tried to have children. There were two early term miscarriages."

"Hope deferred," smiled Rhoades.

"Rachel's passion slowly turned toward the just-being-born state of Israel: If she could not be a mother, she would be midwife to a nation."

"Which is why she didn't pay any mind to me that day at Lake Success," Rhoades concluded. "You recognized me immediately, asked me what I was doing there."

" 'Watching,' you said," Monty remembered. "Just like the first time we met. And just like the first time, I asked you what you were watching for. Do you remember what you answered?"

"Most likely what I always watch for: Trouble and Opportunity."

"That's it."

"So what became of Rachel?"

"Left for Kibbutz Artzi in 1949. I didn't mind. Better to be deserted than harassed for not believing."

"And you took up the ribald life of a young eligible bachelor and citizen of the world."

They reached Monty's bungalow. He stopped by the front door. "I don't love the oil business but I know it. That's why they sent me to look at Abadan."

"In the event they have to build one of their own when we get booted out of here and the Iranians run Abadan into the Shatt-Al-Arab."

"Something like that."

Rhoades studied Livingstone. "You miss her?"

"Rachel? It was just on the flight over here I realized I don't. The truth is I've been running on empty ever since…" He looked down.

Rhoades watched. "What are you thinking about, son?"

331

"Just a Russian girl I met at a dance in Berlin after the cease-fire, back in '45."

"She the one?" Rhoades smiled while Monty continued staring at his feet.

Monty looked up. "She was the one who taught me there isn't one."

Rhoades smiled, glancing around at the silent empty courtyard on which the guesthouses in this part of the embassy compound open. "What do you make of the politics around these parts, cowboy?"

Monty studied Rhoades with curiosity. "Just what I read in the papers. The young hothead clerics are pushing from one end, the communist radicals are pushing from the other. But it looks like Ayatollah Koshani is backing Mossadeq and his democratic nationalists. That's going to make it hard for the Shah to get his way."

"The Shah will have to back nationalization of the oil industry," Rhoades said matter-of-factly.

"Will Britain go to war with Iran?"

"That depends," Rhoades said, glancing back and forth around them again. Monty could see he was coming to something so he waited. Rhoades looked down at the pavement walkway, then up at Livingstone from under his wide-brimmed white hat. "Still want to be a spy?"

"I gave up on that pipe dream years ago," Monty laughed. "Why? Have you got a job with AIOC they'll give me if I promise not to meddle."

"No," Rhoades said, watching Livingstone through narrowing eyes. "But I've got a job of work for the British government and I could use some help."

"You're not kidding?"

"No."

"But I'm not, I – I've done nothing to prepare."

"Life prepares you, son. I'll train you."

"To spy?"

"You could call it that. Are you ready?"

*****

It was the first week of March 1951. His training was supposed to begin with a chatty tour of Iran. But Rhoades took a fateful detour. He wanted, before they left Tehran, to pass by the Shah Mosque and observe the funeral of an important Mullah.

"It's a big deal," Rhoades told him. "Everybody will be there."

Sitting in the passenger seat of the British embassy's two-tone green, 1949 Cadillac convertible while Rhoades drove across the hot, dusty city threading between donkey carts, goatherds, half-ton trucks full of farm produce and three decades of American reject automobiles, Monty asked what he would need to learn to do the "job of work" Rhoades mentioned.

"On-the-job training," Rhoades grinned. He changed the subject. "When did we first meet?'

"The first time? 1942. The Biltmore Conference."

"That's right," nodded Rhoades, remembering. "You asked me what I was doing there."

"And you said you were watching," Monty interrupted. "We've been over this."

"Trouble and opportunity. That was the beginning of your training."

"What?"

"You said you were about to graduate from Harvard. Wanted to get into the war, be a spy. You said you were at the conference to see what it was like."

"That was stupid college-boy stuff."

Rhoades glanced at Livingstone. His eyes were intense. Monty could see he was very serious. "I knew before you told me. I was using you. The place was full of Jews. Talking to you like a mentor made me look like I belonged. Cover. Hiding in plain sight. What did you learn that day?"

"Not much."

"Because you had no context. I saw the American Jews take over leadership of Zionism. That shifted the goals and power of the movement. The same day the communist party held its first meeting here in Tehran and formed Tudeh, its Iranian arm. Small events, big patterns. Did you get to be a spy?"

"I enlisted and applied. They turned me down."

"Why?"

"Why should I tell you?"

"They found out about your father."

"That's right."

"What happened?"

"You ever try to get out of the U.S. Army?"

"So you got to know war from the blood in the mud up."

"Me and the rest of the 102nd Infantry. We fought our way to the Elbe River. But instead of being transported back to France and shipped off for the Pacific war, I got lucky. They found out I was a college boy and assigned me to headquarters duty."

Rhoades slowed the car. In the distance a large crowd was gathered before a magnificent sprawling tan brick structure decorated with tile work in magnificent shades of blue. Great minaret towers loomed over an arched, tile mosaic entryway in two-story high brick walls. The entryway led to a courtyard. Beyond the open space of the courtyard, Monty could see the dome of a cathedral-sized mosque. The crowd, hundreds deep, spanned the width of the great building and filled the courtyard. The noise of the crowd was cacophonous with chants and counter chants in Farsi, screaming, raging zealots calling for death to the British, taunting the Shah or challenging the manhood of their opponents. Trumpets blared, drums snared, angry feet stomped and frenzied hands clapped. Lines of blue-uniformed police and green-uniformed soldiers ringed the mosque plaza, but they kept a safe distance from the seething provocation, warily watching and uneasily waiting.

The traffic jam kept the car at a distance. Monty stared at the crowd. "Looks like combat experience might come in handy."

Rhoades pulled the car over and parked. "Here's your chance to watch how they do things in Tehran."

"How they go to church?"

"Do things by religious doctrine here," Rhoades grunted, getting out of his side of the Cadillac while Monty got out on the other.

"So what they do in church is what they do."

Rhoades walked up next to him, raised a pointed left index finger and smiled. "Watch and learn, son." He watched Livingstone watch the demonstrators. "First thing you see is the white shirts. That's Tudeh, the masses. Russians run that."

"There's a small group in more western-looking clothes trying to push their way to the middle of the crowd."

"The pro-Shah crowd. They're well dressed because when they're not doing politics they're doing well for themselves, whatever it takes. They're pushing because they want to cause trouble."

"Why?"

"Demonstration was called by the National Front. They're the ones dressed like everyday Iranians. But their leaders dress like politicians, because that's what they are. Tudeh – the white shirts – and the Islamists – the ones in the traditional pajamas – signed on just to make it harder for the Prime Minister."

"The Prime Minister?"

The small, western-dressed bunch pushed into the crowd but a line of muscular young men – some in white shirts, some in the traditional Islamic baggy pants and long shirts, some wearing suits or slacks with dress shirts and tiea – pushed them back.

"Let's walk forward," Rhoades said after glancing right and left. As he and Monty moved forward, Rhoades went on explaining. "Prime Minister Razmara is coming here today for the funeral of an Ayatollah friendly to the Shah. Razmara was put in office by the Shah and is AGAINST nationalizing the oil industry. Everybody here but that well-dressed little gang of troublemakers is FOR nationalizing the oil industry."

"So if they make enough trouble to get the police to break up the demonstration before Razmara gets here, no confrontation."

Two cars drove past. The lead vehicle was a police car, its roof lights flashing. The second was a big black Cadillac limousine. The police car pushed forward through the crowd as far as it could without provoking the crowd. When it stopped, two men emerged from the following Cadillac. A line of soldiers trotted forward, formed up around the two men and escorted them through the stunning, blue-tile archway into the mosque's courtyard.

The crowd, momentarily parted and subdued, now resumed its frenetic declaring.

Monty looked at Rhoades. "Well, that's that."

"Not quite," Rhoades said. "He still has to come back out." He made the gesture with the pointed left index finger. "Watch and learn."

"What am I watching for?"

"Trouble and opportunity."

Monty studied the crowd. It certainly was different than the pro-Israel demonstrations at the UN Rachel had dragged him to, he thought. Suddenly, like a hallucination, he saw a small female figure among so many angry young men. He felt dizzy. It could not be — could it?

Yes, he saw her. He remembered her. Vividly. The streets of Tehran were teeming and screaming, a momentous collision of possibilities, and she was here? Yes, she was. It was the small, slender athletic form and graceful movement, the white-blonde hair peaking out from beneath the headscarf, the vibrant yet angry and hungry blue eyes watching, always watching and ready.

After they had fought their way across Europe, most of the 102nd Infantry shipped out to France for the crossing to the Pacific war. He was one of the lucky ones assigned to headquarters duty. He met her at a dance. Tekla. Secretary to the Russian liaison. And here she was, now, in Tehran. Time stopped and it all came back. The dizziness. The ache.

And then, "Bang!" And "Bang-Bang!" And "Bang!" He knew that sound. A pistol. A Colt .38 revolver, an Officers' Match model, the one he carried across Europe. The crowd was in panic, people were screaming, Rhoades was pulling Livingstone back, away from the demonstration. The funeral attendees, now a panic-driven mob, came rushing out from under the grand arch decorated so beautifully with intricate sky-blue tile work.

The political chanting stopped. People were screaming. Behind Monty, police and military commanders were blowing whistles and shouting commands. Their men deployed around the entire panorama, halting the crowd's retreat, trapping Livingstone and Rhoades inside their net. At first, hundreds of demonstrators tried to escape, wrestling with the men manning the perimeter, taking blows or facing rifle point and bayonet for their resistance. But soon they settled down, milling afraid, awaiting the next development, the explanation of the gunshots and the panic from inside. Rumors of the assassination of Razmara began to rumble through the crowd.

Just as Livingstone and Rhoades, surreptitiously mingling at the margin of the crowd's milling, began to hear these rumors, another police car arrived, this one with siren blaring as well as lights flashing. A tall, sturdy man with thick black hair and a black, pencil-thin mustache in a worn dark suit emerged from the passenger side front seat. Suited men from the driver's side and the rear seat followed as the tall, mustached man led into and through the milling crowd toward the archway. As he passed Rhoades, he stopped.

"Rhoades," he said quietly in a gravelly voice.

"Afshartus," replied Rhoades, his voice tired but his eyes wary.

"Where were you and what did you see?"

"Outside, watching the demonstration. We heard the gunshots, four I think. Saw nothing."

Suddenly, the crowd parted with gasps and cries and shouts as soldiers came running through carrying a man while another siren sounded and an ambulance arrived. The men following Afshartus pushed demonstrators away to open a path for the ambulance. The soldiers carrying the wounded man reached the ambulance. Wails sounded as men all around repeated "Razmara!" and "It's the Prime Minister!"

Afshartus waited and watched as the soldiers loaded the bloody, unconscious Prime Minister into the ambulance and sent it off, its siren wailing, into the distance. Afshartus then turned back to Rhoades.

"We?"

Rhoades gestured toward Monty. "Police Captain Afshartus, Mr. Livingstone, an American oil man. I was showing him the mosque."

"You picked a curious day for it," Afshartus said dubiously.

"Why would I want to shoot the Prime Minister? He was on our side. You should go question old Mossy's little army."

"I will decide who to question."

A policeman dragged a slender young woman to them. "Tudeh," the policeman reported.

Monty stared at her in utter astonishment. It was not a dream but a bizarre, perverse coincidence. It was her. It was Tekla.

She angrily yanked herself free of the policeman's grip. Smaller than the men around her, she peered upward from angry, wary eyes, a sullen, unintimidated beauty. And then she saw Monty. Layers peeled away from her expression in the unguarded instant before she dropped her head to regain her composure.

Both Afshartus and Rhoades observed the apparent recognition. "You know this girl?" Afshartus asked Monty in English, establishing it as the language to be used. Rhoades watched, waited.

Monty studied the scarf over the top of Tekla's head. "She's a Russian. We worked in the same offices in Berlin in 1945. I recognized her. All the guys talked about her. She was a fanatic. They said she would be good in bed if you were Stalin and dead weight if you were anybody else. Things like that. You remember."

Afshartus turned to Tekla. "A fanatic, eh? Enough to assassinate a Prime Minister?"

"We were here demonstrating FOR him, you ass," Tekla snapped, looking up at him fearlessly. "Which you would know if you knew something about politics besides who bribes you."

"You little Russian slut!" Afshartus snapped back, raising his hand to slap her.

Monty grabbed his arm. "She didn't do it."

338

Afshartus pulled his arm away from Livingstone and eyed him angrily. "And you know this how?"

"I was watching her. She's nice to look at, isn't she?"

"American defending Russian?" Afshartus sneered quietly. "Just like the good old days during the war, eh?"

A police officer approached and whispered something to Afshartus, who replied with orders in Farsi and dismissed the man. "A poor worshipper has turned himself in for the murder," he reported.

"So I can go?" Tekla asked impatiently. "Or do you want to question me for something else?"

Afshartus looked for a moment at Tekla. "We have information he was shot with a military pistol."

"An Officer's Colt .38?" Monty asked.

Afshartus' head snapped toward Livingstone. "How did you know that?"

"That's what it sounded like," Monty answered.

Afshartus turned back to Tekla. "How would a poor Muslim obtain a military pistol?"

"From a mullah or a politician who did not want Razmara to prevent nationalization of the oil?" Tekla demanded.

"Perhaps Tudeh supplied it."

"If I had supplied a pistol it would be a Makarov 9-millimeter automatic, not an American revolver."

"You have such a weapon?"

"Do not be ridiculous," Tekla laughed.

"Do not be ridiculous, you have such a weapon?" Afshartus asked. "Or do not be ridiculous, you do not."

"Do not be ridiculous, I would never answer such a question," she laughed.

Afshartus glowered at her. "Go," he grunted. "But do not go anywhere new or do anything unusual. We know where Tudeh is."

"You could not find a snake if it was coiled around your leg," Tekla muttered angrily. She threw a flashing glower at Monty, pivoted and stalked off.

Afshartus turned to Rhoades. "You will remain in the country?"

Rhoades smiled genially. "We are motoring to Kermanshah to inspect the refinery. Then perhaps a visit to Isfahan, for the young man to appreciate the glories of ancient Persia."

Afshartus eyed Rhoades suspiciously. "You have no business there?"

"What kind of business would I have in Isfahan?" Rhoades grinned.

Afshartus stared hard at Rhoades for a moment and then answered the Brit's grin with one of his own. "Go," he said.

The rotund, wrinkled, leathery Britisher hurried Livingstone back to the Cadillac and sped off through back streets and alleys until, quickly, they were out of Tehran and onto the rough, narrow, winding asphalt highway running northwest into the Zagros foothills.

After sitting quietly while Rhoades negotiated at unsafe speeds the unpredictabilities of the city, Monty finally turned to him. "What the hell was that all about?"

"I might ask you the same. She's the girl you told me about?"

"That's not important. What were all those monkey shines with the police captain about?"

"Afshartus knows as well as I do that the poor bastard they arrested was just a dupe," Rhoades replied, concentrating on driving. He thought a moment and his wrinkled leathery expression erupted into a grin. "And we both know whoever brings in the real assassin will have the gratitude of the Shah and the loyalty of the people."

"I thought the people were angry with the Shah because of his association with the British?"

"The people are like a mistreated wife, long-suffering but loyal. Razmara was the Shah's man. Whoever killed him must be brought to their brutal

340

justice. Afshartus knows I will be looking for the assassin, as will the girl and her Tudeh comrades. And the mullahs."

"Look for a guy with a .38 revolver who can fade into a crowd at a mosque," Monty said disinterestedly, taking in the immensity of the north-central Iranian plateau, the hot early spring sun beating down hard on the slopes of the chill Zagros, wide patches of unaffected snow still laying in the shadows of the snow-capped peaks.

"I will," muttered Rhoades as he settled back to drive. "You ought to learn Farsi."

"I wasn't planning on being around long enough to need it."

Rhoades chuckled. "The best laid plans, you know."

They drove on in silence. When they reached the small city of Kermanshah in northwestern Iran, Rhoades drove to the Anglo-Iranian Oil Company refinery, where they were greeted like family. The company executive gave them a gourmet luncheon worthy of Baedeker's highest star rating. After eating, they walked the grounds, observing the small but state-of-the-art refining capabilities. At one point in the tour, the executive led Livingstone into a laboratory and began explaining a technical aspect of the fractionating process.

Spying a group of Iranian laborers taking a break and jovially chatting, Rhoades did his best "huffing fat Britisher" act and sat on a pile of crates near enough to hear them. At their suspicious and insincere inquiry in Farsi, Rhoades feigned not understanding the language but with gestures assured them he was not having a heart attack. They laughed among themselves about "fat Britishers" and went on with their conversation in Farsi, a language Rhoades both spoke and understood in even its idiomatic working-class variations.

Rhoades listened as one of the men recounted reports he had heard, via Radio Tehran, that a former co-worker, Kahlil Tahmasibi, had been arrested. Another gruffly mocked the idea that Tahmasibi, known for his slow-wittedness, could be anything but a dupe. The men began reminiscing about a carpenter who worked with them the previous winter and had been aggressively recruiting for Fedaeen-I-Islam.

"Navab?" one asked.

"Didn't he spend a lot of time talking with Kahlil?" asked another.

All looked at each other with nervous realization. One glanced nervously at Rhoades, and the others warily followed his eyes. When Rhoades continued to sit huffing, seemingly oblivious to them, they all looked at each other and laughed to release their tension. The one who remembered Navab told them he now clearly recalled that Navab had spent a lot of time recruiting Tahmasibi, the accused assassin, to the Fedaeen-I-Islam. Another worker pointed out it was time to go back to work. The others agreed.

As they walked away, Rhoades heard one say something to the other about the Fedaeen-I-Islam recruiter, Navab, working now at Abadan. When they disappeared into the refinery works, Rhoades leapt from his passive posture into action. To Monty's complete surprise, the refinery tour ended abruptly and, as soon as the Cadillac's gas tank was filled, they were on a narrow, twisting asphalt highway headed south. As he drove, Rhoades explained what he had overheard. They got a cold supper and spent the night at the Masjid-e-Suleimann oil works. Despite Monty's interest in the operation there, Rhoades got their gas tank filled immediately after the sumptuous breakfast the camp directors gave them the next morning and they set out again, driving southwest.

Near midday, after crossing rolling desert barrenness in seasonal sweltering heat, they reached Khorramshar and quickly crossed the Karun River via the

Bahmanshir Bridge. In Abadan, Rhoades brusquely dispensed with the security guard at the company gates and sped to the small, two-story administration building. As they moved from the car to the offices, Monty recognized the familiar pungent refinery stench, the smoky, eye-irritating air and the constant just-below-loud, ear-numbing hum of machinery near and distant.

In the AIOC administrative offices, Rhoades identified himself and asked how to find where the carpenters lived. When a clerk told him it depended on where the carpenter worked, he asked for the personnel files. After some confusion, they eventually tracked down the Iranian in charge of such sketchy, Farsi language files. He was a small man with thick glasses and scraggily hair wearing a dingy white shirt and wrinkled tie. Pretentiously, he began giving excuses about how difficult it would be to find one Iranian worker. Impatiently, Rhoades interrupted the man's multi-syllabic diatribe about the difficulties of an administrator's duties.

"Navab!" Rhoades exclaimed adamantly. "Just down here from Kermanshah!"

The bureaucrat instantly stopped talking and stared at them in astonishment.

"What?" Rhoades raged.

"Representatives of Tudeh were here looking for the same man, not an hour ago! His mother just died in Tehran. They came with a Mullah, bearing the sad news. They will take the grieving man home for the funeral."

"Take us to him!" Rhoades demanded.

The man turned slowly for the file on his desk and continued telling them what the Tudeh people who arrived earlier said. "His poor mother choked to death on a British sweet biscuit. Too dry, dreadful things. Navab's name was on her dying lips."

"Now!" Rhoades screamed.

Dragging the bureaucrat with them, they leapt into the Cadillac and followed his frantic directions along the blacktopped streets of the refinery office section of Abadan. As they came into the section of the island where the transient Iranian workers' were housed, the car bumped onto refuse-littered, oil-splattered dirt roads.

"What would Tudeh and a Mullah do with him?" Monty asked Rhoades between the bureaucrat's gasped indications for turns.

Rhoades glanced at the Iranian. "Explanations later, after we're sure the grieving man is safe."

Rhoades demanded the bureaucrat point out the carpenter's shanty from a distance. When he did, Rhoades pulled the car over, into a weedy vacant lot full of filthy watery, oily puddles. He turned to the man. "Go back on foot and come with a team of the company's security officers."

"I can fetch the police!" volunteered the little man, getting into the urgency of the drama. "Or the military!"

"No!" exploded Rhoades furiously. "Company security ONLY! And HURRY!"

"Right!" The man grinned. He turned and ran back up the gravel street.

Monty looked at Rhoades. "Now what?"

"First we've got to find out what Tudeh and their Mullah are up to. It would be very bad if they got the credit for catching and turning in the assassin. Follow."

They snuck to the back of the carpenter's shanty. At a crack of the shabby hut's wall, Rhoades peaked in and listened while Monty kept watch. Both could easily hear the Farsi conversation inside. Rhoades whispered a summary translation. "The man insists he did not kill Razmara. He says he was at the mosque with a gun..." Rhoades stopped, listened and chuckled.

"What?" Monty whispered anxiously.

"The carpenter says he was on a holy mission so that Allah can deliver the people of Iran from British enslavement."

"And?"

"When he drew his pistol," Rhoades went on, "he was too afraid and could not force himself to pull the trigger. But just then a man in a uniform stepped up behind, drew a revolver and shot the PM."

"A man in uniform?" Monty asked. "I thought Afshartus said they arrested a poor believer who confessed."

Rhoades listened again to the interchange inside, his wrinkled face tense with concentration, and then turned to Livingstone with a grin. "Says he knows that man from the Kermanshah refinery. Says he is crazy."

"Who is that questioning him?"

"I know the Tudeh man. Faddey, a Russian, the head of the Iranian communist movement. Mullah must be one the communists bribe. The girl is with them."

"The girl?" Monty asked, his excitement unintentionally revealed. He angled to a crack, peaked in and saw, across the shanty away from the men in the tiny kitchen, Tekla sitting with a Muslim woman and little boy.

"Probably the carpenter's wife and son," Rhoades whispered.

As Faddey stopped talking, the Mullah began. Rhoades resumed the translation. "The Mullah echoes what Faddey just said. It was a great deed to murder the Betrayer and the man should take credit because it was his boldness that made it happen."

The carpenter began speaking. Rhoades translated. "He says he is a dutiful servant of Allah and will do whatever the Imam thinks is right."

Suddenly, the front door on the other side of the shanty exploded inward and Iranian police came pouring through, rifles ready. Behind them, as the dust of the crashing entry settled, Afshartus and a pair of suited deputies walked in. Faddey and the Mullah emerged from the corners of the shanty they had sought at the intrusion. The carpenter knelt in the center of the floor, in the prostrate posture of prayer.

Monty noticed, in the shanty's kitchen, Tekla continued to shield the carpenter's wife and son with her own body.

Afshartus began giving orders. The policemen dragged the carpenter to his feet, taking him into custody. Faddey interrupted. Afshartus and Faddey argued.

"Faddey is trying to convince Afshartus the man is in the custody of Tudeh," Rhoades explained to Livingstone. Quietly, Rhoades laughed grimly when Afshatus replied calmly to Faddey's protests, turned to his policemen and barked orders. The policemen dragged the carpenter out the door.

345

"What's so funny?" Monty asked, continuing to watch through the crack as Tekla comforted the carpenter's wailing wife and little boy. Rhoades stepped away from the shanty as Afshartus followed his men out the front door.

"Afshartus told Faddey and the Mullah the man was his prisoner and had already confessed. They protested, said it was impossible. Afshartus said the only thing remaining is for the man to discover how happy he was to confess after being questioned."

While Monty watched Tekla inside and listened to Rhoades chuckle at Afshartus' grim humor, Faddey and the Mullah stomped angrily out behind the police. Monty heard Faddey's loud, harsh voice from in front of the hut. He saw Tekla hear the angry interchange. He watched as she tearfully took her leave of the wife and little boy, who remained in the disheveled shanty, the little boy weeping in his weeping mother's clutching arms.

Monty turned away and looked at Rhoades who had stepped back from the shanty, waiting. Neither spoke. Finally, Rhoades said, "Excellent training mission." He turned back toward the car. "Come on," he said, walking away. "Let's check in at the Riverside Guest House and get some supper. I'll introduce you to a few people tomorrow morning before we start back for Tehran."

As Monty and Rhoades walked back up the rough gravel road toward the vacant lot and the Cadillac, Monty glanced over his shoulder at the little shanty. At that distance, he could now see where a crowd of locals had formed. A few policemen kept them away from the police car where other officers loaded in the handcuffed carpenter. Afshartus and his deputies were already gone. Across the road, Monty saw Tekla and Faddey. He was too far to hear what they were saying but he recognized the postures and expressions of intimate domestic hostility. He tried to discern how much domestic and how much hostility but he could not study the couple closely without drawing Rhoades' suspicion. He looked away.

"I think we shall drive to Isfahan tomorrow," Rhoades announced as they reached the Cadillac. He looked at Livingstone, who was getting into the car. "You have probably never been to Isfahan?"

"No."

"Good!" Rhoades said, slumping in behind the big Cadillac's steering wheel. "You must see Isfahan. We must pass again through Khhorramshar and then on to Isfahan."

Something about the way Rhoades mentioned Khorramshar gave Monty the impression it might be the more important place on Rhoades' itinerary.

*****

"Don't cut my throat, I may want to do that later myself." ...Casey Stengel

The Anglo Iranian Oil Company's Riverside Guest House and Mrs. Vera Flavell, its proprietress, offered gracious accommodations. There was tropical verdure outside and simple, fashionable elegance within. They had a gourmet cold supper, courtesy of Mrs. Flavell, and then made their way to comfortable, cozy quarters for a restful night in cool, clean-sheeted comfort.

Following a sumptuous British breakfast, they again drove to the AIOC administrative offices. In an elegant boardroom overlooking the Shatt-al-Arab, busy with tanker traffic, they sat in on a morning meeting with oil company executives. The executives outlined Abadan operations for Livingstone. When chat drifted to the subject of the previous day's arrest, two of the executives expressed racist contempt for the Iranian carpenter and other ethnic workers.

"These bloody nationalists," a third executive added, "are stinking cheeky. A right to our oil? Merely because we found it inside questionable Persian borders a sodding half century ago?" His wrinkled face smiling genially, Rhoades used the mention of Persia to turn the conversation. He mentioned the caravan roads, the magnificence of Isfahan and then reminded the AIOC men he and Livingstone had to get a petrol refill and be on their way.

After crossing back over the Karun River on the Bahmanshir Bridge, they drove through Khorramshar. At the eastern edge of the little city, Rhoades pulled the Cadillac to the side of the rough two-lane asphalt highway, allowing traffic toward Isfahan to pass them by. He turned off and drove on a dirt road to behind a low, white, mud-walled multi-family complex surrounded by goats, junk and idle pick-up trucks. Children played on the empty desert plains beyond. Livingstone looked at Rhoades, awaiting instruction.

"This will be in English," Rhoades said very quietly. "Do not be perturbed by their conversations between themselves in Farsi. They are bound to our safety by the laws of hospitality. Do you understand?"

"The laws of hospitality? Yes, I have read Homer."

"This is serious business, son." He made the gesture with the up-pointed finger. "Watch and learn."

Monty smiled and nodded 'yes,' deferring to the older man.

A heavy-set, bearded man with thick, black-rimmed eyeglasses in worn, western-style clothing and the traditional keffiyeh head covering approached, escorted by two other men, similarly built, clothed and groomed but without eyeglasses.

"Sheik Omar!" Rhoades exclaimed gleefully. "Meet my American partner, Captain Livingstone."

Omar did not seem to share Rhoades' glee. As soon as he had Rhoades' attention, he pivoted and led the group to the far side of the white mud building-complex whose many separate apartment-like dwellings opened onto a quiet central courtyard. At the side farthest away from the highway, Omar led them into a shadowy alleyway.

Following, Rhoades glanced at Livingstone, read his anxious expression and whispered, "Now you will observe the greatness of our capitalist economic system."

In the privacy of the dark alley, Omar turned to Rhoades. "My clan has protected the British since the time of the first German war. There is no Bakhtiari clan more loyal to the British."

"Sheik Omar," Rhoades replied grandiloquently. "You do not need to explain this to me."

"But you need to explain this to me!"

Moving like sudden cats, the men with Omar seized Monty. One laid a serious-looking piece of glistening cutlery at his throat. Monty's eyes widened with terror and darted frantically from the blade at his throat to Rhoades and Omar.

"You cut off my oil?" Omar ranted. "This is how I am rewarded?"

Rhoades' eyes narrowed and met Monty's. That was when Monty first saw it, the dangerous piercing from deep inside the otherwise apparently innocuous Britisher's eyes. "Don't resist, Livingstone. That will make it more dangerous. Just wait." Rhoades said. Monty calmed. Rhoades turned to the Bakhtiari leader but continued talking to Monty. "We will settle this. Sheik Omar does not want to make his situation worse."

"Worse?" Sheik Omar exclaimed. "You have cut off my oil! The gatekeepers at Abadan no longer allow my tanker trucks to fill! I can deliver no shipments to the clans." He pointed out of the alley to the field where men loitered among the pickup trucks, obviously empty oil barrels scattered around.

"Did you pay the baksheesh to the soldiers on the refinery lot?" Rhoades asked.

"Am I stupid do you think?"

"Perhaps one of your men decided to keep the baksheesh?"

The sheik nodded at the man holding the knife at Monty's throat. "Do you call this man a liar?"

"Kill him if you must," shrugged Rhoades.

A rush of terror again rippled through Monty. Rhoades saw it and held up his left index finger to Monty, the "watch and learn" gesture. He turned back to the sheik. "Do what you will, but if you harm him the Americans will bomb your villages and all your people to dust."

Sheik Omar ignored this threat. "When my men were taking gasoline from our pipeline, the Shah's military drove them off!"

"This is Riahi's doing. Mossadeq's General."

"Is the Shah no longer ruler? Has the military turned against him? Must I now kill you and deal with Riahi?"

Rhoades frowned, not wanting to explain political complexities. Then he smiled. "How would you like to have your own oil wells and refinery?"

"That is what I have, do I not? This is my world! I allow you..." He turned and studied the knife at Monty's throat, then pivoted back to Rhoades. "Or I do not allow you."

"We're going to take Mossadeq down!" Rhoades said with quiet elation. "The Shah will make you not just the leader of a wealthy clan but the wealthiest, most powerful clan leader in all of Khuzistan!"

Omar looked suspiciously from Rhoades to Livingstone and then back at Rhoades. "Talk."

"How would you like to have your own sea-going oil tanker?" Rhoades whispered, his eyes gleaming.

"Promises."

"Why do you think I come with Captain Livingstone?"

Omar studied Rhoades thoughtfully. "You plot with the Americans?"

"Were they not instrumental in both German wars?" Rhoades asked sincerely. "Were they not in both wars our allies?"

"Persians are not fools like Germans. We conquered the world when Germans did not know what Aryan meant."

Rhoades smiled. "Which is why this time we BEGIN with an American alliance."

"So what do you ask of me?"

"Little," replied Rhoades, hurrying to present his terms. "I will see that your oil supplies open up again. And I will keep them open as long Britain runs Abadan."

Omar eyed Rhoades in silent suspicion. "What do you want?"

Rhoades smiled broadly. "Two things: For now, only time. Later, when we go into action, I want your people in the streets of Tehran, screaming for the British cause and for your monarchy."

"I am a businessman. I have no interest in politics."

"This is strictly business," Rhoades replied, his genial smile only widening. "There will be baksheesh for the people in the streets."

"You will pay only to me," Omar answered sternly, his eyes beginning to smile. "I will take care of my people."

"Of course!" exclaimed Rhoades, thrusting out his hand to shake on the deal. "Now can you let the American go?"

With one hand Omar gestured for his men to release Livingstone while, with the other, he shook on the deal with Rhoades. Monty stepped quickly away from his captors and moved toward the sunlit end of the alley, shaking his head and breathing hard to regain his composure.

"Did Riahi cut off my oil?" Omar asked Rhoades. "Or did you cut off my oil to make this deal?"

"Sheik Omar," Rhoades groaned. "Have you no trust?"

"The Arabs have an expression, Britisher. 'Trust Allah but tie up your camel.'"

"It is a wise expression," replied Rhoades, his meaninglessly jovial expression once again masking his wrinkled leathery face in enigma.

Omar stared at him for a moment, waiting for a better answer. When it did not come, Omar grunted "Fine." He turned to his men, muttered a command in Farsi and they stomped past Rhoades and Livingstone, out of the alley.

Rhoades walked to Monty. "Are you all right?" he asked, putting his hand on Monty's shoulder and looking hard into his eyes with an expression of deep concern.

"Like you really care!" Monty pushed Rhoades hand off his shoulder and walked away, out of the alley.

"You were never in any real danger," Rhoades called to Monty's back as he followed to the Cadillac. Back out in daylight, Rhoades caught up to Monty as they neared the car. "Honestly," Rhoades insisted. "You never were. I knew exactly where the deal was going all the time."

Monty turned on Rhoades. "I DIDN'T!" he yelled.

"Omar did," Rhoades replied calmly.

"THE BASTARD WITH THE KNIFE AT MY THROAT DIDN'T!" He pulled open the car's door, jumped into the passenger seat and slammed the door behind.

Rhoades walked around the car, got into the driver's seat and turned to Monty. "You're going to have to trust me, Livingstone."

"What's in it for me?"

"First," Rhoades replied instantly, "I'm going to teach you how to operate here."

"Why?"

"Because someday, maybe very soon, this whole network is going to be yours to run."

Monty turned and looked at Rhoades in astonishment.

Rhoades went on. "Do you think your being in Iran, our encounter, were just happenstance?" He watched Livingstone think and saw Livingstone admitting the truth to himself. "We know your personal life, your history, your war record. We recruited you, son."

Monty simply stared at Rhoades. "I don't know what to say," he finally muttered.

"Say nothing," Rhoades smiled, reaching for the car's ignition. "That is always advisable." He turned the car engine on. "Now let's go see Isfahan." He accelerated and steered back out onto the highway.

"Do you have friends like them in Isfahan?" Monty asked.

Rhoades smiled. "Not really. But there are some chaps you should meet."

"Great," Monty groaned, looking east.

Rhoades drove and launched into a diatribe on the greatness of capitalism. They reached Isfahan after dark, took hotel rooms at a place Rhoades was familiar with and turned in. The next morning, while Rhoades checked out of the hotel, Monty stepped out the door into a landscape of unexpected beauty.

Isfahan in the spring, Monty discovered, was truly an exotic vision. They wandered cobblestone streets into ancient Persian mystery and grandeur, set off against the towering snow-capped Zagros Mountains in one direction and verdant rolling plains in another. Mosques and palaces of medieval architectural magnificence stood amid graceful sprawling plazas and blossoming gardens of fecund elegance. Early in the day, they walked the swarming, exuberant bazaar and the meditatively still holy places while Rhoades lectured Monty on the architectural symphony of garden, platform, porch, gateway, dome, arched chamber and minaret and the colors and textures of building materials that modulated the spaces.

Soon, though, Rhoades moved from aesthetics to tradecraft and began describing techniques for walking without being followed and following without being seen. Through the day he drilled Monty on these basics, having him inconspicuously follow people on the street or walk ahead and attempt to elude his teacher. At Livingstone's developing facility in these skills, Rhoades showed great satisfaction. As evening fell, he announced they had a dinner meeting at a café not far from the bazaar.

"How and when did you arrange that?" Monty demanded.

Rhoades smiled. "I have men here I trained. They know how to be seen without being noticed."

Monty studied Rhoades with surprise. "You mean the arrangements were made today, while I have been with you?"

"Yes," nodded Rhoades. "But don't feel foolish. These men's lives would be ruined if they were seen talking with a British agent. They work carefully."

"I will have to take your training more seriously."

"That would be wise," Rhoades agreed, smiling. "Ah, here we are." He led Monty into another alley, this even darker and more threatening than the one that morning because the sun had set. Monty hesitated before stepping off the street. "Come on," said Rhoades. "It's safe."

"Didn't you say something like that this morning?"

"And wasn't I right? Now follow," Rhoades demanded. "We can't stand here bickering. We'll draw attention."

Monty took a deep breath and followed. After a few steps into the alley's darkness, Rhoades stopped, turned back to Monty and whispered. "One more thing: These are military men. They can know nothing of the smugglers in Khorramshar."

"You think that's something I'm going to want to tell funny stories about?" asked Monty angrily.

"One never knows," smiled Rhoades.

Despite Monty's anxiety, the meeting was nothing more than a friendly get-together over kababs. The two off-duty military officers clearly felt safe in the out-of-the-way café. Like the smugglers, they complained of failing oil supplies and diminishing baksheesh. But they made no threats and welcomed Rhoades' announcement that political action was coming.

After supper, the soldiers arranged rooms for their guests upstairs from the café and returned to the army base. Bright and early the next morning, the café host brought Livingstone and Rhoades pitchers of clean water and cups of hot Turkish coffee. Soon, they were driving north.

On the ride back to Tehran, Rhoades droned on about the four Iranian political factions, the pro-British monarchists, the pro-Mossadeq National front, the Islamists and the Tudeh communist party. Monty feigned attention. But he was really thinking about her. He was putting her back into the story of his life. He had removed her until he saw her in that shanty on Abadan, though from the moment he had seen her at the mosque after Razmara's assassination he had been resisting the memory of Berlin.

*****

"Being with a woman all night never hurt no professional baseball player. It's staying up all night looking for a woman that does him in." ...Casey Stengel

It was a hot Berlin summer night on the patio of the American Liaison Office temporary quarters. He had been to several weeks of these obligatory social gatherings with the international delegations: Cheap wine, bad food, dull bureaucrats, each more tedious than the one before. This particular evening, the sky had just turned blue-black, the lights were twinkling on and the small band was playing a popular American tune.

Would you like to swing on a star,
Carry moonbeams home in a jar,
And be better off than you are,
Or would you rather be a mule?

A mule is an animal with long funny ears,
Kicks up at anything he hears,
His back is brawny but his brain is weak,
He's just plain stupid with a stubborn streak,
And by the way, if you hate to go to school,
You may grow up to be a mule.

Or would you like to swing on a star,
Carry moonbeams home in a jar,
And be better off than you are…

He was leaning against a wall, trying not to be caught in conversation. She walked unexpectedly out of some strange shadows and passed by him. She was brushing at something on her uniform skirt. She somehow made the exceedingly dull Russian uniform look like something Ingrid Bergman or Lauren Bacall might wear. Thick, blond, wavy hair cut short; thoughtful, understanding blue eyes; a slender, graceful way of carrying herself. He could not turn away. He felt compelled to look at her, to enjoy just looking at her.

…Or would you rather be a pig?

A pig is an animal with dirt on his face,
His shoes are a terrible disgrace,
He has no manners when he eats his food,
He's fat and lazy and extremely rude,
But if you don't care a feather or a fig,
You may grow up to be a pig.

Or would you like to swing on a star,
Carry moonbeams home in a jar,
And be better off than you are…

She stopped wiping at whatever it was on her skirt and looked up. Her eyes met his. She did not know why he was looking at her. He did not want to stop. And in that instant, he felt her inviting him to smile, to walk over to her, to say hello, to ask her to dance.

"Well, yes," she said, in a gentle Russian accent. "I like to dance."

And he led her out onto the little, nearly empty, concrete space for dancing in front of the band. They did a bit of a foxtrot and although he was not a great dancer, somehow they moved easily together and their movements felt smooth, almost synchronized, because she knew just how to follow him and it made it easy for him to lead strongly.

…Or would you rather be a fish?

A fish won't do anything, but swim in a brook,
He can't write his name or read a book,
To fool the people is his only thought,

And though he's slippery, he still gets caught,
But then if that sort of life is what you wish,
You may grow up to be a fish.
A new kind of jumped-up slippery fish

And all the monkeys aren't in the zoo,
Every day you meet quite a few,
So you see it's all up to you,
You can be better than you are,
You could be swingin' on a star!

And then the band played "In The Mood" and everybody got up to dance because, ever since Glenn Miller's plane had gone down, the song was a reminder of how short and unpredictable life could be and how important it therefore was to dance when the music played.

So they danced again, a gentle swing, and it was even better, smoother and more exciting. While they were dancing, he glanced at her and saw her looking at him. So he asked if she knew who Glen Miller was. She smiled with a melancholy he had never seen in an American girl and said "yes" and he smiled and said "good" and they went on dancing. He felt something he had forgotten he could feel, something he remembered from before he had slogged across Western Europe with the 102nd Infantry.

So he kept dancing and she did not object and soon they were dancing like two parts of the same feeling and laughing like two characters in the same funny story and both of them forgot they were real people, one Russian and one American in a world rapidly coming apart at the seams. And because neither of them could tolerate the thought of letting these feelings fade away, they kept dancing until the band stopped playing. And when he offered to walk her back to the Russian quarters she said, "Of course."

And when they were alone on the street, he pulled her into the shadows and kissed her with intoxicated passion. And she kissed back with the same hunger. So he pulled her down a back street to an empty alleyway and they kissed and fondled until both were near exploding. He caressed her soft round places with masculine possessiveness and she moaned and worked at the waist of his trousers and took his manhood with her firm warm hand and then with her soft, wet mouth and he moaned, so she pushed him against a wall and pulled down her panties and pulled up her dress and hooked a leg around him and mounted him and put him inside herself. And both of them gasped and froze and the world stopped. Until neither could hold still any longer, each going completely out of control with madly unconquerable

356

rhythmic coupling, a wild cascading to an utterly satisfying culmination. And the world stopped again.

And then they kissed again, still connected at the root of their beings, warm kisses reaching for the other's essence, until his to-this-moment long-unsatisfied arousal resuscitated at the sheer intimacy of her loving groans and subtle, loving pelvic nudging. And they rose once again, and this time exulted and exclaimed at their deeply satisfying mutual conclusions, an emptying for him and a fulfillment for her. And then they looked at each other as if for the first time and fell desperately, hopelessly, endlessly in love with what they saw. And he walked her home and asked her if she wanted to meet him the next day for lunch and she said, "Of course."

There might not have been a more desolate, desperate place in the summer of 1945 than Berlin. But for Tekla and Monty, assigned to complimentary official liaison staffs, it might as well have been springtime in Paris. The grimness of Berlin did not intimidate her. She was a tough girl, quick and confident of the streetfighting skills the Russian army had taught her. She was also feminine, passionate and seductive. The post-bombardment city's indignities and deprivations were irrelevant. They were full with each other, with lovemaking and companionship, with hopes and dreams. They found black market indulgences of exotic French forbidden fruits. They had barren building assignations of steaming eroticism and found countryside secret places where they could believe nature would always give forth and renew impossible things. It was utterly romantic. Until Enola Gay dropped "Little Boy" on Hiroshima and Bockscar dropped "Fat Man" on Nagasaki.

The day after the second bomb, Tekla did not show up for their usual secret lunchtime meeting behind the Russian horse barn. Monty waited but eventually concluded the bombings had caused her offices increased activity. He went back to work, looking forward all the more to their next meeting. He was sure his old unit, on the way to duty in the Pacific Theater, would now be mustered out. He was sure the war was over. He was going home. And he was planning to take her home with him.

His afternoon turned busy. Frantic communications were coming and going from all the international offices. He could not get away until late. He went straight to what they called their "supper club," a bombed-out apartment building's intact basement where they had found a functioning electrical outlet, brought a table and two chairs, plugged in his contraband radio, opened bottles of black market wine and danced the nights away. Again, though, he was disappointed. Tekla did not turn up. When it was clear to him she wasn't coming, he went back to his barracks. There had been other nights when she couldn't get away.

When she again did not come for lunch the next day, he decided to walk by the Soviet liaison offices on his way back to work, just to see what was going on. Nothing was going on. The Soviets were gone. The Iron Curtain was coming down.

*****

By the time Rhoades drove them into the British embassy compound, the discourse on Iranian politics was complete. The essence of it, to the extent that Monty understood, was that the Anglo Iranian Oil Company was everything to everybody. To the Shah, it was rightfully his and the key to modernizing his country. To the British, it was rightfully theirs and the cornerstone of England's economy. To Mossadeq and his National Front, the oil rightfully belonged to the Iranian people and it was the key to making them fit for self-rule. To Tudeh, oil was the resource the Soviet Union's southern neighbor should have to turn itself into the People's Republic of Iran, one of the nations that could join with the Soviets when the workers of the world united. And to the Islamists, oil was Allah's gift to a righteous Islamic Republic and Satan's temptation to non-believers.

But as Rhoades dropped Livingstone at his guest bungalow on the embassy grounds, Monty had only come to one conclusion and it was not about oil: He must find out why she left him in Berlin. He must find her. But how?

"Don't forget the reception tonight!" Rhoades called out, driving off in the Cadillac. Monty turned toward his bungalow thinking only about making his way into the streets of Tehran, this city he did not know, and finding his way to Tekla, this woman he was only now beginning to remember.

He had been functioning for so long by doing the next thing expected of him. How long? He wondered as he dressed for the reception. At least since he married Rachel. He was still doing it: As expected, he walked into the stately embassy reception hall at the appointed cocktail hour, dressed smartly in dinner jacket and black tie. He glanced around the crowded reception room. He had been to many such functions during his years with Socony-Vaccuum. He knew this situation, these people, well. Fifty or so men and women in perquisite evening dress with champagne glasses and cigarettes, sipping, smoking and chattering. Most also with unseen agendas, hidden cards and strings on power. Little interested him as he scanned the room until, to his surprise, he saw a gathering of some 20 children around a pair of adult-sized characters dressed up as clowns in a far corner of the reception hall.

Rhoades came from the crowd and across the room at him, huffing and hulky in his dinner jacket, his wrinkled face rumbling into a smile as he shook Livingstone's hand, stepped near, hooked his left arm in Monty's and whispered, as his left index finger pointed upward, "Watch and learn."

"Tell me again what this is all about."

"Fourth birthday of the granddaughter of the editor of Iran's biggest pro-Shah, and I might add pro-British, newspaper," Rhoades muttered. "Ambassador's determined to do it up big."

He pulled Monty across the room toward a dynamic-looking young man with wavy black hair, deep dark eyes and the proud profile of a leader. "Irdeshar Zahedi," whispered Rhoades. "Father's a General. Good man. Bit of a bastard during the war but what do you expect? Natives hate us. The boy's a whole other story." He beamed and made the introduction. "Irdeshar Zahedi, Montgomery Livingstone. American. Pro-Shah."

"Pro-Shah or pro-British?" Irdeshar asked with a smile, shaking Monty's hand with firm warmth.

Getting a good feeling from him, Monty smiled back. "Both until I started working with Rhoades. Now I'm just in it for the oil."

Irdeshar laughed. "That's all Rhoades is interested in, I'm sure." All three chuckled.

"Excuse me, Irdeshar," Rhoades interrupted, spotting someone across the room. "I've got to have a word with a Major-General."

Rhoades bustled off, his barrel-chested bulkiness wobbling through the guests on lean, tired legs. Irdeshar turned to Monty. "Have you been to Tehran before?"

"No," shrugged Monty. "I'd like to get to know it better."

"From what I hear of Mr. Rhoades' plans, you will."

Monty could not stop himself from showing surprise at this remark and what it implied Irdeshar knew, but before their conversation developed further, a question interrupted them. "Is this the American you and Rhoades are interviewing, Irdeshar?"

Monty turned to see a stunningly beautiful, slender, dark woman with shining black hair, creamy skin and intelligent, penetrating, smoldering brown eyes wearing an elegant black sheath cocktail dress.

"Yes, Princess Ashraf, this is him," Irdeshar replied with a happy disdain.

"My goodness," she exclaimed. "He IS American! Just like Robert Taylor."

"Princess Ashraf, Montgomery Livingstone," Irdeshar said quietly, formally.

"You know Hardy Rhoades?" Livingstone asked her.

"Doesn't everyone?"

"I'm beginning to understand that."

Suddenly the doors at the far end of the room, near where the children were gathered, burst open and a group of kitchen workers rolled a cart through it. Atop the cart was a huge birthday cake with concentric circles of candles alight. At the clowns' vigorous signaling, everyone in the room joined them in singing "Happy Birthday." The clowns brought the delighted little birthday girl front and center as the singing continued and the children, giggling, exclaimed gleefully at the excitement.

Suddenly, one of the clowns threw something liquid into the center of the cake. It splashed and burst into flame. Flames leapt to the linen on the table and the table itself caught fire. Screaming, panic and desperation flashed through the room. Thinking fast, the good clown pulled the birthday girl to safety. Many of the children instinctively fled for their parents. Adults in proximity grabbed the ones too terrified to react. The bad clown meanwhile had leapt to a nearby chair and begun raging at the assembled.

"OUT BRITISH! IRANIAN OIL FOR IRANIANS! BRITISH GO HOME!"

Terrorized, not knowing what might come next, the roomful of dignitaries and business reacted like a mob. Some, especially the parents, scrambled madly forward to protect their screaming, crying, fright-petrified children. Others took cover behind tables or columns or retreated into nearby hallways or escaped out the room's several doorways. Security people pushed toward the madman at the front of the room but struggled against the panic-driven mob in retreat.

"DEATH TO THE SHAH! DEATH TO BRITAIN!" the clown screamed, now leaping from the chair and dancing madly around the flaming cake.

"IRANIAN OIL FOR IRANIANS! BRITISH GO HOME!" A seam in the mob opened up before Monty and he stepped back at the bizarre vision before him. The clown cackled in mad exhilaration. At the height of his perverse joy, the liquid accelerant on the clown's hands caught a spark from the fire on the cake. The clown suit ignited and the man was instantly ablaze from the waist up. Now he went into a horrible rage and charged in the direction of the last group of children left in the room as nearby adults tried to get them to safety out the kitchen door. Seeing this, Monty reacted without thinking. He raced through the seam in the crowd at the flaming clown and tackled him around the ankles, bringing him down before he could get to the children.

As soon as the man went down, Monty came to his senses and rolled away. The flaming clown rolled around and around on the floor, wailing in agony and horror until he just lay still. A few steps across the floor, Monty got to his knees and watched as the man died. A cook now emerged from the kitchen and doused the dead clown with a big bowl of fruit punch, leaving him steaming and smoldering.

All of the children and most of the adults were now out of the room. The cook, some kitchen help, the security men and a few courageous others were left looking on the gruesome scene. Irdeshar Zahedi and Hardy Rhoades came across the floor from opposite directions and helped Monty up.

"You saved those children!" Zahedi told Monty admiringly. "You saved them!"

Rhoades was all smiles. "Did I tell you about this boy!?!" He exclaimed. "Did I tell you!?!"

"Are you all right?" Irdeshar asked, looking Monty over. "Did you get burned?"

"I seem to be fine," Monty said, checking himself over.

The three looked up anxiously as they heard a commotion at the far side of the room.

"Let me in, damn you!" It was Princess Ashraf's voice and it was angrily impatient.

"Your brother will hang us if you come to harm!" a security man protested. "We must get you out of here!"

361

"Not until I thank the American!" She pushed past them and came across to Monty, the two guards trailing at her heels. "Robert Taylor!" She exclaimed on seeing him standing, unhurt. "You saved the children's lives! The Shah will hear of your heroism!"

"My name is Livingstone, Princess. I'm no movie star," Monty smiled. "I just had a chance, that's all."

"Your name will be Hero of Iran before this week ends, Mr. Livingstone." Catching up, the bodyguards positioned themselves on either side of her and began moving her back toward the door. "Forgive me, but I have the welfare of my bodyguards to worry about. They will have heart failure if I don't allow them to take me away from here."

"You must get to safety, Princess," Irdeshar admonished her. "Mr. Livingstone understands that. We will see to him."

"And the Shah will see to his reward!" the Princess exclaimed as her bodyguards pulled her from the room.

"She's quite a woman, isn't she?" Monty asked Irdeshar.

"Not your type, son, so don't go getting any ideas," Rhoades warned Livingstone.

"That's not what I meant," Monty said.

"Still, you Americans can't be trusted around royalty can you?" Rhoades went on. "King Edward and Mrs. Simpson and so on."

"What I'd really like is a little fresh air," Monty said. "Maybe a walk around the block or something."

"Do you feel up to a stroll in the city?" Irdeshar asked.

Monty looked around the room. "Looks like the party's over, isn't it?"

"Pretty fair assumption, that," said Rhoades.

"Yeah, a walk around town, that would be just great," Monty said.

They walked out of the embassy gates onto Ferdosi, through the square and down Winston Churchill Avenue to the business district. They walked briskly and quietly, enjoying the air and exercise. As the evening waned, the shop-lined streets fell into shadow. They turned on Kokh and walked past a grand neoclassical building behind a wrought iron fence with a wrought iron-gated, stone archway.

"What is that magnificent old building?" Monty asked, stopping to admire it.

"The Majlis Building," Irdeshar replied. "The seat of the only constitutionally-empowered, democratically-elected parliament in the Levant," he added proudly, stopping by Monty's side to appreciate the structure's enormous stately presence. "The Prime Minister's home is that way."

Monty looked in the direction his host and guide pointed and then looked the other direction, where a few smaller old stone buildings, across the street and down the block past a big grassy square, housed charming storefronts and upstairs offices. One storefront caught Monty's eye. "What's that?" he asked, pointing at a shop window with Russian Cyrillic letters identifying it.

"The sign says it is an import/export company. But it is a front for the Tudeh Party 'Rahbar' newspaper," Zahedi answered. "Not welcomed, but tolerated. Tudeh has uneasy associations with the National Front. And they buy some of the clerics with donations to their mosques."

"Yours is a strange and beautiful country," Monty smiled, staring at the Russian lettering on the storefront window. He turned to Zahedi and said, as if finally coming to a conclusion, "I want to get to know it better."

"And we want you to," smiled the young Iranian.

"But not tonight," Monty said. "I'm ready for supper and a good night's sleep."

They walked back to the embassy living quarters making small talk. When Irdeshar started telling tales from the ancient and modern history of Iran, Monty's mind started down its parallel track, thinking about Tekla. But now he had a focus: If that office housed Tudeh's newspaper, Tudeh officers and members must surely come and go from it.

The next morning, when Monty joined Rhoades for a breakfast meeting in the embassy cafeteria, he told his mentor his walk with Zahedi had inspired him and he would like to know more about Tehran. He then looked at Rhoades and waited.

363

"Splendid," the British agent replied beaming. "Because word comes back. From the highest levels, mind you. The Shah's palace. Tehran would like to know more about you."

"So what? Take classes at the University?"

Rhoades laughed. "Nonsense. You're an oilman. You have appointments, meetings. Deals will be cooking."

"How does that make me more familiar with the city?"

"Your meetings will be everywhere. In the embassies below the foothills, in the Majlis district, in offices south of the bazaar. You're the oilman, boy. You work it out. As you go, I will accompany you, helping you develop tradecraft along with a knowledge of the city."

Over the next weeks, Monty fell into the routine of breakfasting with Rhoades at the embassy and then taking up his day's work. Often they retreated to a private office where the British agent lectured and trained him. There were networks to understand, relationships to develop, contacts and codes to know. And the most important thing, as Monty had hoped, was the development of street skills: The arts of patience and geniality as displayed in properly chosen kebab cafes and Turkish coffee houses; the meeting and winning of trust from Iranians already inclined toward the monarchy and the oil company; and the knowledge of who was coming and going and what they were up to. After an initial training period, Livingstone frequently volunteered to take to the streets of Tehran on his own. Rhoades, ever the agreeable enigma, did not object.

When Livingstone went out on his own, he used Rhoades' tricks to be sure he was not being watched or followed. He had good reason to be alert. Rhoades had made it clear his movements would be of interest to the British, Russian and American embassies and the Shah's military as well as the other Iranian factions struggling for power. Methodically, Livingstone perfected his tradecraft. He cultivated a purposeful presence in the life of the street. He always had a good reason for going where he went and spending time where he spent it. Sometimes he made his way through the city with announced purposes and specific destinations. Other times, he played the tourist and gawker, used unusual routes, detours and stop-offs, as would any sightseer, until he knew with certainty if he was followed and, with the nonchalance of the slightly befuddled daytripper, elude his follower.

Most importantly, he made certain nobody could tell the center of his attention was the Russian newspaper office. He watched it in regular irregular intervals, over weeks. Usually, he merely passed by. Other times, he held business meetings in front of the Majlis and took a position from which the Russian newspaper office fell in his line of sight so that while discussing oil or American politics he could study the office's comings and goings. Sometimes, he had lunch in the square across the street from the Majlis and down the block from the newspaper, munching on a kabab from a street vendor while checking the journalists' lunchtime habits and meetings. At the evening commute time, he frequently borrowed one of the embassy cars and drove past the office, fell in behind an employee or customer as they left and followed. Or he parked a car beside a curb nearby and appeared to wait or nap while watching comings and goings. Slowly, he began to recognize the office's staff and patrons, the editors and writers, illustrators and tipsters, salesmen, suppliers and rabble rousers, clerks and bookkeepers, even the janitors and those who pedaled sandwiches at lunchtime or religion all day long. He soon spotted Faddey, and Tekla with Faddey. When he saw her, he made no immediate move to confront her. He desperately wanted to. Instead, he went on watching. He saw politicians of every stripe and tribe, whether or not they were welcome. Some stayed and were presumably heard. Others left abruptly. He saw the Mullah from Abadan, with and without bearded companions in Islamic garb and the white-shirted communists. He saw the small and nattily dressed, the fat and bearded, those with and without scars, the tall with and without hats, the small with and without boots, some with Faddey, some with Faddey and Tekla, some alone and pensive, many in large, boisterous, contentious groups.

All the waiting and watching gave him too much time to think and his thoughts rambled a gamut of possibilities, from sentimental melancholy to existential fear and despair. Fortunately, Rhoades' exercises in spy craft methodically taught him to jettison the unnecessary. Memories of his Chicago and Oklahoma origins seemed irrelevant. His lifelong struggle to resolve the conflicting impulses of his Chicago-born Californian mother and his French-born Oklahoman father no longer held his attention. The trouble he got into when he went back to the oil fields during a high school summer and got caught running hot oil was only preparation for the harder fight he fought in the war and in—this—whatever this might turn out to be.

Rachel? Rachel was a wonderful idea but it could never really have worked. She chose him because of what she thought he was, not who he really was. And he chose her because she chose him. Things happened between people—either the people responded and adjusted or they couldn't. Who would have predicted the birth of Israel or that its on-going jeopardy would seduce Rachel? If she had not found this other, more demanding lover, he would still be with her. He had never expected Rachel to be Tekla.

He had decided to forget about Tekla when she disappeared from Berlin. He had resolved to never feel that kind of pain again. It had not been easy, but he had done many things in his life that were not easy. Maybe the hardest was the thing he did the day he went back into the office at Socony-Vacuum after the honeymoon with Rachel on which he found out for certain what a struggle the marriage was going to be. Waiting for him on his desk when he got back to the office was the letter from Tekla. He looked at it a long time before he decided what to do. He sent it back unopened. And then he blocked Tekla from his memory and tried to make his marriage work. It did not.

When he was satisfied he knew the practices and routines of the Tudeh newspaper office well enough, Monty was ready to make his move. His objective was to catch Tekla alone and confront her. Every Monday for the five weeks Monty had been watching, Faddey and Tekla had arrived together on Faddey's beat-up red Vespa very late in the afternoon. On this hot Monday evening in late April, Monty borrowed a British embassy car and parked across Kohk Avenue and down the block, with a view of the newspaper office's front door. They arrived later than usual. Shadows cast by the sharp spring sun falling behind the Majlis building and rows of three- and four-story Tehran sprawling to the west were lengthening when Faddey parked the scooter. As they started into the office, the Russian reached to put an arm around Tekla as he replied to something she was saying. Monty was too far away to hear. But he saw her push the arm away and snap at Faddey. The Russian shrugged and walked ahead of her into the newspaper office. She stopped, stared at Faddey with obvious frustration and, finally, followed inside.

Monty sat in the car and waited for what he expected would come next. Twenty minutes: Anytime now. A half-hour: Longer than usual. Thirty-five minutes: That was interesting. Forty minutes: What the hell was that about? Forty-five minutes: What the HELL was THAT about? Damn! Fifty minutes: Something must be wrong. Maybe that bickering exploded. Was she all right? Fifty-five minutes: Dammit. Break cover? No, never. The watcher's only edge. But was she all right? Just as he was reaching for the car door's handle, Faddey and Tekla emerged from the newspaper office, obviously arguing. Arms waving, heads bobbing, fingers pointing. Monty began wondering if this argument had aborted the routine, if it would go on through the night, perhaps ending in a passionate reconciliation. Just then Faddey pivoted, threw his arms up in an "I'm done with this" gesture and stomped back inside. Tekla stood on the street, staring at the newspaper office door, arms dropped helplessly at her sides. Watching carefully, Monty saw equanimity, not despair, on her pale, beautiful face, flush with life but not taut with rage, the bright blue eyes intensely alert and pensive, not wounded or afraid, the slender, graceful body held with confidence and poise, not loss.

She appeared to have reached a very necessary decision, one in which she seemed rather confident of the outcome. She turned and walked east, as she did every Monday evening after the meeting at the office.

When she was far enough away, Monty stepped out of the car and followed. As he expected, she turned south. He lost sight of her but he knew where she was going. When he rounded the corner at Ferdosi, he saw her moving south. She seemed to be enjoying the walk, the shop windows and the cool evening shadows. He lost sight of her again, just past the National Museum, when she jogged west toward Kayyam, but he remained confident, expecting to pick her up as she headed past Golestan Palace. When he came around the corner, however, he did not see her.

He slowed and studied the street before him. Moving forward cautiously, his mind raced. This should not be happening. What mistake did he make? Where could she be?

From a shadow, something came at him. In an instant, he was off balance. In the next instant, he was turned and bent helpless, his arm locked behind his back. He was pushed into an alleyway off Kayyam, released and spun around to face his attacker.

"Monty."

He raised himself straight and peered into the darkness. Lights splashed shadows below a star-smattered blue-black evening sky. She was standing in the reflected light of a shop window smiling the elegant and profoundly melancholy smile he had forgotten until this moment. Emotion held back his voice.

"You must stop following me," she said.

He looked at her, hesitant to speak, uncertain if he could. She was so beautiful, so desirable.

"You have no idea how dangerous it is," she said commandingly.

Finally, he had to reply. "You don't even want to know why I am following you?"

"I assume you wish to compromise me."

"This is not about politics," he blurted.

She remained calm. "Politically or emotionally. You cannot."

"Just tell me why," Monty said quietly.

"Why what?"

"Why you left me."

She stared at him without reply, her blue eyes steely.

"You have no answer?" he asked.

She hung her head, her shocks of blond hair falling down. "Its not about you, you self-obsessed bastard," she said quietly.

"What?"

She looked up. She was angry. Her bright blue eyes flashed lightning. "Its not about you!"

"You left Berlin without a word."

She looked at him hard, her anger transmuting to a thought, and then a feeling more complicated. "I loved you."

"Why did you leave me?"

"To save my family! Why did you not come for me?"

"You left me! Without a word! How could I know you wanted me to come?"

"I wrote."

"Years later."

She looked down. "Perhaps you have heard of the Iron Curtain," she muttered, then remained quiet.

He thought about the Iron Curtain, the obstacles between them, but said nothing.

"You must stop following me," she finally said, quietly.

He stared at the top of her head, her blond hair falling down over her face. He waited. She looked up at him, saying nothing. He looked back. There was only silence. She started to speak but stopped herself and dropped her head again.

And then a thought came to him. "Why did you do it this way?" he asked her.

"What?"

"You could have warned me off without a confrontation."

"It is very dangerous…" she began without looking up.

"All the more reason to warn me off without seeing me. Without seeing me alone."

"Monty…" Her head remained down.

"You wanted to see me alone!" He stepped nearer to her.

"Monty."

"Nobody but my parents and you ever called me Monty."

She looked up at him. Tears rolled over her pink, suntanned cheeks. "We are two people who once loved each other and are furious with each other because we still do."

He smiled, stepped to her and started to kiss away her tears.

"Wait, Monty. Think. This is impossible."

"Didn't I see you at a dance somewhere a long time ago?"

Recognizing the old familiar jest, she looked up at him, smiled and gave the old familiar reply. "I like to dance."

He kissed her. The old feelings sparked, then flared, then burned. Slightly awkward embracing quickly became longing groping that quickly became separate people moving into oneness. Moans answered moans. Grasping became irresistible grinding. Longing inspired lust which inspired passion until both were slightly mad with wanton, loving wanting.

369

Finally Tekla pulled away. "Monty!" She exclaimed. "Monty, Monty, Monty. I have not felt like this since Berlin! Shall this be like that first night? Do you want to do it here, in the alley, in the dark? I need you!"

He looked at her, looked around at the alley and came back to her. Finally, he realized the foolhardiness, the risk in what they were doing. "We are no longer innocents, Tekla. And both of us know now it is not a safe world."

She stepped to him and placed a palm on his cheek. "What do we do?"

"Do you know a safe place?"

She thought. "No."

"The car," he finally said.

"What car?"

"Come on..."

They were now alert to detection but the streets were dark and Tekla knew the city. In a few minutes they were back at the car Monty had been watching from. When he pointed to it and told her to get in, she laughed. He asked why.

"We have had reports of the British watching the 'Rahbar' office from their cars. Your tradecraft is terrible."

"And yet here we are," he smiled.

"Drive," she told him. "We will improve your ability to get to me undetected," she added laughing, "if you prove yourself still worthy of the attention."

Hours later, off a dirt road on a ridge of the Alborz foothills overlooking the sleeping city, they lay naked in the back seat of the spacious Frazer, caressing each other, breathing each other in, reminiscing and tentatively beginning to fill in the gap of years.

"Your mother and your father," she said. "Did they reconcile after the war?"

"No," he smiled sadly. "My mother is back on the road, singing with a band. She hates communists more than ever. My father spends most of his time in Hollywood. He's fighting red-baiters now."

"And, like theirs, your marriage was unhappy."

"Not all the time."

"But no children?"

"No. Rachel supervises the pre-school kids on the kibbutz now. What is this Faddey to you?"

"Is he my lover, you mean?"

"Yes."

"When they ordered me home from Berlin, my only thought was to get to you. Until my commanding officer called me in, revealed he knew about you, and meanly mentioned my family was looking forward to my return. He then said something about my brothers' places in the party."

"They could have protected your mother."

"Or they could have been sent to work camps for having a sister who defected. No one knows how many disappeared before the war. For even more meaningless things."

"Faddey?"

"I went back to Kiev and waited to hear from you."

"Without leaving any word that you wanted to."

"And, finally, smuggled the letter to you. Which you never answered."

"You never got my answer?" he exclaimed, quietly elated to learn the nastiness of returning the letter unopened had miraculously been erased. "I answered!"

She stared at him, her expression revealing ugly feelings lifting. Not knowing how awful his nonreply reply had been, she now felt remorse for giving up on him and remaining angry all these years, only to now learn it was apparently the state and not Monty who had failed her.

He interrupted her thoughts, anticipating the rest of her answer. "So you were angry at me and succumbed to Faddey's advances."

371

She looked away, out the car window. "Yes," she nodded. "He is an agent, like your Rhoades, and now leading Tudeh, on Moscow's orders."

"Do you love him?"

She looked back at Monty. "Love is very complicated, isn't it?"

"Yes."

"But when I saw you at the mosque, I knew instantly I could never feel about anyone else the way I feel about you." She put her hand on his chest, over his heart. "You know what I mean, don't you?"

He nodded and they kissed. Their kiss aroused them and their hunger for one another took them on yet another whirling journey of one another's bodies into each other's souls.

Sometime later, after they fell asleep together, blue began peeking into the distant eastern sky. After opening his eyes, he gently waked her and they dressed. As they drove down slowly from the foothills, they began looking toward the day with general comments about political goings on, the Razmara murder, the investigation, the rumors of dark plottings. Each was reluctant to mention the other's loyalties but they found they had a common antipathy for the radical Muslims.

"The assassin's trial begins today," Monty said. "Will you be there?"

"There will be no trial."

"What?"

"Did you read that no Imam would lead prayers at Razmara's funeral?" she asked him.

"Yes. The Shah even offered a huge donation to the mosque of an Imam who would lead the prayers."

"But Kashani declared Razmara a betrayer of the faith. Publicly praying for him would be suicide in an unholy cause. Even the Shah does not have enough money."

"But that's religion, not law."

"In Iran they are the same. The clerics say the assassin did Allah's bidding. There will be no trial." They came to the edge of the city. He stopped the car where she indicated and opened the door to a silent, empty street. "I will make my way from here."

"When will I see you again?"

"You will go on ignoring me in public," she dictated.

"Of course."

"And you will stop following me?"

"Until my tradecraft meets your approval."

"I will contact you," she said, getting out of the car.

He smiled. "See you at the dance."

She smiled. The smile. Her smile. He drove off, and back to the embassy, happier than he could remember ever being.

Later that morning he joined Rhoades, as previously arranged, and they walked together across the city to the Palace of Justice to observe the trial of the accused assassin, Kahlil Taramasibi Fedayani. Monty made no mention of Tekla but now, as Rhoades lectured about ways to move through the streets minimizing detection, and pointed out things about the car and foot traffic around them worth taking notice of, Livingstone paid stricter attention. He now knew his ability to move stealthily and keep track of what was going on around him was vital, if not to life, at least to love.

At the magnificent palace that housed the Iranian State Supreme Court, they waded through throngs milling on the broad marble steps outside. They squeezed into the courtroom among throngs of passionate Muslims whispering in anticipation of the trial. Before Monty got comfortable on the elegant hardwood benches of the trial chamber, the Judge—a cleric and, by the terms of the Iranian constitution of 1906, the sole authority in legal matters (including capital crimes such as murder and adultery)—dismissed the case. The believers exploded in joyous celebration and carried the weeping Kahlil from the courtroom to the steps outside.

Rhoades and Livingstone followed and stood on the palace portico above the apparently spontaneous demonstration. Milling throngs cheered the brave but now unmartyred hero as he modestly spoke a few words. When he finished his hesitating sentences, the crowd erupted in frenzy.

"This turns my stomach," Rhoades muttered to Monty.

"What did he say? I heard the word Allah."

"He said he was only submitting to the will of Allah."

"What is that chant?" Monty asked of the crowd's repetitive cadences.

"Death to the British. Death to the Shah," Rhoades muttered quietly, shaking his head. "Death to infidels and those who steal from the people."

"Infidels and the people?" Monty asked, smiling grimly. "Is that some kind of hybrid communist-Muslimism?" Rhoades did not answer. Monty looked away from the crowd to Rhoades and saw the British agent staring at a tall young man with large, dark, tired eyes, a heavy nose and big lips wearing the traditional loose clothing and turban of the clerics. The young man was talking to a smaller man wearing western clothes who was scribbling into a notepad as the cleric talked. "What?" Monty asked.

"You recognize that one?" Rhoades asked.

"Cleric," Monty replied, shrugging.

"Obviously," said Rhoades, walking away from Livingstone, toward the cleric.

Monty followed. In a nonchalant way, they walked near enough to the cleric to hear what he was saying. Rhoades lingered. The cleric went on talking until he noticed Rhoades and Monty. When he looked up and stared hard at them, Monty saw a seriousness and rage and pain in the deep sad eyes like nothing he had ever seen before. The cleric stopped talking and held Rhoades in his gaze. For an instant the Britisher squeezed his eyes into the piercing squint Monty had seen when Rhoades was dealing with the smugglers who had the knife at Monty's throat. But this was in Rhoades' eyes only for an instant. Suddenly, he grinned, and his big, round, wrinkled, leathery face became almost clownishly innocent. "So sorry. Didn't mean to interrupt," Rhoades bubbled. "Carry on." He led Monty away.

When they were at a distance, Monty glanced back. The cleric went on talking and his companion resumed making notes. "Who was that guy?" Monty asked as he followed Rhoades across the palace plaza to the far side.

"Young firebrand," Rhoades replied, still thinking. "Ruhollah Khomeini." As they walked, young men handed them flyers. "Heard of him?"

"No," Monty answered, studying the flyers that, printed in Persian, meant nothing to him. "What was he saying and why was that guy writing it down?"

"Chap with the notepad was a reporter. Khomeini was telling him Mossadeq has   forsaken   Islam."

"Even Mossy isn't good enough for him?"

"Kashani is the politician. He thinks we will eventually compromise on the oil. Says we eventually must let Iranians be patriots. But his strength comes from believers like this Khomeini. Nationalists and fundamentalists. Works as long as Fatwas condemn our oil company."

"But the radicals are going to want to condemn the Shah, aren't they? Or the elected parliament?"

"Uneasy lies the crown," smiled Rhoades.

Livingstone thought about the revolving, evolving alliances and the many players. "Hard to figure," he said, deciding he still did not understand. He would definitely take this up with Tekla. As they stood across from the mob, Imam Kashani stepped before the crowd of celebrants on the steps of the Palace of Justice and began speaking. Intermittently, he paused and the crowd chanted again, in phrases Monty was beginning to recognize.

"Death to the British! Death to the Shah! Death to infidels and those who steal from the people!"

Rhoades studied the flyer.

"What's it about?" Monty asked.

"Another rally. Big do. Anti-British, anti-Shah. Called by Tudeh and the clerics." He nodded toward the crowd. "This is just the beginning." He looked up and his eyes tracked a group of men leaving the plaza. "Look," he said, nodding again. Monty recognized Faddey among the small coterie of white shirts and others. One or two of them were among those distributing flyers. Monty did not recognize any of the others but noticed they were dressed similarly to the oil smugglers who threatened his life in

Khorramshar, in worn western style along with the traditional head coverings. "Let's see just how well you are doing with your tradecraft," Rhoades muttered, following after the group.

They trailed Faddey's group off the plaza and then around the palace and down Khayyam toward the bazaar.

"Just a fraternal bunch of chaps off for a kebab and a nip," muttered Rhoades with sarcastic meanness.

"They don't look like they're having much fun," Monty replied.

"Astute."

Several in the group began glancing around and there appeared to be muttering among them.

"Follow me!" Rhoades commanded. "Double time!" He cut sharply across Khayyam and, indicating a shop, walked straight through the entrance as if he owned it. As soon as Monty followed him inside, Rhoades pivoted to the window and peered, past fabric rolls and boxes of ribbon and buttons, along the street.

Monty followed Rhoades' stare. "They disappeared," Monty said in surprise.

Rhoades glanced around the shop. A slender, unshaven man came from a back room, tentative at the unexpected entry of westerners. Rhoades waved him off, then looked again at the street. "They're up to something," he muttered. "Planning something or settling something."

"Where?"

Instantly assessing the possibilities, Rhoades nodded up the street. "In that alley. Let's see if we can get close enough to hear."

Moving surprisingly quickly, the British agent strode out onto the street and across, Monty at his heels. As he went down the block toward where the alley turned off, he motioned with a discreet wave of his hand behind his back for Monty to do as he was doing, keeping very near the shop fronts at the building facades and giving the appearance of hasty window-shopping. Two doorways from the alley, he turned to Monty, put a finger to his lips and whispered, "THESE chappies put a knife to your throat, all you can do is pray, fight or run."

Monty stared at him in shock for an instant and then nodded that he understood. Rhoades turned back. Suddenly, a commotion sounded from the alley and the whole bunch burst out into the street. The ones in the worn everyday-wear and keffiyehs backed into the street as the white shirts, yelling angrily in Farsi and led by Faddey, drove them and pushed them from the alley.

Rhoades pushed Monty into the nearest shop. "Duck!" he whispered. Following Rhoades' lead, Monty dropped below the level of the shop's window display. Rhoades listened intently to the shouting.

"What's going on?" Monty whispered.

"Shsh!" Rhoades cut him off.

The fracas and yelling at the mouth of the alley continued. Rhoades cautiously rose from his crouch and peered out.

"What can you see?" Monty asked.

Rhoades glanced at him with an impatient, silencing expression, and quickly looked back.

As in the last shop, a shopkeeper came from a back room, this one smiling happily and chattering. "Get rid of him!" Rhoades commanded.

Monty pivoted to the small, rotund, chatty shopkeeper. When the man took in Rhoades apparent surreptitious activities and heard the shouting on the street, he turned pale with fright. Monty grabbed him, turned him away from the window and began pointing at the jars and urns lining the shelves over the counter. "English?" he asked the terrified curly-headed little man. "English?"

With desperation, Curly-head shook his head 'no' and stepped back. Not wanting him to do something disruptive in his panic, Monty grabbed him by the shoulder and pointed at the urns. "Chili peppers?" he asked quickly. "I want to make a Mexican dinner for my British friend here. Do you have chili peppers?"

The bewildered, terrified shopkeeper shook his curly head in helpless incomprehension.

Suddenly, the shouting in the street stopped. Monty turned back to Rhoades. "They're splitting up, going their separate ways," the agent reported without looking away from the window. Monty took his first deep breath in long minutes.

After waiting for the street to clear, and having made amends with the put-upon shopkeeper by handsomely overpaying for a package of herbal laxatives promised to cure whatever ailed, Livingstone and Rhoades walked up Ferdosi on their way back to the British embassy.

"What do you think it was about?" Monty asked.

"Don't know," shrugged Rhoades, studying the Farsi label on the herbs. "Only one way to find out."

"Really?" asked Monty.

"Really," nodded Rhoades. "Must get to the big rally, don't you think?"

"The Tudeh rally?" asked Monty.

Rhoades looked up from the package. "Death to infidels and those who steal from the people, eh?" he smiled at Livingstone as they walked on.

Despite investing much time and imagination wondering when and how he would hear from Tekla, no word came that night. After a short debriefing with Rhoades over supper in the embassy cafeteria, he treated himself to a much-needed night of deep restful sleep.

Late the next morning, as he was studying an introductory text on the Farsi language in the embassy library, Rhoades barreled into the otherwise empty room. "Time to go protest," the agent grinned, plopping his broad chest and belly and narrow hips onto the table at which Monty was working, beside the textbook.

Monty looked up. "I thought it was late this afternoon?"

"Ah," smiled Rhoades. "For the patriots, it is indeed. But you must observe the planners."

"The planners?"

"You might want to put on a rally sometime yourself," Rhoades replied, lifting himself back onto his bowed legs and starting for the door. "These commie chappies know how it's done!"

They went downtown into the Grand Bazaar. Rhoades was jovial and talkative as they made their way along the winding aisles of merchants. He handled the merchandise of woven cloth and fabric traders. He bargained with fruit, vegetable, meat and fish vendors. But the only item he bought was a single exotic blue blossom he paid for without debate and tucked into the buttonhole of his white suit's lapel. A signal? Monty wondered. No, just vanity, he decided.

Rhoades appeared to be the very picture of the perfect tourist and shopper, uninterested in the crowd around them, except that every so often he nodded nonchalantly toward a white-shirted man moving among the patrons and hawkers. Monty understood the implication. Tudeh organizers were working the bazaar to develop a big crowd for the rally.

Satisfied they had toured the almost inexhaustible marketplace of Iranian retail and wholesale possibilities, Rhoades circled back and treated himself to a snack from one of the Bazaar's many stalls, then another, and then another. A cup of yoghurt and honey here; a handful of kumquats there; a freshly baked and rolled bread sweetened with raisins and butter. "Not indulgences," he explained to Livingstone. "Purely cover. But it is time for lunch, isn't it?"

They took an outside table at a café along a major lane of the Bazaar. Rhoades enthusiastically enjoyed a lamb and rice stew, nodding each time a white shirt passed. Monty simply watched. More than once it occured to him he was in an ideal situation to receive a covert communication, were one seeking him. But all he got was more of the same from Rhoades and a blatant lesson from the Tudeh operatives in how not to be inconspicuous in a crowd.

After lunch, they again wandered the Bazaar. Finally, late in the day, Rhoades led him back out into Tehran's streets and north to the square opposite the monumental Majlis building. Official Iran watched from the parliament house, calculating, while white-shirted Tudeh foot soldiers set up for the rally. On another side of grassy Majlis Square, Monty followed Rhoades up a set of outside stairs to the British agent's prearranged perch on a second floor office porch overlook. It was just down the block and around the corner from the Tudeh newspaper office.

The well-made crowd, already gathering when they arrived, soon almost filled the small square, though streams of pedestrians still flowed in from the middle and lower class sections of the city to the south, east and west. Pairs of Tehranian police cars strategically placed at intersections channeled the gathering throngs to the rally space. On the far sides of the streets defining Majlis Square, a picket line of uniformed Tehranian police officers kept vigilant watch at arm's length.

Almost entirely male, the crowd was nothing like the anarchic swarms demanding Israeli statehood Rachel had dragged Monty into at the Lake Success UN meetings. This crowd was quietly seething, yet orderly. Dozens and dozens of white-shirted Tudeh foot soldiers passed among them, handing out pre-made placards and signs printed or painted with pro-Mossadeq slogans and images. Others, organizers, moved more slowly through the crowd, calling small groups to them and authoritatively lecturing.

"Captains," Rhoades remarked when he saw Livingstone watching one of the organizers. "The reds don't leave anything to happenstance."

"But wasn't he in that bunch we followed yesterday?" Monty replied, nodding toward one of the men talking to a group in the crowd.

Rhoades studied the man. "B'lieve you're right," he concluded. "Keep an eye on him. Shouldn't be hard to do. Captains'll make themselves conspicuous."

"Maybe the others were Captains, too."

"Good theory," Rhoades nodded. "Keep an eye out."

By this time a small group had made its way to the center of a makeshift platform stage, Ayatollah Kashani and Faddey among them. As the Ayatollah stepped to the speaker's podium and began praying, Monty spotted Tekla, once again wearing the headscarf and modest coverings expected of a woman. She was near and behind Faddey on the platform. He watched her. His eyes sparkled with admiration for the poise and beauty he saw in her as he indulged himself, watching her watch the crowd and the unfolding of plans she no doubt had been integral in forming.

"See something?" Rhoades interrupted, turning Monty's pleasure guilty.

Startled, Monty recovered his poise. "The woman." He nodded toward Tekla. "From the mosque and Abadan."

"Obviously Tudeh leadership. Wogs keep their women in sacks but the bloody Reds know what the ladies can do. Someday maybe we'll have them carrying our water."

"Right," grinned Monty. "A Lady Churchill."

"Don't kid yourself," Rhoades smiled. "Winnie's mum was a right stern one."

They were interrupted when, the Ayatollah's benediction done and a rabble-rouser now at the podium, the crowd responded to his opening harangues by erupting in passionate chanting.

"Here we go," Rhoades muttered, his grin dissipating at the sound of what Monty now recognized without translation as "Death to the British!"

The rally became a sweaty, noisy event in the warm afternoon sun, a political version of an athletic contest except here the entire crowd rooted loudly and passionately for one side. Speaker after speaker stepped up to the podium, each explaining and then proclaiming, more vehemently than the one before, why – in Rhoades' translation – the oil belonged to the Iranian people! The British must go! They are Cheats! Thieves! Invaders! Usurpers! Murderers! Crusaders!

There was also ample condemnation of the decadent anglophile Shah. This degenerate, corrupt Shah surrendered precious Iranian treasure for paltry British pounds! This Reza Shah Pahlavi of the depraved Pahlavis was not even good enough to call a Khan or an Ottoman! He was no heir of Cyrus and Darius, no Shahanshah, no King of Kings! He spilled the blood of the Iranian soil into barrels and sold it for the Queen of England! He was a jester from the British court, a pretender to the Peacock Throne!

As the speakers made their rhetorical points, the Captains leaped up and rallied the mobs into roars of approval. Once they got them cheering, the Captains led them into the familiar chants and – intermittently, at a nod from Faddey – rousted them to their feet to march up and down, and even out and around the Majlis Square. As the Captains goaded them, the wild crowd waved its signs and placards, clapping and clamoring its frantic adamant assent to the speakers' most vicious anti-British, anti-Shah assertions.

Standing at the rear of the crowd and at arm's length from it, the heat of the afternoon and the cacophonous, rhythmic, meaningless Farsi chanting lulled Monty into an over stimulated trancelike numbness. When Rhoades' elbow bumped him, he startled alert. The barrel-chested white-suited old man wiped streams of perspiration from his forehead with a now sweat-dampened Irish linen handkerchief. The crowd was momentarily settling down. Ayatollah Kashani was again stepping to the podium.

"You'll want to see this," Rhodes smiled, watching Livingstone come alert.

Kashani remained silent as the crowd quieted. The distant cry of a muezzin reminded all it was time for the evening prayer. The Captains and their assistants walked among the gathered, sharing ceremonial barrels of water for the cleansing, even as Kashani did his bathing from a bowl of water brought to him at the podium. The Ayatollah then initiated the prayer procedures and all joined in the familiar rituals. When the prayers were complete, Kashani stood silently, solemnly, before them. He smiled. The solemnity of the moment turned to anticipation. Finally, he spoke. He spoke quietly, reasonably, at first. But then he began crescendoing into passionate diatribes, an angry summary of all that had been said before, and he ended with a booming call for the gathered masses to follow him to the Sa'adabad Palace and show the decadent Shah the force they represented and scream out the change they demanded. In a hysteria of unequivocating commitment, the throngs—led by the Captains among them—followed the Ayatollah forth, marching en masse into the streets of Tehran and up Vali Asr Avenue toward the Sa'adabad complex, wailing and cheering.

Rhoades lingered on the balcony. Monty, assuming they would eventually follow the marchers, glanced around the emptying Majlis Square scene. His eye fell on a small gathering of men around Faddey and Tekla by the foot of the speakers' platform at the far end of the now quiet, nearly calm square. "Rhoades!"

"See'em." The agent was already moving down the stairs and toward the gathering. Making his way through the last lingerers in an indirect manner, he gave the impression he was simply joining the protest. Monty trailed him. In a few minutes, they were able to almost nonchalantly slip through the dissipating throng and position themselves unnoticed around a corner of the speakers' platform yet very near the group around Faddey and Tekla. Monty did not understand the harsh, angry verbal interchange between the outsiders and Faddey's group, but it seemed to be a continuation of yesterday's hostilities. This time, though, the outsiders' leader had a few more men with him and they all carried short clubs or wore knives at their belts. One or two had a threatening, pistol-like lump at his waist under a loose-hanging shirttail. Faddey's white-shirted Captains gathered protectively around their leader and Tekla.

Seeing Tekla caught in the middle of this escalating danger, Monty felt helpless and desperate. "What is it?" Monty hissed at Rhoades.

"These men are Qashqai," Rhoades whispered, still listening.

"What the hell is that?"

"Tribesmen from the northwest. Used to be Turks. Treacherous men."

382

"What's their problem?"

Rhoades, listening, did not answer.

Monty watched the argument. It was primarily between Faddey and the Qashqai leader, the same man who faced off with Faddey the day before in the alley. It grew more intense, as did Monty's fear for Tekla.

"Rhoades!" Monty hissed. "Answer me!"

As the men went on arguing, Rhoades turned and looked at Livingstone calmly. "Their problem? In a word, oil. They had a deal with the Shah's men. Faddey promised them a better deal if they supported the Tudeh-Nationalist alliance. But Mossadeq's general, Riahi, cut them off. Sound familiar?"

Rhoades turned back to the argument but continued whispering. "The Qashqai leader, Ibrahim Muslit, demands restitution, baksheesh. Faddey is giving him commie sophistry. Not going over."

"What the hell does the Qashqai want with the oil?" asked Monty angrily. "They're tribal people, right?"

"Ibrahim says Sheik Ahmed Hamad, the leader of the clans, has truck convoys, railroad flatbeds and tankers, even a pipeline. Not getting enough oil to keep them running. But Riahi's boys still want their baksheesh."

Monty watched Tekla. She remained calm despite the raging between Faddey and Ibrahim and the violent men around her watching one another for a sign to strike. He saw Faddey arguing angrily, passionately. "What the hell is he saying?"

"Commie claptrap. Crack down on the clans."

Monty watched Ibrahim laugh and then reply angrily. "What's that?"

"Ibrahim says his clan has fought the monarchy since before the Ottomans! Maybe its time to crack down on the new oppressors. He wants protection for his oil smuggling operations and baksheesh for the military guards. Says Faddey promised it."

Rhoades grunted a dark laugh as he translated Faddey's reply. "Don't worry, you are the people, the Tudeh. What goes to the government is yours. This is the new system."

Ibrahim stepped back, saying nothing, and looked hard at Faddey, then walked around Faddey, as if he was studying something from another world. Finally, he turned and looked at Tekla. He smelled her, touched her face, looked into her eyes. She stared back fiercely.

Finally, Ibrahim spoke and, though Rhoades did not translate, Monty, in terror, understood exactly what he was saying. He wanted Tekla. Suddenly two of Ibrahim's men leaped to Tekla. One held her arms. Another cradled her head with an arm around her neck, a knife blade at her throat with his other hand. Faddey protested furiously. Ibrahim replied.

"Translate!" Monty again hissed.

"Ibrahim demands the woman," Rhodes said. "According to his tribal system. A kind of payment."

Ibrahim gave a hand signal to his men and they all began backing away, retreating with Tekla, their hostage as much as their prize. They moved slowly, triumphantly, toward the end of the platform around the corner from where Rhoades and Monty stood.

Faddey put a hand on his hip and smiled, casually slid the hand from his hip to the small of his back, in a flash drew a pistol, pointed it at the head of Ibrahim and barked at the Qashqai. It needed no translation: They let the girl go or Faddey shoots Ibrahim. The hands of the Qashqai men moved for weapons. Faddey's white shirts prepared to attack. The men holding Tekla backed to within two long strides of Rhoades and Monty.

Though Monty virtually trembled for Tekla, he could see no fear in her expression, only fierce rage. He glanced at Rhoades and was astonished and terrified to see Rhoades signaling silently. By pointing and hand gestures, the old man was signaling a plan of attack. Monty shook his head 'no' vehemently, seeing only danger and death in the plan. Rhoades nodded 'yes' firmly, that piercing intensity coming into his eyes. Silently, he held up one finger, then two, meaning to go into action on three.

Suddenly, a police siren blared and two police cars accelerated from the street onto the grassy square and closed on the scene, trapping everyone between the cars and the platform. The men froze. Afshartus and three detectives emerged from one police car while five uniformed officers came out of the other. As all eyes turned to the police, Rhoades whispered "Now!" like a war cry and flew at the men holding Tekla. Though Monty was terrified, he instantly realized it was now even more dangerous not to follow Rhoades into action.

He leaped ahead of the quick but bulky Brit, grabbed the forearm wielding the knife at Tekla's throat and pulled it away with all his strength. Simultaneously, Rhoades tackled Tekla and the unarmed man restraining her arms, driving them in the opposite direction from Monty and the man with the knife. Afshartus shouted in Farsi as his policemen reached for weapons. Ibrahim pivoted and ran, his Qashqai men scattering at his heels.

Faddey fired once at Ibrahim but missed the moving target. His eyes darted. He saw the knife-wielding Qashqai raise it to stab Monty. Faddey fired again. The Qashqai groaned, dropped the knife and fell at Monty's feet. Faddey's eyes kept darting. He saw the tribesmen scattering and the police bringing their weapons to the ready. He threw down his pistol. Tekla's Qashqai captor now gone in the melee, she pulled free from Rhoades' grasp, jumped up and ran to Faddey. White shirts gathered protectively around them.

Afshartus waved for several of the police officers and a pair of the detectives to chase the fleeing Qashqai, then turned and walked to Rhoades. The detective offered the Britisher an arm to lean on as the barrel-chested, bandy-legged man climbed to his knees and then stood. "You again?" Afshartus said in Farsi, smiling.

Rhoades offered a quick smile but no reply as he dusted off his white suit. "Bloody grass stains," he muttered.

Afshartus now looked at Monty but said nothing more. Behind the Police Captain, a detective picked up Faddey's pistol, looked at it carefully, walked it to Afshartus and displayed it. Afshartus turned away from Rhoades and Livingstone, took the gun, looked at it carefully, nodded, handed it back to the detective and muttered instructions. The detective pivoted away, went to a police car with the gun, got in and drove away.

"Another dead body," Afshartus said in English, turning back to Rhoades and Livingstone. "Explain."

"Never seen a kidnapping gone bad?" Rhoades snapped back.

"It was a kidnapping," Afshartus said sternly. "It is now a homicide."

"Bloody right," Rhoades answered contentiously. "Bastard tried to stab my American mate for trying to help the little lady. Russian shot him. Good job, I say. Not as if YOU or your coppers were about to do anything."

"But the shooting was done with the same type of pistol that killed the Prime Minister."

"We are unarmed, Afshartus," Rhoades said.

Policemen brought Faddey and Tekla to Afshartus. It was a replay of the mosque scene after the Razmara assassination. All eyed one another uneasily: Rhoades watched Monty watch Tekla. Faddey watched Tekla watch Monty. Afshartus watched Faddey and Rhoades. Nobody said a word until Afshartus finally broke the tension. "Another coincidence," Afshartus smiled. "If I did not know better I would think the British and the Communists plot together."

"To what purpose?" smiled Rhoades.

"Absurd," Faddey spit.

"You both want Iran's oil," Afshartus suggested. "As long as we refuse it to the British, we will refuse it to the Russians as well."

"You will eventually deal with Comrade Stalin," Faddey told him. "He knows oil."

"We are late for cocktails." Rhoades interrupted. "Either arrest us or let us go."

Afshartus intently studied Rhoades, then Faddey, for long silent moments without replying. Finally, he shrugged and smiled at Rhoades. "I would not want to inconvenience you."

Rhoades smiled. "I thought you might feel that way. Come along, Mr. Livingstone."

With one last glance at Tekla, Monty followed the British agent as he walked away. At a safe distance, he finally asked his question. "What was that all about?"

"Afshartus is smart," Rhoades said. "He knows he'll have to deal with the bureaucrats if he gets too pushy."

"You think that was the gun that shot Razmara?"

"Doesn't matter," Rhoades shrugged. "Afshartus knows who he's playing for. They aren't looking for Razmara's assassin. They don't want anybody but the religious hero to get blamed."

"So they won't arrest the Russian?"

"Just as much mess for Afshartus with Russian bureaucrats," Rhoades smiled. "But tell me, sonny," Rhoades said in a more conversational style as he led Monty north on Farahzad Boulevard toward the British embassy. "What did you learn from today's big doings?"

"Same thing I learned at the mosque," Monty shrugged. "Expect trouble."

"And opportunity. Would've thought you learned that in 1944," Rhoades answered impatiently. "Bloody Yanks always were the sodding optimists."

"What did you learn?"

Rhoades stopped and turned to Livingstone. "What we need here," he said intently, "is a demonstration for our side."

"With politics being what they are," Monty said, "It's not likely to be much of a demonstration."

Rhoades turned and resumed walking. "Nonsense, my boy. Her Majesty's money will buy a much bigger demonstration than Uncle Joe Stalin's money."

Rhoades chuckled at his own humor. Monty walked beside him. Nearing the embassy, Rhoades announced he wanted a bath before eating and Monty agreed. Admitted by the military guards through the gates of the embassy, they walked up the drive and were not far from where they would take separate routes to their respective bungalows when Rhoades asked a question.

"How do you know she isn't just using you?"

Monty stopped. "Sorry?"

Rhoades stopped and looked at him. Without saying a word, his expression said 'you heard me.'

Monty studied Rhoades. "She isn't," he finally said to his British mentor.

"How do you know?"

Offering no reply, Monty wondered who he could believe in – His mentor? Tekla? Himself? "I don't," he finally said.

"If I can find out about her, Tudeh will find out about you."

"So?"

Rhoades studied Livingstone, then turned and walked up the driveway. "Don't say you weren't warned."

Monty watched Rhoades walk away, wondering what he was being warned about. Questions without answers rushed at him. Doubt was daring him to go on. Rhoades disappeared into the embassy compound. His new reality was spiraling beyond his control. Yes, he thought, beyond his control. He threw up his hands in a gesture of helplessness. Time for a bath. He turned and walked to his room. Later, he joined Rhoades and other embassy personnel for dinner in the cafeteria. The talk was all about the big loud but uneventful Tudeh rally. After eating, he walked back toward his bungalow looking forward to a well-earned rest, wondering if all the noise and fury meant anything at all.

The next day, Rhoades excused himself from their usual morning meeting. He had arrangements to make, he explained, and there would be big news when the arrangements were complete. He said nothing more about Tekla. Monty resumed his "cover" work, sending out official Socony-Vacuum business inquiries. In the afternoon mail, he found an innocuous, typewritten note on the letterhead of a Tehran oil trading company he did not remember contacting. It thanked him for his inquiry about an import/export deal. He recognized Tekla's handwriting in the postscript at the bottom. It read, "I hope I will see you at the dance tonight."

As the sun fell below the city's horizon turning the sky blue with swaths of red and yellow at the edges and deep black highlighted by twinkling stars spreading out from above, Monty drove an embassy car slowly past the Tudeh newspaper office and circled the block. The second time around, a lone female figure stepped out from between buildings and walked along the street. When he recognized the slender figure's graceful execution of a foxtrot quick-quick, slow-slow, he slowed the car. As he caught up with her, Tekla jumped in. She directed him into the high desert beyond the far western edge of the city where, she informed him, she had secured for them an official "love nest." Some miles out, he saw a line of mud huts on a dirt road off the highway. She directed him to park behind the last hut.

Explaining the property was abandoned, she led him into a little cabin and lit a kerosene lantern. In the lantern's glow, the cozy room was charming, if bare. A bed, a sink, a cabinet for supplies, a table, a couple of chairs, a privy: Clearly she had spent time cleaning and preparing it. "It is the nicest place we have ever had together," he said, taking her in his arms and kissing her hungrily.

She laughed. "It is the only place we have ever had together!" She began pulling his clothes off. "Undress me, Monty!"

"You've forgotten those wonderful Berlin alleys and bombed out basements, have you?" He laughed, pulling her white shirt over her head and falling hungrily on her small round breasts and their proud, happy nipples.

"Not a one!" she exclaimed as he laid her back on the bed, still caressing her chest with his wet tongue. She moaned deeply. "Oh Monty..."

He kissed his way down her naked torso to her waist, opened the zipper at the side of her skirt and pulled both it and her white underwear away, throwing them on a chair across from the bed. He kissed back up her legs, quickly coming to the center of his attention, enjoying the strong scent of her womanhood, even now opening at his attentions.

He gently lapped at her with his tongue. Her moans became deep, inarticulate gasps. With his fingers he began rhythmic strokes intuitively coordinated with her inner rising. She reveled at his attentions, writhing in pleasure. Finally, she shuddered and trembled. When she calmed and her breathing slowed, she looked down at him and grinned happily, exuding a rejuvenating joy.

Seeing she was ready for him, he rose from between her legs, dropped the last of his clothing on the floor and fell over her onto the bed. She reached excitedly for him and placed her other hand on his chest, holding him over her. She stared up into his eyes. Neither spoke in this less hungry and more loving moment than any they had ever shared. And then she splayed herself wide and fell back, pulling him down into her even as she rose up wantonly.

The night in the car had been lustful. Young, passionate longing voraciously rejoined. This was a reunion of undefiable love, a star-crossed unbelievability that, like existence itself, refused to not be. They would join, they would love, the heat of their having each other would send waves outward to the very rhythm of the music of the spheres, a beating of rising and falling arching upward, two becoming one, a sinuous contrapuntal harmony of thrust and roll and grunt and moan to a conjoined crescendo explosion in waves rolling higher and deeper joining and joining and he felt she and she felt he and she was screaming "MontyMontyMonty" in climactic ecstasy and he was moaning "I'm there, I'm there, I'm there" and she was screaming "YesYesYes!" as he grunted and thrust and grunted and thrust and she screamed "Come to me, Monty!" and he exploded from himself into her and there was a deep red blackness and motionlessness and utter silence. And it was over.

There was sweat and breathing. There was a glow from the lantern in the darkness and shafts of light fell across the strange little hut. There was the faint sound of a truck driving up the distant highway. Moments passed. Bodily needs returned.

"I must," he said, rising up from the bed.

"Yes," she smiled. "Me, too."

"Go ahead."

"You first."

He smiled, raised himself to a sitting position, slipped barefoot and naked into his shoes and walked across the room to a chamber pot. He raised the lid and sat, urinated while looking around the lantern-lit room, rose and walked back to the bed. They passed halfway, she, too, naked and barefoot but for her heavy leather shoes. He kissed her forehead as they passed, then shucked his shoes and laid down on the bed, waiting naked, listening to the tinkle of her urine on the hollow inside of the chamber pot.

When she again lay naked beside him, he smiled at her.

"The miracle of a second romance?" she asked.

"Yes. Better than the first time."

"In a way," she said. The glow of the lantern on the table behind her cast a halo around her that quickly dissipated in the deep darkness of the shabby hut. "More miraculous. But that is because it is so much harder to believe in."

"You have doubts too?"

390

She studied him. "Yes, of course. It is true, we did find each other, and, yes, we are still…" She hesitated, trying to find words.

" 'We.' "

"Yes, exactly. We are still a 'we.' But…"

"It's no longer so easy to believe," he nodded, following shafts of lantern light into the hut's dark corners.

"And it was not easy then. In Berlin."

"But in Berlin we thought it was our reward. For winning the war."

"For surviving the war," she corrected him.

"Yes."

"And now," she concluded, waving her hand and throwing shadows into the halo-glow of the lantern. "I am not sure there is any reward."

"And the war never ends."

"I was innocent then," she said almost to herself. "I believed in love."

"You don't now?"

"The world is full of true believers, Monty. Your wife believes in Israel. Faddey believes in the party. The assassins believe in Islam. The Shah believes in the monarchy. The British oilmen believe in Britannia's right to rule. My mother hates the Germans and believes in Mother Russia. Your mother hates communists and believes in America. Your father believes in the American right to stand up to people like your mother."

"What about this guy opposing the Shah? Mossadeq."

She turned her head and looked at him with a curious smile. "He is like us, is he not? Caught in the middle of it all. What does he believe in?"

"Yes. That's what I'm asking."

"What do we believe in?"

"I don't know."

391

"Maybe that is the best thing," she said almost dreamily, laying her head back on his chest. "Passion without reason does not seem to end in anything but violence."

"And us?"

"I do not know," she said, drifting near to sleep. "Whatever it means, it is probably the best we can hope for. I am so tired, Monty." Her eyes closed. She slept.

Wearily, he looked at her beautiful, peaceful face, smiled to himself, closed his eyes and whispered, "See you at the dance."

In the gray light of dawn, Tekla roused Monty and they drove back into Tehran. Groggy from little sleep and the early hour, both sat quietly. Near the city center, they passed a truck unloading newspapers at a traffic circle kiosk. "Morning news," Monty observed. "An international ritual."

"Here each paper has a ritual chant," Tekla answered, laying her head against the seatback. "The pro-Shah papers blame Tudeh and the Nationalists for the bad economy. The pro-Communist papers blame the British and the Shah. The pro-Nationalist papers blame the Shah and the monarchists."

"I suppose you believe your side?"

She raised her head, turned and looked at him. "Do you believe your side?"

He glanced at her. She watched him. Instead of answering, he looked at the road ahead and drove. They remained quiet.

"You know what baseball is?" he asked.

"What?"

He smiled. "Sounds like I'm coming from left field, huh?"

"From where?"

"Do you know what baseball is?"

"Yes. The American team sport."

"Exactly. And every team has a manager. And there's this team in the states called the Yankees. They've got a manager named Casey Stengel."

"And you are telling me this for a reason?"

"Absolutely. Everybody used to think Stengel was a clown. But his team has won the championship the last two years. He has this crazy, complicated, brilliant strategy but when they ask him to explain it, he just starts talking and clowning, naming players and making up wise sayings and describing things that already happened. Pretty soon they forget how successful he is and start laughing at him."

"So he never has to explain his secret."

"Exactly."

They rode a little longer in silence. "Seems like it all starts with the oil," Monty finally said.

She laid her head back again. "They all want it. They are all part of the problem. If they make a deal, there will be no problem. If they continue being greedy, it can only end in violence."

He drove up to the quiet, empty Majlis Square from the west, just as the sun flashed in their eyes between buildings on the city's eastern horizon. He stopped the car but kept the motor running. Anxious not to linger and be seen, she popped open the door and jumped out. "Go!" she ordered, and immediately began walking up the street toward the Tudeh newspaper office.

Instead of quickly driving off, he rolled along the street beside her, leaned across the passenger seat and rolled down the side window. "How long will it be?" he called.

She looked with annoyance, then turned away and continued walking. "You will get us both deported!" she said through clinched teeth.

"How long 'til I hear from you?" he grinned. "'Til I can breathe again?"

"Get out of here!" she seethed. "Before I have you arrested for committing an indecency!" Her head snapped back and forth as she quickly scanned around her. "I will see you at the dance!" she snapped, then burst into a run. She dashed in front of the car. He slammed on the brakes to avoid hitting her. She disappeared into an alleyway across the street.

Alone again on the street, he now realized his risk and glanced nervously into the rear view mirror and around for observing onlookers. He relaxed again when he saw the streets were still empty. He smiled to himself, steered the car into a U-turn and drove off toward the embassy, shaking his head. Playful, he thought. Dangerously playful.

*****

*"If we're going to win the pennant, we've got to start thinking we're not as smart as we think we are." *...Casey Stengel

The next day Rhoades, ebullient, joined him at breakfast and happily announced the news. The higher-ups liked the idea of a pro-British, pro-Shah rally. He had permission to begin planning it.

"Planning it?" Monty asked, confused. "What do we do, gather the employees here at the embassy and sing 'Rule, Britannia'?"

Rhoades grinned. "Now you will meet our friends."

Later that morning, they stopped at the embassy operations desk to pick up two large, gift-wrapped boxes, one deep and rectangular, the other wider, flatter and square. "One from you and one from me," laughed Rhoades. Taking an embassy car, Rhoades drove them to a group of large estates among pine trees in the foothills at the northern edge of the city. He turned into a wide driveway. A pair of heavy, swarthy men in western slacks and sport shirts stood before eight-foot high wrought-iron gates in a long, high, thick stucco wall. Monty noticed bulges of handguns at the mens' waists, under their shirttails. When Rhoades identified himself, the men waved him through. He drove to the end of the driveway and parked beside the stately two-story house amongst a half dozen other large, shining, late-model American and British cars.

As they left the car, each with his gift box, they heard noise, beyond the house, recorded music, laughter, shouting men and women and water splashing. "Pool party," Rhoades muttered. "Good idea. Noise."

Rhoades led him through the house's grand, wide-open front door. Carrying their big gift boxes, Monty with the more awkward large, flat, square one and the British agent with the deeper, rectangular one, they were observed all along their way by more pairs of men in fashionable western casual wear with hanging shirt tales poorly concealing telltale handgun bulges at their waists. They walked toward the noise, through a large foyer and a family room, into a breakfast room full of people chatting and grazing over a large

394

table full of "brunch" for eastern and western appetites. Most of the men attending the party were in the familiar sportswear but many also wore suits with ties. There were many more men than women but the women stood out. All wore stylish, clinging swimsuits, some with light, gauzy or diaphanous scanty wraps over the swimwear. In heavy make-up and expensive hairdos, most of the women did not appear to be there to swim. Seeming to enjoy their roles, the women chatted and laughed with the men and each other, a small bevy of hostesses, or perhaps paid entertainment, at what otherwise would be a stag smoker.

Livingstone took in the food, the women, the partying, and looked to Rhoades. The big Brit was looking back, smiling gluttonously. "All on the menu, son. Every tasty morsel. But business before pleasure." He led out through sliding glass doors to the patio and pool area. More of the same men and "hostesses," some even in the pool cavorting. A sound system played big band music. "Perhaps they will have some of your mother's recordings," Rhoades remarked as he led Monty toward a small pool house at the rear of the property where four of the sport shirt-wearing men stood double-guard duty. One recognized Rhoades and they were sent inside.

Rhoades stopped just inside the pool house and waited. Three groups of men in suits or military uniforms stood chatting and smoking cigarettes in the white stucco room. It was spacious but dark because heavy curtains were drawn across its ample windows. Rhoades caught Livingstone's eye and nodded toward a long picnic table across the room's tile floor. Five men in military uniforms sat talking. Four of them, it was immediately apparent, deferred to the stern, commanding man with a hawk nose, large, fierce dark eyes and a full head of black hair at the head of the table. While Livingstone and Rhoades watched, the commanding man spoke authoritatively and listened to responses. Rhoades muttered to Livingstone. "General Fazlollah Zahedi. Shah's man. Will be P.M., sooner or later."

"Zahedi," Monty said. "Irdeshar's father?"

Rhoades glowed. "The very same." The Brit scanned the room. "Ah!" Irdeshar Zahedi came toward them from one of the clusters of men. Monty recognized the proud, dynamic young man he had met at the embassy just before the clown disturbance. He now recognized the General's Roman profile, deep dark eyes and wavy black hair in the son.

"Mr. Livingstone!" Irdeshar beamed, shaking Monty's hand warmly. "You must meet the men I was just talking with. They are locals with immeasurably valuable contacts."

Rhoades leaned toward Irdeshar. "We bear gifts," he whispered. "Is he here?"

Still shaking Monty's hand, Irdeshar turned to Rhoades. "Indeed he is," Irdeshar told Rhoades, still smiling. "Follow me."

As they turned and made their way across the room, Monty saw Rhoades whisper something to Irdeshar. Irdeshar shook his head 'no' as he led through a door behind the picnic table. The military men went on talking, though General Zahedi pointedly noticed and nodded as Rhoades and his son passed. The door led out to a rear patio. Two sport shirted bodyguards followed them out.

On the patio, a large, portly, middle-aged man with big hands, recognizably Iranian and working class by his dark, heavy features and worn expression, sat alone at another picnic table. His apparent reverie over the lush pine forest landscape just off the patio and spreading down across the hillside was instantly interrupted when he heard Livingstone, Rhoades and Irdeshar coming and turned to study them. As he did, Monty saw in his small, dark eyes something he had never seen before. The man seemed to be peering out from deep inside his head. The eyes seemed less like a window into his thoughts and feelings than a protective covering.

The man made no move to rise. Irdeshar, Rhoades and Livingstone seated themselves at the picnic table across from him. Rhoades set his gift box on the table between them and nodded to Monty to do the same. Monty was happy to get the large, flat, awkward load out of his arms. The man spoke in a harsh voice to Zahedi in Farsi.

"English, please," Irdeshar smiled. "We must think of our guests." The man snapped again in harsh Farsi. "Yes," smiled Irdeshar unruffled. "I do regard you as a guest. But these are representatives of Britain and America."

"The Britisher I know," the man said in English. "And I know he speaks Farsi. So we speak English for the American?"

"The Americans have always been our friends, Mozzafar."

"Fine," Mozzafar muttered in his deep, harsh voice. "What do they want with me?"

Rhoades smiled. "We had hoped you would enjoy the General's hospitality."

"The SHAH'S hospitality," Mozzafar corrected Rhoades, "does not appeal to me. It is bought with British money that should rightfully go to Iranian oil workers."

Polite smiles masked reactions from Rhoades and Irdeshar. Monty watched. When Mozzafar's expression remained stern, Irdeshar took a deep breath. Rhoades glanced at Livingstone and, seeing the American's incomprehension, simply raised his left index finger. "Watch and learn," the familiar gesture told Monty.

"First," Irdeshar began with sincerity. "Please convey our best to Hussein Makki."

"Makki is Mossadeq's man. I speak for the oil workers," Mozzafar grunted. "Get on with it."

"One of these gifts…" Irdeshar indicated the boxes from Livingstone and Rhoades. "…is from the British to the Shah."

"As I said," Mozzafar replied sternly.

"Yes," smiled Irdeshar. "But the other. The other."

"Get on with your bribe," Mozzafar snapped at Irdeshar.

"It is not a bribe, my friend."

"If I am your friend, give me back the pistol your men took away!"

With self-possessed diplomacy, Irdeshar smiled. He looked up at the bodyguards, standing by the door to the meeting room. "Ezatollah!" He waved one of them to him and pushed Rhoades' deep, rectangular box across the table to the bodyguard. "See that to accounting. Tell my bookkeeper to enter it as petty cash and keep it in the safe for the General's personal use." As the guard moved away with the large gift box, Irdeshar looked again at Mozzafar, who stared back coldly. "Our American friend has a gift box for you," he said. "It is better than a pistol."

"And what is it I must do to have this gift?"

"Show him the box, Mr. Livingstone."

Monty slid his flat, square box across the table. Mozzafar stared at it for a moment and then reached with one big hand, pulled the ribbon from it with a snap, lifted the top, looked inside disinterestedly, dropped the lid back on the box and looked at Irdeshar again, his cold stare unchanged. "What am I supposed to do for this fortune in cash?"

"Untraceable, unrecorded, unassigned cash," Rhoades muttered.

Mozzafar turned his stare on Rhoades. "But not without obligation. What do you want?"

"We don't want trouble from your oil workers," Irdeshar interjected. "Like we have had in the past."

"Good," Mozzafar rumbled angrily. "You finally agree it was inhumane to answer striking desert oil field workers' demands by cutting off their water supply. You give us cash instead."

"We will get nowhere if we dwell on old grievances, my friend," Irdeshar replied gravely, with compassionate reasonableness.

"Good again," Mozzafar answered, his voice rising. "We will talk about a new grievance! Your mercenaries opened fire on protesting strikers."

"All we ask is an agreement signed by Hussein Makki," Irdeshar said sincerely. "To stop oil workers' strikes until we work through this political turmoil."

"You ask NOTHING! You BUY! You think you can put yourself behind strong walls and buy your way to safety and power? You forget how high oil workers build derricks, how deep they drill holes, how easily they move earth and rock. Your walls mean NOTHING to us!" Suddenly, he shouted loudly. "Hey-Yah!' Men with rifles pointed at Monty, Rhoades and Irdeshar came running from the nearby forest to the edge of the patio.

The lone bodyguard at the meeting room's door started to go for the pistol at his waist but Irdeshar gave a 'no' command with cool calmness. "Take the money," Irdeshar told Mozzafar. "No gunplay here. It would be a bloodbath."

"Your riflemen are not so thoughtful when they answer our pleas for better housing, food, drinking water and a bit of wash water for ritual cleansing before prayer."

"We will talk about these things, Mozzafar."

Mozzafar stood and picked up the box of cash. "Yes," he smiled. "When we are ready." He stepped around the picnic table and started toward the forest. As he passed between Irdeshar and the riflemen, Irdeshar lowered his arm and slapped upward hard on the big flat box. The awkward load popped up from Mozzafars's hands and bundles of American money spilled out all over the patio. Seeing tens of thousands of dollars scattered across the concrete was a great distraction to Mozzafar's impoverished soldiers. They came rushing forward, eyes on the money.

"Now!" Irdeshar exclaimed, pulling a pistol from beneath his shirttail and firing on the riflemen while simultaneously pushing Monty, who was unarmed, under the picnic table and dropping to one knee. At Irdeshar's command, the bodyguard at the door also pulled his pistol and opened fire and, to Monty's surprise, Rhoades took a pistol from beneath his white suit jacket, dropped from the bench to one knee and calmly started shooting as well.

Instantly realizing his situation, the disarmed Mozzafar dashed into the pine forest and down the hillside, bellowing for his men to retreat with him. Three of them had already fallen in the gunfire. He and the others disappeared into the woods as an army of bodyguards charged out of the meeting room and from the pool area beyond, firing handguns as they came.

Turning to see these reinforcements, Irdeshar spotted the bodyguards' captain. "Chase them!" He ordered, pointing into the pine forest with his pistol. The captain's head pivoted, picking men. An instant later, he was shouting orders while leading a half-dozen of the bodyguards into the woods in pursuit of Mozzafar. Behind them on the patio, another half-dozen bodyguards gathered around Irdeshar, Livingstone and Rhoades.

Still on one knee, Irdeshar turned to Monty. "Are you all right?" he asked anxiously.

Shaken, adrenalin rushing, but unhurt, Monty climbed out from under the table. Both he and Irdeshar allowed bodyguards to help them as they climbed to their feet. Behind them, General Zahedi and the other uniformed officers came out of the meeting room to survey the situation. Not wanting to speak rashly, Monty held his impulses firmly in check and dusted himself off before replying to Irdeshar's question.

"Are you all right?" Irdeshar repeated anxiously.

By the time Monty stood upright and looked around, Rhoades stood chuckling, his pistol holstered. Behind them, the military officers stood waiting, all eyes on Monty. He looked at Irdeshar for a pregnant moment. "Nice party," he finally said.

Irdeshar looked at his father, General Zahedi, and smiled. The general nodded and stepped over to Monty. "You must accept my sincerest apology, Mr. Livingstone."

"Any chance I could get a soft sofa in a quiet room to go with that apology, General?"

This brought laughter from General Zahedi and the others around them. 'Of course, Mr. Livingstone! The very sort of thing I had in mind!" the General beamed.

General Zahedi led Rhoades and Livingstone to a library/office upstairs in the stately house. He arranged for food and drink and, when he was sure all Monty's needs were attended to, General Zahedi left Monty and Rhoades to Irdeshar and excused himself to resume his planning conference.

Over the next few hours, they nibbled a sampling of the downstairs buffet brought to them by a parade of beautiful, exotic hostesses in swimwear. Irdeshar artfully led Monty through lighthearted conversation, Rhoades joining occasionally with meaningless wit or pungent asides. Sometimes they paused to eat and sometimes they paused to flirt with the servers. Intermittently, guests visited the room and joined the chat. In this way, Monty met Nossey and Cafron, a pair of import/export men, and Bahram Shahrokh, a locally well-known Radio Tehran personality. He also chatted with a newspaper editor and the manager of the Tehran Bazaar's street performers. Finally, they were visited by Sayfollah, Ghodratollah and Asadullah Rashomian, three brothers very different in size, personality and profession but in some unspoken way profoundly unified in purpose.

After the three Rashomian brothers left, Irdeshar saw Monty wearying and nodded to Rhoades, who made their excuses and led Monty back to the car. As they drove back toward the embassy, Rhoades did not directly answer Monty's questions about the day but, instead, enigmatically observed that the day had been a "stunning victory for our side" and promised, "Your new acquaintances will sooner or later turn out to be far more valuable than you can know." As they arrived at the embassy, Monty asked if that would also be true of Rhoades' new acquaintance, a dark-eyed hostess who the Brit had promised to return for and escort home.

"Her value should be apparent to you, sonny," Rhoades chuckled lecherously as Monty climbed out of the car at the embassy gates.

"Would your monarch approve?" Monty smiled.

"We have had no real monarch since Victoria," Rhoades sighed nostalgically. "I honor Victoria by my work for the Empire. But even in the Victorian age one's personal pleasures were one's own," he laughed. "So – out of the car!"

Wearily, Monty walked up the driveway toward his bungalow, where he found in his mail another letter from Tekla's oil trading company. Her handwritten scrawl at the bottom of the otherwise ordinary business letter mentioned "...the dance next week on the day after the rally for the Shah" and added, "Why don't you join me before the dance at our usual place for cocktails and conversation, say around sunset?"

With everything to anticipate and nothing else to do, Monty threw himself into the work of rally planning. Over the next week, he was at Rhoades' side almost all day every day. Initially there were planning sessions at the embassy or private homes in the wealthier, northern parts of Tehran. In these meetings Monty frequently recognized faces he had seen at the Zahedi "brunch." He learned how widespread the Rashomian brothers' contacts were. And he learned why the Grand Bazaar entertainers' manager and Bahram Shahrokh of Tehran Radio were important in the scheme.

After the preliminary arrangements were set, Rhoades and Livingstone took to the streets. They visited Rhoades' contacts, associates and informants throughout the city, meeting and greeting, scheduling and instructing and, most importantly, doling out money as fast as the barrel-chested, broad-bellied British agent could get his heavy, leathery hand from his trousers' deep pockets to the open palms of his local patronizers.

"You would think," Monty observed as Rhoades sampled his way along the food stands in the bazaar one midday, "those hundred rial notes you hand out were flyers announcing the rally."

"Even better," Rhoades replied with a mischievous grin as he licked tahini sauce from his fingers. "They announce the rally AND the promise of a reward for attending."

On the day of the rally Rhoades announced over breakfast in the embassy cafeteria, not very much to Monty's surprise, they would begin, as they did the day of the Tudeh rally, in the Grand Bazaar.

"Building the crowd?"

"Building the crowd where the crowd is," grunted Rhoades, gobbling down a last slice of bacon. "Come along."

They walked through Ferdosi Square and down Churchill Avenue in the early morning stillness, past carpenters hammering together the speakers' platform and manual laborers setting up police barriers around the Majlis Square on Kokh. At the Grand Bazaar, the frenetic predawn wholesale crowd had dissipated and the morning shoppers were arriving. As Rhoades walked the produce stalls, indulging his unperturbed gastronomical pleasures, he pointed out to Monty the now familiar faces of his organizers. Packets and envelopes full of small bills changed hands. Soon retail business in the marketplace picked up as the rial notes – Rhoades "flyers announcing the rally" – were spread around. Boys and young men ran from the bazaar to take the word to the poor neighborhoods in other parts of the city: Opportunity had come to market. On the streets where the runners went out, people began wandering back in, anxious to protest for pay.

The bazaar's entertainment manager, a small, thin man with narrow eyes and a perfectly trimmed, groomed mustache, walked sleepily in from Kayyam Avenue. With a wave of his hand, he sent a boy for a Turkish coffee. He stood watching the slowly growing buzz in the marketplace until the boy returned with the stimulant. The entertainment manager drank the Turkish coffee down in a gulp. A few minutes later, feeling the coffee take effect, he took a deep breath, smiled, rubbed his hands together and began walking into the curtained-off rear areas of the market's many stalls. Each time he re-emerged, sleepy-eyed men and/or women were pushed out before him or followed groggily. Some wore exotic costumes. Others carried musical instruments. Much earlier than was the custom, entertainment began at the many entrances to the bazaar, as well as in the open spaces where busily trafficked aisles met.

The newly forming numbers crowded around the entertainers and, while jugglers, belly dancers, bouzouki, boron and whistle-players played to delighted listeners and pea-and-shell-operators plied their crafts under determined, competitive eyes, Rhoades' rally organizers passed among them, spreading the word and the "flyers" to people with too little to do and not enough to spend who were delighted to instantly and unexpectedly improve their prospects for both.

By early afternoon, Rhoades' plan had, through the baksheesh-spreading morning, come to full employment. The bazaar was teeming with eager faces impatient for marching orders. Right on schedule, charismatic ruffians called for the circus to transform into a march. The entertainers immediately responded, leading the marchers into an exuberant parade, drawing in their audiences and most everyone else milling about. Reluctant stragglers responded readily to rumors of rials awaiting their arrival at the square. By mid afternoon, the green space across from the Parliament building was a cauldron of joviality as the well-paid audience enjoyed its bought-and-paid-for street revel.

Livingstone and Rhoades once again climbed the outside stairs to the second floor office porch across from and overlooking the scene. The first speaker, a widely liked member of parliament better known for his wit and charisma than his politics, stepped to the podium. Rhoades explained to Monty who the speaker was and what he was saying. The man introduced himself as the day's Master of Ceremonies. He thanked the crowd for gathering in support of "our cause" and urged them to raise their voices and sound their applause in gratitude "...to his highness the Shahanshah, King of Kings, for making this joyous day possible!"

The walls of the surrounding buildings rumbled and the windows rattled at the cacophonous ovation the gathered multitudes, anxious to be worthy of their rials, rendered their beloved leader (and paymaster). After letting the clamor of the crowd settle, the Master of Ceremonies launched into an energetic opening speech, delighting his audience with topical humor in the best tradition of vaudeville and the music hall, before calming to solemnly introduce the next speaker.

A well-known long-bearded Mullah stepped to the podium. He led the crowd in quiet fervent prayer and then began sermonizing reverentially on the burdens and the blessings of tradition. He slowly unfolded a profoundly logical and deeply comforting justification of their blessed monarch and the peacock throne. When the Mullah left the podium, the crowd was silently pondering. Rhoades raised his hand over his head and held it still, palm open. Both he and Monty watched the crowd below and saw heads, turned watchfully toward them, respond to the signal by leading the groups around them in a fitting but not offensively boisterous approval of the Mullah's solemn sentiments.

The Master of Ceremonies returned to the podium and thanked the Mullah in respectful tones that underscored the profundity of the remarks. He then announced a change of pace and welcomed entertainers to the platform for a musical interlude. He stepped back and musicians came forward playing Iranian folk music. The crowd's attentiveness relaxed. Rhoades watched the crowd and Monty watched Rhoades. After a few minutes, the wily British agent saw the crowd's relaxation turning to disinterest and once again raised his open-palmed hand. The Master of Ceremonies returned to the podium and the musicians, stepping back, faded their music out.

The crowd quieted in anticipation of the Master of Ceremonies' next words. He stood at the podium without saying anything. The crowd became alert, wondering what he was waiting for. As the silence went on, it became more pregnant. Finally, the Master of Ceremonies recognized the crowd's readiness, looked up at Rhoades and nodded. Rhoades, making his own assessment, agreed. "They are ready," he muttered, and nodded back.

The Master of Ceremonies saw Rhoades nod and raised both arms as he said, "And now…" He paused, repeated a little more loudly "…And now…" paused again and, with finality, bellowed "And NOW!" This was the moment men in the crowd were pre-positioned and prepared for. As the Master of Ceremonies proceeded to introduce "…the man who will deliver today's keynote address…" Rhoades' men moved toward the speakers' platform. The audience, its attention galvanized, politely received the carefully selected speaker. The man eased gracefully into his rhetorically perfect pro-Shah, pro-British seduction, every eye in the crowd hypnotized to him. Monty saw a look of self-satisfied delight begin to form on Rhoades' face. But then the Britisher's eyes narrowed fiercely.

"What?" Monty asked quickly, turning back to the crowd.

"Tudeh," Rhoades muttered.

In the crowd, even as the keynote speaker launched into the first of his passionate, carefully crafted cadences and the attentive throngs exhibited utter acceptance and Rhoades' men moved into position to lead approving responses, white shirts in groups of three and four moved forward in the crowd.

"What do you think they're going to do?" Monty asked.

"Not cheer us on," Rhoades said quietly through clinched teeth.

To Monty, there seemed nothing they could do. In answer to the questioning faces beginning to turn toward him, Rhoades raised a fist and made a vigorous hammering motion, signaling uncompromising commitment.

At the same time, Rhoades quietly filled Monty in on the gist of what the speaker was saying. He talked about times past, when Iranian oilfields were working without interruption, and then adamantly made the point that

"...when the Shah controlled the oil industry, he brought great wealth to Iran!"

As he translated for Monty, Rhoades raised his fist over his head and swung it in small circles. The bought men in the crowd shouted and waved to their bought men. Mild clapping and random calls of assent turned to insistent clapping and loudly shouted approval until cheering erupted.

Watching the white shirts, both Livingstone and Rhoades saw them look across the street toward the Majlis building, or more specifically to the stone wall around the Majlis building. Taking advantage of its height, spectators stood on it watching and listening, holding on to the wrought iron fencing atop it. From the second floor balcony, it was easy for Rhoades and Livingstone to see what, or more precisely who, the white shirts in the crowd were looking at. Faddey stood atop the wall, Tekla next to him. Faddey was waving his hand, as if signaling his men in the crowd forward. He then pointed. The man he pointed at yelled "Iranian oil for Iranians!"

The speaker at the podium paused, looked at the man who yelled and shook his head as if to say, "What rudeness." "An Iranian national oil company," he exclaimed, "would squander our wealth!" He paused again and waited for a response but there was no spontaneous response from the crowd because the interruption had ruined his timing, leaving his exclamation hanging powerlessly. Angrily, Rhoades again raised his fist and swung it in circles. His men responded, their men responded, and they got the crowd going, but it was a muted enthusiasm.

The speaker resumed, elaborating on the beneficent relations the oil company and Iran had under the Shah. Rhoades signaled for cheers but, before they started, Faddey pointed to another white shirt, who screamed: "The British keep our wealth for themselves!" At this, the crowd's incipient response broke off.

The speaker was now visibly angry. "The British turn our oil into wealth!" he yelled reflexively.

Rhoades' men burst into action but once again, before their actions brought affirmation from the hesitant crowd, a white shirt yelled. "British wealth!" And once again, the crowd quieted.

Seeing the speaker fume in frustration, Rhoades waved a man standing near them on the balcony to him, whispered in his ear and sent him running. As the man entered the crowd he whispered to others and sent them spreading through the crowd toward Rhoades' leaders. Meanwhile, the speaker attempted to slow down and regain control.

"Before the British came to Iran there was nothing. Now we have cities and newspapers and businesses. Before his highness Reza Shah, progenitor of the Pahlavi dynasty, exalted be his name, may he stand at Allah's side in Paradise…"

At this mention of the Shah's father, the founder of modern Iran, the crowd quieted and was drawn back to the speaker until a white shirt yelled again. "Deposed by his son! A tool of the British!"

The speaker paused. Fuming, he stepped around the podium and forward to the edge of the platform. "Who dares such an insult!?!" He looked around. Rhoades' men leapt up, pointing at the white shirt. "There!" the speaker screamed, pointing at the man. "There! Traitor! Infidel! Russian dog!" Rhoades' men barreled through the crowd, seizing the opportunity to carry out instructions just arrived from Rhoades via the foot soldiers. Four strong men pounced on the white shirt while his three companions struggled to protect him. Faddey vigorously waved his arm in a circle. White shirts waded into the crowd. Rhoades was swinging his fist in wide angry circles as the rest of his men, too, struggled toward the fight. As the goons met, fists flew.

Everywhere innocents screamed, turned and ran, barreling into other uncomprehending but suddenly panicking innocents in the out of control mob. Fighting erupted at various points throughout the melee and quickly spread outward. Madness ensued. Those angry few surging forward to join the fray exploded into the terror of the many desperate to escape it. Screams. Stampede. The most frightened and helpless went down and were trampled. The stronger, struggling to resist and help the helpless, soon succumbed, many falling under the stomping. Utter panic reigned.

Now there was the sound of sirens coming from the distance and racing toward the wildness even as the uniformed police at the barriers of the scene began wading into it. More than half-panicked themselves and swinging billy clubs indiscriminately, the police moved forward with a new force, raising a greater screaming and worse wild madness from the helpless innocent masses caught in the crush of an adrenalin-driven machine-like brutality. In what seemed like a never ending eternity to Monty as he watched the horror unfold before and below him, but what was no doubt an incomprehensible instant without hope of escape to the poor souls caught in it, gunshots sounded. Police sirens surrounded them. The beaten and wounded were falling bloody all over the field.

Monty could no longer stand to look. He turned on Rhoades in rage. "You see what you've done!" Suddenly, his voice locked and his mind froze. There was nothing but smiling satisfaction on Rhoades' face. Rhoades did not reply and went on watching the scene with unchanging placidity. Monty regained his voice. "Do you hear me?" he demanded.

"What I've done?" Rhoades asked, still smiling as he watched the violent riot. He turned to Monty. "Yes. Bought us a pro-British demonstration that everybody is sure to hear about on the radio for the rest of today and tonight and read about in the all the papers tomorrow. Those who hate us have nothing more than they began the day with, except perhaps more hatred for Mossy's police. And I've bought sympathy for the pro-British side, who ugly Tudeh interrupted and shouted down."

Monty was so incredulous he could not respond. Rhoades smiled. "Now we must make sure the blame for this falls where it should. Come."

As Livingstone followed the barrel-chested, bowlegged British agent down the stairs, he saw bloody, bruised, battered people limping away weeping, leaning on others or being carried away by their friends. Suddenly, his rage rose up again. "You sacrifice innocents and create this brutal ugliness to make a political point!?!" He yelled at Rhoades' back.

Now at the bottom of the stairs, Rhoades stopped and pivoted to Monty. The big man's face came very near Monty's. "Son," Rhoades said quietly, his eyes once again small and piercing. "You don't know what ugly is. It is going to get so ugly in these streets it will make today's show look like child's play. Now follow. We have work."

Their work consisted, first, of a visit to Bahram Shahrokh at Radio Tehran, where Rhoades was quickly on the air in an interview about the rally. He indignantly bemoaned the lapse of political dialogue into Tudeh-provoked violence. And he sincerely promised British medical assistance for all who were injured. Next, they visited Tehran's newspapers and the wire service offices one by one. At each one, Rhoades methodically repeated his radio statements in serious but chatty conversation after friendly but serious chat. He bemoaned lost civility in Iranian society and the sad transformation of political dialogue into violent confrontation with Tudeh. And he promised British medical assistance for all who were injured. Late in the hot miserable day's night, Monty stumbled back to his bungalow and fell exhausted on his bed without undressing, grateful to be too weary to think before falling into a heavy sleep.

*****

"You have to go broke three times to learn how to make a living." ...Casey Stengel

The next day Monty avoided Rhoades. He stayed in his bungalow and relived the rally over and over in anguished letters he wrote and then destroyed before putting into envelopes. Finally, he could not think about the rally anymore. He turned to tedious, organizing tasks he had long been postponing. He alphabetized his oil industry client list and brought his address book up to date. When the sky turned blue-black, he took an embassy car and drove down Ferdosi and then along Kohk slowly, watching for Tekla to step out of an alley. The city was quiet and Parliament Square was eerily empty. Curiously, she did not appear. He circled the area and made another pass. Once again, she did not appear.

His mind came alert. She was late. Maybe she was not coming. Maybe she could not come. His mind went into high speed. The possibilities presented themselves too fast for him to answer: She was in trouble; she was injured in the riot; she was angry about the riot; Faddey had turned on her. His emotions, dormant since the night before, ran rampant. Struggling to control himself, he circled, making pass after pass, each time more slowly. She did not appear.

It was now growing dark. Sundown shadows disappeared into inky night and transformed into the longer, darker more indiscriminate shadows of dull streetlights. Not knowing what else to do, he circled again and again. Nothing. Tradecraft, he finally thought. Tradecraft.

He had already been far too obvious, he realized. Variation, he told himself. He circled in a completely different pattern, returned to Kohk from a different direction, parked on the far side of the street and waited. Nothing. The street remained silent. He watched the street in the rear and side view mirrors. Nothing. Now his hope began waning. This was not going to happen. Something was wrong, terribly wrong. He checked the mirrors. Nothing. His mind was racing around a circle that began with self-condemnation and ended with danger and fear. The mirrors. Nothing. Now what? She might have...

The passenger side door opened, startling him. "Let that be a lesson to you," she told him. "You watch behind you and neglect everything else. It will get you killed."

"I..."

"Drive," she said. "We will talk about tradecraft later."

He had already started the car and before she finished her sentence they were traveling west. Though Tekla remained silent, he began to relax before they reached the outskirts of the city. "Why were you late?"

She stared straight ahead. "Because I was late."

"That is not a reason," he explained. "I was worried."

"It is your tradecraft we have to worry about."

"I want to know why you were late!"

She turned to him. "You do not want to know!" She stared at him for a moment and again looked straight ahead.

Unconsciously, he accelerated. "Now I MUST know!"

"NO!"

He was speeding. "TELL ME!"

"You are driving too fast," she said quietly, suddenly calm, still looking straight ahead.

He accelerated. The road curved. The speed and momentum of the big car carried it toward the road's dirt shoulder. He swerved back, tires screeching.

"Watch your driving!" She demanded.

"DON'T TELL ME HOW TO DRIVE!" He yelled back. "TELL ME WHY YOU WERE LATE!"

"NO!"

He gritted his teeth in rage, jammed the car's accelerator pedal to the floor and sped down the highway in silence. A few minutes later, he recklessly swerved onto the dirt turnoff leading to the row of abandoned mud brick huts, veered off behind the huts and slammed on the brakes, bringing the car to a rough, skidding halt in darkness amid a patch of weeds. He turned off the engine and angrily slammed his body against the seatback twice, then sat still and looked down at the car's silent, shadowed dash.

She sat and waited, looking straight ahead out the windshield into the dark night. Quiet closed in. The faint sound of high desert insects came through the open windows to them, the same sound heard on this harsh plain by the first wanderers who migrated to it millennia before. "Faddey found out about you," she finally said.

His head snapped toward her. He stared. So many new questions now ran through his mind but he was so agitated he could not ask anything.

She waited. When his questions did not come, she went on. "I told him I am turning you," she said. "That I am going to use you against the British."

He turned away from her and stared out the windshield. There was only darkness and silence. He thought long and hard about Rhoades' question: "How do you know?" He looked at Tekla again. At first the words would not come. "Tell me how I can know that is a lie?' he finally asked.

She looked him and waited. Finally, she spoke. "What is in your heart?" she asked.

He looked hard at her again. Love and fear suddenly overwhelmed him and he felt like they might pull him apart. He reached desperately, clumsily for the door handle, twisted it hard and exploded out of the car, leaving the door open behind him. Not knowing where he was going, he walked back down the dirt road toward the highway.

He heard Tekla close up the car and follow him. She caught up with him as he stood in moonlight beside the highway, looking up at a sky full of stars.

"This is insane," he said quietly. "This whole thing. This complicated country. This weird war of fanatical ideas. It has to stop."

"If only," she said quietly.

"I thought there was one thing that made sense."

"When one thing makes sense, the rest becomes intolerable."

He turned to her. "So we let it pull us apart? Like before? We let go?"

"I thought of that," she said. "It might work. When we were worlds apart, it was not too hard living without it. But can we let it be over when we are only streets apart?'

"But such streets," he said.

She stepped to him and put herself against his chest. Almost involuntarily he responded, folding his arms around her.

She looked up at him. "About this I cannot be strong, Monty. You must decide."

He leaned down, kissed her forehead, then looked at her, her blue eyes shining in the moonlight. Suddenly, he knew. He did not know how or why he knew, he only knew. He took her face in his hands and kissed her deeply. She felt in his kiss that he had broken the barrier and she kissed back. In this one kiss, both knew only the one true thing: If the world was going to go crazy, it might as well start with their love.

He swept her into his arms and carried her toward their love nest, kissing and laughing and stumbling as they went. He kicked open the door, strode across the quiet, waiting room and laid her on their rough palette in the moonlight. He turned away, lit the lantern, closed the door and turned back to her. She was naked atop the bedding, arms spread wide, legs open.

He quickly shed his clothes, fell on her and met her hunger with his own. They moaned together in passion, both quickly ready for coupling. "Do it, Monty. Quickly. And all night. It is all we have against the rest of it!" Soon he was inside her completely and she had him wholly and they were rising and falling as one, breathing heavily and moving intensely, having and having and having, until the wave crested and fell away and then rose again like another stronger sensation rising and rising and rising again, the having and having and having until the cresting and falling and peace.

They fell apart, panting, but almost right away turned again toward each other. They kissed and touched and indulged their eyes in the beauty they saw in each other. Soon his hunger returned yet again and her moist soft warmth was still ready to be met by his renewed fullness. Once again he rose over her, slid into oneness with her, and they rolled reciprocatingly together, riding the waves upward, igniting each other to higher excitement. His capacity to be with her love, to be inside her love lasted longer now so that her hunger could reach its peak and when she got there she lost all control as she took her welcome, shuddering gratification, slamming her pelvis upward into him, gasping, "Monty, Monty, Mon-n-n-n-tiiiieey!" And her exhilaration swallowed him in its fulfillment, bringing him a second and wilder, deeper, more paralyzing satisfaction, matching hers, and then he fell on her and rolled to her side, their arms and legs remaining unremittingly intertwined as gasping became heavy breathing became drowsiness until they drifted off into the sleep of satiation.

They slept to the gray light of dawn when, together, they awakened to the realization that the world was no different and they must rise to deal with it. Both were mature enough to accept that awareness without hesitation, smiling together, grateful for the night before, expectant of more such nights to come. They went about their morning ablutions in a quiet easy dance of moving toward their own needs and out of the way the other's. While they dressed, it occurred to him to ask what she thought of the rally.

"You really want my opinion?" she asked hesitantly.

"You think I don't know it was bad business?" he asked, opening the hut's door.

"Well," she shrugged as she finished dressing and moved out the door he held open for her. "You are an American oilman so I suppose you know a lot about bad business."

"They would settle this whole thing in two minutes," he said.

"Who, the Americans?"

"The oilmen," he said, following her to the car.

"You are saying it is the politicians who mess it up."

"The power brokers," he said, climbing behind the wheel. "The more I read the papers, the more I worry about the Mullahs. They'll be dangerous if they ever wise up about how things work."

They closed their car doors and he started the engine. "Have you read anything by the British writer George Orwell, Monty?"

"No."

She chatted as he followed the highway back into Tehran. "He wrote a book called 'Nineteen Eighty-Four' a couple of years ago."

"Oh yeah," he said quickly as he turned into the city and drove past the trucks dropping off the morning papers. "Some strange futuristic thing."

412

"It's about using language to govern, to twist the truth until there is no truth. The best book about governing since Machiavelli. His imaginary government uses a language they call "Newspeak." They make up phrases like "War is peace" and "Freedom is slavery.""

"Sounds a lot like Casey Stengel," he smiled.

"Over there," she added pointing to the place on Kohk Avenue she wanted him to drop her.

He glanced at her. "It probably makes a lot of sense on your side of the Iron Curtain."

"It makes a lot of sense wherever you live in this world," she smiled, as he pulled the car over. "Casey Stengel would do well as a Soviet politician. But I was thinking about another "Newspeak" aphorism when you were talking about the Mullahs: 'Ignorance is strength.' Do you understand?"

After pulling the car over at her drop-off, he turned to her. "I think we're saying the same thing from two different points of view. You know them by the strength they get from the ignorant masses. I wonder if that strength will ever be used by somebody who's power hungry."

"Yes. Exactly. Different ways of saying the same thing." She threw open the car door. "I must go." She jumped out, closed the door behind her, started away, then pivoted back, bent to the window and grinned at him. "See you at the dance." With that, she dashed off. He turned north and drove up Churchill Avenue toward the embassy, wondering how he could be so happy in such a confused world.

After putting the car away and cleaning up, he walked to the embassy cafeteria for breakfast. As he filled his tray and walked across the crowded room to join Rhoades, he noticed the room was filled with excited chatter. Many of the diplomats and residents were catching their associates' attention and pointing to newspapers they usually read in silence.

"What's up?" he asked, sitting down.

"Big stuff," Rhoades snorted. "All the papers are railing about the rally. Casualty figures, who to blame, that sort of thing."

"And?"

"All good for our side," Rhoades smiled. " 'Tudeh's violence at the pro-Shah rally,' that sort of stuff."

"Now what?"

"This, sonny, is just the beginning. Got it right from the top. Ambassador Shepherd his own self. 'The educating of Iranian opinion,' he called it."

Monty gestured around the room. "That's what they're so excited about?"

"That's just part of it. Big doings in the Majlis today. They're going to name the Shah's man Zia PM."

"He's your man?"

"Wouldn't have it any other way!" Rhoades grinned. "Lets go down and watch the doings," Rhoades suddenly proposed.

"But I don't know the language," Monty protested.

"You know I'll fill you in," Rhoades smilingly replied.

From the distance of the out-of-the-way, dimly lit visitor's gallery, surrounded by respectful political aficionados and attentive members of the press, Monty at first found the spectacle of dignified democratic proceedings in an unknown language fascinating, if slightly inscrutable. But the action soon became repetitive and dull, despite Rhoades' best efforts to add drama by interpretation of word and event. Monty was sleepily letting his chin drop to his chest when the abrupt absence of Rhoades' droning translation jolted him alert. A compelling, unexpected drama on the floor of the grand hall had galvanized Rhoades' attention, bringing him to a tense silence.

As Monty shook his head and studied the floor, a portly, dignified man was walking away from the speaker's podium. Heads were slowly turning to a lean, bald man with sad eyes and a large nose in a front row seat. The lean old man sat motionless and silent for a long, long moment as, all around, the House members coughed nervously or shifted uneasily in their seats.

Finally, the old man rose, went to the podium and began speaking. Immediately, there was murmuring at what he was saying. Before Monty could ask for the translation his companion was not providing, Rhoades began muttering expletives and a clamor rose in the House. When the old man delivered a resounding climactic declaration, passion obvious in his every dynamic, melodramatic gesture, the House erupted. The Chairman

414

pounded his gavel repeatedly and called for order. The clamor faded some, allowing the Chairman to call for a vote. But he never got to the 'nays.' When asked for their 'ayes,' members exploded in near unanimous agreement, leaped from their seats, surrounded the old man who had incited this wild, joyous display and followed him from the room in triumph while the Chairman irrelevantly gaveled the proceedings to an official close.

Up in the gallery, around Livingstone and Rhoades, the aficionados raced off to join the celebration. The press dashed to report the news. Rhoades sat in stunned silence. After the noise and turmoil had receded, the gallery around them empty, Monty turned to Rhoades, who was staring at his feet, mostly silent but occasionally muttering vulgarities.

"Come on, Rhoades, give. That was Mossy, wasn't it? They made him P.M.?"

"That's not the worst of it," Rhoades muttered, still looking at his feet.

"What?"

Rhoades looked up. "He told them he wouldn't accept the job if they didn't put through nationalization."

"It looked like they voted 'yes' for both."

"Sod it all," Rhoades muttered, dropping his head again.

The next question was obvious, but Monty waited. Before he could ask it, Rhoades looked up again. "Good news and bad news," he said grimly.

"The bad news is pretty obvious," Monty said. "We didn't do much educating of Iranian opinion yet and it could cost your country their oil. There's good news?"

"Good news for you and me. Our jobs are secure. We've got a lot of educating of Iranian opinion to do."

From that day on, the frequency and violence of the political confrontations and demonstrations escalated. While Monty tagged along, Rhoades' visited his Iranian agents over and over, urging them to push back against Tudeh and the Islamists. A mosque was burned. Tudeh was blamed. Tudeh publicly protested and blamed British spies. A National Front leader was assassinated. Tudeh blamed the British and Rhoades hit the streets, pointing out to Radio Tehran reporters and newspaper editors that the political leader was pro-Shah and had been demanding the National Front negotiate with the oil company. Virtually daily, there was either a demonstration that turned violent or a clamorous session at the Majlis or an act of terror on the street. Daily, Livingstone protested the violence to Rhoades. The British agent always shrugged, told Livingstone he was only doing what must be done and repeated his now daily declaration. "If you don't have the stomach to fight this war, you can be replaced. Go home." Knowing this would mean leaving Tekla, Monty merely mumbled and turned away.

Against a mounting tide of public opinion and a slowly building avalanche of Tudeh-inspired political actions by Mossadeq's National Front against them, Rhoades and the British embassy worked to weaken the Prime Minister and win back the United Kingdom's failing foothold in Iran. Mossadeq's popularity made it impossible for the Shah to resist signing the decree nationalizing the oil industry. But Britain placed battleships in the Shatt-al-Arab, stopping all oil exports from Abadan, bringing the facility to a standstill. In addition, they embargoed Iranian trade. Mossadeq demanded that Britain relent and insisted the Anglo-Iranian Oil Company (AIOC) turn over control to the National Iranian Oil Company (NIOC). Though they could not stop the Iranians from coming into the Abadan facilities, the British employees resisted the changeover at every office doorway and every desk, every derrick and every truck, every holding tank and every pipe, every cracking tower and every chemistry lab, every rail line and every ocean tanker. But, facing the inevitable, they also sent the women and children of Abadan's ex-patriot British community home to England, leaving only the company's workforce behind as potential hostages.

Livingstone and Rhoades and the rest of the ambassadorial attaches worked harder now, lobbying anywhere and everywhere they could, trying to bring Mossadeq's government to the bargaining table. One day, they wandered through the Grand Bazaar from contact to contact and food seller to food seller. While Rhoades grazed, Monty asked why Mossadeq was so dead set against making a deal with the British.

"You'd think it was only right, wouldn't you?" Rhoades said snidely.

"You found the oil out there," Monty said.

"And it didn't find easily," shrugged Rhoades, indulging in a plump strawberry.

"And you built the world's greatest refinery."

"They'll run it into the mud sludge of the Shatt-al-Arab," Rhoades said casually.

"Mossy says his people can do most of the work and they'll hire oil technicians from all over the world to do the rest."

Rhoades looked up at Monty. "It's a magnificent refinery. Might take 'em three or four generations, but they'll ruin it. Promise."

"Some of them must know what they can and can't do. Why won't Mossy make a deal?"

"Partly because he can't and partly because he won't."

"Explain."

"Can't because Tudeh and the Mullahs don't want a deal, they want the oil company. Won't because the company men are bastards and think the oil is really theirs so they won't give him anything like decent terms."

"So where does that lead?"

"Nowhere," said Rhoades, popping another strawberry whole into his big leathery face. "Let's get back to work."

The heat of midsummer settled on Tehran and the city turned too lethargic for political turmoil. Meanwhile, the vying parties did everything possible to avoid resolving the dilemma amicably. In the U.S., Wisconsin Republican Senator Joseph McCarthy ranted. In Korea, the Chinese army rolled south and President Truman fired General MacArthur. Britain decided to take the oil matter to the World Court at The Hague. Iran refused to participate, insisting it was not a dispute between nations but a contractual dispute between the Iranian government and the oil company. The court announced it would deliberate over the question of jurisdiction. When Monty asked Rhoades' opinion on the value of the legal proceedings, the Brit's face tightened. "Fat lot of good it'll do 'em," he told Monty. "But it'll buy time to bring the buggers to their knees economically," he smiled, referring to the embargo. "We'll make 'em so bleedin' hungry they'll try to drink the bloody oil. And when they choke on it, they'll come crawling to us for a deal."

Another month went by. Livingstone and Rhoades continued to work on eroding support for Mossadeq and nationalization. They expanded their network of well-paid pro-Shah operatives. While peace talks on Korea in Kaesong filled the headlines, a U.S. State Department delegation began commuting between London and Tehran. Averill Harriman, a legendary diplomat and President Truman's personal representative, and George McGhee, an oilman and Rhodes scholar, exercised virtuosic diplomacy in arranging an August summit between the British and Iranian governments.

Once under way, the talks proceeded slowly. While they went on, Livingstone and Rhoades – after their own very complicated maneuvering – obtained an audience with Ayatollah Kashani, one of Mossadeq's most committed supporters. Intending to intimidate the Ayatollah into compromise, they planned to hint at the havoc their pro-Shah/pro-British network could create if Mossadeq's National Front/Tudeh/Islamic alliance remained intransegient. But Kashani set a disinterested tone quickly when he started the conversation by observing, "Foreigners in Iran are evil and not to be trusted."

"Not very diplomatic," Rhoades smiled condescendingly.

"The British are the worst," Kashani smiled back disdainfully.

"Bah!" Rhoades exploded, and stormed from the room.

Kashani turned to Monty. "You remain, Mr. Livingstone?"

"I am an oilman, Ayatollah. Perhaps we can talk about oil."

"There was an American oilman here before the war," Kashani told Monty, staring coldly. "The people regarded him as an Infidel. He was shot on the street by a Believer and rushed to the hospital by a Samaritan. A mob followed, burst into the operating room and butchered him on the operating table."

Monty stared at the holy man, silently seething and wondering what to say. Finally, he decided to reveal some defiance. "Perhaps you think you are threatening me, your Eminence," Monty said. "But I was an officer at the Battle of the Bulge. For twelve days my men and I were trapped in freezing foxholes with dwindling supplies and ammunition. I do not scare easily."

Kashani smiled. "There was no harm in trying."

Monty was not amused. "I waited at the Bulge for the fog to lift. I will do the same here."

"You may wait," Kashani said. "But if Mossadeq submits to the British he will meet the same fate as Razmara."

418

"So it is true."

"What?"

"There is nothing for us to talk about," Monty said.

"Mr. Rhoades already realized that," Kashani replied.

*****

"Now there's three things that can happen in a ballgame: you can win, you can lose, or it can rain." ...Casey Stengel

By the end of August, the talks had failed. The British refused to offer the same 50-50 deal every other oil-rich nation in the world was getting from other oil companies and the Iranians continued to demand 100% ownership for what they did not create, find or produce. At The Hague, the World Court ruled the Iranians were correct to believe the court had no jurisdiction. Still playing for the time required to make the embargo felt, the British government announced it would take the matter to the United Nations Security Council. To Rhoades' delight, worsening economic conditions in an Iran stripped of its oil industry began causing real pain. Mossadeq's power began eroding.

Mossadeq's dilemma became clear when he arrived at the Majlis on September 25, to announce a new decision concerning AIOC at Abadan. His popularity had so waned that, for the fourth session running, there was no quorum to hear him. Melodramatically, he stepped to the podium weeping and mumbled a few disconsolate words but said he would not deliver his speech without a quorum. He then lurched from the House floor and stumbled outside, leaning on his loyal ally Ayatollah Kashani and followed by his remaining legislative minority. On the street, Tudeh white shirts, Kashani Islamists and all the idlers who could immediately be gathered formed into a crowd around the old man and the members of his coalition. Theatrically bemoaning his fate, Mossadeq seemed to take heart when his loyalists cheered him and chanted for him to read the speech he had come to the Majlis to deliver. He wept tears of bittersweet joy and praised the loyal few.

Whether spontaneous or prefabricated, the moment now had a momentum of its own. Mossadeq enthusiasts turned a lemonade pedlar's cart on its side and lifted the old man onto it. To cheers and adulatory applause, he announced his fateful decision: The British oil company must abdicate entirely by

419

October 4, 1951, or face forceful expulsion by the Iranian military. Already, he told the gathered faithful, General Riahi's army and Admiral Shahin's navy were taking up reinforced positions around the refinery and the island. The proletarian throngs shrieked their approval and paraded around the Prime Minister cheering. Members of the press dashed for their offices with a genuine scoop. Kashani stepped up on the overturned lemonade cart beside Mossadeq and declared the coming weekend to be religious holy days reserved for celebrating Iran's triumph. He called for all Believers to join him in a pilgrimage to Khorramshar, where there would be a festival. On Saturday, he proclaimed, the festival would end with a march of national pride and solidarity culminating in a joyous demonstration at Abadan's Islamic cemetery.

Rhoades and Livingstone returned to the embassy when Mossadeq left the street rally. The big Brit announced he was feeling "peckish" and led Monty to the cafeteria for a late lunch. Many of the embassy people were still eating when word-of-mouth reports brought in the first word. Radios in the room came on and personnel from around the compound started gathering. Soon, Radio Tehran news flashes confirmed what nobody in the British delegation wanted to believe: The oil company was lost. Meetings promptly convened.

Rhoades, outwardly unperturbed, declined to attend the emergency meetings. After polishing off his "snack," he led Monty back to the streets. The two began the most serious network building footwork Monty had ever done. But by the weekend, there was upheaval in and around Abadan. The streets of Tehran were full of rumors and becoming threatening for westerners. Hints of worry were emerging in Rhoades' wrinkled leathery face. By Saturday night, reports of violent demonstrations at the refinery reached Tehran and Monty could easily see Rhoades was anxious. Early Sunday morning, Rhoades roused Monty and told him their car was waiting. The overnight intelligence from operatives at Abadan was very ominous. As soon as Monty could ready himself and get to the car, Rhoades jumped behind the wheel. He drove ferociously, wrecklessly, heading southwest across the desert toward the island refinery.

As they drove, they picked up news reports over the car radio, Rhoades translating. Mossadeq was accusing the British of the new riots and subsequent deaths and injuries. He announced that several British reporters had been forcibly expelled from the country as a demonstration of his serious intent. He warned the remaining oil company employees they were running out of time. He ended his speech with another promise of military action if the oil company resisted.

As on their previous visit, they drove onto the island across the Bahmanshir Bridge, this time at breakneck speed. On Abadan, Rhoades was forced to slow by the chaos and upheaval in the normally orderly, business-like refinery. Naffars, the native oil field and refinery workers, were fleeing on bicycle and foot, pulling and pushing carts full of children and meager possessions. Squads of Iranian military and police patroled the roads and loading docks, some accompanied by machine-gun mounted jeeps or small tanks. Pairs of British security guards escorted groups of company employees from the residential sections of Braim to transport craft at the piers that ferry them to Basra in Iraq or the safety of the waiting British naval vessel Mauritius anchored at sea. Lone British civilians, company officials, scurried to and from their offices in obvious desperation.

Security at the company gates was now more rigid but Rhoades readily identified himself and gained admission. Inside the company offices, clerks packed, shredded and burned papers frantically. Iranian officials and military officers came and went, attempting to interrupt the proceedings despite the company men's best, most polite efforts to be curt and unhelpful or ignore them. Amid the turmoil, an executive secretary recognized Rhoades and waved him through the outer offices. He quickly entered a long hallway, Monty moving quickly to stay at his heels. He turned into the boardroom where their previous meetings with company executives had taken place.

"Got to be quick," Rhoades told Monty. "It's getting too busy around here." On a wall of the meeting room across from the windows looking out on the Shatt-al-Arab was a painting of Queen Victoria Monty had paid no attention to on their first visit. "Pardon me, your majesty," Rhoades said quietly, lifting the painting away to reveal a wall safe. Rhoades studied the dial and then began turning it. Up to this point, Monty had been silently taking in what was all too obvious to require explanation. Now, however, he was angrily perplexed.

"You had to come all the way down here, to this battle zone, to empty out a safe?"

"Nobody else knows the combination."

It was only moments until Rhoades got the safe open, scooped the three notebooks and two bank bags that were its contents into his arms, and turned for the door. As Monty followed him back down the hallway toward the front offices, he was now simply angry.

"You're going to walk right out of here with an armload of records and money?"

"Mine," Rhoades said bluntly. "Come on."

Sure enough, nobody on the premises even took notice of them. All seemed more than occupied with similar concerns of their own. Outside, as they were about to get back into their car, five police cars drove up quickly, lights flashing and sirens blaring. Rhoades tossed the notebooks and bank bags into the car's back seat. "Have to bluff this one, sonny. Ready?"

"Ready to act like I don't know what the hell's going on?" Monty snapped quietly, through clinched teeth. "That's not acting."

"Detective Afshartus!" Rhoades exclaimed cheerily when he saw Tehran's Chief of Police emerge from the lead police car. "You're here just in time!"

Afshartus stared suspiciously at Rhoades and Livingstone as he walked toward them. Behind him, plainclothes officers emerged from the police cars in groups of four and five. He waved them into the oil company offices. As they swept around him, he smiled grimly at Rhoades. "You are always so much happier to see me than I am to see you."

"Because you represent the forces of law and order," Rhoades replied smarmily.

Afshartus ignored Rhoades, glancing from Livingstone to the car, back to Livingstone and, finally, to Rhoades. "You are here because?"

"We have no reason to be here now," Rhoades beamed. "The embassy was worried there would be theft and destruction. But that will not happen with you in charge!"

Because this seemed to obliquely imply Rhoades and Livingstone had not yet been inside, Afshartus decided it was the case. "So I have arrived just in time?" he said, suggesting a meaning of his own as well as a trite answer to Rhoades' smarm.

"As you always do, Chief Detective," Rhoades smiled.

Afshartus concluded Rhoades and Livingstone represented no threat. "I have no time for this," he said, waving a hand dismissively. He turned to follow his men inside, but stopped and turned back. "Don't make the mistake of getting caught doing something you should not be doing here, Rhoades. The old man is going to put Riahi in charge of the refinery. He will kill you before he lets you sabotage this takeover." He turned again and walked toward the offices.

"You were always a good friend, Afshartus," Rhoades smarmed at the Police Chief's back.

Afshartus laughed a cold, grim laugh and disappeared inside without looking back.

As soon as he was gone, Rhoades jumped again behind the wheel and Monty had barely got his door closed when the older man sped the car through a U-turn and screeched away toward the center of the refinery complex. Both were silent as Monty waited to see what came next and Rhoades picked his way through narrow streets treacherous with flight and chaos. Suddenly, Rhoades sat back in his seat. "Did I replace the painting of the Queen?" he asked Monty.

"I don't remember."

"Neither do I, sod it all. We better make fast work of this."

After a short drive, they pulled up in front of a block of neat two-story buildings. Behind them, there was a tall tower with a flame coming from the top of it.

"That's a cracking tower," Monty observed.

"Experimental," Rhoades muttered as he jumped from the car. "Easy access." He grabbed the things from the backseat and raced inside. Without stopping to reconnoiter, he dashed through the empty building.

"What is that stuff?" Monty asked impatiently.

"Nothing much," Rhoades muttered. "Just an agent's lifeline. Money. Passports. Visas. Identities. And a few random tidbits on some important people that might encourage cooperation."

As they went out the building's back door and onto the blacktop behind it, Monty saw the small, scraggily-haired man with the thick glasses who had helped them find the carpenter right after Monty had started working with Rhoades. Standing at the base of the tall tower, the little man appeared to be wearing the same dingy white shirt and wrinkled tie.

"Are you ready?" Rhoades asked impatiently as he rushed across the blacktop to the man. The man pointed to a pit in the dirt at the base of the tower with an open, empty, half-buried metal box in it. "Perfect," Rhoades grunted, bending to it.

Amazed, Monty looked at Rhoades. "You had this prearranged?"

"Prior planning, sonny," Rhoades replied disinterestedly. Kneeling, he slid one of the notebooks and one of the bank bags into the metal box, pulled the cover closed and latched it tightly. He paused a moment and hung his head. "The only thing I forgot was to replace the Queen."

"Better hurry," the little man said nervously.

Monty studied him. "What are you afraid of?"

The little man looked at Monty. "Being shot for treason," he said bluntly.

"He's right," Rhoades said while he covered the metal box with dirt. "Both of you get outside. Wait in the car. If they show up, tell them you're waiting for me."

"If who shows up?" asked the bureaucrat, looking around nervously.

"Nevermind," Rhoades answered impatiently, standing up and wiping the dirt from his hands. "Get out." He looked hard at the bureaucrat. "You know what to do."

The little man from administration nodded 'yes,' pivoted and did not wait for further instructions.

Rhoades picked up the remaining two notebooks and the moneybag, turned to the iron door on the cracking tower and pulled it open, revealing the fire burning inside it.

"You're going to burn that?" Monty asked.

"Phonies," Rhoades replied. "Something for them to find in the ash."

"Thorough."

"But for the Queen," Rhoades said with melancholy, watching the fake notebooks and counterfeit moneybag burn. His voice suddenly turned blunt. "Get out of here, Livingstone."

Monty shrugged and started after the bureaucrat until Rhoades called to him. "Livingstone." Monty turned. The rotund, leathery-faced Brit stood by the intense fire of the cracking tower, smiling. "Do you remember Razmara?"

"The Prime Minister who was assassinated?"

"That's right," nodded Rhoades. "Remember one more thing: A smuggling network becomes a revolutionary network when there's nothing to smuggle."

"I watched," Monty smiled, holding up his left index finger. "I learned that."

"Good," Rhoades smiled back. "Wait for me in the car. If Afshartus shows up, you don't know where I am. I told you to wait there."

"Right."

When Monty reached the car, the bureaucrat was nowhere in sight. On Rhoades' instructions, he waited in the car. For the first time on this visit, he noticed the refinery's familiar pungent stench, the eye-irritating smokiness and the constant ear-numbing hum of machinery.

Two police cars, sirens blaring and lights flashing, roared up and skidded to halt. Afshartus and a platoon of his men emerged. The Police Chief quickly walked to Monty and leaned into the car. "Where is Rhoades?" he demanded. The others charged into the building.

"Don't know," Monty shrugged. "I thought you already said your good-byes."

Afshartus studied him. "Before the war, you Americans were such innocents. The British ruined you."

"You don't think it had anything to do with Hitler?"

Suddenly there was commotion at the building door. Afshartus turned. Three plainclothesmen dragged Rhoades out of the building forcibly. Another followed, carrying a shovel horizontally in front of him. In the dish of the shovel were the charred remains of the decoy notebooks and bank bag.

Afshartus walked to Rhoades, smiling. "I have waited for this Rhoades."

"Indeed you have," Rhoades replied grimly.

"INFIDEL!" One of the trailing police officers suddenly screamed, pulling a revolver. "INSOLENT INFIDEL!" He rushed at Rhoades, stuck the barrel of the pistol to the back of his head and fired point blank. The bullet exploded the back of Rhoades' head, penetrated through and burst from his forehead, scattering blood and brain matter all over Rhoades and the plainclothesmen restraining him. His body instantly a dead weight, it slumped to the ground.

The gunman threw the pistol down and ran. The other detectives were frozen in momentary shock and disbelief until Afshartus, in fury, screamed at them in Farsi and they all gave chase.

Afshartus bent to the fallen man. Feeling suddenly heavy, Monty effortfully pulled himself from the car and started to Rhoades' body. Afshartus finished pulling Rhoades white suit coat off as Monty neared and started to bend down. Afshartus rose, pivoted, stopped Monty halfway through the stooping motion and stood him up. "You don't want to see this." Monty stepped back. Afshartus bent again and used Rhoades' suit coat, bloody red and linen white, to cover the lifeless, mangled head.

Despite his seething rage, Monty knew to restrain himself. Rhoades was always in control, Monty told himself. Rhoades did not vent his rage, he used it. Not wanting to reveal his feelings to Afshartus, he looked away, staring in the direction the chase for the shooter had gone. There was nothing there now, the pursued and pursuers having disappeared into the refinery complex. Now there was only the familiar pungent stench, the eye-irritating smokiness, the constant ear-numbing hum of machinery. He hung his head. Unconsciously, his eyes scanned the ground without thought. Until he saw it. "The pistol," he said.

Afshartus, staring blankly at the body, shook his head to clear it and looked at Monty.

Monty nodded at it. "A .38 revolver," Monty said to Afshartus. He remembered Rhoades last question: Do you remember Razmara?

Afshartus' eyes followed Monty's nod to the pistol.

"Was your man at the mosque the day Razmara was shot?" Monty asked.

Afshartus walked to the pistol, picked it up and examined it. "Standard military issue," he said.

"Was he military before he was a cop?"

426

"Most of my men were," Afshartus said, continuing to study the pistol. "I never trusted that one."

"A religious fanatic," Monty said, hanging his head, thinking of what he so recently said to Tekla, that the real danger in Iran was not the politicians.

"He certainly wanted us to think so," Afshartus replied. "But to tell you the truth I always thought he was a British sympathizer. Or, at least, pro-Shah."

"If that was true, why would he kill Rhoades?" Monty asked condescendingly.

Afshartus looked hard at Monty. "Do you know what our military does to a man arrested for spying BEFORE they shoot him?" He looked down and shook his head. "If you don't think Rhoades planned for all eventualities, sonny, you didn't know him very well."

Knowing how thoroughly Rhoades did indeed plan, Monty could not reply. There was a long silence. "If only he hadn't forgotten about the Queen," he finally said.

"What?" Afshartus asked sharply. But they were interrupted by the return of the bureaucrat. He walked up from out of nowhere and went straight to Afshartus, glancing nervously at Rhoades' body. "Mr. Livingstone?" He asked the policeman. Afshartus shook his head irritably and indicated Monty. The bureaucrat walked to Monty. "You're to see Mr. Mason."

"Mason?" Monty asked, puzzled.

"The company's man," said Afshartus, still irritated.

"Yes," nodded the bureaucrat. "Mr. Rhoades had me arrange it. It would've been for the two of you but…" The small officious man did not seem to think an explanation was necessary.

Monty looked at Afshartus, then at Rhoades' body. Just then, the police officers returned without the shooter. Afshartus was not pleased. "Go with the little bastard," Afshartus barked at Monty, then turned toward his men. "My men will take care of the body."

Monty drove. The bureaucrat rode with him. Following the bureaucrat's directions north to Khorramshar's residential community, Monty pulled up in front of a large house bustling with activity just as the bureaucrat repeated yet again his apology and explained yet again he only did what Rhoades told him to do. Getting out of the car, Monty stopped and stared at the unending procession of British and Iranian officials and functionaries coming and going from this house. When he looked back to ask the bureaucrat how he was supposed to get to Mason amid this hubbub, the little man was gone. Monty shrugged and began threading his way through the crowd.

Inside, he spotted a tall man with stooped shoulders and a high, worried brow constantly moving from room to room, always followed, frequently handed paperwork to consider or sign and always answering questions. Discouraged about getting anywhere near the busy executive, Monty considered leaving until he decided that if Rhoades had requested this meeting, it must be important. Working his way through the crowd, Monty placed himself in the busy executive's path but Mason was waylaid and then diverted. After repeating this effort enough times to begin feeling ridiculous, Monty again considered leaving but decided to look for a place to sit and reconsider first. While looking for a place to sit down, he came face to face with Mason.

"Mr. Mason," Monty announced abruptly, "I am Montgomery Livingstone. Hardy Rhoades arranged to see you. He has been killed."

Mason stopped in his tracks and looked up from the paperwork he was studying. The men around him stopped talking. Without a word, Mason handed off the papers. Taller than Monty, he looked down at him ponderously, then stepped forward, draped an arm around him and walked him toward a corner, their backs to the room. As they walked, he raised his other arm behind himself and waved. Suddenly, three men stepped between the rest of the crowd and the huddle Mason had created for himself and Monty. "You are certain he is dead?" Mason whispered hoarsely.

The image of the big burly Brit sprawled on the ground, his blood red and linen-white suitcoat over his head, his white shirt oozing red blotches, rushed at Monty. He pushed the image away but Mason saw the pain of loss on Monty's face. He did not wait for Monty to speak.

"The contents of the safe?"

"Hidden," Monty answered, quickly shifting from the image of Rhoades to the question of whether this man should be told where the safe's contents were.

With the insight of a man who read other men and the tact of a diplomat, Mason quickly continued. "You will keep the location confidential."

"Yes sir."

Mason's expression became gentler, more intimate. "I will be gone from here forever in hours. As an American, you may stay or go. Do you want me to arrange safe passage with our last people on the Mauritius?" He studied Monty and waited for a decision as if he knew much hung in the balance.

Monty's first response was surprise. He had not yet thought of escape. Then he thought of Rhoades, who left him with information on which he could act. He could carry on the work. The smuggling network would now become a network for change in this country. With the thought of Iran's political turmoil came the thought of Tekla. Monty leapt to his conclusion. "I have work in Tehran," he told Mason. The executive nodded and held out his hand. Monty shook with a firm, steady grasp and looked Mason in the eye with a firm purpose.

"Well done, son," the British executive smiled, sharing the firm handshake and unspoken commitment to what neither knew was coming.

Monty made his way back to the car and drove northeast. Along the heavily guarded highway, he was allowed to continue only because he was able to identify himself at each checkpoint as an American returning to his post in Tehran. Each time he identified himself, a stern Iranian reminded him threateningly that British spies were shot. After dark he arrived in Ahwaz and found his way to the Shush Hotel, the only accommodations in the small desert town used by westerners. By this time, the oil company personnel exodus had passed Ahwaz by on its way to Abadan. Monty had no trouble getting a room for the night. For a few extra rials, he got a meal of leftovers in the hotel kitchen. He then went to his room, wet his face at the low-ceilinged, stuffy cubicle's only working tap and collapsed atop the bed's covers for a few hours of forgetting.

He woke, uneasy, in morning gray light. He immediately knew he would not fall back to sleep. He again splashed water from the tap on his face and wearily returned to the car. A long day of hot dusty driving followed. He was torn between the aching loss his unremitting memories of Rhoades brought on, and the only thought that would assuage the pain, the longing to see Tekla, to tell her everything, to cry on her shoulder.

Some hours after nightfall, he arrived in Tehran. The embassy was in turmoil. He considered reporting to Sir Francis but decided the facts had no doubt already been transmitted. Anything he could add would wait until morning. Returning to his bungalow, he quickly checked his back mail and was disappointed to find no letter from the front company Tekla used.

Wearily, he stripped from the clothes he had worn for two days and nights, and bathed the dust and sweat from his body. Despite failing to cleanse his heart of its ache, he fell damp into his bed and a serious sleep.

The next morning he woke feeling uneasy, as if everything was the same and yet different. He walked to the cafeteria. The intense scurry of the embassy complex all around him affirmed his irrational feeling that the world was not the same and somehow dangerously tilted. It was not despondence but an emptiness mixing explosively with a new sense of uncertain purpose. He took a table alone and was sitting over porridge and coffee, steeling himself for the necessary recounting of events to the ambassador, when Sir Francis walked up. Clumsily, Monty stood.

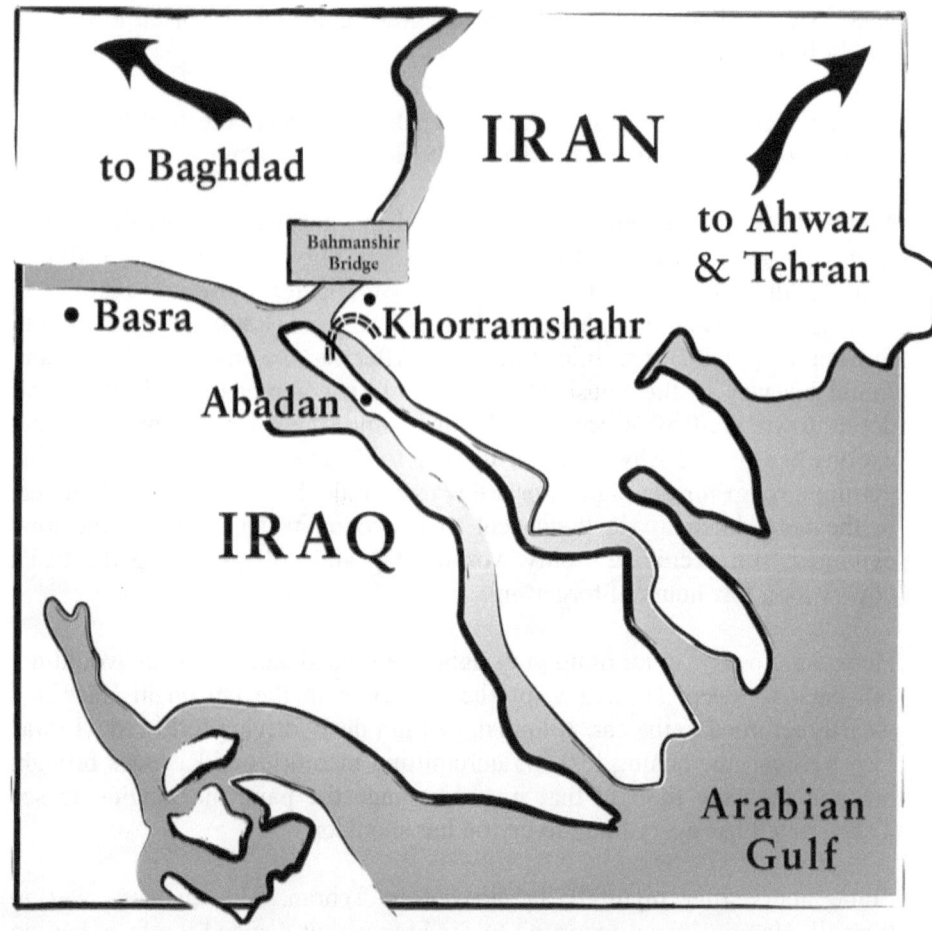

Stern-faced, the ambassador was curt. "We've had the communications from Abadan, Livingstone. Mason says you've got the situation in hand."

Monty's mind raced. In hand? "More or less, sir." It was a phrase an Englishman could appreciate.

"Quite," Shepherd replied. "It's a loss to us all. A terrible loss."

"Yes sir."

"You'll want to check in with Ambassador Henderson at your own embassy."

"Yes sir."

"We'd like you to stay on here. Carry on with your – uh – work." Shepherd's churning hand gestures and unspoken instructions spoke volumes. "The oil business and so on. You understand."

"Yes sir."

Still fighting the feeling of facing a world turned upside down and desperate, Monty returned to his room. Checking the morning mail, he found nothing from Tekla. He began to wonder what to do next. Business as usual? What was that now? He decided, as Shepherd suggested, to check with Ambassador Loy Henderson at the U.S. embassy. He walked down through the British embassy gates into Ferdosi Square. A little Iranian boy approached. Not in the mood to be harried, he waved the boy off but the boy kept coming, yammering in Farsi until he was close. He held out an envelope and went on yammering. Monty glanced around cautiously. Nobody was paying attention. He grabbed the envelope, gave the boy all his pocket change and walked away quickly.

Without stopping, Monty walked through the square and down the length of Ferdosi, instinctively using evasive maneuvers. When he was certain he was not being followed, he ducked into a storefront. He made a show of examining the pots and pans on display but waved off the shopkeeper. Working at casualness, he browsed until he "noticed" the envelope in his pocket and, feigning his best disinterest, opened it. It was a brief, handwritten note on Tekla's front company stationery. After its "apologies for short notice," it requested an "urgent meeting" and suggested "tonight at the usual time and place."

Monty struggled to maintain his poise. As casually as possible, as if he was disregarding it, he stuffed the note and envelope into his pocket and resumed his show of browsing the pots and pans, his mind racing. He had been so

431

absorbed in the events of the last three days he had not considered Tekla. Was her situation now "urgent" too?

He walked to the U.S. embassy. While he waited for admission at the gateway in the imposing walls of the compound, he glanced across the street at the equally imposing walls of the Soviet embassy. Walls, he thought. When his name was identified and the Marines on guard passed him in, he walked through the sprawling complex to the ambassador's office and reported. After a long, tedious wait, during which he pondered fruitlessly the many possible implications of Tekla's note, and the walls between them, he was called to the ambassador's office.

Ambassador Henderson was frantically busy. Between taking phone calls and signing off on cablegrams, he thanked Monty for reporting, told him the State Department was aware of his activities and suggested he keep a low profile for the time being and stay in touch. One secretary entered to notify Henderson of another phone call from the Royal Palace. Another was at the first's heels with a pair of cablegrams from Washington to be read and signed. Moments later, Monty was walking back toward the British embassy with no answers and more questions.

The rest of that seemingly endless day, Monty felt slightly desperate and utterly helpless as he pondered the possibilities of Tekla's situation and his own. As evening finally fell, Monty went to meet her. Again, she was not at their meeting place. Again, he waited and worried, this time using more precise tradecraft. This time, though, his patience and caution were unrewarded. After hours of vigilant panic, he decided it was time to act.

He chose an investigative technique Rhoades called "walking back the cat." Starting at the only place he was sure Tekla had regularly been, the Tudeh newspaper office, he would try to pick up a trail to her. Hoping the office would be closed for the day so he could sneak in and scour records, he was frustrated to see all the lights on and the journalists working into the night. Gritting his teeth in frustration, he shook his head. "What to do?" He looked into the office. It was his only lead. He felt something harden inside. The image of Rhoades suddenly turning serious came into his mind. His eyes, like Rhoades, focused. He studied the office a moment, then burst through the front door.

"Faddey!" he shouted. "I need to see Faddey!"

Several young men came at him from desks behind the front counter, shouting in Farsi and pushing him back. He went on shouting. "Faddey! I need to see Faddey!"

Senior people quickly emerged from offices at the far end of the room. One, a portly, middle-aged, balding Iranian man with glasses hanging from a cord around his neck, began pulling Monty's attackers away, authoritatively shouting at them in Farsi. When the room finally settled down, the man studied Monty. "I am the editor of this newspaper," he said. "You are the American working with the British."

"And with Faddey," asserted Monty. "Where is he? Is he here?"

"I know nothing of what you are talking," the editor replied.

"If you want the deal I am working on with Faddey to succeed, you better find out!" Monty yelled in only half-feigned desperation.

"Deal?" the editor asked quizzically, his eyes darting around the room.

Monty studied the man and then glanced at the others. "Maybe we'd better talk about this in private," he suggested.

"Yes. My office. Follow." He pivoted, calling back instructions in Farsi. Monty followed him to a small office at the back of the building with a small window opening onto the rear alley and a ceiling fan whirring and creaking. The editor closed the door, its opaque glass top panel offering complete privacy. He stepped behind the desk. Monty started to sit in the visitor's chair. "No need to sit," the editor said, turning to face Monty. "I know nothing of a deal."

Monty eyed the man who, Monty saw, was leaning in the direction Monty wanted him to go. "This is off the record."

"No."

"Forget it then," Monty said, turning toward the door.

"Fine, fine," the man said quickly. "Off the record. Background."

"Good. Faddey and I have been trying to put together an oil deal between the U.S., the Soviets and your country. To keep the peace and save Mossadeq."

"Save Mossadeq?" The editor said, astonished. "This could save the world from nuclear war. I know nothing of it."

"You know President Truman likes Mossadeq."

433

"Yes."

Monty started to explain further, but stopped. "You don't need to know anything else right now. I've got problems from Washington. If I don't get in touch with Faddey and get them smoothed out, this thing could fall apart."

"But..."

"Do you know where he is!?!"

"He was here earlier," the editor said, obviously thinking as he talked. "Sending and taking cablegrams. Then he left. Perhaps to the house he keeps with his staff. Something about taking someone to the airport."

"The airport!" Monty exclaimed. "I've got to catch him. Where is the house!"

"Just down Kohk," The editor shrugged. "Behind the Prime Minister's residence. Number 29."

Monty dashed out of the office and down the street. When he was far enough from the newspaper storefront to feel confident he was not being pursued, he slowed to a fast walk. Striding quickly past the Prime Minister's wall-enclosed, well-guarded residence, he moved forward cautiously as he approached number 29. A car stood in front of the house, its engine running, its driver patiently waiting. Monty stepped off the sidewalk behind an old linden tree and watched. Moments later, Tekla came from the house carrying suitcases and moving quickly. Faddey followed more deliberately, one hand in his jacket pocket. She dropped the cases beside the car, plopped into the backseat and slammed her door closed. Monty could see her sitting in the car, staring straight ahead, her arms folded across her chest. Faddey came to the car, put the suitcases into its trunk, got in the front seat and waved the driver on. The car passed Monty on its way up the street and turned onto Churchill Avenue in the direction of the highway to the airport.

Monty sprinted behind the car to the busier end of the street and watched as it faded into traffic. His outlaw summer in Oklahoma flashed through his mind and he thought of hotwiring a nearby car until he realized a taxi, readily available in this part of the city at this time of night, would be less conspicuous and troublesome at the airport. The taxi he hailed did not catch the car carrying Tekla but he saw it unloading her and Faddey as his taxi drove up to the terminal. He waved his driver past them, to the shadowy far edge of the quiet airport. He kept watch on the Russians out the rear window. The taxi driver said something to him in Farsi.

"Wait," Monty answered. He watched Faddey walk Tekla, again carrying her own suitcases, into the terminal. Monty threw a handful of paper rials onto the front seat and bolted from his taxi. He walked quickly into the terminal behind the Russians. Keeping a distance and to the shadows, he noticed Faddey keeping his right hand in his jacket pocket while Tekla talked to the man behind the ticket counter. Though the man paused every so often to make an announcement over the airport's public address system, he eventually completed the paperwork and held up a ticket folder. Faddey stepped forward, handed the man a stack of bills with his left hand and took the ticket folder. When the transaction was complete, Tekla turned, picked up the suitcases, and said something to Faddey.

Monty was too far away to hear what she said but he could see it was belligerent. Faddey snapped back and waved the ticket at her with his left hand. She answered back instantly, still angry. Faddey made a clumsy gesture, a movement with his right hand from inside his jacket pocket. It was not an overt gesture but a bank robber's gesture and Monty read it easily. There was a pistol in that pocket to make certain Tekla used the airplane ticket. At Faddey's gesture from inside his pocket, Tekla, still carrying the suitcases, pivoted angrily away from the Russian and walked off toward the rear of the terminal building. Angrily, Faddey followed.

Remaining inconspicuous, Monty trailed behind them through the very light, late night traffic and bustle of the airport. The public address system periodically interrupted the subdued clamor.

At the ladies room, Tekla dropped her suitcases by the door and stomped in, letting the door bang noisily in Faddey's face. After she went in, he turned, leaned against the wall by the suitcases and lit a cigarette. Seeing a meager but probably singular opportunity, Monty moved swiftly out a side exit and ran for the outside windows at the back of the terminal building that vented the restrooms.

Grabbing a nearby trash barrel, Monty upended it beneath the narrow, open vents, and jumped atop it. Peering cautiously, he did not see her. She must be there, he thought, glancing quickly from stall to stall. But they were all unoccupied.

"Get down from there," he suddenly heard her whisper behind him. "Before someone thinks you are a pervert."

He dropped back to the blacktop and embraced her.

"Your tradecraft is much improved," she said, embracing him as tightly as he did her.

"What is going on?" he suddenly asked, stepping back.

She took a deep breath, folded her arms across her chest and spoke in a cold voice. "My mother is dying. Faddey is using it as a wedge. He knows how I feel about you. He can see it. He has threatened my brothers with ruin if they do not intervene. My brothers love the party more than they love me. If I go back, I am their captive. If I do not, I will never see my mother again." Despite herself, tears rolled down her cheeks. "I do not know what to do. I cannot stay." She looked at him and dropped her arms. "But I cannot go!"

He stepped forward and took her in his arms. There was a long silence as he held her and thought. "It adds up to one thing," he finally said. "You've got to go."

She wept "No, no. I cannot"

"Think about it, Tekla. This place is about to blow up. The way they treat foreigners here, you're lucky if they just shoot you and don't torture you first."

"Why are you saying this?"

"I'm saying it because it's the truth. Even if you gave in to your impulse and stayed, you'd regret it. Maybe not right away, but eventually. You couldn't live with yourself knowing you deserted your mother."

"What about us?"

He looked at her wearily, feeling nothing but sadness. "I'm no hero, Tekla, but you know what I've got to do here. If you stayed, you'd have no side."

"But this was our second chance!"

"This IS our chance, Tekla. Our chance to make a choice. Between not so good and worse, but we get to choose. Sure, we could try to run. But eventually it would catch up with us. That's the way it works. I don't know why. I only know you've got a plane to catch. I guess if it was possible to get it right, we would have. We didn't. So you go back to Russia and do what you have to."

"And you?"

"I stay here and watch the place come apart."

"And us?"

"What we had, nothing can change. What is coming is bigger than us." She looked at him, her expression fragile, her lips and eyes quivering. An announcement inside the building on the airport's public address system broke the silence. "Is that you?" he asked.

"Yes." Her voice trembled.

Suddenly, Faddey stepped out of the darkness. "Is this not sentimental?" he remarked with snide meanness. "Like a scene from one of your romantic American films.
" 'Casablanca', perhaps."

"Tehran is a little like Casablanca these days, don't you think?" Monty replied, his voice suddenly hard.

"And just like the film, I have a gun in my pocket."

"And just like the film, we both agree the girl's got to get on the plane," Monty snapped back, protecting Tekla.

"And if she changes her mind, I can always shoot her hero," Faddey smiled.

"You won't do it," Tekla told Faddey.

"Just go get on the airplane, Tekla," Monty said quietly, urging her out of harm's way.

"I won't shoot him here in public like this," Faddey told Tekla. "Unless you make me."

She dropped her head and stared at the ground. None of them spoke. Finally, she raised her head and looked at Monty, tears streaming down her cheeks. "See you at the dance."

She turned and marched to the plane without looking back. Monty watched her walk away, forcing back tears with rage. Faddey stood behind him, triumphant, his right hand on the pistol in his pocket, wary of both Monty and Tekla. Her head held rigid, facing forward, she boarded the plane. When the passenger door closed and the plane rolled slowly toward its take-off, Monty turned to Faddey. "This isn't over."

Faddey smiled. "Tonight I have my way with you. Someday my country will have its way with yours."

"I'm looking forward to it already," Monty said, pivoting and walking away. Thinking now only about the man with the gun at his back, Monty did not watch the plane take off, so he did not see Tekla, still weeping profusely, looking out the window of the plane, watching him walk away.

Faddey, though, was still watching with a gloating smile as the plane rolled swiftly by and he caught sight of her watching Monty and weeping. The Russian's smile faded and he turned away angrily as the airplane lifted off with a roar.

Monty walked out the front of the terminal and then along the highway. He did not want a taxi, he wanted to walk. And remember Tekla. And wonder while he walked: Was he ready for any of it? No. "Watch and learn," Rhoades always said. What did he learn? To be ready.

*****

August 15-16, 1953

"Most ball games are lost, not won." ...Casey Stengel

The normally silent post-midnight Tehranian streets were alight, rumbling and popping. The glow of celebratory bonfires and flaming destruction haloed the skyline. Intermittent explosions punctuated the ongoing rat-a-tat of pistols and rifles and the odd boom of a tank or rapid-fire machine gun burst.

The soldier leading the way turned suddenly to Irdeshar, whispered with desperate panic and backed toward them.

"Here!" Irdeshar Zahedi whispered, pulling Monty and then the soldier back into the darkness of an alley. They pressed themselves against a wall and watched the military patrol's jeep, carrying its officer, go by, a platoon of foot soldiers around it in escort.

"What do we say if they stop us?" The soldier whispered to Irdeshar.

438

"He wants to know what we say if they stop us?" Monty asked Irdeshar in English with grim irony.

Irdeshar gave a harsh, quiet laugh. "There is no answer that will stop them from arresting us, torturing us and shooting us," Irdeshar told the soldier in Farsi.

The soldier's visible terror now ratcheted up. Monty leaned toward him. "So shoot first," he told the terrified man in Farsi.

"Yes," agreed Irdeshar.

"You want to stay in this alley all night?" Monty asked Irdeshar in English, checking his handgun one last time.

Irdeshar smiled grimly, waved the soldier forward and they moved cautiously into the treacherous streets. One block was quiet, the next filled with a crowd around a trashcan fire. One intersection was empty, the next filled with people frantically celebrating the burning of a government building or a pro-Shah newspaper or the home of a pro-Shah politician. At one such burning house, Irdeshar turned to Monty.

"They were ready for this," he said in a quiet, bitter voice. "They called out all their thugs."

"Yeah," Monty agreed. "Whoever the informer was, he let them know some time back what was coming and then got word out it was tonight."

"I want him," Irdeshar said like a vow as they moved forward past the blazing house and the celebratory crowd.

"You?" answered Monty with frustration, carefully watching the crowd and then glancing suspiciously at shadows in the empty street beyond it as they moved on. "I didn't spend the last two years carrying secrets between Tehran and London and Washington because I like flying."

"You made it happen," Irdeshar whispered as, beyond the fire, the street quieted.

Monty smiled thoughtfully at a fond memory. "Rhoades would be proud of us."

"Of you," Irdeshar insisted. "You were the genius who found common cause for the CIA and MI6."

Livingstone laughed self-consciously. "It didn't take a genius to figure out they were more worried about the Soviets than each other."

"You think the one who sold us out is Tudeh?"

"No. Military. He knew when Nasiri was going after Riahi." Then Monty thought. "But he could be working through Tudeh. Or maybe the police. Afshartus."

"Afshartus is dead," Irdeshar answered matter-of-factly, cautiously scrutinizing the route the soldier leading them chose. "He investigated the wrong murder."

"His replacement?" Monty asked.

"Riahi's man," Irdeshar answered. "He knows nothing."

They walked silently up an alley behind the Majlis building, circled it and came out at the back of a crowd in front of the Prime Minister's house. The crowd let out a ringing cheer, then quieted. A speaker on a makeshift platform by the wall around the Prime Minister's house continued. Monty, Irdeshar and the soldier remained in shadow at the rear, unobserved, listening. The speaker railed.

"Fatemi," Monty said.

Irdeshar nodded 'yes' with great weariness. "Mossadeq's rabble rouser. He should be in jail right now."

A big commotion rippled toward them from the front of the crowd as the onlookers jostled and shifted to better see what was happening. On the platform, Fatemi pointed at the source of the commotion. "Prisoners!" he exclaimed. "The cowards and fools who thought they could betray you, the people of Iran. You see their reward!"

The soldier with Monty and Irdeshar moaned and the crowd cheered as Mossadeq's soldiers marched Nasiri and his pro-Shah men, in handcuffs, leg irons and chains, before the crowd. The prisoners' heads hung down. Their faces and uniforms showed harsh treatment.

"They have confessed their treason!' Fatemi proclaimed.

The crowd roared its approval.

Monty looked at Irdeshar, who stared in torment at his captured soldiers. "I want that betrayer, Livingstone."

"I know."

Suddenly, the man with them shouted in terror. "AHH!" He dashed past them. Where the soldier had been standing, a military squad just coming into place turned toward the shout and movement. The military squad saw a man in uniform running and two more, carrying sidearms, staring back at them with panic on their faces.

The squad's commander shouted orders and blew a shrill whistle. His men readied their weapons.

With a quick glance, Monty saw that another squad on the other side of the crowd had already responded, moved into position and was at that moment capturing their fleeing soldier.

"Into the crowd!" Irdeshar yelled, pulling his Luger and charging forward. Monty pulled his revolver and followed at Irdeshar's heels.

At first the crowd did not give way, and the two were forced to push and shove. Some in the crowd pushed back and the struggle became desperate. Monty did not think of using his pistol on innocent bystanders. He pushed more frantically at the mass of bodies pushing against him. Irdeshar, however, did not hesitate. Shots rang out. A man fell. People everywhere began screaming, shoving and fighting. Terror and panic took over. Forces hit against Monty from all directions, driving him back and forth, left and right. Through grunting and cursing, falling and stomping, pulling and forcing, heaving, lifting and dragging, wailing, weeping and pleading, Monty followed Irdeshar's lead and they struggled together, in the same direction, away from the pursuing military. With this singular advantage over the seething masses who did not know who they were escaping or what they were caught up in, Monty and Irdeshar finally emerged at the forward edge of the insanity's rising wave and were thrown free into the space vacated at the first sign of trouble by the prisoners and their military escort.

Bursting finally from the crowd, Monty's momentum hurled him to his knees at the front edge of the now-empty speakers platform. Frantically looking everywhere for his companion, he unexpectedly spotted Irdeshar below and ahead, slithering under the platform. Monty dropped to his belly and followed. They squirmed to the narrow open space between the rear of the platform and the wall around the Prime Minister's house. Continuing to

441

crawl in the dirt beside the wall, they eventually made their way around the margin of what had become a full-scale riot. As the sirens of arriving police troops wailed, Monty and Irdeshar cautiously rose and inconspicuously slipped up a side street. As soon as they could be sure they wouldn't be noticed, they broke into a full run. Darting from shadow to alley, they did not slow down until they had made their way back to the protection of the British embassy. As he stumbled past the armed guards at the embassy gate gasping for breath, Monty was soaked with sweat and filthy but grateful, for the moment, to still be alive.

"WE HAVE GOT TO FIND OUT WHO BETRAYED US!" Irdeshar exploded as soon as he could squeeze the words out between his own gasps for breath.

Monty was about to agree when a young British man in a clean white shirt and neatly knotted tie approached. "Mr. Zahedi?"

Irdeshar turned, still catching his breath. "Yes."

"Sorry to interrupt. The guards at the gate had orders to report your return. Mr. Roosevelt wants to see you at once."

"And I want to see him!" Irdeshar answered bluntly. "Lead on!"

*****

In a secluded bungalow at the rear of embassy grounds, a tall, lean American in khaki sat with a small, select group of Iranians. And Monty. In the quiet of the waiting, expectant room, the upbeat sound of a Broadway orchestra playing a popular showtune, *Luck Be A Lady*, came from the record player in the TV-radio-HiFi console against a far wall. Kermit Roosevelt, clean-cut and professorly in his thick glasses, stood and stepped to the center of the room. Someone lowered the volume of the music. "Tonight, despite my grandfather's advice to 'Speak softly but carry a big stick' you roared," he said. "And it fell on deaf ears. Big or small, you have only the stick left." He looked around at them.

Monty first met this group two years before, in 1951, through Rhoades. Kermit Roosevelt met the Iranians through Monty, through Irdeshar Zahedi or through Irdeshar's father, General Fazlollah Zahedi, who was not present now.

"My message to you is simple," Roosevelt said. Then he stopped again. The only sound was the faint crescendo ending of "Luck Be A Lady." Roosevelt looked each of them straight in the eye, starting with Monty, leaning against the far wall. Next, he turned to Nossey and Caffron, the import/export men the CIA had promised Roosevelt were unfalteringly reliable. They sat at the small, round table before which Roosevelt stood. Bahram Shahrokh, the dark, handsome Radio Tehran personality everybody knew would not come through until their triumph was a certainty, sat at the same table. On a sofa against the wall away from the room's door, were Sayfollah, Ghodratollah and Asadullah Rashomian, the very different brothers with the unspoken, profoundly unified purpose. And, finally, in an armchair away from the others, was the beautiful Princess Ashraf, hardheaded firebrand sister to the Shah, who sat with a grimly serious expression.

"Bahram, nothing is going to involve you for days," Roosevelt began. "Get out of here."

"But I must know what is going on."

"No. When we come for you, you will know. Until then, play it straight. Now get out."

"Colonel Roosevelt…"

Roosevelt turned to Irdeshar, who sat in a chair behind him. "Call your security."

"Fine, fine," the radio personality exploded, standing suddenly and stomping toward the door.

Irdeshar stopped him, threw an arm around him and whispered. "You are safer this way."

Shahrokh looked at Irdeshar with a start, realized it was true, nodded and left. When he was gone, Roosevelt looked at Irdeshar as he resumed his seat. "Well done."

"He is a better diplomat than soldier," Princess Ashraf remarked. Roosevelt and Irdeshar exchanged knowing glances with her and, as Roosevelt turned to the Rashomians, Irdeshar looked hard at the Princess with an "enough" gesture of his hand that she waved off angrily.

"Asadullah," Roosevelt said to the oldest Rashomian, "you and your brothers have done great work for your country. But it has come to nothing."

"We were betrayed!" the bulkier of the three handsome, dark-featured men on the sofa protested.

"Which is why..." Roosevelt interrupted, "...I am going to ignore the coded messages Washington is sending. You people have one more chance. And it has to happen fast."

"How much time?" Asadullah asked in a surly manor unlike his fine banker's suit, tie and starched white shirt.

"Days," Roosevelt replied. He looked at the faces around him but said nothing. The room remained silent, waiting. He finally continued. "I'm going up to Shimran now to tell General Zahedi the same thing. But remember: I'm not here. I never was. No matter how this plays out, no representative of the United States government or any of its agencies had anything to do with this."

Nossey sat forward, glanced back at Monty and then looked up at Roosevelt. "Can we keep Livingstone?"

The group chuckled. Roosevelt gave them the moment, then answered officiously. "Mr. Livingstone is here doing oil company business. Officially, the U.S. government has nothing to do with him." Nossey smiled and nodded. "Unofficially," Roosevelt's voice turned suddenly stern. "If anything happens to him I will punish you because his mother will never sing "Let's Call The Whole Thing Off" for me again." He smiled at Monty. "O.K., that's it." He looked at Ashraf and gave a slight bow of his head. "Princess."

She smiled. "Give General Zahedi our regards, Colonel."

"I will." He turned to Irdeshar. "They're all yours. Get me out of here."

Irdeshar stood, stepped near Roosevelt, shook his hand and whispered, "Tell my father we will find the betrayer."

Roosevelt smiled, nodded and walked to the door of the room, which a soldier opened. The soldier checked outside as a large, late model Cadillac drove up. Meanwhile, Irdeshar stepped to where Roosevelt had stood at the center of the room. He began speaking in Farsi and the small group of ringleaders listened intently while they watched, behind Irdeshar, Roosevelt get down to his hands and knees on the backseat floor of the Cadillac. The soldier threw a blanket over the man who was Theodore Roosevelt's grandson and Franklin Roosevelt's nephew, completely concealing him on the floor. The soldier closed the car door, nodded to the civilian driving and the car moved off. The soldier turned back to the bungalow and closed the front door. Irdeshar continued talking.

"Nobody will know when the move is coming. On personal orders from Colonel Roosevelt and the General, I will say go. Meanwhile, we have three objectives. One – prepare to prove the validity of our claim on power. That means making the firmans known in every way, everywhere." He looked at the two Rashomian brothers sitting next to Asadullah. Unlike their older brother, they were not dressed like bankers but like street merchants. "I expect to hear concrete plans at our next meeting." They nodded. He turned to Caffron. "Pass on any ideas your people have." The burly man in street Arab garb nodded. Irdeshar continued.

"Two – discredit Mossadeq. This will be easier, of course, when the content of the firmans is known, when the people know the Shah has officially replaced Mossadeq with the General. But we need a campaign accusing Mossadeq for letting this lawlessness come to our country."

"Blame Tudeh," Asadullah said abruptly.

"Yes," nodded Irdeshar, "That is number three. And blame Mossadeq for Tudeh."

"What about the Mullahs?" Princess Ashraf asked.

Irdeshar looked at her. "We will leave the Mullahs out of this for now. If the blame for chaos begins falling on his allies, Kashani may come over."

"Breaking the Mullahs' power could be the key to breaking the Mossadeq coalition!" Princess Ashraf asserted.

"But they could be the key to our success if they come over to our side. We will leave them alone for now."

"That is a mistake," she answered.

"We will see," Irdeshar cut her off. "But not tonight." He looked at her sincerely, an unspoken plea to let the issue go in his expression. She replied with a frustrated facial expression and then nodded 'yes.' Irdeshar went on. "We are all tired. We have people on the streets. We should sleep while we can. We will meet tomorrow evening, hear reports, plan and begin again.

The room emptied quickly as the exhausted men said quick goodnights. When only Monty, Irdeshar and Ashraf remained, the Princess stood up and

445

spoke to Irdeshar harshly. "You left out objective number four: Find our betrayer!"

"That is objective one!" Irdeshar answered angrily. "But our betrayer may have been in the room. I will not talk about it, I will do it. I will find him and butcher him."

"You are talking about it now," Princess Ashraf said snidely, with a dismissive snap of her wrist.

Irdeshar threw up his hands.

Monty smiled. Ashraf did not. She walked to the door, turned and looked at Irdeshar. "Are you coming?"

Irdeshar looked at Monty and shrugged. Monty's smile grew bigger at his surprise in discovering a relationship between Zahedi and the Shah's sister. Irdeshar smiled back. The Princess left the room and, with a warm goodnight to Monty, Irdeshar followed.

A little later, as Monty approached his embassy compound bungalow, a girl emerged from the darkness. "Livingstone," she said in a quiet, firm voice.

Startled, he snapped alert, his eyes reading the darkness until he recognized her. "Sanaz."

"You did not pay me."

He smiled, breathed deeply, stepped to the door and opened it. "Tonight?"

She held out her hand, palm up, and looked at him with dispassionate eyes, awaiting payment.

He smiled. He liked the ones who challenged him. After Tekla, he no longer believed in love. But he needed even more to desire. He replaced love with sex. He could feel nothing now for women like Tekla, lithe and bright with sparkling eyes. Now he lusted for the passionate, dark-haired, dark-eyed Persian professional girls. There were many before Sanaz. There would be more. He liked getting to know them until his desire waned. And it always waned. He had intended to break it off with this one by not paying her, but she apparently had her own desires.

She remained in the dim yellow glow of the bungalow's small porch light, her palm up and open, fearless. He studied her, reached a decision, removed a roll of rial bills from his pocket and counted them off into her hand. "Last night," he said, and continued laying out the bills. "And tonight."

Inside, they were both soon naked. She was warm. He took his pleasure and slept.

Waking up next to Sanaz late Sunday morning, he padded to the toilet and thought about the day. Standing naked at the sink and splashing water on his face, he was halfway through plans to discharge the girl when he thought of something better. He pivoted, walked across to the bed, grabbed her bare ankle and shook her awake.

"You missed morning prayer," he said sarcastically. "Let's go for a walk in the city."

Groggily, she looked up at him, skepticism and resentment on her half-awake face. Without replying, she rose naked from the bed and walked stiffly to the toilet. After she sat a few moments thinking, she looked up to where he was, shaving at the sink. "A walk in the city? You have become a romantic overnight?"

He laughed. "No. You will be my escort."

"I will be paid?" She asked, wiping and rising.

Using his razor, he chuckled. "I have known women who went for a walk with me for the sheer pleasure of it."

"I will be paid?"

"Of course."

"Let me bathe."

Tehran was calm. Sunday being the middle of the work week, the shops were open and people went about their daily business. But there was an undercurrent of unease. Military patrols rolled by intermittently. Policemen, tired from a long, tense night, walked beats slowly and dealt with citizens irritably. There were burned buildings and broken windows along the nonchalant stoll Monty and Sanaz took through the city. The Shah's palaces, as well as many fine estates, had armed guards and locked gates.

They heard rumors, in whispers, of trouble. Prime Minister Mossadeq, people said, put down a rebellion, a coup attempt. Some said it was the

447

Mullahs. Others said it was plotted by the Shah with the American General Norman Schwartzkopf, who had visited recently. When Sanaz asked Livingstone if he knew anything about the rumors, he replied with a question. "Do the rumors frighten you?"

She laughed. "If the Shah takes over, it will be easier than it is now. If the Mullahs take over, it will be more difficult. Either way, I will go on doing what I do."

As the afternoon waned, Monty turned back toward the British embassy. At Ferdosi Square, she stopped him. "You want me again tonight?"

"No. Not for the next few days. Go home."

"It is not safe."

Having just walked the same streets together, they both knew she was lying. He studied her a moment, then smiled, took a roll of rial notes from his pocket, grabbed her wrist and slapped the entire roll into her palm. Her fingers instantly closed around it. "Will this make it safe?"

She smiled. "Very safe."

The same small group gathered Sunday evening in a back bungalow of the embassy compound and, once again under Irdeshar Zahedi's leadership, formulated a set of actions along the lines Irdeshar had proposed the previous night. Until they turned the tide of public and political opinion, there would be no further direct military action.

"But we now begin making every kind of trouble," Irdeshar told them. "Suggestions."

"I have people spreading the rumor that General Riahi is contending with Mossadeq for control," Caffron, the thick-chested, balding Arabic CIA operative said.

"Good. Develop that," Irdeshar replied.

"But we have people putting the blame on Tudeh," Ghodratollah Rashomian, the chubby middle brother objected.

"That is not a problem," Nossey, Caffron's small, wiry Persian CIA partner, replied. "Contradictory information will cause paranoia."

448

"And conspiracy theories," Irdeshar nodded. "What else?"

"We have a network of old women," Sayfollah Rashomian said. "They are complaining of the destruction by Tudeh in the demonstrations."

"Excellent!" Princess Ashraf smiled quietly.

Monty looked from the Princess to Caffron. "Can you make the Tudeh demonstrations more destructive?"

"It could get violent," Caffron replied.

"Do I look like someone who cares?" Monty answered.

Caffron looked at Irdeshar. "They are your people."

Irdeshar looked from Ashraf to Monty to Caffron. "Do it." He turned back to Princess Ashraf. "Now about these firmans."

"They are the key to our legitimacy," the Princess told him. "By signing them my brother risked everything."

"But the people did not elect my father," Irdeshar replied. "Until they believe in the Shah's right to make these firmans law, Mossadeq will remain Prime Minister."

"Roosevelt has the New York Times reporters at Shimran tomorrow morning," Monty told Irdeshar. "They must see the originals of these decrees. You get that story into the Times tomorrow and by Tuesday it will be everywhere in the world."

"Except Tehran," interrupted Asadullah Rashomian.

"Fine," Irdeshar snapped. "We will get the word out here ourselves. We have all night tonight. I want photostats. I want typists. I want mimeo machines. I want paper..." His voice rising, he went on describing the delivery of the Shah's firmans – his monarchical decree of Pahlevi power and his appointment of General Zahedi to replace Mossadeq – like an assault on Tehran.

These leaders went on plotting and planning while foot soldiers marched in with reports of action on the streets and out with assignments for more action. With occasional breaks to eat or nap, this core group worked all night and into the next day, relentlessly discussing, improvising and assigning.

Late Monday morning, Irdeshar and Monty fetched the original firmans from the embassy safe and took them to General Zahedi's Shimran basement hideout. In a secret interview Kermit Roosevelt had arranged between the General and two New York Times reporters, Zahedi laid out the case for the coup and validated it with the firmans. The reporters were convinced and left assuring the General his message would go out to the world with the next edition of the Times.

Monty and Irdeshar returned to their headquarters confident the world would soon believe in the legitimacy of their cause. At command central, they found their fellow plotters working with the radio on. The Radio Tehran broadcaster was disinterestedly reporting grain prices.

"You have given up hope and are preparing to become farmers?" Irdeshar asked.

"No, no," Asadullah Rashomian laughed as he heard the radio announcer finish the grain reports. He reached to the radio and turned up the volume. "Listen."

The room quieted and they sat listening as the announcer introduced General Riahi and explained the interview would be brief because of the General's many responsibilities to Prime Minister Mossadeq. As the questioning went on, the leaders eyed each other expectantly but said nothing. After five minutes of platitudes, at which the Rashomians, Nosey and Caffron rolled their eyes incredulously, the announcer mentioned he had a last question.

"Is Prime Minister Mossadeq now fully in charge?"

The tone of Riahi's voice revealed he was perfunctorily and inattentively answering, mentally already on his way out of the radio studio. "Of course. But Iran and its people and the Army of Iran are more important than any figurehead."

"Truly," agreed the interviewer. "But more important than the Prime Minister?"

"More important than the Prime Minister, the Shah or anyone. We work for Iran and the people of Iran."

"Thank you, General Riahi."

"Thank you."

As Radio Tehran went back to more farm prices, the leaders in the room sat silently, looking away from one another, the monotone of farm price reports the only sound. "Nothing there," Asadullah said sullenly, snapping the radio off.

"Wrong," Sayfollah, his younger brother, suddenly said.

All eyes turned to him. "What?"

"Is Riahi about to take over?" Sayfollah asked. "He said the people and the army are more important than the Prime Minister or the Shah. Is he going to make a grab for power?"

"Ridiculous," Asadullah answered with a dismissive wave of his hand.

"No," interrupted Irdeshar. "Sayfollah is right." Irdeshar stepped across the room to Sayfollah. "Get some of your old women to work on that. Tell them to ask their husbands who is in charge. Tell them to ask their sons in the army who is in charge. Very good. It is another question about this administration. Mossadeq is an old and emotional man. He can only stand up to so many questions."

"Especially when they're coming at him from every direction," agreed Monty.

"Good!" Exclaimed Irdeshar, excited. "Let's get back to work. We have our one true claim going out and they have doubt and dissension."

"How are we doing with the work against Tudeh?" Monty asked Ghodratollah.

The middle Rashomian brother smiled. "Tudeh is working the story that the coup was created by the Shah with the American General Schwartzkopf."

Monty's brow wrinkled. "Schwartzkopf was here to tell the Shah we were developing something. That's all. The State Department sent him because he had done so much work organizing your police and military after the war. It was a good excuse for the visit."

"Unfortunately, Tudeh did not believe this," Ghodratollah said. "But fortunately your embassy resents being accused of lying. They have aggressively attacked Tudeh and suggested Tudeh is behind the coup. All the papers are reporting the story."

451

"Cold War news," smiled Monty.

"Yes," Ghodratollah nodded. "Tudeh answered with a march and a demonstration. With a little help from some of our people, the demonstration turned into a riot."

"Excellent," Monty smiled.

"And Tudeh has called for a candlelight march after prayers tonight."

"We'll have people there?" Monty asked excitedly.

"We are moving carefully. We do not want Tudeh to react, to stay out of the streets."

"Their leader isn't that smart," Monty told him. "Turn up the heat."

"That is dangerous," Ghodratollah said. "It could get violent."

"Good!"

Ghodratollah turned and looked at Irdeshar. Once again, Irdeshar pondered the question of violence, but finally nodded 'yes.'

As Ghodratollah turned toward the door, Monty was already talking to Irdeshar. "I want to start rumors that Mossy is organizing a military counter-coup against the Shah."

Irdeshar had looked down at a newspaper. He looked back up. "How many different ways can we turn this?"

"As many as we can think of," Monty told him. "Until all the people want is their Shah."

The room continued to buzz with activity through the day and the night. Runners from the streets brought in reports of demonstrations and speeches that had to be answered. Flyers, street gossip, radio interviews and orders for street actions went out. Meanwhile, the National Front and Tudeh were generating radio news and newspaper reports. Events spiraled toward more and more hostile confrontation. Speeches became demagoguery turning demonstrations regularly into riots. This necessitated extra editions of newspapers and breaking news radio reports into the night, which started the command center up on a new round of planning and new, more desperate responses. Formulated, the new actions were sent by runners into the streets.

452

Predictably, the actions sustained the cycle of events. Before there could even be a result, Irdeshar was demanding speculations on outcome and countermeasures.

As Monday night wore tensely and wearily into very early Tuesday morning, reports of destructive overnight demonstrations mounted and rumors of violent incidents grew. Nossey and Caffron, reporting to Irdeshar after spending the night in the streets, pointed out that the most recently reported beatings and shooting deaths were not the result of direct action but simply of chaos.

"We do not want unnecessary violence," Irdeshar told the CIA agents. "That is why I am holding in check the pro-Shah military potential."

"Yes," Nossey replied. "This mayhem is merely factions settling old scores. To be sure we have people in place spurring it on." He glanced at Monty. "That is what you ordered, was it not?"

The room quieted, waiting to measure Irdeshar's response.

Irdeshar hung his head.

Monty stood. "Yes," he said to Nossey. "That was the plan. That IS the plan. Good work."

Nossey, Caffron and others continued to watch Irdeshar. Finally, the Iranian leader raised his head, sadness in his eyes. He nodded 'yes.' The room resumed its activity.

A little later, a runner, a young boy in blue jeans and tee shirt, came in breathless to report bands of Tudeh had ransacked a Pan-Iranist splinter group's headquarters near Majlis Square.

Irdeshar, once again studying a newspaper, looked up. "Was anyone hurt?"

The runner shook his head 'no.'

"More importantly," Monty interrupted, "What was the group's reaction?"

"I can answer that," Nossey interrupted Monty, breaking out of a whispered consultation with one of his own runners newly in from the streets. "The Pan-Iranists have contacted one of my people. They want to make a deal with us."

Shouts of approval matched grins around the room.

"That's not all," Ghodratollah Rashomian shouted over the noise, hanging up a telephone receiver. "I have word from people I put into Third Force."

"That's a Marxist bunch, isn't it?" Monty asked.

"Ghodratollah nodded 'yes.' "More communist than the Communists. And there is fighting between those factions, too. The Third Force has abandoned the Tudeh cause."

Again the room erupted in shouts of triumph. By the time Irdeshar had calmed the room down and got his people back to work, dawn was emerging in diffuse grey-blue light outside the bungalow's windows. Boys started arriving with early editions of the day's newspapers. All the leaders grabbed copies and quickly started reading. The room fell silent.

"They're all defending the National Front," Ghodratollah Rashomian said quietly.
"The Pahlevi dynasty is over..." he read.

"But look at this!" Asadullah Rashomian interrupted to announce gloatingly. He held up a newspaper headlining SHAH APPOINTS ZAHEDI – FIRMAN UNSEATS MOSSADEQ. The older Rashomian smiled. "My man."

Irdeshar looked from the headline to Asadullah. "Have our people steal and burn as many of the papers that don't report our story as they can get to." He turned to the rest of them. "We have work to do."

The morning was turning bitterly bright, heralding more harsh summer heat, when Sayfollah Rashomian came in from a meeting with his operatives near the market. He reported to his older brothers. They conversed quietly. As Sayfollah went on reporting, all three Rashomians began stealing glances at Monty.

Monty did not notice because he was showing Irdeshar something he had found in the back pages of a newspaper. "Its from the AP, part of your father's statement: 'Be ready for sacrifice. Be ready for loss of life for freedom, the monarchy and Islam threatened by infidel Communists.'"

"How did that get in there?" Irdeshar wondered aloud.

"Probably an accident," Monty smiled. Irdeshar turned away to other business. Monty sat down at the round meeting table in the middle of the

454

room and went on studying the paper, searching for more reporting "accidents" planted by U.S. agents.

Sayfollah now walked quietly to Monty.

"There was a girl."

"There always is," Monty answered without looking up from the newspaper.

"A dark-haired girl. A professional girl. She said she was a friend of yours."

"Did she have a name?"

"Sanaz."

"What about her?" Monty asked dismissively, anticipating a request for money or favor.

"She got caught between the factions. She was shot."

Monty looked up. "By who?"

"It is impossible to know. She is dead."

Monty stared at Sayfollah for a moment, hung his head and shook it. Then, startling Sayfollah, he quickly looked up. "Why do you come to me?"

"Dying, she said to tell you."

Monty's tone became hard, his only revealed emotion a cold anger. "So you told me. Take care of the body. I will cover the expense." He looked back at the newspaper. Sayfollah nodded politely and walked away. The room went on buzzing, unchanged from moments before, but now Monty began growing weary. Surely it was the many hours' work without rest or resolve. Shaking his head did not clear the sudden burdened feeling.

Reports now started coming in of the day's Tudeh and National Front events, the rallies and speeches set up to sustain support. On hearing these reports, Irdeshar walked to the center of the room and began yelling, demanding plans for responses to every event, disruptions at the demonstrations, declaimers interrupting every speech. The activity around Monty became frantic as the leaders called in lieutenants and they called in foot soldiers and the hubbub of assignments and groupings got discussed and debated. The room seemed intolerably loud and tense to Monty. He stood, whispered to Irdeshar he needed to take a break, and left the bungalow.

Too keyed up to return to his own rooms, Monty once again set out for the streets of the city's center. Immediately he saw that Sunday's everyday normality was now agitated by much greater tension. Though the shops were open, fewer people went about their business. Shopkeepers were watchful but not for deliveries. Shoppers were alert but not for bargains. There were fewer chats and more guarded whispering.

As the heat of the day set in, Monty moved cautiously through Tehran. A band of Tudeh marchers paraded past, chanting anti-Shah slogans. "Destroy everything the Shah built! Everything he stands for!" They handed out flyers announcing a speech by Fatemi, Mossadeq's top propagandist, as they went.

Monty watched two middle-aged, heavy set, slightly bent, weary-looking women dutifully accept the flyers and hold them until the marchers passed. When the street was again quiet, both women crumpled the flyers, tossed them to the ground and turned into a nearby fruit stand. Monty followed them. He made himself inconspicuous by picking over oranges in a shadowed corner and listened. As they picked through pomegranates, peaches and potatoes, they muttered to one another about the madness of these vulgar young people and their angry politics. Monty smiled, happy to see his side's tactics were working.

A young woman, pudgy and sleepy-eyed, came in off the street pushing a baby in a stroller and dragging a little girl by the hand. Seeing her, the old man sitting at the back of the fruit stand listening to a small table radio and watching over the place, leaned back on his stool and called out the rear door. "Ziba!" He listened, then answered. "Roshni!" with a jerk of his head toward the inside of the fruit stand.

An older woman came in the back door of the fruit stand wiping her hands on her apron and chattering a combination of greetings to and admonitions at the young mother. "It's so good to see you! The children look happy! You shouldn't be out on these crazy streets!"

Monty laughed to himself, not at these women but with them, enjoying the laughter that came with a domesticity he never had known.

"We have to have food, don't we?" Roshni, the young mother, answered Ziba, the older one. "If you aren't going to bring it to me, I have to come and get it, chaos or not!"

"Ah, it is chaos isn't it?" Ziba sighed.

"It is worse than chaos," one of the middle-aged, heavy-set women joined in.

"That's right," her companion agreed. "It is dangerous chaos!"

Monty listened as the women dissipated their fear among themselves by chattering on about what they could do nothing about. "They will be ready to accept us soon, Hardy," he muttered quietly to his memory of Hardy Rhoades as the women chatted on.

The monotonous drone of farm reports on the radio ended abruptly. An announcer told listeners to stand by for an important statement by the Prime Minister. Shushing the women, the old man turned the volume up. The women stopped talking.

"Good morning," Mossadeq's high-pitched, nasal voice exploded from the radio. The unrest on our streets is unacceptable. Under the brave leadership of General Riahi, the military has taken the ringleaders of the actions against the government into custody. Order will be restored.

"Because of the turmoil, however, the current Majlis is split by untenable tension. I am today, therefore, using the proper authority of my office to dissolve the 17th Majlis. We are in the process of arranging for new elections in the autumn…"

"AH!" The old man angrily snapped off the radio. "It will only make everything worse!" he exclaimed.

The women looked at him tenuously, but he ignored them, staring down at the bin of apples in front of him and muttering epithets against politicians. The fruit stand was uncomfortably silent. One of the middle-aged women caught the eye of the other, nodded her head toward the potatoes, and they turned their attention back to their shopping.

"Here," Ziba said to Roshni. "Look at these melons."

There was a rough loud engine sound as a large vehicle approached and then stood idling outside the back door. The engine stopped. A truck door slammed. A moment later, a lean, aging man in a green work shirt looked in. When he spotted and then caught the eye of the old man on the stool by the radio, he raised his eyebrows in a quizzical expression. The old man nodded once in vigorous approval. The man in the workshirt disappeared, shouted "Omid!" and there was the sound of another truck door slamming. Soon the man in the green work shirt returned carrying crates of zucchini and eggplant, followed by a big, fat unshaven young man in a dirty white tee shirt, also carrying crates, who was talking as they entered and went on talking as they unloaded the vegetables into the proper bins, returned to the truck and brought in more crates.

Omid was recounting to Firoz, the green-shirted truck driver, events he witnessed the night before. He told of speeches, fistfights, guns brandished, people running and buildings set afire. Firoz ignored Omid and went on unloading vegetables silently. But the women were in awe of the incidents the fat boy told of, agreeing over and over with him the situation was dire. In a corner of the fruitstand and unnoticed, Monty listened, smiling.

When Firoz and Omid had unloaded the last of the produce, Firoz stepped to the old man by the radio and muttered something. The old man nodded, reached into a drawer, pulled out a stack of rial notes and counted them off. Finishing, he looked up at Firoz, who nodded.

A noise of heavy engines working hard approached on the street in front of the fruit stand. All looked toward the street in terror. They saw the cab of a huge truck pass, pulling a flatbed trailer. Laying on the flatbed, on its side, was part of a broken, polished bronze statue. Right behind came another truck, pulling a similar load.

"You see!" exclaimed Omid. "You see! It is the statue of Reza Shah Pahlevi. They have torn it down!"

The older women gasped in horror.

"It is a desecration," Ziba said.

"I remember when Mohammad Reza Pahlevi dedicated that statue. So grand," the old man said quietly, his toothless gums smacking the words with emphasis. "I remember his father riding that horse."

A third truck now rumbled past, this one carrying the huge bronzed haunches and hind legs of a horse on which the previous pieces had rested.

"It was such a magnificent horse," Roshni, the young mother, said quietly.

"Reza Shah would not let this happen," Firoz muttered, turning away. "Omid." He walked out the back door. Omid followed with a barrage of questions about the founder of the Pahlevi dynasty.

"If he were here, he would put things in order," the old man muttered, turning his attention back to the apple bin.

While the women's attention remained on the rear of the store, Monty quietly slipped away. He walked up the street. It was quiet. He decided to see if there was a response to the Prime Minister's announcement at Majlis Square. He walked up Churchill Avenue in silence, then turned onto Kohk where, as he approached the Majlis, he first heard and then saw another cortege of Tudeh white shirts chanting and dispersing flyers in the square. Stopping at a safe distance, he took in the celebratory scene. He glanced across the square at the wall around the Majlis Building. Cold venom ran through Monty as he saw Faddey atop the wall, surrounded by followers and admirers, directing the celebration.

It was the first time he had seen Faddey in almost two years. Since the airport. And then he caught a glimpse of something and his body trembled: Was that Tekla, in that group of people arguing with Faddey? He quickly shifted his position, moving forward to see through the crowd. But people were moving all around Faddey. By the time Monty's view was again clear, the group of people he had seen, or thought he had seen, was gone. It could not be Tekla, FORGET Tekla, he demanded of himself, as he had since she had left. It was a ridiculous, hopeless, romantic's dream, a dream that had been dead since Tekla's plane flew off for Russia. The last thing he needed now, just as he was about to complete what he had started then, was to dwell on past loss. Only future triumph mattered now.

Monty turned and started walking vigorously up Ferdosi, away from the square. His emotions roiling, he did not want to confront Faddey. He might act violently, he might attack Faddey, and that would create sympathy for Tudeh. At just that moment, Faddey emerged from an alley and stood in Monty's path, surrounded by a gang of white shirts and followers.

"Now I know the end is near," Faddey smiled. "All the rats are coming out of their holes." As Faddey gloated, Monty forced himself to look away, knowing that if he met Faddey's hateful gaze he would react. Scanning the crowd behind the Russian, Monty saw a familiar face. Where had he seen that face before? Despite his street clothes, the man looked military.

"You avert your eyes," Faddey smiled.

"Perhaps I have more important things on my mind than you," Monty replied disinterestedly, scanning the group behind Faddey for more familiar faces but finding none. Who was the one with the stern face and military bearing? He looked so out of place among this group of activist and radical followers.

"Yes," Faddey gloated. "Americans are always thinking about profits."

Faddey's followers laughed.

Monty interrupted the laughter. "You are here for a reason," he hammered at Faddey, finally turning his gaze directly into the Tudeh leader's. "Come at me or say what you have to say."

Faddey smiled but remained silent. Monty waited. He instinctively knew that identifying that familiar face was more important than anything Faddey and this bunch could say or do to him. Monty looked over Faddey's shoulder, surreptitiously studying the man.

Faddey realized he was failing to intimidate Monty and spoke. "I don't know what hole you have been hiding in with your British friends for the last two years, but we have been here, in Iran, building a movement. This uprising of the people is the culmination of all our planning..."

Planning, Monty thought, shuddering at the thought. Planning! The pool party!

Misunderstanding Monty's startled reaction, Faddey interrupted himself. "You Americans do not know what patient planning is, do you?" He paused, awaiting Monty's reply.

The man behind Faddey was at the pool party, one of the officers at the table with General Zahedi! What was he doing with Faddey and Tudeh? A betrayer? A betrayer. Monty suddenly understood, even as he realized the men facing him were silent, waiting for him to reply to Faddey.

Monty did not even remember the question. He could only think of one phrase. He looked at Faddey, smiled and raised his left index finger. "Watch and learn."

"Ever the arrogant American," Faddey replied, his tone grim. He half turned to his followers. "Teach him humility.

But in the instant Faddey turned away, Monty dashed. The men beside Faddey were watching their leader, not Monty, and did not react. The men behind crashed into those in front as they charged forward. Monty got a head start. Sheer fear and Oklahoma outlaw instincts took over. He knew these Tehran streets as well as a native. Dashing up the right alleys and leaping the right stone walls, he easily beat them in the long foot race to the gates of the

British embassy. Well-armed, stern-faced British Marines admited Monty and warned off his pursuers. He was safe, he knew who the betrayer was and Faddey did not know he knew.

Without stopping to catch his breath or wipe off his sweat, he barreled into the headquarters bungalow. "Now we're ready!" he exclaimed.

Late that afternoon, Ezatollah Mumtaz sat shackled to a chair in the middle of a bare, concrete basement, head hanging to his chest. Asadullah Rashomian stood over him, looking down on him. Monty and Irdeshar stood away, against one wall, watching. Nossey and Caffron stood across the room, against another wall, also watching.

"Look up at me," Asadullah said calmly.

Mumtaz slowly raised his face. It showed no sign of beating or torture. "You cannot hurt me enough to make me betray the people of Iran," he said defiantly.

Rashomian's face grew stern. "I have no time for that," he said quickly. He looked at Nossey and gave a quick nod of his head toward the room's door, then looked at the prisoner. "You must believe only one thing: What I am about to tell you, I mean."

Nossey returned with a woman wearing a veil, three little girls and a boy toddler. Sobs came from behind the veil. The children were all weeping in terror.

"My family!?!" Mumtaz exclaimed. "My family!?!"

"One!" Rashomian shouted. "You have already betrayed the Iranian people!"

"You would bring my family here and speak to me of betrayal!" Mumtaz shouted.

"Two!" said Rashomian. "I serve the Iranian people. You serve communist dogs."

"You do this and talk politics!"

"Three!" shouted Rashomian, stepping very near Mumtaz, putting his hands around the restrained man's head and his mouth by the man's ear. "You can agree to do my bidding now." He waited. Against the restraints and Rashomian's strong grip on his head, Mumtaz shook his entire body in a 'no'

461

gesture. "I will begin by tearing that veil from your wife's head," Rashomian continued, whispering, "tearing her robes from her body and raping her in front of you and your children."

"No!" wailed Mumtaz.

"Yes," smiled Asadullah. "And then, when your daughters know what to expect, I will have them raped, too. One at a time." He paused. "Of course, you will have the opportunity at any time to save any one or all of them."

Mumtaz quivered with rage and fear. "Nooooo!"

"I will save the boy for last. Shall I castrate him and then kill him?"

"No," Mumtaz pled, weeping. "No, no, no…"

"Or shall I just castrate him?"

"No, no, no…"

"Or just kill him? Nevermind. I will decide later."

"No, no, no…" Mumtaz was sobbing.

"But first, your wife." Rashomian walked to the woman. With a quick snap of his arm, he ripped away the veil.

She screamed, weeping hysterically, and backed away. The children screamed, cried in fear and ran to her, grabbing her legs. Unable to move away, she begged for mercy. Rashomian grabbed her black gown at its neck and pulled her forward. She was madly shaking her head 'no' and shrieking. "No! No! No!" The children held her in place. Rashomian yanked forward. The children lost their hold and fell away. He put his hand on her head, bent her at the waist, and snatched the gown over her head. Now wearing only a thin white cotton undergarment, she tremblingly backed away from Rashomian, toward an empty corner where bare concrete walls met, closing her in. Her terrified sobs of "no, no, no" alternated with choking weeping,

Rashomian turned to Mumtaz. "She is a beautiful and passionate woman. I think I will enjoy this."

"No, no, please, no," Mumtaz moaned.

"All you have to do," Rashomian answered, "is promise to do as you are told. Or," Rashomian paused, "you can wait and see what I do."

Rashomian waited. The woman's sobbing and the childrens' terrified crying were the only sounds, echoing in the room's hollowness.

"What do you want me to do?" Mumtaz asked in a weak, beaten voice.

Rashomian turned away from Mumtaz's wife, looked at Monty and Irdeshar, and smiled.

A little later, in the same room, the woman, now dressed and veiled, sat huddled with her children in a corner, sobbing and weeping quietly with them, muttering endearing phrases and reassuring lies to them. Mumtaz, still in the chair, was unshackled. He sat hunched, in a submissive, broken posture. Monty, Irdeshar, Caffron and Asadullah Rashomian stood around, looking down on him.

"Tell me," Rashomian said quietly.

"I am so thirsty," Mumtaz said in a hoarse, dry, hard-to-hear voice.

"Tell me," Rashomian repeated, now threateningly.

"Give him water," Irdeshar said.

"When he tells me," Asadullah insisted.

"Fine," Mumtaz submitted. "I report to Faddey. "I tell him you have given up."

"And how do you prove it?" Monty asked.

"The American spies left for Ankara," Mumtaz effortly croaked in his fading voice. "Please, just a cup of water."

"What else?" Rashomian demanded.

"Just one cup."

"What else?"

"The CIA men and the Rashomian brothers have gone to Baghdad."

"Very good," Rashomian smiled. He turned to Irdeshar. "Now you can give him water."

"You give him water," Irdeshar snapped back, turning away.

"How do we know he will keep his word?" Monty asked Asadullah.

The big Iranian, still smiling, nodded his head toward the woman and children.

"Please could I have a drink of water now?"

"And I have ears inside the Prime Minister's house now," Caffron added.

"Just a cup," Mumtaz said quietly, his head falling to his chest. "One cup."

"Your ears can report out?" Irdeshar, turning toward them, asked.

Caffron nodded 'yes.'

"Please," Mumtaz begged.

"He must return for his family," Rashomian said. "He cannot expect to leave with them until we see he has done his job." He turned to Mumtaz and lifted the man's head up by the hair. "Do you understand, traitor?"

"Water," moaned Mumtaz.

Suddenly, Mumtaz's wife screamed at them from across the room. "Can you not give the man a sip of water!"

Looking from Mumtaz to the woman in irritation, Rashomian dropped Mumtaz's head, stomped to a utility sink in the corner, ran dirty water into a metal cup and returned. "Here," he said impatiently, handing over the cup. "Now shut up."

"You are too generous with him," Caffron told Rashomian while Monty and Irdeshar walked away, deep in planning for their final moves.

"I know," the bulky Iranian replied. "I am weak that way."

They smiled at one another as Mumtaz desperately gulped the water.

*****

464

"Ability is the art of getting credit for all the home runs somebody else hits."
...Casey Stengel

The next few hours were slow and tense. Monty and the other ringleaders spent them in the headquarters bungalow. They chatted quietly about their coming actions. Princess Ashraf sat near Mumtaz's wife and children in a far corner and talked quietly, comfortingly. No staff remained. To enhance the deception they hoped to create of having disbanded, Irdeshar had sent all his people out on the streets, readying action. Certain ones, the most trusted, were given secret instructions to return late that night. Others among the trusted were sent to monitor Tehran military bases, with instructions to report in only if there was a change in military status.

After several hours, Mumtaz turned up. He swore he had done as they had demanded and begged to be let go with his family. Irdeshar told him he would have to remain in custody until they had confirmation his mission had been accomplished. Princess Ashraf demanded Irdeshar put Mumtaz and his family alone together in a guarded room. When a glance at Asadullah Rashomian and Caffron told him they saw no point in punishing the man and his family further, Irdeshar told Monty to see to it.

The waiting went on. Toward the middle of the night, those assigned to the military bases started coming in. Their reports were consistent. There was a general stand-down from the 'alert' status of the last three days. A growing sense of anticipation began to fill the room. Just before midnight, as some of those assigned to return began straggling in, a runner came in with a message for Caffron. After a lengthy whispered exchange with the runner, Caffron sent him back out and turned to them.

"My ears in the Prime Minister's house confirms," he told them. "Mumtaz came and went without incident. His visit created great happiness in the Prime Minister's staff and Mossadeq was ecstatic when they took the information to him. They all talked of triumph. The Prime Minister asked General Riahi if a stand-down order could be given, the General consented and the order was dispatched."

When Caffron finished reporting, he looked at Irdeshar and waited. Irdeshar turned to Monty and smiled. "Are you ready?"

Monty looked at him intently. "Yes. And your people are ready. They want you to give them back their Shah."

Irdeshar turned to the two younger Rashomians and Nossey. "Send out runners. Begin the final outrages." As they leapt into action, Irdeshar looked from Princess Ashraf to Monty, Asadullah and Caffron. "All flyers and propaganda go out tonight. A copy of the firmans for every man, woman and child in Tehran."

Asadullah smiled. "Two. And three copies of General Zahedi's statement: 'Be ready for sacrifice and loss of life for freedom, the monarchy and Holy Islam threatened by the infidel Communists.'"

As Asadullah walked away, already busy, Irdeshar looked at Princess Ashraf. "It is time to contact that Cleric. Your brother's boyhood friend."

"Ayatollah Fazal," she said.

"Yes. He promised to go to Ayatollah Borujerdi in Qum. We need the Fatwa calling for jihad against the Communists Borujerdi promised us."

"You will get it."

"Copies to all the mosques in the city by the time of morning prayer."

"I am a princess, Irdeshar," she said indignantly. "Not a Greek goddess."

"You are a goddess to me," he smiled, and turned to Caffron. "Get messengers to our military loyalists in the provinces. Tell them it is time to start for the city."

"Already working," Caffron replied.

"Good. Put them on the street as soon as they come in. Send them to get Nassiri and their comrades out of jail. By force if necessary. Tomorrow the pro-Shah demonstrations start early and I want our military in control of the streets when they start. We should be converging on the Prime Minister's house to serve the firmans by noon. Everybody reporting in, every step of the way. No surprises."

"Along those lines…" Caffron replied hesitantly.

"What?" snapped Irdeshar, tensing. "I just told you: no surprises!"

"You need to know this. My ears says there is a Soviet delegation at Mossadeq's house."

"A delegation from Russia?" Monty exclaimed. His mind raced. Could this be the group he saw, or thought he saw, at the square with Faddey? Could Tekla...Stop! He screamed at himself. Stop! He turned to Irdeshar. "We should take this opportunity to get rid of the Tudeh leadership."

Irdeshar looked from Caffron to Monty. He thought carefully about what Monty had said. "It is tempting. But is it worth an international incident?"

"Target the leaders," Monty urged him. "You and I can do it. Just pistols."

Irdeshar was still processing the idea. "That would be the only way. Unofficially. An accident amid the chaos and violence."

"Assuming there will be chaos and violence," Caffron said.

Irdeshar looked at him. "There WILL be," he said threateningly. "You get to work and make SURE of it."

After Caffron walked away, Irdeshar turned to Monty and smiled grimly.

"Back out on the streets?" Monty asked.

"On the streets? Definitely," Irdeshar replied. "But assassinations? We will see."

The night, which before had passed so slowly, now seemed to disappear. They ordered an army of passionate, or paid, civilians into action, spreading the word via rumor and broadsheet. Tens of thousands of copies of the firmans and General Zahedi's call to action statement were spread across Tehran. They announced the Shah's intention to return to Iran and assume control from Mossadeq, with General Zahedi as his Prime Minister. In his firmans, the Shah asserted his constitutional right to assume this control and called on his military to fulfill his instructions and follow Zahedi's orders.

At the same time Irdeshar and his people were setting these massive moves in motion, they were coordinating the arrival in the city from provincial garrisons of military units loyal to the Shah. Their arrival needed to coincide with the uprising of pro-Shah units at Tehran's military barracks. With poor timing, the pro-Mossadeq forces led by General Riahi could fight and defeat the separate segments of the pro-Shah forces. But the military assault, planned so carefully by Zahedi and his loyal officers, came off with perfect coordination and succeeded. The good news came in from agents in the streets: What troops Riahi was able to muster despite the general stand-down ordered the night before were retreating to the Mossadeq compound or scattering.

Amid these huge movements of people, panic set in when the command center got reports Mossadeq's police had seized the one pro-Shah newspaper left in operation. The cold terror of another betrayal froze the command center. Asadullah Rashomian voiced their fear: "Maybe Riahi's troops were only pretending to stand down." But no further reports of pro-Mossadeq action came in. They decided the newspaper office attack must have been an independent, vindictive act. Irdeshar sent word for the newspaper staff to disperse without resistance, promising his soldiers would put them back in the office before midday.

By dawn, the Tehran military bases were under the command of Zahedi's most loyal officers. They led forces out to take control of key city locations. Small- arms battles followed. Pro-Shah units took the city's police station and prisons and freed loyalists arrested in the failed action of the preceeding weekend. Other units attacked the secret police holding the newspaper office and routed them. Finally, pro-Shah forces in heavy trucks and tanks emerged in formation from the military bases and took control of the streets around the city center and the marketplace. Under direct orders from Irdeshar, they did not approach the Majlis or the Prime Minister's walled, fortified estate. With the city securely in his possession, Irdeshar sent out orders for his military to hold their positions, rest and eat, in preparation for the final, decisive day.

It began with the civilian population at the bazaar. Securely guarded by the military, which kept a protective but discreet distance, Asadullah's hand picked street leaders, including the circus of performers Hardy Rhoades had long ago developed, gathered a crowd to them and started a spontaneous rally. Nossey, Caffron and the younger Rashomians all had people ready to respond in support. The rally became a demonstration and the demonstration became an uprising, an overwhelming expression of the Iranian people's love for their Shah and resentment of the chaos, violence and destruction wrought by the communists and the usurping Prime Minister who dared to align himself with the communists.

"FOR ALLAH, KING AND IRAN!" they chanted. "FOR ALLAH, KING AND IRAN!"

When their numbers swelled beyond what the marketplace and its surrounding streets could contain, the leaders marched them toward the Majlis. Along the way they encountered small groups of Tudeh, unaware of how different their situation was this new morning until they were subdued, and often worse, by the now openly hostile citizens. Some Tudeh marchers fled, carrying word of the new circumstance to their leaders and fellow travelers. Others were beaten by the mob-like segments of the pro-Shah demonstration. Still others were taken into custody by the military and humiliated, forced to join the march and chant pro-Shah slogans at gun- or bayonet-point.

The march up the avenue toward Majlis Square became a wild and joyous celebration. At the pro-National Front Bahktar-I-Emruz newspaper offices they pillaged and burned, and then repeated the actions with more zest at the Tudeh Rahbar newspaper offices.

At the square, they were met by Ayatollah Fazal, the Shah's boyhood playmate, and Ayatollah Borujerdi from Qum, Fazal's loyal, if politically uninformed, coreligionist. The Ayatollahs stood on the familiar makeshift platform at the head of the square, patiently waiting. At the far end of the square from the Ayatollahs and across the street, on Hardy Rhoades' cherished second-floor outside-porch overlook, Monty, Irdeshar, Nossey, Caffron and Asadullah Rashomian stood and watched the demonstration form.

After the massive crowd assembled, Fazal gave a benediction. Borujerdi stepped forward and solemnly read his Fatwa, condemning Mossadeq and his National Front government "for collaboration with infidels." Spurred by the pro-Shah ringleaders among them, the gathered throngs cheered lustily. When he finished reading, Borujerdi looked up as if he did not understand the crowd's response and it frightened him. He stepped back. Fazal stepped forward again and lead another prayer. He was about to remind the congregation of upcoming midday prayers and dismiss them when one of the marketplace ringleaders leapt to the platform.

The ringleader, exuding patriotic fervor, reminded the gathered masses there was one stronghold of collaborators and infidels remaining. Grandiloquently pointing in the direction of the Prime Minister's estate, he chanted "Right there! Right there! Right there!" He looked out on the tens of thousands gathered and waved his arms, encouraging them to join him in his chant. The collaborators among them joined in. "Right there! Right there! Right there!" Soon the entire throng was chanting. "Right there! Right there! Right there!" When they appeared aroused, he started a second chant. "Do we want it? YES! When do we want it? NOW!" "Do we want it? YES! When do we want it? NOW!" Again the crowd joined in. Now others from the marketplace, pro-Shah men, leapt to the platform and began screaming to take the protest to the Prime Minister's house and chase the usurper from office. Within a few minutes, the crowd was raging and their leaders marched them the short distance up the street for the final showdown. As the rally moved out of the square, the people chanted. "SHAH PIRUZ AST!" "SHAH PIRUZ AST!" "SHAH PIRUZ AST!" Asadullah, Caffron and Nossey moved quickly from the balcony into the crowd to coordinate the last actions. Monty and Irdeshar inconspicuously followed at the rear of the marchers, accompanied by a threesome of loyal runners, young pro-Shah men who had been serving in and out of command headquarters throughout the action.

At Mossadeq's walled estate, the crowd's easy progress ended. The Prime Minister's military ally, General Riahi, had used his remaining loyal troops to fortify and arm the compound. Sherman tanks ringed the property, their 75mm cannons facing outward, their turrets still. Grim men with machine guns lined parapets above the walls and a manned machine gun sat threateningly on the roof, behind protective sandbags. Within the compound, there was no movement, no sound. At this silent, solitary last stand of National Front resistance, the passions of the multitudes came to an unexpected halt. The throngs milled, giddily celebrative. At their rear, Monty and Irdeshar did not share their joy.

"He is not there," Monty told Irdeshar.

"Yes."

"But you want the house."

"He will have no place to run." Irdeshar turned back to a runner and nodded. The young man moved purposefully into the crowd.

"What about that Soviet delegation?" Monty asked Irdeshar.

"They will come out when the shelling starts. Our diplomats can deal with them."

"And the Tudeh leaders?"

Irdeshar looked at Monty, smiled grimly, took his Luger from its holster and checked the slide mechanism. "There may be casualties in the action." He turned back to another runner and nodded. The young man dashed away. Irdeshar looked at Monty. Monty nodded, understanding and ready.

They waited. Soon there was a roiling at the front of the crowd. The chant began again, at first from a few lone voices but soon from the howling mob.

"SHAH PIRUZ AST!" They screamed, proclaiming the Shah's triumph. "SHAH PIRUZ AST!"

Irdeshar smiled as the din of the chant rose. "They will not tolerate this long inside those walls," he said.

"SHAH PIRUZ AST! SHAH PIRUZ AST!"

Monty looked at Irdeshar but said nothing about the price he knew these paid agitators and innocents would momentarily pay for drawing the first shots in this final battle.

There was a burst of machine gun fire from the walls and roof. Screaming at the front of the crowd followed. In the next instant, thousands were retreating in panic. Monty and Irdeshar moved forward, toward the battle, making slow progress against the fleeing melee of madness. Monty remembered something Tekla had said to him when they were discussing that Orwell book about the future. "In a nation of fools," she had said, " a wise man always moves against the crowd."

Even as the marchers stampeded wildly away, a loud rumbling came up the street toward the battle. It was a column of Sherman tanks, rolling slowly forward. Five, six, seven of them, thundering to the rescue at their top speed of twenty-five miles per hour. The desperate crowd parted before the tanks, dozens of the unfittest falling underfoot. While those unwilling to fight dispersed in fright, the tanks came on. At the perimeter of the engaging battle, they peeled off in military precision, one to the left and the next to the right. They formed an arc around the house and its defenses on three sides, outflanking the Riahi forces pouring machine gun fire down on them as they came. The pro-Shah tanks wheeled into facing positions. The tanks defending the house opened up with their cannons. Irdeshar's tanks quickly returned fire.

Explosions rattled the streets and surrounding buildings. Fallen remnants of the marchers, lingering around the scene like survivors of a disaster, screamed with horror as the walls around the house began crumbling. A pro-Shah tank exploded into flames from a Riahi tank direct hit. Burned and crippled soldiers came out of the escape hatch under it, crawling. Machine gun fire from the walls stopped them.

Now heavy troop trucks sped onto the scene, squealed to a braking halt and dispersed units of pro-Shah foot soldiers under the command of loyalist officers, once again with military precision. The first unit moved to the left and the next to the right, until the troops had replaced the bulk of the crowd that fled. The house defenders increased their fire, soldiers racing along the walls and up to the roof carrying belts of machine gun rounds while the tanks rotated their turrets rapidly and blasted their attackers almost incessantly, their targets too easy and falling fast in gory blood-red slaughter. Then the pro-Shah tanks began exacting a toll from the house defenders. Sections of the house's crumbling walls caved in. Machine-gun positions were blasted apart, bodies and body-parts raining down in the rubble-filled open space between the faced-off tanks. A Riahi tank, and then another, and then another, exploded into flames from direct hits. As tank crew remnants came out of underbelly escape-hatches crawling for survival, pro-Shah foot-troops' guns denied it. Monty and Irdeshar grimly watched flesh pile and blood pool on the rubble as the stench of charring human filled the air.

The runner Irdeshar had sent for the tanks and troops emerged from the chaos around the estate. "Sir!" he reported anxiously. "People are escaping over the rear wall into the estate grounds!"

Irdeshar's expression turned from grim to outraged. "They did not secure the far side?" he screamed. He turned to Monty, his fury obvious.

"Let's go!" Monty exclaimed, turning and heading out around the battle perimeter without waiting for a response.

Irdeshar sent the runner with orders for a platoon to follow and went after Monty. They made their way around the outer edges of the firefight and carnage, moving slowly toward the rear of the house. Recognizing the World War II equipment and tactics, Monty felt slightly nostalgic and slightly panicked but did not have time to dwell on his feelings, thinking only of running down what he was certain were Tudeh escapees and settling his score with Faddey.

The runner and the summoned platoon caught up and fell in behind Monty and Irdeshar just as they came around the far corner of the house side wall. People were dropping off the rear wall one by one and racing into the tree-covered estate grounds that separated the compound from the surrounding city. Irdeshar turned to his troops, pointed at those fleeing and shouted furiously. "Get those people!"

Monty was about to follow with the troops when he recognized the big heavyset figure that next dropped from the wall and stumbled into the dirt. "That's our man!" he exclaimed. He was two steps into a vengeful dash at Faddey when he froze with astonishment. Tekla dropped from the wall and more gracefully hit the ground behind the Tudeh leader.

Faddey effortfully found his feet and started running without looking back. Tekla landed like a cat and sprinted after him, her loose Russian skirts flapping.

"There!" Irdeshar yelled, and gave chase.

This shook Monty back into action and silenced the riot of emotion inside. Chasing through the forest-like estate rear grounds, he was at Irdeshar's heels in a few strides. A few strides later, he passed Irdeshar and Tekla and hurled himself forward, tackled the big Russian around the knees and brought him down into the dirt and brush with a thud. Faddey tumbled to a stop before clumsily climbing, grunting, back to his feet. Monty, meanwhile, sailed through the tackle, rolled agilely and jumped back to his feet, blocking Faddey's escape route.

They faced off for an instant and Faddey lunged. Monty sidestepped and shoved down on the Russian's shoulder hard, letting the big man's own momentum take him to the ground again. Faddey wound up on his back. Monty stepped quickly to him, dropped a knee into the big man's gut, a forearm across his throat and glared into his eyes, for the first time revealing the full force of his hatred for the Russian. Just then, Tekla, not realizing Monty was the man she saw looming over her fellow Russian, hit him hard in the chest with her shoulder, knocking him off Faddey. They both rolled backward on the dirt floor amid the tall trees.

Faddey was gruntingly climbing to one knee, gasping for breath, when Irdeshar arrived and slammed him across the back of the head with the butt of his Luger, knocking the Tudeh leader to the ground again.

When Monty and Tekla stopped rolling, both jumped to their feet. Seeing for the first time who she was fighting with, Tekla froze in an astonishment of her own. "Monty!"

He looked at her with fury. "What are you doing here?" He asked in English, the language they had always used.

"A diplomatic mission!" she blurted out. "I'm part of a Soviet delegation to Mossadeq's government!"

"I know that," he said quickly. "But why are you running away with this bastard," he pointed to Faddey. "After what he did to you."

"He wants to put Tudeh back out on the street, to go at your military. I'm trying to stop him. I've been trying to stop him since I got here three days ago."

"But he didn't listen to you," Irdeshar smiled darkly, looking down at Faddey as the big Russian struggled back up to one knee, the back of his head bleeding from Irdeshar's blow. "If he had, we might not have been able to bring this government down."

"You SEE!" she screamed at Faddey. "You see!" Turning away in disgust, she looked at Monty. "And what are YOU doing here? We heard you went back to the oil business in America."

"Cover," Monty smiled. He turned to Irdeshar. "Go ahead," he said, nodding at Faddey, who was still on one knee. "Shoot him. He's trying to escape."

"No!" Tekla exclaimed, jumping between Irdeshar and Faddey.

"What are you doing?" Monty demanded, drawing his own sidearm. "Get out of the way!"

Before he finished the demand, Faddey was on his feet, a knife drawn from his boot at Tekla's throat, her body a shield between himself and the pistols. Faddey backed away from Irdeshar and Monty, smiling at his sudden control of the situation. He looked at Monty. "The gallant American will not risk the shot, will he?" He turned to Irdeshar. "But will the Persian?"

In this instant, as Faddey was stepping back on the uncertain terrain of the forest-like grounds and glancing from Monty to Irdeshar, Tekla pivoted and, with the gathered momentum of her spin, twisted Faddey's knife arm down, around and back up, plunging the knife deeply into his abdomen. She did not stop with simply planting the knife but allowed her own driving force a full follow through, slicing across the abdomen and into his thorax and heart. Blood gushed out as his "oof" and "ach" turned into a pathetic if chilling gurgling sound. Finally, she let go, her momentum carrying her quickly past him. He dropped to his knees, his face a mask of incomprehension and agony, and then fell to on his face and lay still.

Tekla turned. She looked down at the body, then up at Irdeshar and Monty. By this time, the sounds of the firefight at the front of the house had faded to sporadic machine gun bursts. In the opposite direction, beyond the estate rear grounds, there were intermittent gunshots as the soldiers chased down escapees. "Are you satisfied?" Tekla snarled at Monty, her eyes wide with rage and terror, her body quivering.

"Are you?" he replied.

She was silent for a long moment, staring at Monty, still quivering with intense emotion. She turned her head and looked again at Faddey. Neither Monty nor Irdeshar spoke. The sound of gunfire in front of the house was dying away. She turned back to Monty. The quivering passed. She visibly calmed. "Yes," she said. "He was a horrible man."

"Then I am satisfied, too."

They remained standing silently, looking at one another. Each realized how much they had longed for the other in the intervening two years. Tekla glanced at Irdeshar. Monty, too, looked at the Iranian. "Don't you want to assume command out front?" Monty asked him.

Realizing he was only in the way, Irdeshar nodded. "Yes." He pivoted. "Join me at headquarters when you can," Irdeshar said to Monty as he walked away.

Monty looked at Tekla. "How did you get out of Russia?"

She looked at him, then looked down at the front of her white shirt, now covered in blood, and then up again at Monty. "Let's get out of here." She strode away. He stepped to her side. They walked through the woods, back toward the city. "After my mother died," she told him matter-of-factly, "I remained silent until I won the trust of my brothers."

"They are still important in the party?"

"They are still apparatchiks, party hacks," she shrugged. "Easy to play for fools. When the call came for this mission, I was a natural choice." She stopped walking and looked at him. "I thought I would never see you again."

"Me, too."

"Monty…"

He stepped to her, took her in his arms. "I didn't know until this moment how badly I ached to kiss you."

He kissed her and she kissed him, a climactic coming together neither expected to know, a passionate yet enduring moment beyond words, beyond understanding, a fulfillment only love could know, a completion beyond comprehension.

The kiss lasted until each knew, in some intuitive yet almost magical way, to pause and look at the other.

"But what now, Monty?"

He looked at her with exaggerated sadness. "I can't go back to Russia with you, can I?"

"Don't mock me Monty!"

"Shall we go to America? Take a nice little house in the suburbs?"

"It would not be a very friendly place for a Russian, would it?"

"No, I don't think it would. You know how my mother feels about Russians."

"There is nowhere for us."

He smiled. "Well, then, we'll go nowhere. I have heard the Shah is going to bring an international consortium into this country to run the oil industry."

"No!" She exclaimed.

"I think I might be able to get a job at Abadan."

She beamed gleefully.

"And there's a metal box in a hole in the ground beside a cracking tower there, full of money and everything else we need. Passports. Identity papers." He held out his arm in a sweeping motion, indicating that they should begin walking back toward the city from the woods. "What do you think?"

She hooked her arm around his and led him forward. "It sounds like the beginning of a beautiful new life."

"In the oil business."

End of Part III

Epilogue

How did you find out about all this? I asked.

Kermit Roosevelt was here shortly after. He told me.

Did you sing "Let's Call The Whole Thing Off" for him?

She laughed. As a matter of fact, I did. And he asked for one he said was Monty's new favorite. Do you want to hear it?

I'd love to.

She walked to her piano player and whispered in his ear. He played an introduction and she started singing a song. It was from a popular Broadway musical:

> *They call you lady luck*
> *But there is room for doubt*
> *At times you have a very un-lady-like way*
> *Of running out*
>
> *You're on this date with me*
> *The pickin's have been lush*
> *And yet before the evening is over*
> *You might give me the brush*
>
> *You might forget your manners*
> *You might refuse to stay*
> *And so the best that I can do is pray --*
>
> *Luck be a lady tonight*
> *Luck be a lady tonight*
> *Luck if you've been a lady to begin with --*
> *Luck be a lady tonight...*

The End

BIBLIOGRAPHIC NOTE

As with the first book in this series, *OIL IN THEIR BLOOD: The Story of Our Addiction*, the first acknowledgment must be to my reading of Daniel Yergin's *The Prize* and my listening to Professor Arnold Weinstein's Teaching Company lectures on the timeless greatness of Herman Melville's *Moby Dick*. It was that coincidental encounter which inspired my (regrettable?) impulse to take on this project

Part 1

Details of the Paris peace talks come from Margaret MacMillan's brilliant *Paris 1919* and from David Fromkin's *A Peace to End All Peace*. The elements of the Red Line Agreement were thoroughly laid out in Yergin's book. Laurence Bergreen's *Capone: The Man and the Era* was instrumental in helping imagine the episodes set in Chicago. Sources for my portrait of the 1920 Republican convention can be found in my essay "Scandal—A Short History of the Teapot Dome Affair" from the 2005 edition of the Petroleum History Institute's *Oil-Industry History*, a link to which can be found at the website for this book, www.oilintheirblood.com. Elements of the Black Sox scandal were recreated from the David Pietrusza's *Arnold* and his *1920*, from Eliot Asinof's *Eight Men Out* and from John Sayles' film version of the book. The picture of barnstorming was partially drawn from biographies such as Mark Ribowsky's *Don't Look Back: Satchel Paige and the shadows of baseball* and Arnold Rampersad's *Jackie Robinson*, as well as from many fine histories of the "Negro" (African-American) leagues such as those by Ken Burns, et. al., Bruce Chadwick and John Holway. The film of *The Bingo Long Traveling All-Stars & Motor Kings* and its novelization contributed as well. Sources for the portrait of the oil field boom town were numerous. They are listed in my essay "A Brief History of Oil Industry Folklore" from the 2006 edition of the Petroleum History Institute's *Oil-Industry History*, a link to which can be found at the website for this book, www.oilintheirblood.com.

Part 2

These characters' and adventures are most closely modeled on the true-life experiences of Betty Thorpe Pack, as recounted by Mary S. Lovell in *Cast No Shadow*. But the pastiche could not have been complete without *Sisterhood of Spies; The Women of the OSS*, the account of so many other women's heroic and patriotic espionage efforts by Elizabeth P. McIntosh. Also vital to creating my tale was Alexander Klein's *The Counterfeit Traitor*, the true story of oilman Eric "Red" Erickson. I also reviewed the George Seaton film of Klein's book. The encounters with Ibn Saud come from *The Desert King; Ibn Saud and his Arabia* by David Howarth, *Arabia Reborn* by George Kheirallah and *Allah's Oil* by I.G. Edmonds. Background on Saudi Arabia in this period also came from going through the online archives of *Saudi Aramco World*. The glancing portrayal of Pretty Boy Floyd was borrowed from the Larry McMurtry/Diana Ossana historical novel *Pretty Boy Floyd* (on the assumption that the legend in this case was preferable to the facts). My understanding of the historic importance of and details about the brave men who flew on the Ploesti raids came from *Ploesti; The Great Ground-Air Battle of 1 August 1943* by James Dugan and Carroll Stewart. Background on Romania during the period came from *The Quality of Witness; A Romanian Diary 1937-1944* by Emil

478

Dorian. Gerstenberg's massage treatment came not only from my own clinical experience, but from *The Devil's Doctor* by John H. Waller as well. My deep gratitude to Baseball Hall of Fame Librarian Claudette Burke for help with details of the 1942 Ball and Bat Fund/Army-Navy relief all-star game in Cleveland.

Also, thanks to Paul MacCready, the genius of human-powered flight, for reminiscences and research on the Aeronca and other small planes of the 1930s.

Part 3
My first and best source on the 1951-53 turmoil in Iran was *All The Shah's Men* by New York Times writer Stephen Kinzer. (And my thanks to Vinnie Destefano for loaning it to me.) In the NY Times' "Secrets of History" section of its online library, "The C.I.A. In Iran" has most of the Times' original reporting associated with the subject in that era, including historic photos. It also links to original C.I.A. reports (as do conspiracy theorists across the web). Kermit Roosevelt's memoir, *Countercoup: The Struggle for the Control of Iran* becomes greater than itself when read in conjunction with these historical achives. Other books consulted included *Faces In a Mirror* by Ashraf Pahlavi, sister to the Shah; *Iraq: The Untold Story; An Insider's Account of America's Iranian Adventure...* by Mohamed Heikal; *Escape to Adventure* by Fitzroy Maclean; *Envoy to the Middle World* by Ambassador George McGhee; *British Petroleum and Global Oil, 1950-1975* by James Bamberg; *The History of the British Petroleum Company, Vol. 1...* by R. W. Ferrier; *Abadan; A First-hand Account of the Persian Oil Crisis* by Norman Kemp; and *Oil, Power and Principle; Iran's Oil Nationalization...* by Mostafa Elm. I learned much about daily life on Abadan from various personal reminiscences posted at Iranian.com

Without Google and Wikipedia, I would be like a blind man in the Knot Hole Gang.

The brilliant cover design and the illustrations are the work of Jennifer Egger.

Many thanks to Phillip Garcia for his generous assistance with online and layout mysteries.

The last word of gratitude must go now and always to my wonderful patients and readers who give me the unfathomable gift of their belief and support.

If you enjoyed this book, be sure to read **OIL IN THEIR BLOOD: The Story of Our Addiction**, the first book in the series. It tells the tall tales of the three preceding generations, from the end of the Civil War to the end of the Great War. You can find out more about it at the **OIL IN THER BLOOD** website, http://www.oilintheirblood.com.

And for the latest from the world of energy, visit this author's newsblog, **NewEnergyNews** at http://www.newenergynews.net/

Email inquiries: herman@newenergynews.net/

www.ingramcontent.com/pod-product-compliance
Lightning Source LLC
Chambersburg PA
CBHW020920020726
47495CB00002B/268